# HER GRACE

## S. R. HOYER

S. R. HOYER

www.srhoyer.com

Edited by Kathryn Moore

ISBN: 978-0-6456016-0-2
ISBN: 978-0-6456016-1-9 (ebook)

*For Harriet and Henry, my greatest creations.*
*Dream big, make noise and love without restraint.*
*Now put the book down. You're too young for this.*

# HER GRACE

# Contents

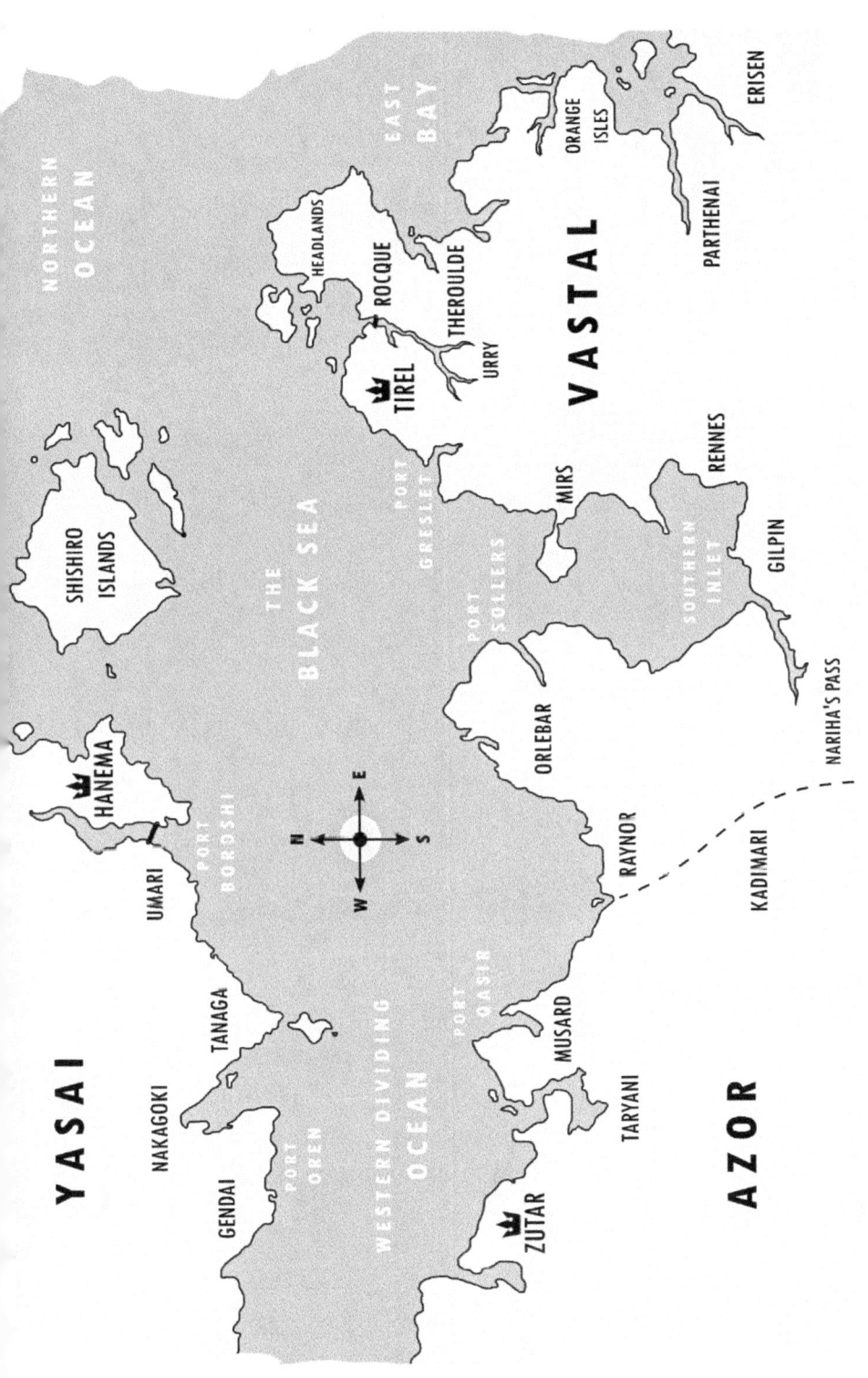

# One

The skies of summer's end offered no relief to Theroulde's hillsides. With a constant blue from sun-up to sundown, the leaves crisped, and the hounds hadn't the strength to shake the flies from their pelts. Even in the shade of her duelling partner, Penn's breeches clung to her legs like a second skin. Truthfully, they clung no matter what the weather, for they had not been cut for a woman's figure at all.

Though the castle courtyard was stagnant, Penn was grateful for her temporary freedom. Anywhere but the marketplace with Maud, its suffocating stench of fish and horse dung ripened by the heat, not to mention the village boys who laughed at the sight of her *every single time,* all because she didn't dress like the other girls. Gods, she would slap them all if she could—the boys who called her a freak and the girls who fawned over them. Fools, the whole damned bunch. Yes, Penn was exactly where she wanted to be. The great oak may not have made for much of a challenge, but it was the only partner she had.

No matter how dirty her tunic or enthusiastic her sword arm, Penn would never pass as a boy. At just seventeen, she was all woman, save for the good graces. But that was okay; Penn didn't care much for silken gowns or court gossip. She had grown up with a father and two brothers, playing tug-of-war and sparring with wooden swords. Her tea sets and dolls lay covered in a layer of dust, untouched for some eleven years. She liked it that way, but most thought her uncouth. They blamed her father's lack of discipline; they blamed her mother's death; they blamed old Maud and her dwindling mind. They blamed everyone but Penn, the poor thing who had to be pitied because she would never find a husband with an upbringing like that. That's what her stepmother said, anyway.

As Penn channelled her energy into the scarred trunk in her combat dance, footsteps sounded from behind. Just like she had practised, Penn spun around, took a fighting stance, and faced her opponent. Was it father, come to fight for the last slice of cherry pie? It had been months since they had sparred together, and Penn was getting rusty.

"How many times must you be told to stop this nonsense?" came the familiar voice of her stepmother, a less welcome sight.

"At least once more, Lady Torteval." Naturally, Olivia insisted that Penn and her brothers call her 'mother', but she had never seen her with such affection. How could she when Olivia had been so very different from her own mother? She had not sat by her bedside when Penn fell ill or held her when lightning filled the sky. With her sickly pallor and endless skirts of blue, her stepmother was as miserable as the place she hailed from, Port Greslet.

"Mind your tongue, *Lady Prestcote*." Olivia bowed facetiously. "Gods, can we please stop doing this? You're hard pressed to find a husband as it is with your … interests. An attitude certainly won't be tolerated." Olivia frowned as Penn tossed her stick into the garden with a sigh.

In truth, Penn wasn't losing sleep over the prospect of growing old alone. What she really wanted was to do something useful, something brave, something … memorable. A housewife didn't exactly fit that criterion. Penn's brothers, trained in the arts of knighthood, would have songs written about them and their names scribed in their great grandchildren's books. For Penn—for any woman—to be remembered for something other than being ordinary was absurd. Yet Penn never stopped dreaming.

"I've told you and father time and time again; I don't want a husband," Penn said. The repeated argument was exhausting.

Olivia chuckled. "I'm not sure why you're under the impression you have a choice in the matter."

Penn shut her eyes to keep them from rolling. "All I have to do is wipe my mouth with the back of my hand in the little lord's company and nobody will even consider me for a wife." Penn had been successfully sabotaging her matchmaking dinners for months, much to Olivia's disgust.

"Oh, Penn. Your father and I are pushing you on this because we care about your future. I know you think I'm rotten and that I'm trying to shove you somewhere out of sight—"

"Why would you think that?" Penn asked abruptly.

"Because I heard you." Olivia scowled. "A fortnight ago. Whining to your father after you sent that poor Lord Humbridge home with a black eye."

Penn knew she ought to have checked her father's chambers before opening her mouth. The memory of Gregor running from the castle at an amazing speed brought a smile to her face.

"He was pompous and boring. Could anyone blame me? And he had the audacity to comment on the size of my thighs, which is rich considering that heinous wart on his nose."

"Penn..." The pulsing vein on Olivia's temple had made an appearance, but her voice was laced with concern, not anger. "You have no idea how lucky you are. Girls all over the country are marrying boys they've never even met. In Yasai, marriages are still arranged at birth."

Penn sighed. "Well, if I was in Yasai, I'd do something about that."

"Life isn't that simple. The man I married before your father wasn't of my choosing, but that was the way of it. I was very lucky the second time around."

Penn had scarcely heard Olivia speak of her first husband, a gambler and a cruel man. There had been a great debt to be paid after his death, and who had saved the day? Her father, Lord Prestcote, of course. He was always helping others at his own expense. She was sure he only married Olivia to get her out of that grimy town. It couldn't have been love. Penn's entire family had been changed by her mother's death; the grief had never left her father's eyes.

"Come now," Olivia said, breaking Penn's reverie. "This heat is unforgiving, and your father would like a word." Olivia turned, skirts flinging around with a whoosh that sent debris a foot into the air.

Penn's interest piqued. "Is it Florent?" She followed on Olivia's tail with a growing feeling of excitement. Penn's older brother had recently been ordained and had been sent to Port Sollers on some secret business; she was almost certain it was to apprehend slavers, although his letter had been vague. Slavery had been outlawed almost two years prior, but those who made fortunes off selling souls were not easily discouraged.

"No, still no word." Penn's spirits dropped. "It's for your father to share. He's where he always is."

At that, Penn shot past Olivia and along the pathway that led to the keep, past the grove of dragonsnort, slowing by the pond. The water had always made her anxious, or at least since her younger brother Gillot had slipped and plummeted in. Though she was only seven, Penn dived into the green ooze and pulled the boy out by the neck of his tunic. Nowadays, Gillot insisted he couldn't remember any event that resulted in being saved by a girl, let alone his sister. Maybe now that he was in service of the Crown, his ego had abated. Or her father's news was of some trouble he'd gotten himself into.

Penn wouldn't be surprised if the knight he squired for had changed his mind and was sending him home.

It was much cooler inside, the stone so thick that the castle never really warmed. Penn took the stairs in twos and was breathless by the time she reached the third landing. It *had* to be good news. Penn was so tired of bad news. If the Crown needed crops again, Theroulde's people went hungry. If the village taxes went up, Lord Prestcote would undoubtedly offset them. That meant another midwinter with no festival, so they would all suffer. Penn needed it be good news.

"Father?" She called, peering through the crack in the doorway to his study.

A rustling and the clearing of a throat sounded from within. "Penn, yes, come in," his gruff voice beckoned.

Penn heaved open the wooden door to find her father in his usual spot, perched on his velvet armchair, leaning over a pile of parchment with a quill in hand. Durant had spent the last thirty odd years in service of the Crown, and it showed in the deep creases on his forehead. Castle Theroulde had been a reward for his service before he married, though Penn wondered whether it was really compensation for the leg wound that had left him with a limp as eternal as his frown.

Durant looked up, dropped his quill, and laced his fingers together on the smooth oak surface of his desk. "You've been messing around in the courtyard again." His voice was stern, his lips barely visible beneath the scruff upon his jaw. A mass of long, greying hair pooled around him like a nest. It was a comical sight; the humidity was not his friend.

Penn ducked her head in apology, knowing that her activities didn't really bother him, only Olivia. She couldn't help that being a boy agreed with her more than being a girl.

"Never mind that. I've had word from Rocque," her father said, averting his gaze.

"Rocque?" The northern town was a three-day ride, halfway between Theroulde and the Vastal Headlands. Penn had never visited, and as far as she knew, her father had no business there.

"Yes, Duke Wymark Bondeville has lost a maid. Of the sweat, it seems."

Penn's stomach clenched like it always did when somebody mentioned the notorious sickness. Her own mother had died of it when a plague had swept through Theroulde a decade ago. They were lucky nobody else in the castle had fallen ill because few of those who caught it survived. Durant gave her a sympathetic look and motioned for her to take a seat.

"That's awful," she said sincerely as she dropped into the wingback armchair. But what importance was the loss of a nameless maid to her father, anyway? Duke Wymark was the king's youngest brother and a born prince. It went without saying that his household was very rich and very close to the Crown. Duke Wymark owned all of Rocque and its outlying villages and was a prominent scholar, much like Durant.

"Yes, indeed. A terrible thing, the sweat," Durant said. With glassy eyes, he looked to the window.

Did he still think about her mother even after remarrying? For ten years, Durant refused to speak of her, batting away Penn's pleas to talk with a cautionary look. All Penn had of her mother was her memory and the silly stories Florent spun.

"Naturally, the duke will be needing a new maid."

Penn's already-tight stomach did a somersault. There could only be one reason her father would endeavour to share this news with her, and she had a terrible feeling their conversation was not going to end in her favour.

"We're the closest noble house with an unmarried daughter, and the duke has always been good to me. It is my duty to accept the offer." Durant could not speak the words without looking away, for he must have known how she would react. Her insides had been catapulted halfway across the realm along with her hopes and dreams of ever doing anything meaningful. A maid? *Her?* The idea was absurd! Her head swam with words she couldn't articulate.

"Good, it's settled. Duke Wymark is third in line, so you'd do well to be on your best behaviour. None of your tricks, none of your tree-climbing and bare feet in the dirt."

"Father, wait!" Penn exclaimed. "You talk of this like it's certain. Please tell me I have a say."

"I'm afraid this time you do not." Durant sighed and narrowed his eyes at the parchment before him. "It's not forever. And it'll do you some good, I'm sure of it."

"Good?" she shouted, jumping to her feet. "I can't think of anything worse!"

Durant set the parchment down and leant back in his chair with a pained expression. "Just last week you said you'd rather drown in the pond than marry. You wanted another option, and I'm giving you one. You'd best be grateful." Durant massaged his brow with a groan, evidently tired of her protests.

"How is braiding hair and stitching hems any better? I said I didn't want to be a housewife. A maid is no different!" Penn's face was hot, and her vision clouded with unshed tears. "I want to do something that matters. Why couldn't you have sent me to be a page when I was seven? I'd be a squire—a great squire—to some southern knight by now. I'd be a better squire than Gillot, and you know it! Why couldn't you have sent me to Tirel instead?"

"Because you are a *woman!*" Durant boomed.

Penn stilled. The very air in the room stilled.

Durant took a deep breath as he tidied a stack of parchment. "Enough, I've had enough. Olivia has had enough. This nonsense has gone on for too long. Women marry, men fight. You don't want to marry, so you will serve other women who will. That's just the way it is, Penn. You can't change it, and neither can I." He crossed his arms.

Penn shook with fury. She sank back into the velvet armchair and brought her hands to her face. Maybe Rocque was a nice place, and maybe the king's brother and his daughters were kind, but Penn couldn't be a maid. She wasn't good at anything remotely ladylike. It would end in complete disaster, and she would shame her father and her family name.

"When do I leave?" she croaked, wiping a tear from her cheek. There was no sense in arguing with him anymore; the decision had been made.

"At first light tomorrow. I know it's sudden, but it's a long ride."

Penn's heart faltered. Tomorrow? That meant she only had the afternoon to spend in Theroulde. She might not see her father again for years, and what chance did she have of seeing Florent and Gillot? It was rare enough she had word of them while home; she would never hear from them if she was stuck up north. The only person Penn would be glad to see less of was her stepmother.

Penn scowled. "Who am I to serve, then?"

"Lady Lovetta, the duke's third daughter. Your age, I believe. Very bright, I hear." Durant returned to his parchment.

Penn came to her feet. "May I be excused?" She ought to be alone with her thoughts for a while. It would take some time for her to come to terms with her father's decision.

"Of course. Have Maud fill you a bath, then pack your things." Durant narrowed his eyes, then waved his finger in the direction of her well-worn breeches. "You won't be needing those."

Penn skulked out of her father's study and down the stairs to her own chambers, throwing herself onto her four-poster bed. She turned to her side and faced the wall, too angry to make the most of her last afternoon in Theroulde. It was far easier to lay there and resent her father than it was to pack her trunk or play a final game of hide-and-seek with Maybelle, her half-sister. If only Florent were home. He wouldn't let her be sent away.

Eventually, the light faded with the setting sun, and Penn had to face their housemaid and the dreaded wooden tub.

"I bet their castle is at least three times the size of your father's," Maud said, nearly swooning as she soaped Penn's hair. "The king's youngest brother! You'll be invited to every ball and festival in Tirel, you will." Maud said enviously. "You should be excited, Lady Penn! Oh, the opportunities you'll have..." She trailed off as she pulled at Penn's scalp.

"I think you and I have different perspectives of what constitutes an opportunity," Penn said, closing her eyes as a cascade of cool water dropped over her head.

"Nonsense. You'll meet all kinds of men in Rocque and Tirel. Men much more sophisticated than the boys you're used to around these parts. Things will change for you, deary. You'll see."

"Meeting a nice nobleman isn't going to solve all my problems." Another wave poured down her back.

Maud laughed. "Problems! Goodness me. Well, you can't stay like this forever, you know. Eventually you'll have to marry, or else you'll end up like me. Old, overworked and surrounded by ungrateful children. Be good to Lady Lovetta for a year or so, meet a nice man with a good family name, and marry while you're still young. It won't be long before the proposals stop coming, Lady Penn. You're already seventeen," she chastised.

Penn snorted. "I'd rather eat frogspawn."

Maud grumbled something and wrapped a drying cloth around Penn's shoulders. "Keep your mind open, child. Don't make a mistake you'll spend the rest of your life trying to undo."

Penn climbed out of the tub and began to rub herself dry. "Sounds a lot like marriage to me."

Maud gave in and wheeled the tub from her room, leaving Penn to dress and pack her things alone.

# Two

Theroulde sat south of the Vastal Headlands and stretched wide, covering every inch of land from the Tirel River to the eastern coastline, although most of it was farmland. Rocque followed the Tirel River north and covered much less ground than Theroulde but was home to the great Rocque Bridge. The enormous stone structure passed over the river, connecting Duke Wymark's land to Tirel, home to the remainder of the royal family. Penn had never seen the famous bridge; the closest she had been to Tirel was Port Greslet when her father remarried, and all she remembered was the rain and how damned long it took to get there. She was not looking forward to much over the three-day ride, but seeing the great bridge was considered something to write home about.

First light was approaching, and the stable hands had saddled the packhorses. Penn would travel in the carriage led by four horses, two men-at-arms and her father's steward. Penn's own horse, a young mare she called Primula, was amongst the party. Her father had at least granted her that luxury.

"Penn, Penn! Will you write to me?" came the sad squeak of her sister, a blonde and curly haired girl of six who was all skin, bones and silken dresses.

"Of course I will!" Penn grinned, picking her up from the underarms and spinning her around, skirts ruffling in a very unladylike manner. Maybelle squealed. "And when I get back, I'll be blinded by your beauty!" Maybelle giggled as Penn put her down. "Don't *you* forget to write, so you can tell me all about your husband." Penn winked. Maybelle screwed up her nose as if she'd just been presented with a large cake of horse dung. Penn couldn't help but smile; Maybelle was not a silly girl, and she would be very beautiful. Lords and ladies from all over Vastal had already expressed an interest in her, and in a few years, she would start receiving official marriage proposals. Penn hoped her sister had a stronger aptitude for womanly graces than she had. Olivia would not let her only daughter follow in Penn's footsteps.

Penn kissed Maybelle on the forehead, ruffled her hair, and turned to the keep where Olivia and her father had emerged. Olivia motioned for Maybelle to return to her with a look of concern, and her sister obeyed with a frown. Olivia needn't fear; Maybelle could be corrupted by Penn no more.

Durant limped forward, one hand clutching the cane that supported him and the other holding something small and purple. "You may work as a maid, but you are still a lady of Theroulde," he said, thrusting the small package into Penn's hands.

It was a purse made of velvet, heavy and clinking. Penn looked inside. Coins: silver and golden aur, enough to outfit herself in the finest threads for years to come. Thanking her father, she closed the purse with haste, as if merely looking at her wealth was a sin. The village was in far greater need of coin than she was.

Durant waved it off. "You are to be clean and well-dressed at all times. If your hem is torn, you will repair it. If your shoes are scuffed, you will buy new ones."

Penn nodded, the grief from the night before still stinging her eyes.

"You may be the only maid with a horse of your own, so Primula will be your responsibility." Durant cleared his throat and placed a hand on Penn's shoulder, grasped it firmly, then let go.

Olivia gave her a rare smile and tucked a strand of hair behind Penn's ear. "Keep your hair like that. You look like a real lady," she said in her most maternal voice.

Penn could no longer meet her eye. Olivia looked at her as if she were searching for something, but Penn's mind was elsewhere. She could hardly breathe in her travelling attire. Maud had pulled Penn's hair into a tight braid and laid out a beige tunic, a pink girdle and hose, and brown ankle boots for Penn to wear. The sun had only just made an appearance on the horizon, and Penn was already beginning to sweat. She was not looking forward to changing into a heavy bodice and skirt when she arrived in Rocque. Gods, what if the lady's maids wore heels?

Penn said her goodbyes and took a final look at her home. Though the castle was not glamorous from the outside with its sun-scorched gardens and cracked stone, she had never known anything else. Penn would miss the battered tree trunks, the unkempt pond and the feel of the hot, dry soil beneath her bare feet. Even more so, she would miss her dirty breeches and her father turning a blind eye to her ways. Penn climbed into the carriage, took a final, fleeting look at her family through a cloud of unshed tears, and forced a smile. The door clicked shut behind her, and she was thankful. She couldn't have Maybelle remember her wet-faced and begging to stay. Penn sniffed back the tears and took a deep breath. It was all that she could do. Be strong.

\* \* \*

It felt like a week had passed by the time the carriage slowed and Penn's riding party set up camp for the night. Penn had not spent a night on the road in years and was surprised by just how much she enjoyed the crisp evening air and woodland smells. She sat cross-legged in the dirt beside the fire, eating rabbit with her fingers like a peasant. Her father's men-at-arms—though they looked slightly bewildered at first—did not say a word. Penn didn't know the men well; she had seen them a handful of times on castle grounds, but their names escaped her. However, she did know her father's steward Brennan, who eyed her quizzically.

"I do hope you aren't planning on eating like that in the Bondeville household," he said. "Not that I mind. Puts this lot at ease." He chuckled, then sucked on a greasy finger.

Penn smirked. "If it gets me sent back, maybe I will. In fact, I'll go a step further. I'll eat like you." She tossed her scraps into the fire and ran her tongue all the way from her forearm to her fingertips, cleaning up after herself in a much more grotesque fashion than Brennan had, purely to make a point. After a hearty laugh from her riding party, Penn took a stroll through the trees to wash up. The rabbit had left an unpleasant taste in her mouth. She had never liked eating meat, but fresh game had been on the table for as long as she could remember, and her father insisted that she could not live on cabbages, bread and cherry pie alone. It was a shame—she loved cherry pie.

They had camped just shy of the Tirel River, only half a mile from the road to Rocque. Far from any villages, Penn could explore without the fear of company, and by the water, she found a small alcove bordered by moss-dappled rocks and a great weeping willow. As Penn rolled up her sleeves and dipped her hands in the shallow water, her earlier misery returned. She was on her way to serve a family she had never met, in a place she had never been, doing work she would probably fail at. Part of her hoped that a bandit would leap out of the bushes and kidnap her.

In her dreams, she was often whisked away to another place by a shadowy figure who had discovered how clever, brave and talented she was. They would find her work doing something she was really good at, and the people she passed in the villages would remember her name, as they would her brothers. But Penn wouldn't find anybody like that in these woods. People like that existed purely in stories, not the waking world. The only souls she would meet alone on the road were thieves and rapists, or so Olivia said.

That was what she reminded herself of as she rinsed her mouth and washed her face in the alcove, and what she'd remind herself of again if she considered running away during the remainder of her journey. Who knew how long she would serve as the Bondeville girl's maid? Perhaps she could muster up some mischief and get herself sent home before making a total fool of herself. Surely that would make her father understand she simply wasn't suited to women's work. He would have no other option but to find her a job somewhere else far from sewing needles and frilly dresses. Her father might even train her to be a steward so that when Brennan retired to his old home, the Prestcote's affairs stayed in order. Penn didn't know much about maintaining estates, but she was good with numbers and didn't mind traveling at the drop of a hat. Oh, the places she could see! The villagers would have no choice but to respect her. She might even find her name in the history books: the first lady steward! Gillot would be beside himself with envy. Now, Brennan was older than their father, so his retirement couldn't be too far off. Yes, this was a much better plan than sneaking off in the middle of the night, and Penn thought about it until the sky grew silver with morning light.

\* \* \*

Thoughts of sabotage consumed Penn the following day. She could have filled an entire roll of parchment with potential tricks, from things as childish as stuffing a toad under Lady Lovetta's pillow to braiding weeds into her hair. It wasn't until the third and final day of her journey that she began to think about the repercussions her mischief might have. If the Bondevilles sent her home, it would bring disgrace to the Prestcote name, and the whole of Theroulde would hear of it. Her father might not forgive her. Instead of finding her more suitable work, he might denounce her in front of the entire village, and she would be forced to gut fish for a living or—even worse—be sent to the convent. Was there truly no way out of this? Gods, she despised Lady Lovetta and her hundred sisters already! They probably slept on sheets made of silk and ate peacock for breakfast, all while Penn soaked gravy spots from Lady Lovetta's gowns and chewed on mouldy bread. Some opportunity, Maud.

Her brain thoroughly exhausted with all these thoughts, Penn stretched her stiff muscles. The carriage was small, and the scarce soft furnishings were hardly pleasant to sleep on. Even the most luxurious wooden box would give somebody bedsores after three days. Peeking through the miniature window for the umpteenth time, Penn finally saw something of interest. The road had widened and was bordered by a vast meadow. A scattering of cattle grazed in the distance. After a long game of counting cows, Penn started to see grain fields and pastures, which could only mean one thing. They had arrived in Rocque.

Eventually, the carriage slowed. As the dirt road made way to gravel, Penn changed into her bodice and skirt, and by the time she stuffed her travelling clothes in her case, they had come to a complete stop. Unhooking the latch, she opened the door a crack and peered out, feeling cool air waft into the carriage. Brennan and her father's men-at-arms had dismounted and were conversing with what looked like two of the Bondeville's men-at-arms. One was thickset with jet black hair and a bushy eyebrow that failed to break in the middle, something like a caterpillar. The other man was much younger, blond and handsome in a self-assured way. Brennan spied Penn peeping from the carriage and swung the door open, offering an arm for her to climb down. If she were anywhere else, she would have jumped down on her own.

"Lady Penn Prestcote of Theroulde, welcome," greeted the older man with the caterpillar eyebrow. "My name is Roderick Pippery, and this is Sir Ulrich Rochford."

Penn realised that Sir Ulrich was a knight by his title. It explained the way he held himself, like he could recite the code of chivalry in his sleep. Penn curtsied to the men-at-arms and half-smiled, suddenly very nervous of the many ways she could make a fool of herself and bring shame to her family.

"We're pleased to see you've arrived safely. Lady Lovetta has been eagerly awaiting your arrival," Sir Ulrich said in a silky voice.

Standing tall with his chest puffed out and nose in the air, Penn thought of Florent and Gillot. Sir Ulrich was a portrait of the knight her brothers aspired to be, what their father might have been if it weren't for his injury and the loss of a great love.

Roderick, on the other hand, was thickset with drooping shoulders and ruddy cheeks. He wasn't handsome, but he had a cheerful face. His smile alone could sell water in a flood.

"Pleased to meet you. Is Lady Lovetta well?" Penn asked politely as the party surged forward. After passing through the tallest archway she had ever seen, Penn found herself on a drawbridge, hovering over a moat, like something from a folktale.

"Quite well, indeed," Sir Ulrich said, too sharply. "A picture of health."

"It seems the maid's illness was an isolated event," Roderick added. His caterpillar eyebrow furrowed. "We haven't received a single report of the sweating sickness since. Don't worry yourself, my lady." He smiled earnestly.

Penn nodded and clasped her hands to keep them steady, her eyes fixed on the path ahead rather than the dark water by her side. She would allow the men to think her nervous about illness in the castle, a reasonable concern. She would not allow them to know her true fear: the bridge's collapse and plummeting into water so deep she couldn't find her feet. Breathing shallowly, she fell into a daze until they reached the end of the bridge.

Roderick said something and Sir Ulrich laughed in response. What was funny? The death of a maid neither seemed able to name, or was it Penn they laughed at? Had they seen the way she looked at the water or heard her great sigh of relief as she crossed the last plank? Or had she said something odd in her daze? Gods, she probably had. There was so much Penn didn't know: when to talk and when to stop talking. What questions to ask, and what questions would cast her as a fool. What rules was she to follow now she had entered a life of service? Penn had only ever served herself.

If only she had paid attention to Maud or listened to her governess. Penn's father had been so lax in his discipline (and she had been so uninterested in her classes) that she couldn't remember a thing that might be of use to her, save for her lady's title. Being the king's niece ought to make her princess, but for reasons unknown to Penn, Duke Wymark had rejected his own title and duties as prince. Thus, Lady Lovetta and his other daughters were to be treated as any duke's children. Highly respected, regarded higher than a lord's daughter such as Penn, but not royal. She could only hope the duke's daughters saw themselves in the same light. Her own father had assured Penn that the Bondevilles were good people, but good people to a lord could be very different to those who served them. Penn calmed her nerves by reminding herself that it *was* Duke Wymark who had rallied for the abolition of slavery. Surely that was a good indication of the family's character, was it not?

As the group passed through the inner wall, Penn was taken by surprise. She stood in an extravagant courtyard very unlike anything Castle Theroulde had to offer. The road before her forked into three paths, one that veered to her left and disappeared amongst the pristine shrubbery, one that surged forward to a great entrance, and one that veered to the stables on her right. Lining the paths were roses, dahlias, hydrangeas and ferns, stone-bordered streams swimming with multicoloured carp, and two great water wells smothered in creeping vines. It was otherworldly.

"This way, Lady Prestcote," Roderick called from up ahead. Penn had stopped in her tracks without noticing. She looked to her right to see her father's men-at-arms leading her mare to the stables. "Your horse will be looked after, I assure you," Roderick added, continuing on the centre path to the great stone building with Brennan and Sir Ulrich by his side.

As if the courtyard had not been grand enough, the castle foyer took Penn's breath away. Two wide marble stairwells stood sparkling before her, separated by a stone archway twice as tall as Sir Ulrich. Every muscle in her body urged her forward, but to her disappointment, the Bondeville men-at-arms led Penn and Brennan through a passageway to their left. Soon she found herself in a maze of dimly lit corridors and stairwells, passing servant after servant, hearing snippets of conversations and the occasional clatter and thump from the rooms beyond. Just as Penn began to fear the very real possibility that she would lose herself on more than one occasion while attempting to navigate these passageways, Roderick and Sir Ulrich halted at a closed door. After a tap of the brass knocker, the door swung open, and her party was ushered inside.

Penn and Brennan stood in a modest sitting room, home to a scattering of wingback armchairs, a large wooden bookcase, and an empty open hearth that would make anyone pray for winter. It was nowhere near as extravagant as the foyer, but it was still much nicer than any space she had known. In the centre of the room, a heavy-set, middle-aged woman with brown skin curtsied, introducing herself as Osenna, the housekeeper. She wore a tunic of periwinkle blue and hadn't a hair out of place.

"May I present Lady Penn Prestcote of Theroulde," Brennan boomed, a look of utmost pride on his face.

Penn attempted her best curtsey.

"Could use some work," Osenna said, looking her up and down. "Her Grace is in her chambers. You'll need to wash up and change before you're presented to her. Don't expect to see much of me; I handle house affairs. I don't titter with lady's maids unless they're in strife," Osenna said with a hint of a threat, then tipped her head to the right. "Clare will take care of you."

A freckle-faced redhead stood in the corner with her palms clasped before her. She had delicate features and a tunic much like Osenna's but darker, and her blue eyes were tired. At her name, she jumped to attention.

"Now, I must talk business with the steward," Osenna said.

Penn thanked the housekeeper for her hospitality and turned to Brennan, squeezed between the Bondeville men-at-arms. By the look on his face, Penn was sure she would not see him again any time soon.

Brennan placed a hand on her shoulder and put his mouth to her ear. "Everyone must have a place in the world, Lady Penn," he whispered. "It's time you found yours."

That was the moment she knew this was real, her fate sealed in these great stone walls. Her eyes welled up, and she said a quiet goodbye to her days of beating tree trunks with sticks and walking barefoot through the village. Goodbye to her dreams of ever amounting to anything special; goodbye to becoming someone who mattered.

She bowed her head and hoped her voice didn't crack. "Thank you for always looking out for me. I hope to see you and father again soon."

Brennan smiled, then disappeared with Roderick, Sir Ulrich and Osenna in tow through the doorway they had entered from. Suddenly, the room felt much larger.

"Lady Penn, it's a pleasure to meet you," the redheaded girl in the corner said. "My name is Claremonde Mortain, but most people call me Clare. I'll be helping you to settle in to the Bondeville household."

Penn knew immediately that this girl was no noble. Though her words were formal, the girl had a thick, common accent, much like the farmer's daughters and merchant families in Theroulde. Her voice alone put Penn at ease, as she had never gotten along with noble girls.

"Please, call me Penn. I'm just a servant here, the same as you." She tried to smile. Being called a lady never felt quite right.

"Duke Wymark prefers us not to use the word servant, Lady ... I mean Penn." Clare smiled warmly. Penn apologised and Clare shook her head. "An easy mistake. He's a very kind man. He pays a fair wage and treats us as well as family. He says we should never settle for anything less," Clare continued, looking almost smitten as she explained the duke's character.

Penn was a little shocked by Clare's reverence. She had never considered that some people actually enjoyed a life of service, nor that she might be treated with kindness. So far, the Bondeville household was not the awful place she had expected it to be. But she had yet to meet Lady Lovetta, the daughter she would spend an overwhelming amount of her time with. If Lady Lovetta did not share Duke Wymark's compassions, Penn might have a very different experience to Clare.

"Evidently, I have much to learn. I'm so nervous," Penn admitted, as if it weren't obvious by the whites of her knuckles. "Thank you for putting my mind at ease, Claremonde."

Clare laughed and touched Penn's upper arm lightly—familiarly —as if they had known each other for some time. "If I'm to call you Penn, then you're to call me Clare. There's no need to be nervous. We do things quite differently here, and it's my job to teach you. In time, you will love it here, I promise." Clare gently steered Penn toward an open door. Her new companion's formality had dropped quickly, and she seemed to know exactly what to say to quell Penn's anxiety. Had she once felt as Penn did, full of doubt and terrified of failure? Perhaps Penn might be in Clare's shoes one day, happy and singing the praises of Duke Wymark's virtue as a new maid stood shaking in Osenna's sitting room. Oh, Penn could dream.

"Come, there's so much to see!" Clare ushered Penn through the door and the two began their tour.

# Three

Beneath what Penn would have ordinarily called the servant's quarters was a bathhouse. It was the first stop on her tour of the castle. At home, Penn had her own bathtub. Maud would wheel the mouldy wooden tub to her chambers and fill it with buckets of lukewarm, scented water a few times a week. Penn had never been inside a bathhouse before—she didn't even think they existed south of Yasai.

The great stone chamber held a modest changing bay littered with linen baskets, small buckets and soaps. Stretched along the wall beside the bay was a raised trough filled with hot, running water. A scattering of stools and a long, fogged mirror lined the wall, creating a space to wash away the day's dirt to keep the bathwater clean. In the centre of the chamber was an enormous pit filled with steaming water that looked black in the low light.

"Is it deep?" Penn asked, starting to sweat.

Clare shrugged. "Not more than four feet, I'd say, although I've never thought to ask."

Four feet. She could manage that. Bathing with an audience, on the other hand, she wasn't so sure about. Penn had not bathed in front of anyone other than Maud since she was a child, and the thought of stripping off communally made her stomach tighten. She didn't even like looking at her own body, so how would she manage the prying eyes of other women? And they *would* look, just as Penn would look at Clare if she had stripped bare before her. She would appraise the many imperfections that made her human, quietly noting the shape of her breasts and if her inner thighs touched as her own did. Her skin prickled at the thought of seeing other women so vulnerable and of being so vulnerable herself.

"Take your time. I'll go and fetch your uniform." Clare disappeared down the hallway, leaving Penn and the flutter in her chest alone in the steamy bathhouse.

Oh, how grateful she was for the privacy. Penn began in the changing bay where she removed her clothes and placed them in one of the empty hanging baskets. Hiding her chest with her arms, she hurried to the trough, as if the walls themselves had eyes. With a bar of floral scented soap, Penn scrubbed her hair and body, dropping several buckets of water from the trough over herself to rinse. Goosebumps rippled her flesh as she walked over to the bath and made a quick descent into the hot water, which only just reached her chest. Yes, she could manage this. It was no ocean abyss, only a bath. A bath so grand that twenty people could fit in with enough room to kick their arms and legs about.

Penn looked to the high, stone ceiling, sank into the water, and sighed with pleasure. Perhaps she would have shown more of an interest in bathing as a child if she'd had a bath like this. Penn perched on a step and wriggled her toes in front of her, hoping she would be lucky enough to choose an unpopular time to bathe every day. But if Lady Lovetta used the bathhouse too, she would almost certainly have a daily bathing companion. At least it would save her hauling buckets of water to her chambers. Penn sank deeper and tilted her head back, enjoying the feeling of the water tickling her hairline. The air was thick with hot steam that stung her nostrils when she inhaled, and Penn was sure to fall asleep before long.

Just as she had entered a pleasant daze, Clare's voice echoed in the hallway, snapping Penn back to the present.

"I've brought your uniform," she called from around the corner.

"Just a moment!" Penn squeaked, pulling herself out of the bath with a great effort. How she would love to stay there and let the warmth lull her to sleep. Pulling a drying cloth from a basket, Penn tried her best to wring the water from her hair. The air in the bath-house was so humid that no amount of patting her body dry would quite do the job, so she wrapped herself up, the cloth only just falling to her upper thighs. Peering around the corner, Penn found Clare waiting with an armful of fabric. Her new friend dropped her gaze and first passed Penn her undergarments, then her matching tunic, a white girdle, and hose. Lastly, she handed her a pair of sensible leather boots. No heavy bodice, frilly skirt or heels in sight, thank the gods.

After dressing, Clare braided Penn's hair in the preferred style of the household, which looked very much like the way Maud had braided her hair before her ride to Rocque. The style began as two braids, merged into one, then wound around itself in a neat knot secured by a white ribbon. It was lovely, but how could she possibly replicate it?

Penn looked at her reflection critically. She didn't like her hair pulled back quite so tight; her faint eyebrows and lashes made her forehead look bigger than it was. Her chin had a noticeable point, and her sharp nose was dusted with the faintest of freckles, making her pale skin look patchy. She didn't have the smooth, olive-toned complexion that the pretty court ladies did. The only part of her face she didn't mind were her eyes, which were as wide and green as her mothers had been.

Clare chattered excitedly as they continued the tour of the castle. First, they visited the kitchen, where Penn met three kitchen maids and the cook, who was brown-skinned like Osenna. Adjoining the kitchen was a dusty hall that had once been used as the servant's dining room. According to Clare, the duke did not look kindly on royals who segregated their households, and he encouraged his staff to eat in the main dining hall with his family. Penn later learned that the room she had met Osenna in was the housekeeper's study, a gift from the duke to commemorate her tenth year in his service. The more Penn learned about Duke Wymark, the more interested she became in the Bondeville family. They were so unlike the noble families Penn had visited throughout her childhood.

It was late afternoon by the time Penn made it to Lady Lovetta's chambers. During her tour, she briefly met two of the duke's youngest daughters, Dorett, who was thirteen and had more than a spoonful of trouble in her, and Sarra, a shy girl of nine. Both daughters shared Osenna's golden-brown skin, glossy black curls and midnight eyes. Clare told her that all of the duke's children favoured their mother, who had passed six or so years ago. She was from the far west kingdom of Azor, born in the old city of Musard. Marriages between kingdoms were unheard of at that time and tensions high following the cessation of the war. Even now, such marriages were sure to be a scandal.

"Are there many families like the Bondevilles?" Penn asked.

"With shared blood? I couldn't say. If there were any in my village, they were sensible enough to make themselves scarce."

"I'm not quite sure I follow," admitted Penn.

"Awful things happen to people who dare to be different, but enough of that. We're here." Clare went to knock on Lady Lovetta's door, a great mahogany thing that shone with fresh oil.

"Wait," Penn said, stopping Clare's hand. "What's she like?" Her nerves had come alive again.

"Practical ... and independent." Clare closed her hand around Penn's and squeezed it gently before whispering, "In a way, you have it easy. You needn't worry about making up her face or polishing ruby diadems as I do with my lady, Edony. But she is headstrong and no stranger to trouble, so you must look out for her. She may take some time to warm to you, but she has a good heart. I have a feeling she will like you." Clare let go of Penn's hand and knocked hard on the door.

This was it. Everything rested on this moment. To Penn's surprise, the Bondeville family interested her, and she liked the castle and her new friend Clare. If Lady Lovetta was as Clare described, her duties as a maid might not be so bad. Penn could give her lady the space she needed, and she could look out for her, as she had Maybelle. But could Lady Lovetta truly like her when she was everything a lady's maid shouldn't be?

"Do come in," a woman called out, her voice strong and melodic.

Clare turned the handle and the door creaked open. Holding her breath, Penn reminded herself that if Lady Lovetta was a monster, she could simply run away and live with the guilt of ruining her family's reputation. Gillot was only bound to do it in a few years, and she couldn't stand being bested by her younger brother. Her father had to forgive her eventually, didn't he?

Past the threshold, Penn saw a woman with her head in a book, perched on an armchair by an unlit hearth. The book closed with a snap, she rose and walked forward.

Lady Lovetta was everything like her sisters, but also something else entirely. Penn had never seen a face that was both soft and angular. Her eyes were near black, bordered by boldly arched eyebrows and a severe widow's peak. Her lips were plumper than most, deep pink without stain or gloss. Soft curls spiralled to hips that were wide, reserved for the finest of fabrics. Trailing behind her and gathered at the waist was a cream-coloured gown cut low at the front, exposing her generous chest. She was tall, almost a head above Penn. Everything about her lady drew Penn in, from her pristine silk slippers to the manicured tips of her fingers. Oh, her fingers! So long and neatly intertwined, like a thread waiting to be unravelled. How Penn wished to unclasp those hands and hold them in her own, if only for a moment.

Something inside Penn tightened when she looked at Lady Lovetta. Dizzy and with sweat budding on her palms, she savoured the sight before her. This magnificent woman was a whole new world of beautiful. Penn could not decide if she was intimidated, made insecure, or awed by her. Though Lady Lovetta would never wear a crown, she was the kind of woman who, with a single glance, could incite a war.

As Clare introduced Penn, she sank into a deep curtsey and hovered, heart hammering. "Your Grace, I will serve you faithfully, loyally and dutifully, sworn in sight of my ancestors before me, and the gods of our realm," Penn recited. It was the first and hopefully last time she would ever say the oath out loud, and it dripped from her lips with a sincerity she didn't recognise. Was this how her brother had felt at his knighthood ceremony as he pledged himself to the king?

"Stand up, Lady Penn Prestcote of Theroulde," Lady Lovetta hummed. Was that humour in her eyes? "I admire your dedication, but such formalities are not necessary here."

Penn straightened and clenched her unsteady hands. Had she made a fool of herself already?

"From this day forth, you are to call me Lovetta and nothing else. I've never been fond of titles."

"Nor I ... Lovetta." Penn winced as if she had muttered a curse. What great power there was in a single word.

"I think she'll do nicely, Clare." Lovetta smiled playfully. Penn wasn't exactly sure what she meant, but she was certain of one thing. There would be no toads under Lovetta's pillow that evening, or any other evening.

"Has Clare shown you the grounds?" her lady asked. "Our gardens are marvellous."

Penn stiffened. It was her turn to speak again. Gods, why was it so difficult to string a sentence together? "Just the castle, but it alone took the better half of the afternoon," she said, hearing the timidity in her own voice. She was curious about the overgrown path that disappeared into the shrubbery, and she would very much like to see Primula's new lodgings. But both meant leaving Lovetta's chambers, and Penn wasn't sure she remembered how to walk, or even wanted to.

"That won't do! Clare, you must show her the gardens before supper. Oh, look. It's almost dusk. Go now!" Lovetta insisted, staring wistfully out of the window.

"Certainly," Clare said, leading Penn back through the doorway.

Lovetta grinned. "I can't wait to learn all about you after supper."

Clare curtsied and pulled the door shut, and Penn silently thanked the gods for the gift of working legs. Lovetta couldn't wait to learn about her. Her! How absurd. What was Penn compared to her? What was a river pebble compared to a diamond? The idea that Penn's life was of any interest to Lovetta had her head spinning. Who cared about the damned gardens? She wanted to stay right there!

As Clare led her back through the maze of the castle, they passed dozens of frantic women dressed in blue, but none stole Penn's attention like Lovetta had. Women greeted her from every angle, housemaids donning dirty aprons and bonnets, and lady's maids dressed as neat as she. They flitted around her like butterflies, polite yet eager to get on with their duties.

"Is it always this busy?" Penn asked as Clare ushered her around a corner she swore they had passed only a moment ago.

"Certainly not. The duke has been away a week, and he returns tonight. There's to be a feast later," Clare said, followed by a grin. "You couldn't have arrived at a better time. A Bondeville feast is to die for!"

A wave of relief passed over Penn. The household would be too busy fussing over the arrival of the duke to even notice a new maid.

"What took him away?" she asked. The duke must have left Rocque right after sending word to her father.

The change on Clare's face made it quite clear that his trip was not for leisure. "Delivering ashes."

The maid. Penn immediately apologised for the household's loss.

"How kind of you," Clare said. "Did anyone … sorry, do you know what happened to Lady Lovetta's maid? Her maid before you?"

"Yes, my father told me. She had the sweating sickness, didn't she?" A wave of heat washed over Penn, and she wished she had kept her curiosity to herself.

"Yes, we had to … to burn her," Clare replied, her voice cracking. "Or else the sickness might spread. The duke did it himself."

Penn didn't want to remember the burning of her mother's body, but she did. Brennan had done it, as was expected of the family's steward. But that couldn't be Penn's last memory of her mother. When she was deemed ill, all visitations stopped. The illness was too unpredictable; anyone near her mother could have caught it. The last time Penn saw her mother alive was late in the evening, three days before she passed. She had brushed out her daughter's hair before bed while Penn complained about Florent getting a larger serving of pudding. It was such an ordinary evening, yet Penn held it tight in her heart. She hoped that the Bondeville household had fond memories of their fallen maid. By the look on Clare's face, it was clear that someone had cherished her.

"She was from a noble house in the Headlands. Have you ever been?" Clare asked with a hollow smile.

Penn shook her head. "I'm afraid I haven't." The Vastal Headlands were about as far as Theroulde but north. Making a round trip in a week, as the duke had, sounded exhausting. He could have sent the ashes with his staff, but instead chose to deliver them personally. Penn was yet again impressed by Duke Wymark's character. She turned to her new friend who looked ahead with cloudy eyes. Her face had become so pale it was as if the blood had been siphoned from her body.

"You were close, weren't you?" Penn asked gently.

"Very," Clare whispered as they rounded another bend.

Penn couldn't bring herself to ask anything more as they made their way into a large courtyard. It took her a moment to get her bearings, but Penn soon deduced they had entered the gardens from the rear of the castle. Here, the greenery was just as charismatic as it had been at the front, but there were large expanses of grass and decorative stones divided by half a dozen hedge-lined pathways, all leading in different directions. A great fountain sat in the middle of the gardens, shallow enough to wade through on a hot day, if it were permitted. Walking through the impressive arrangement, Penn spotted a winding path that vanished into shrubbery, just like the one in the front gardens. If her bearings were correct, they were one and the same. Perhaps it was her imagination, but Penn could have sworn the shadows were calling to her, pulling her in.

"This way!" Clare called, summoning Penn.

Immediately, her attention was stolen by a plot of tiny yellow flowers surrounding a massive hedge shaped like a horse. Its head was tilted, nose pointing to the road ahead. In the glow of the setting sun, it was astonishing, and the winding path became inconsequential. "I've never seen anything like it. How clever," Penn whispered, admiring the manicured creature. It was no wonder Lovetta fawned over the castle's gardens.

Clare smiled earnestly. "It was my idea, although Mabs did the hard work. It shows the way to the stables."

Penn hurried forward. "Is that where we're going?"

"I heard you brought your own horse and thought you might like to see it. Does it have a name?" Clare asked. A little of her life had returned.

"Primula. She's a gorgeous buckskin. Do you have a horse?" she asked, even though it was unlikely. Horses were expensive, and Clare's accent did not allude to wealth. Clare was silent for a moment, and Penn felt a little guilty for asking.

"I do. She only became mine this week, though. She was left to me, you see..." Clare's voice trailed off to its earlier unfeeling state. Had the maid before her left Clare her horse? Penn felt even guiltier for bringing her up again. The two had been very close, indeed.

They reached the stables, and for the first time since she'd arrived in Rocque, Penn was underwhelmed. An afternoon immersed in the fineries of the castle had her expecting a stable to match. But the stable was like every other, dimly lit, drowning in hay and reeking of dung. Penn spotted Primula standing alone in a generous sized stall, looking worn from her journey. She rested a hand on her neck and Primula sniffed her hair affectionately.

"She'll be grazing and getting fat with the rest of the horses, come tomorrow. Our stable hands spoil them rotten," Clare said as Penn surveyed the timber building once more. It was both larger and cleaner than Castle Theroulde's stables. The duke had twenty or more horses, while her own father had a modest half-dozen and two stable hands. The duke must employ half the village!

Penn scratched Primula's neck. "Spoiled rotten, indeed."

"Over here," Clare called. She had a hand on a stepladder that stretched the length of the wall. Penn looked up and saw what looked like a hayloft. Clare beckoned her forward. "Come on, slow-poke." She climbed the ladder swiftly.

Penn walked forward. "Up there? Why?" Haylofts were no place for a lady, as Olivia would say.

"I promise I won't mug you," Clare said.

"That's exactly what a mugger would say." Penn took a rung and made her ascent, quickly noticing what made the hayloft worth visiting.

The space was small, with a bundle of blankets laid out in the centre, a stack of books, and a rusty lantern atop a wooden crate. Snoozing in the middle of the blankets was a fat tabby cat with several miniature versions of herself nestled close by. Penn could hardly stop herself from squealing with joy.

"They're about four weeks old," Clare said as Penn shuffled closer to the family of cats. "I come up here a lot. To read, to sew, to get away from the noise, and one day this cat was just here all fat and grumpy, and she started having kittens in front of me!"

Penn was in a state of adoration. There were five kittens, two that were ginger like their mother, and three that had darker colouring. One of the darker kittens was smaller than the others and was settled a little further away from the group.

"Do you think they'll be okay up here?" Penn asked.

"I check on them every day. That little one might look like a runt, but it's twice the size it was when it came out."

"What will you do with them?" She was never allowed pets at home. Some years it had been hard enough keeping the horses fed, and Olivia sneezed from just about anything.

Clare smiled. "Oh, I think they'll be just fine right here. They might even keep the mice under control."

Penn grinned. "Wouldn't it be nice to have them in the castle, though?"

"The girls would love them," Clare started, then frowned. "But Osenna hates cats. She'd have my head."

"Is she that bad?" Penn asked, remembering Osenna's stern demeanour.

"It depends on her mood. She's prickly, and I'd rather not risk losing my good reference."

"Reference? What do you mean?" Penn asked as she stroked the back of a ginger kitten. The mewling was music to her ears.

"It's a letter. A statement of my character and the experience I've gained through working in the castle. You need one if you expect to work in any household half as fine as this."

"Oh, I don't think I have one. I've never worked before."

"Lucky," Clare said with a cocked brow. "Although the duke doesn't care for such things, much to Osenna's disbelief. If it were up to her, we would all be from noble houses, like you. She's quite traditional."

"So, she should like me, shouldn't she?" Penn felt a flicker of hope. Osenna sounded strict, and with Penn's poor aptitude for women's work, she could do with a little favouritism.

Clare shook her head. "Sorry, but I don't think so. She doesn't seem to like anyone. In fact, she'll probably expect more from you than she does from girls like me. That's how it was last time, at least." The same look came over Clare again. Vacant, as if she was somewhere else entirely. Earlier, she'd mentioned that Lovetta's previous maid came from a noble house, and Clare's sudden distance made sense. Penn would bet an aur it was Clare's friend who had rubbed Osenna the wrong way.

Feeling grim, Penn pulled away from the mewling animal. "So, we definitely shouldn't sneak the kittens into the castle, then."

Clare's eyes went wide. "Absolutely not. If you step a toe out of line and Osenna finds out, your entire family will hear of it."

A picture came to Penn's mind. Her father shaking his head, hands on his temples in frustration. Olivia glowering at her, Gillot laughing, and, worst of all, Florent saying nothing as he looked at her with pity. Penn would not let that happen.

"Supper will be served soon," Clare said, reaching for the ladder. "We shouldn't stay out much longer." The shadows in the stable had grown longer as the early evening light dipped closer to the horizon. "There's just one more thing I want to show you," Clare called as she climbed down from the hayloft.

Penn said goodbye to the cats and followed her. She'd already seen so much, what else could there be? The shadowy path came back to her. Of course! It was the only path they hadn't yet taken. Penn kissed Primula's neck and hurried out of the stable.

The castle was even more breathtaking as the sun set. Torches had been lit, and the three great pathways that converged at the drawbridge were illuminated, casting reflections that danced on the surface of the waterways between them.

Clare sighed, looking defeated. "On second thoughts, it's too dark. I'll show you another time."

Although Penn was a little disappointed, her stomach had started to gurgle. She hadn't eaten since morning.

As the two set out for the castle's main entrance, a horn sounded from beyond the drawbridge. They stopped to watch the great slab lower, chains clinking, and listened as voices shouted from outside the stone walls. Hooves thumped across the bridge the second it touched ground, and a broad-shouldered man cloaked in black thundered into the gardens on the back of an enormous blue roan, followed by a party of men-at-arms. Though the sky grew steadily darker, Penn was almost certain she had seen this man before.

"Is that Duke Wymark?" she asked, and Clare nodded with a look of pride. As the two moved on, Penn wondered why Duke Wymark looked so familiar. Her father had never mentioned the duke visiting Theroulde, and why would he visit? Why would anyone? She was imagining things, she decided, as she followed Clare through the servant's door and entered another maze.

\* \* \*

The smell of roasted vegetables and spices drifted through the archway to the Bondeville's great dining hall. Two armoured men with straight faces were stationed at the entrance, greeting Penn and Clare as they crossed the threshold. The dining hall was long with a towering ceiling, lit by clusters of candles that made the polished stone floor glisten like water. Tall arched windows interrupted the embossed plaster, and three long tables buzzed in the middle of the hall. Two of the tables were filled with women in clothes much like Penn's, and the head table sat horizontally on the dais, occupied by Duke Wymark and his six daughters.

Clare ushered Penn to a cluster of empty seats and started piling their plates high with baked breads, curried vegetables, beans, greens and savoury pastries. Penn surveyed the dishes before her and quickly realised that something was missing. Where was the meat? She craned her neck to look at the Bondevilles table and found that they ate the same fare as their staff, no glazed ham or peacock in sight.

Clare looked at her quizzically. "What's wrong? You must be starved. Is the food not to your taste?"

"No, it's not that. I just noticed ... did no one hunt in the duke's absence?" Penn returned her gaze to her own plate and the fragrant steam that wafted from it. Gods, it looked good.

Clare cleared her throat and leaned closer to Penn. "Azorians don't eat meat," she whispered.

"Oh!" Penn exclaimed. "I had no idea."

"It's their religion. They believe the lives of animals are just as sacred as the lives of people. It's nice, actually. I think it has something to do with the first gods, but I don't quite remember what," Clare explained. Having never liked the taste of fresh game, Penn wasn't bothered one bit. Rocque was quickly surpassing all her expectations. It seemed one *could* live off cabbages and cherry pie alone.

Evidently, Clare was as just as hungry as Penn because they both cleared their plates at an alarming speed. Throughout supper, Penn stole glances at the duke's table. His daughters, though so very similar in appearance, looked nothing like their father. He was white-skinned, like Penn, while his daughters had inherited their mother's Azorian colouring. He was, however, responsible for their angular faces, above-average height, and their hair, which was thick, glossy, and as dark as a starless sky. Lovetta had the most curl, her hair loose around her shoulders like a veil.

Penn did not spend long with Duke Wymark on her mind once she spotted Lovetta. She was without doubt the most astonishing of the Bondeville daughters, glowing bright without gemstones, powder or kohl. Just as Penn put a heaped spoonful of pudding to her mouth, Lovetta met her eye with a smile. Gods, why did she have to shovel all that in? Lovetta pushed her plate away and stood, two of her sisters following suit. They descended from the dais and walked the length of the hall, right towards Penn. Nervously, she wiped her face with a napkin and swished some water around in her mouth; the last thing she wanted was broccoli in her teeth. Lovetta, who had changed into a delicate gown of pale blue for the evening, sat next to Penn and introduced her two elder sisters, Belsante and Edony. The distance between Penn and Lovetta was scant, and she had trouble looking at her without her nerves reigniting, but how could she look away? It was a sin! There was something about Lovetta that stole the air from the room.

"You're very pretty," cooed the eldest sister, Belsante.

Penn could hardly believe her ears. *Her,* pretty? Not next to Belsante, who looked demure in a high-necked gown of burgundy and wore neat curls pinned close to her head.

"Prettier than the last one," added Edony, who looked softer than her elder sister in emerald green, her curls gathered loosely by a glistening comb. Her neckline was cut precariously low, and she wore half a dozen gemstones on each hand, and a fine gold ring pierced her left nostril. Looking at her was fun. Penn had never seen a woman her age dress so boldly; it was admirable.

Lovetta didn't disguise the reproachful look she gave Edony, and Clare stiffened as if taking personal offence to the comment. But Penn didn't spend long with her eyes on Clare, or on any of Lovetta's sisters. Not when Lovetta herself was there, sitting right beside her smelling of lavender, her fluttering eyelashes nearly long enough to fan away the heat from Penn's neck.

"Oh, I wish my cheeks did that!" Lovetta said with a pout.

Penn's hands flew to her cheeks, hot with embarrassment.

Edony giggled. "That's what rouge is for."

The redness blossomed darker on Penn's face as she prayed for a change in conversation. Ever since she was a child, whenever she felt a strong emotion, the whole room knew about it immediately. Thankfully, Lovetta saved her.

"I'm sorry I didn't come down sooner. With father back, there was a lot to talk about. Did you see the gardens?"

"Yes, your Grace," Penn said without a thought.

"Your Grace!" cried Edony with such drama that Penn flinched. Belsante stifled a laugh, and Lovetta rolled her eyes, then looked pointedly at Penn. "What did I say about titles, *Lady* Penn?" Lovetta smiled in a teasing way.

"I'm sorry!" Penn exclaimed, suppressing a giggle herself.

"Oh, don't worry about it," started Edony with a wink. "It took Clare almost a year to stop calling me 'your Grace', and I'm the least graceful of us all." There was a murmur of agreement, Clare included. Finally, Penn felt at ease.

"But we haven't broken her completely," Lovetta interrupted. "Half the time she still calls us m'lady."

Clare, who had been quiet all throughout the Bondeville's taunts, defended herself. "My father would hang me by the toes if he knew I spoke to you so boldly!"

"Your father would hang you by the toes if you sneezed," Edony said scathingly.

Everyone but Penn laughed, clearly privy to something Penn wasn't.

"Well," Lovetta continued, "in any event, if you must call me something unnecessary while you settle in, please just stick to my lady, or my head will get so big I'll topple over."

The others shrieked with laughter. Penn giggled along with them, quite enjoying the company of Lovetta and her sisters. After they had exhausted themselves of laughter, Lovetta continued, "I bet we aren't what you were expecting, are we?"

Lovetta had indeed read her mind. "Not quite," she confessed. Though Penn was dreading her daily duties as a maid, Lovetta was so pleasant to be around that perhaps life in the castle wouldn't be the torture she had imagined.

"I promise I won't make you scrub the privy, okay?" Lovetta placed her palm on Penn's knee. Her touch startled Penn so much she omitted a terribly off-pitch giggle that she hoped the others thought a cough.

"I'm here to serve you in whatever way that pleases you," Penn said in her most formal tone. "You ought not make any allowances for me that you wouldn't any other maid. I may be new to service, but I promise to work hard and expect no indulgences."

Lovetta laughed. "Oh, that's sweet. I'll be honest with you, when father said I needed a new maid, I told him not to bother." She sighed and her tone hardened. "It's ridiculous, really. I'm quite capable of looking after myself." Edony snorted and received another reproachful look from Lovetta. "Honestly, just look at them all." She waved her slender fingers in the direction of the two full tables of staff. "If I need help, there's no shortage of hands. We just don't need another maid, and a noble at that! It's unnecessary, don't you think?"

Penn couldn't help but feel hurt by Lovetta's words, even if there was truth to them. She didn't seem fond of highborn maids at all, and she talked of Penn's new duties as if they were so trivial that her presence wouldn't be missed. Was there any point in her being there, if Lovetta herself didn't even care for a maid?

An uncomfortable silence followed before Penn could speak, and all those around the table seemed to notice. "I'm sorry," Penn said. "If I had known you felt that way, I mean, if my father had known, we wouldn't have troubled you. The last thing I want is to be a burden."

"Oh, I didn't mean it like—"

"I think it's time for bed," interrupted Belsante, imitating a yawn as she pushed out her chair.

"You're not wrong," Edony added, which was Clare's cue to stand.

"I'll see you at breakfast," Penn's new friend said. "M'lady will be needing me tonight." She gave Penn's shoulder a reassuring squeeze. The three said goodnight and made their way out of the dining hall, leaving Penn and Lovetta alone at the end of the table. The space between them felt even smaller now there was nobody on either side of them, and Penn wondered if Lovetta felt as awkward as she did.

"That came out wrong, what I said. I think you might have gotten the wrong message," Lovetta said.

Penn tried not to sound as dejected as she felt. "It's okay. I think I understand." It was simple; Lovetta, like herself, was a grown woman and did not need or want a maid. Penn would be in the way, but Lovetta felt guilty for admitting it. Maybe her father had written to Duke Wymark and told him of Penn's ineptitude, and he had passed on the message to Lovetta so that she wouldn't expect too much. Maybe Penn was sent to serve Lovetta *because* of this. If she had no use for a maid, it wouldn't matter whether she was any good. Lovetta gave Penn an apologetic smile, only confirming her thoughts. Fantastic.

"I'm glad," Lovetta said.

Being useless was a hideous feeling.

"I suppose we ought to go to bed, too," Lovetta said, looking vaguely at the emptying tables. At least half of the crowd had dispersed, and Duke Wymark's table had been abandoned. Lovetta slid off her chair and brushed the creases from her gown. "Come," she summoned, and the two made their way to Lovetta's chambers by a much simpler route than the servant's maze.

Lovetta's chambers were elegant, with stone floors and embossed plaster not unlike the dining hall. Earlier that day, Penn had been too nervous to appreciate the finery, but now she could take it all in. In the middle of the room stood a large four-poster bed draped in ivory fabric and adorned with an excess of cushions. A long dressing table sat by an arched window, open to the evening breeze. The hearth, fronted by a wingback armchair and a crimson rug, sat still and unlit. A partition sectioned off a corner of the room that held a much smaller bed and a bedside table, topped with flickering candles, a washbasin and spare linens. Penn's trunk sat at the foot of the maid's bed, waiting for her.

"By the way, you don't have to use those awful old passageways to move about the castle. Father hates them, but there isn't much he can do about them," Lovetta said, then started to smile. "Although they are a great hiding place. Edony and I would play in them all the time when we were younger, but only when Bel wasn't around to rouse on us. Do you have any siblings?"

Penn helped Lovetta unlace the back of her gown and prayed she didn't scratch her with a hangnail. Lovetta's skin was soft and warm without a freckle in sight. "Yes, an elder and a younger brother, and a younger sister," Penn said with a hitch in her voice. Why was it so hard to talk with her hands on Lovetta? Penn cleared her throat and continued. "She and I don't have the same mother, though. My father remarried after my mother passed."

"Oh, I'm so sorry. I lost mine too, but father wouldn't dream of marrying again. I couldn't imagine any lady tolerating the six of us, anyway."

Penn laughed as she took a hairbrush from the dressing table. "Your sisters seem wonderful, and six children is a blessing."

Lovetta sat before her, her hair splayed out around her strong arms. What had she done to build muscles like that? Penn had spent every chance she could bounding around Castle Theroulde's court-yards, yet her arms were still pathetic. A lady like Lovetta was far too busy for such nonsense, as Olivia would say.

"What's it like to have brothers?" Lovetta asked. She wiped her face with a damp cloth as Penn started on the ends of Lovetta's hair. It was so thick with curl and tiny knots that Penn had to take care not to rip chunks from her scalp.

"Not the same as having sisters," Penn confirmed. "My elder brother Florent is kind and we've always been close, but Gillot is too competitive for his own good. We've never gotten along. Maybelle is just the sweetest. I adore her. It's impossible not to when she puts my breeches on her head and runs around the castle covered in mud." The memory brought an instant smile to Penn's face, but it quickly dropped when she saw the furrow in Lovetta's brow through the mirror. "They're Florent's breeches, actually. He gave them to me when he outgrew them, but I wouldn't dare wear them outside the castle," she lied.

Lovetta's brows came closer together. "Why not? They're light and comfortable, perfect for riding. Nobody in Azor would bat an eye at a woman in breeches. Personally, I don't see what all the fuss is about."

Penn abruptly stopped brushing. "Nor do I!" she exclaimed. "I only meant that people would talk, and if it came back to my stepmother, she would be furious. If it were up to me, I'd never take them off. I'd sleep in them."

Lovetta laughed. "Oh, I don't know about that. Call me spoiled, but there's nothing like the feeling of bare skin on silk sheets."

The image of Lovetta sprawled out on her four-poster bed stark naked caught Penn off guard, and her fingers began to tremble. When did the room get so warm? Swallowing hard, Penn took the next section of Lovetta's hair.

"You're so gentle. Like a little bird," Lovetta said. "I was going to brush my hair myself, but I'm glad I let you."

"The trick is to start with the ends. That's how my mother did it," Penn said, supressing a smile as she continued her handiwork. "My hair could be a nest at the start, but she was so careful that I barely felt a thing." And then her mother died, and Penn's hair became a nest once more. "I'm sorry, I shouldn't have said anything. Not when you've also suffered a great loss."

"Don't be sorry," Lovetta said. "It's a lovely memory; cherish it. I would have liked that instead of a maid's hands all the time. But with so many daughters, it's understandable. Anyway, I can't imagine my mother would have been as gentle as you. She was firm ... unyielding. And full of light. She couldn't sit still long enough to have her own hair tended to. She would be in such a hurry that she'd have ripped the hair clean from my scalp." A shadow of a smile flitted across Lovetta's face.

"Our housemaid was awfully rough. I'm surprised I've any hair left at all." Penn worked her way through Lovetta's tresses, savouring the heady floral scent. "Can't imagine my stepmother would have been any better."

"You don't get along," Lovetta said matter-of-factly.

"No, we don't," Penn admitted.

"Why?"

Penn placed the hairbrush back on the dressing table. "She believes me a bad influence on my sister because I don't want to marry."

"Interesting," Lovetta said as she leaned forward. She took a small pot and offered it to Penn. "It's for my hair. Only use a little on the ends."

Penn took the pot and swirled her finger in the oil, the source of Lovetta's intoxicating scent. She fingered it through her curls, and when Lovetta wasn't looking, dabbed a little on the inside of her wrist. Then, Penn was dismissed for the evening. She made to close the window, but Lovetta stopped her. She didn't mind the insects, it seemed, as long as she had fresh air. Penn liked that.

Disappearing behind her partition, Penn opened her trunk, changed into her bedclothes, and climbed under the covers, blowing out the candles before settling in. For a while, she laid on her back and stared at the ceiling, replaying the events of the day in her head as she sniffed the lavender oil on her wrist. The emotional whirlwind had left her thoughts in a scramble, and she tossed and turned as sleep evaded her. Penn had entered an entirely new world she had never desired, yet she was excited for morning to come. None of it made sense. What was it about Lovetta that captivated her so?

As the night drew on, Penn became certain of what she would have to do. Come tomorrow, she would try everything in her power to prove to Lovetta that she was the furthest thing from useless.

# Four

It was barely dawn when Penn rose the following morning. Lovetta slept soundly as Penn scribbled a letter to Maybelle, describing the castle and all its fineries. She would like that. Before Lovetta woke, Penn crept out the door, determined to reach the bathhouse before anybody else. To Penn's dismay, though, it appeared that the castle housed several early risers.

Four people bobbed about in the water, chattering and laughing amongst themselves. As Penn turned to head back to Lovetta's chambers, a familiar voice called her name from the water. Penn squinted her eyes and made out Edony's face through the steam, accompanied by Clare and two women Penn had yet to meet.

"Don't be shy. We're all women," Edony called, teasingly.

Penn took a deep breath, stripped off her clothes, placed them in a hanging basket, and tiptoed to the washing bay. She snatched up a wet cake of soap and lathered herself in bubbles, then scooped up enough hot water with her bucket to rinse her body off, taking care to keep her day-old braids dry. She had to make the style last long enough for her to figure out how to recreate it. Eyes stinging from the steam, Penn walked toward the water, far away from the twittering group. Only once submerged did she wade over, red faced and feeling awkward. Clare smiled warmly as if reassuring her that yes, it would get easier.

"Have you met Ysabell?" Edony asked, placing a water-wrinkled hand on the shoulder of a brown-skinned girl who, wet and unkempt, looked much like a slightly smaller version of Edony, though her ears stuck out a little too far. She was the last of the Bondeville daughters Penn had to meet, and a look of total ambivalence was plastered across her face. Penn introduced herself with a smile, but Ysabell simply nodded. "She doesn't talk much. That's why we don't get along," Edony said with a grin, patting her sister's sodden hair. Ysabell returned the gesture with a great splash that left no one untouched. Penn blinked the water from her eyes and looked to the other unfamiliar face in the party, a sickly thin girl a little taller than Ysabell with pale skin and brunette ringlets. She introduced herself as Marion, Ysabell's maid.

"I don't know how I'm going to remember everyone's names," Penn said honestly. "This castle feels bigger than my entire village."

Clare chuckled. "That's how I felt when I got here."

"And me," added Marion, who spoke the same thick, common accent as Clare.

"How long have you two been here?" Penn asked, sinking deeper into the water.

"Almost four years," Clare answered, "but Marion's only been here for two." Two years sounded like a long time to Penn. "I'm sure you'll settle in much faster than we did, though. I didn't know a thing about service."

Penn feigned a laugh, wishing she had an excuse for her pitiful abilities.

"I was so shy that I didn't bathe for two weeks," Marion said with a look of shame.

Two weeks! Perhaps Penn wasn't off to such a bad start, after all. Then, seeing the Bondevilles with their respective maids, a thought dawned on her. "When does Lady Lovetta bathe? Should I have waited?"

"Oh, you know ... I'm not sure. She's never in here when I am," Edony said.

Ysabell shook her head. "Don't ask me."

"She says she prefers the quiet," Edony added. She looked at Clare momentarily, as if exchanging some sort of message. "She calls herself independent, but really, she's just a prude."

Marion chuckled, and Clare glared at her disapprovingly.

Penn considered Lovetta's spiel about independence from the night before. Whatever the reason, it was welcome news. She may not have a bathing companion, after all.

When the Bondeville daughters climbed out with their flushed maids in tow, Penn averted her eyes. Shortly after, she followed, clutching a drying cloth tight to her chest. Clare, who had already pulled on her undergarments, offered Penn a sympathetic look. "You'll come to love being down here, I promise."

The bathhouse was nice, and if Penn had been alone, she would have gladly stayed and soaked a little longer. Parading around naked in front of an audience, though, she very much doubted she could learn to love. Penn thanked Clare for her reassurance, then turned away to change. By the time she left the bathhouse, it was totally empty. Tomorrow she would come just that bit later in the hope of avoiding another awkward run-in.

Once she was dressed and tidy, Penn made her way back to Lovetta's chambers to ready her for breakfast. To her surprise, Lovetta was awake and clothed, sitting at her dressing table. She looked serene in dark blue, running her fingers through sleep-ruffled hair then settling them in her lap, atop her tight-clad thighs. Wait, was Lovetta wearing breeches? Yes, she was! Penn grinned. It was a marvellous sight.

"Ah, I was wondering where you were," Lovetta said with a yawn.

"I'm sorry, I hoped to be back before you woke. I thought it would be a good time to bathe ... in the quiet," she added, hoping Lovetta would understand. It was so hard to take her eyes off Lovetta's legs, her breeches pulled taught across her muscular thighs, just as Florent's old breeches had clung to Penn.

Lovetta laughed delicately. "You definitely picked the wrong time then, didn't you? Mornings are chaos down there." Lovetta winked. "Next time, try closer to lunch. Now, we're going riding this morning, so I suppose you can braid my hair, but nothing too dressy. What are you so happy about?" She eyed Penn.

"I just love mornings," Penn lied, then bit the inside of her cheeks to stop herself from smiling. Before her sat a grown woman in breeches. A beautiful grown woman with royal blood, wearing breeches without a care in the world. Penn could have shouted with glee. Such people did exist! Oh, she couldn't wait to tell Olivia.

"Gods, not another one," Lovetta said with a sigh. "You're free to do what you like, of course. Just don't expect me to rise with you."

Penn stifled a laugh as she took Lovetta's comb, then remembered the task at hand. Her stomach clenched. She only knew a handful of simple hairstyles, and braids were not one of her strengths. She gathered Lovetta's hair in her hands and brought it behind her shoulders. It was soft, and despite its thickness and curl, it slipped from Penn's fingertips with ease.

"I love braids, and I would do them myself, but ... they're just so difficult with hair this heavy," Lovetta said, straightening her woven girdle in the mirror. Penn began to separate Lovetta's hair into sections, but each time she tried, a clump would escape her. "I suppose it gives you something to do, though. Not much happens around here. Ariad almost went mad when she got here."

"Sorry, my lady, I don't think I've met Ariad." Penn twisted Lovetta's hair in an attempt to keep the sections separated.

"Oh, you won't. She's dead now."

Realisation dawned on Penn, and she paused her handiwork. "Your maid? I'm so sorry."

"It's fine. She was perfectly lovely when she wanted to be, but," Lovetta cleared her throat, "I don't think she liked it here. And she certainly didn't like me."

"Surely she did, my lady. I may have only been here a day, but everyone speaks so highly of the duke, and the castle is so beautiful. As for you, well ... what isn't there to like?" What Penn didn't say was that she had come to Rocque crying, but meeting Lovetta had made her want to stay.

"Plenty, apparently. Anyway, she was used to a different lifestyle."

"Oh. She was of noble birth, wasn't she?" Penn resumed her handiwork, slowly coiling sections of hair around themselves.

"She most certainly was," Lovetta said, her tone sour.

Had Ariad thought so highly of herself that she had neglected her duty to serve Lovetta? If that was true, it would make perfect sense for Lovetta to dislike highborn maids.

"I do hope that you can find some happiness here. I appreciate that it must be difficult going from being waited on to waiting on others."

"Please don't worry yourself over me, my lady. I'll be just fine." Did Lovetta think she too would neglect her duties? Was that why she disliked the idea of a new maid? Penn continued braiding, her confidence building with every movement of her fingers, but when she was finished, she surveyed her work with dismay. Loose strands fell from every other segment, and the braid sagged in an unflattering way. Lovetta snapped her head from side to side to scrutinize the style and concluded with an unconvincing 'that'll do'. Penn was going to need some practice before she attempted to style Lovetta's hair again.

Feeling humiliated, Penn silently followed Lovetta to the dining hall for breakfast and took an empty seat between Clare and Marion. Looking at Clare's long, intricately braided locks gave her an idea. "Clare, I need your help."

"Hmm?" Clare mumbled with wide eyes and a mouthful of bread.

"Can you teach me to braid?" Penn asked, spooning thick oatmeal onto her plate.

"You don't know how to braid?"

"Not well," Penn admitted. "Lady Lovetta likes them, and I tried this morning and, well..." She gestured toward the duke's table and sighed. "It was embarrassing."

Clare's eyes widened and she slapped a hand on Penn's shoulder. "It appears you do need help. Of course I'll teach you."

Thank the gods.

Maids trickled into the hall one by one until only a scattering of empty seats remained. It wasn't long until the Bondeville daughters descended from the dais and took their leave, maids scurrying behind. Penn followed Lovetta to the stables where they met Belsante, Edony and their maids, one of which she had not yet met. Belsante's maid, Jehane, was a broad woman with brown skin and a flat face. Though her height alone was remarkable, what stuck out the most to Penn was that Jehane wore a much shorter tunic and a pair of loose, tan breeches underneath. If it weren't for her generous bosom and trailing braid, Penn might have mistaken Jehane for a man. No other maid dressed as she did, not even Belsante or Edony wore breeches. In one day, Penn had met two women who dressed in men's clothing, and one was a lady's maid! Surely Osenna would not approve; neither Olivia nor Maud would.

A moment later, two more women in breeches emerged with the riding party's saddled horses. Penn took a step back, shocked. Were these women stable hands? How? It was commoner's work. It was *men's* work! Overwhelmed by the dream she couldn't seem to wake from, she turned to Clare.

"Are you all right? You're white as a ghost." Clare said.

"I'm quite well," Penn breathed. "Where are we riding?"

"West of the lake. It isn't far."

Belsante pulled herself on top of a towering black stallion with a hand from Jehane. In turn, Edony and Lovetta mounted their smaller mares with ease. They were both blue roans, no doubt to match their father's stallion. Penn sat astride Primula and set off with her riding party, feeling at home in the saddle. As they passed the drawbridge and the outer wall, Roderick and Sir Ulrich silently joined them on the road.

"Do they always follow?" Penn asked as Clare brought her newly acquired horse to a trot beside her. She was a piebald mare, her great black patches like a cow's.

"Without question, but I hardly notice anymore." Clare's horse whinnied and shuddered underneath her. "You can never be sure of what's beyond the wall."

What would it be like to be watched so closely? Theroulde's villages were so small and familiar that Penn had always felt safe beyond the castle walls, even without Maud or Brennan on her tail.

Up ahead, the Bondeville daughters brought their horses to a gallop. Clare struggled with her reigns before she leapt forward. "You're too tense; she can feel it," Penn called back as she came to a gallop.

"I know how to ride!" Clare battled, bounding ahead and overtaking Penn. Penn stayed at the rear and watched with an unexplainable sense of pride as the five women before her surged onwards astride their horses, confident in their saddles. Even Belsante and Edony rode well with heavy gowns billowing at their sides.

As Primula soared beneath her, the summer breeze grazed Penn's cheeks and whipped her own tunic to and fro. The riders rounded a bend in the road bordered by shrubbery that became denser by the leap. Though all three daughters were graceful riders, Lovetta looked the most at home on her mount. Her posture was relaxed, her movements soft; she had either been riding longer than her siblings, or she had a much stronger connection with her horse. Watching her was mesmerising. To Penn's disappointment, Belsante soon signalled for the group to come to a trot. The dirt beneath their mounts gave way to lush pockets of green, and a break in the shrubbery showed a glimpse of water on the horizon. In the distance, Penn heard whinnies and voices.

"Who are they meeting?" Penn asked as she came to Clare's side.

"Lords Hazir, Sahin and Zekeriya Saraq," Clare recited as the group broke through the last of the greenery, entering a clearing adjacent to a great lake. Three young, tall and well-dressed Azorian men sat perched on flattened boulders, their mounts grazing by the water's edge. The maids fell further behind as the Bondeville daughters approached the men and dismounted.

Clare caught her foot in the stirrup as she struggled to the ground. "They meet every week."

Lovetta and her sisters had taken seats with the men, Edony laughing jovially at a comment made by one of the Saraqs. The maids settled themselves on a patch of grass by the lake and watched over the ladies. Penn, remembering they had set off with Roderick and Sir Ulrich in tow, spun around to find that, bewilderingly, they had vanished. "The duke's men —"

"They're still there," Jehane said. "They stay out of sight. Better not to insult the lords." She smirked.

"Are they brothers?" Penn asked, returning her attention to the Azorian men.

Jehane nodded. "Hazir and Sahin are. Zekeriya, the big one," she gestured to the broadest man who sat beside Belsante, "he's their cousin and the oldest." Unlike the others, Zekeriya had a close-cropped beard and short hair, and his eyebrows were severe.

"He's proposed to Belsante about a dozen times now," Clare said, looking bored.

"She doesn't like him?" Penn asked.

"He's handsome enough, but she can't stand his ego," Jehane said. "He talks of marriage like he's doing her a favour, just because she's two years older than he is."

Penn looked over to Zekeriya, who was watching Belsante intently. The eldest of Duke Wymark's daughters was twenty-one and incredibly beautiful, even if she was a little older than the usual age of betrothal. Penn wondered why she hadn't married already, why none of the Bondeville daughters were married or at least engaged.

"If she doesn't want to marry him, why does she keep meeting with him?"

Jehane raised her eyebrows. "It's not Belsante who wants to meet with the Saraqs."

Penn shifted her gaze to Edony and Lovetta, sitting close to Sahin and Hazir. A smile pulled at the corners of Lovetta's mouth.

"Edony never stops talking about Sahin," Clare said.

The man beside Edony was leaner than his brother and cousin, and he had a playfulness to his demeanour that the others did not. His hair was oiled back into a knot, and he had a gold hoop dangling from one ear.

"And Lady Lovetta?" Penn asked.

"With Hazir? Maybe," Clare said. "She never talks of such things."

"Can you blame her?" Jehane scoffed. "After what happened?"

Clare looked at Jehane with fire in her eyes. "Don't. Not when she isn't here to defend herself."

"Sorry," Jehane whispered.

"Ariad?" Penn asked, confused by the exchange. Clare and Jehane nodded in unison, neither looking directly at her. "Something happened between them, didn't it?"

Clare sighed. "I suppose you'll find out eventually. There was a rumour, but Ariad never meant to start it."

"What kind of rumour?"

"That Lovetta was ... different."

Jehane narrowed her eyes at Clare. "Ariad called her a *queer.*"

Penn cocked her head. "A what?" She had never heard the term before.

"Never mind what it was, she didn't mean it. Not like that. It was a question," Clare said in obvious defence of Ariad. "Can we please talk about something else? It's bad enough that she's not here, that there's someone in her place."

"I'm so sorry, I shouldn't have said anything," Penn interrupted. Clare's eyes glittered with unshed tears. Today might have been the first time Clare had rode without her friend, and Penn had put her foot straight into her mouth.

"It's all right. Just don't go talking about it to anyone. Osenna will have your hide," Clare warned.

"I won't, I promise." Penn didn't know what to make of the rumour, but she couldn't press Clare on it anymore.

Penn turned back to Lovetta and Hazir. He was handsome like his brother, but half a head shorter and rigid in posture. He and Lovetta talked quietly, and she held her arms taut around her knees. Belsante and Zekeriya, on the other hand, did not appear to be speaking at all. It seemed the only people actually enjoying themselves were Edony and Sahin, who bellowed with laughter every few minutes.

Penn practiced her braids on Jehane with Clare's instruction, and by the time the Saraqs took their leave, the sun shone high overhead. While Clare helped Edony into her saddle, Penn approached Jehane. "What did Ariad mean when she called Lady Lovetta a queer?" Penn whispered.

Jehane cringed at the word, then answered, "That she has an appetite—Ariad's words, not mine—for women."

*What?* Penn mulled over Jehane's words, trying not to laugh. Who on earth would believe a rumour as far-fetched as that? She tried to imagine Lovetta the cannibal in a lovely white gown speckled with blood, an innocent housemaid spread out before the hearth with a bite out of her arm.

"I'm sorry," Penn said, unable to keep her laughter in any longer, "but you must be joking. Nobody would believe that."

"Whether they believe it or not is beside the point. An accusation like that can ruin somebody's reputation, and Ariad should have been sacked. Not that it matters now." Jehane sighed, then took her horse by the reigns and walked over to Belsante.

Penn called Primula and hoisted herself into the saddle, and soon the group had set off through the undergrowth once more. Lovetta and Belsante rode quietly ahead, with Edony behind, singing as she galloped. The entire time, Penn pictured Lovetta sampling the flesh of maids as if each one was a fine wine, and she could barely contain herself. When they reached the castle, the stable hands came to fetch their horses. Again, Penn ogled the women in breeches with a kind of envy, then wondered if they might be her lady's next victims.

Looking sombre, Lovetta left to bathe before lunch, while Edony chattered away to Belsante, who seemed quite unimpressed. The maids were dismissed. Jehane took to the castle, and Clare disappeared into the stables. Suddenly, the world was Penn's oyster. She made to follow Clare, then stopped. There was somewhere else she wanted to go first. With the gardens empty and plenty of time before lunch, Penn made her way up the winding path to the side of the castle, letting the shadows pull her in.

Trees loomed overhead, keeping the path pleasantly cool. Penn walked in awe, identifying plants she had only ever seen in books: great vines of white ivy, tufts of fingerfern and strings of golden pothos. Pulled along by the darkness and the scent of wet soil,

Penn's heartbeat quickened and her hesitancy turned to hunger. Her heels clapped the stone beneath her feet, bringing rhythm to the many rustlings and calls of tiny creatures. The further she walked, the colder and darker it seemed to become, but was it just her imagination? How far had she come? Time seemed to slow here, every twist in the path identical to the last. Eventually, a light flickered in the distance, growing brighter with each step. She had come to the end of the path.

Was that it? No pile of dismembered bodies, no secrets. It was just a corridor of greenery that could do with a good trim. Penn wasn't sure of what she had expected, but it was certainly more than that. Feeling a little disappointed, Penn took the castle's back entrance and made her way to the dining hall.

# Five

Penn's unexpected excitement of the Bondeville household faded quickly. It had been over a month since she had arrived in Rocque, and she regularly found herself agitated from boredom. Penn had expected Lovetta to run her ragged from the moment she arrived, but she couldn't have been more wrong. Lovetta hardly spent any time with her at all.

Often, Penn thought about home and what she might be doing if she was still in Theroulde. She would probably be sitting beside Maybelle, working on her embroidery under their governess' watchful eye, just as bored as she was now. What would her father be doing? Was he in his usual spot, bent over his desk with parchment in hand and a scowl on his face? A long time ago, his usual spot had been the garden. He would sit in the sun with a book, smiling wide as Penn ran towards him, filthy from play. That was the man she imagined reading her letters, not the stern, sullen man he had become.

Perhaps it was better that Penn was in Rocque. At least now, she had Lovetta. She was never bored when she was with Lovetta. In fact, any time at all with Lovetta excited her in the most peculiar way. Even tidying her chambers while Lovetta silently nursed a drink brought a smile to her face. If only she didn't disappear so damned often. Between her classes, archery practice and visits to

Edony's chambers, Lovetta didn't have time to entertain a maid. So, she found her own routine. Once Lovetta took her leave, Penn would make the beds, fluff the pillows, wash the linens and refill the basins. By late afternoon, she had darned their clothes, trimmed the candlewicks and visited the bathhouse, which was always empty at three o'clock. Then, she twiddled her thumbs until Lovetta returned. Not once did she find a blood splattered gown or a human bone charred in the hearth.

Her favourite nights were those spent with Lovetta. Clare was fun, but with Lovetta, her entire body hummed with a tension she couldn't make sense of. Like a bee with veins full of honey, forever buzzing and warm in the strangest of places. Lovetta would sit in her armchair making small talk, and Penn would study her as if appraising a work of art. Sometimes she would catch Lovetta looking at her, and she wondered of the things that filled Lovetta's head. Did her body hum as their eyes met, her skin prickle as their hands brushed? Or was her mind somewhere else entirely, perhaps back at the clearing by the lake? Every now and then she talked of Hazir with a smile that didn't quite meet her eyes, and on the days they met, she would fall even further away.

Nevertheless, those weekly meetings were sure to entertain, much like a travelling circus would. Belsante made polite but awkward conversation with Zekeriya, who always looked as if he was holding a breath in. Edony swooned under Sahin's gaze, while he spent more time fixing his hair than he did anything else. Lastly, Lovetta huddled with Hazir, whispering as if planning to overthrow an empire. Penn would sit in the background listening to Clare and Jehane bicker about the most trivial things. They clashed frequently, but all was forgotten the following day. It was amusing, even when Penn didn't know what they were arguing about.

Often, Penn would simply watch the Bondevilles, and by the month's end, Lovetta alone stole her attention. Her dress, the way she tucked her hair behind her ears, and how she sat with Hazir, angled away with her arms always crossed, as if she was ready to run at a moment's notice. Something about Hazir bothered Penn, but she couldn't put a name to it. One morning he brought a book to lend Lovetta, and she beamed with gratitude. She spent the next week buried in the damned thing, leaving Penn to seek out Clare for company.

Penn was grateful for Clare and the hayloft, their usual meeting place. Sometimes Marion would join them, and they would share a bottle she had smuggled from the cellar. Clare would help Penn with her embroidery, and in return, Penn helped her bond with Ariad's horse. They would gossip about the household, take bets on when Sahin would propose, and they would play cards, which Penn nearly always won (courtesy of Florent's teachings). Spending time with Clare was easy. She could simply be herself. Having left the Orange Isles on the back of a potato wagon to escape her drunkard parents, Clare wasn't one to cast judgement.

If only Penn could drop her guard around Lovetta as she did with Clare. Despite all the mornings and evenings spent together, Penn felt they barely knew each other. Lovetta would ask Penn about her life in Theroulde but would give so little of her own life away in return. She drank too much. She disappeared too often. She kept herself an arm's length from everyone, even Hazir, who tried so hard to impress her. But why? Was it because of Ariad's absurd rumour, or was it the loss of her mother? Whatever it was, Penn prayed for it to release Lovetta.

"Bugger!" Penn cursed. It was a crisp day; the weather had cooled down markedly since her arrival. Penn and Clare were cutting flowers from the back courtyard to replenish the vases in their lady's chambers.

"I told you to wear gloves," Clare said as she handed Penn a handkerchief.

Penn wrapped the patterned cloth around her bleeding finger. "This is why I don't like roses. They look nice from a distance, but once you get close, they stab you with their horrid tiny knives."

Clare rolled her eyes. "It was a thorn, and it pricked your finger. You're going to be just fine."

"Well, I won't be able to sew tonight. We'll have to do something else," Penn said as she pulled the handkerchief away. Her finger had already stopped bleeding, but it was tender to touch.

"Any excuse," Clare said, taking back her handkerchief. "I was going to give you a night off, anyway. I'm busy tonight."

Penn frowned. "*Again?* What is it this time?" Clare had spent the previous evening with Marion, and the night before that, with the kitchen maids. Penn had hardly seen her.

"Edony wants to drink."

"Of course she does." Penn sighed. "Will Lovetta be joining her?" She hoped not. When the sisters drank, they drank until the early hours of the morning, and often more than they could handle. That left Penn alone, eyelids drooping, waiting for Lovetta to stumble through the door. She told her not to wait up, but Penn worried that if she didn't, Lovetta would knock over her bed light and set fire to the room.

"No, Lovetta is all yours," Clare said.

It was a strange thing to say, and Penn's reaction stranger still. Heat prickled at the nape of her neck, and she had the sudden urge to look away.

Penn changed the subject as she cut free another rose. "What do you think the duke is up to?" Duke Wymark had left for Tirel that morning. He was always away on business of some kind, and when he returned, there was always a feast.

"It can't be Ysabell again, surely. Not if he's gone for two weeks," Clare said.

One of the Bondeville daughters had been offered a position as a lady in waiting for Princess Anais, King Segarus' youngest child. Ysabell had not responded to the offer, but they were all quite certain she would decline, given her hysterical laugh at the letter.

"I really don't know," Clare said as she clipped a pristine white rose from the shrubbery. "It isn't like him to spend this much time away from home. At least not since…"

Penn paused her scavenge. "Not since what?"

Clare's brow knitted. "Well, since his campaign to end slavery." She nodded to herself. "Which means that whatever he's up to is probably big."

Penn shrugged her shoulders as she took one last clipping. "Maybe he has a secret lover."

"Maybe he's looking for your replacement," Clare joked, then returned to her handiwork. "I'm so sick of white. Can we pick the pink roses next time?"

"Absolutely not!" Penn laughed. "Lovetta hates pink. White roses are her favourite."

Clare looked surprised. "How could you possibly know that? I've known her for three years and only just discovered she's allergic to jasmine, and it was Edony who told me!"

Relief washed over Penn. "I thought it was just me who she kept in the dark."

"Gods, no. She's in another world most of the time," Clare said plainly.

"Well, whatever world she's visiting, it's hurting her." Penn pulled the leaves from her last rose.

Clare gave Penn a faint smile. "How sweet. You care for her."

"Of course I do. I only wish I knew what troubled her. Do you think it's Hazir?"

"Hazir Saraq?" Clare laughed, and Penn wondered just how many Hazirs Clare knew. "I highly doubt it. Lovetta's moods have always been fickle." At that, Clare rounded up her bundle of roses and wrapped them in cloth. "Actually, she's better now than she has been in a long time."

"Truly?" Penn wrapped her own bundle.

Clare nodded. "A few months back, she threw her fist through the mirror in her room, and Ariad found a shard hidden beneath her mattress."

Penn felt the blood drain from her face faster than she could take a breath. "You don't think she meant to—"

"Why else would she keep it? To spread jam?"

Penn felt sick to the stomach, but strangely, she was also relieved. *She* wasn't the problem. Hazir wasn't the problem. So, what was? Was Lovetta melancholy by nature, or had something broken her? Ariad was the first person to come to mind, but Penn wouldn't dare speak ill of her to Clare.

"Anyway, there's no need to worry yourself. Edony talked some sense into her and she promised not to do anything quite so rash again," concluded Clare, handing Penn a length of twine to tie her bundle.

Penn hoped Lovetta meant it; a world without her had quickly become unimaginable.

When night threatened to fall, Penn returned to Lovetta's chambers to light the candles and, for the first time, the hearth. As she pulled the curtains closed, Penn heard the door swing open, then close with a creak. Lovetta walked to the hearth in a golden gown that shone exquisitely in the light of the fire. A smile pulled at the corners of her mouth. "I've missed this," she cooed, gazing into the flames as they flickered from red to yellow.

"The fire, my lady?" Penn watched Lovetta intently, haunted by her earlier conversation with Clare.

"The weather," Lovetta said. "I love summer, I do, but I can't think of anything better than cosying up by the fire on a cold night."

Penn smiled, feeling nostalgic. Though she was a summer child through and through, when she was younger, she would sit with her father by the fire, and they would read themselves to sleep. She missed those nights.

Lovetta sighed, then looked to her dressing table, where Penn had positioned a large vase of fresh white roses. "Oh, they're lovely!" Lovetta cried, hurrying over and scooping up a rose. She tucked a few loose hairs behind her ear, then held the rose to the side of her head and examined her reflection.

"That won't do," Lovetta said, making a clicking noise with her tongue. She turned to Penn with a mischievous smile and looked her in the eye. Penn said nothing as Lovetta let out the braid at the back of Penn's head, snapped the head of the rose from its stem, and placed it behind her ear. "You suit it better than I do," she said.

"You're too kind." Penn bowed her head in the hope of concealing her pink cheeks. Lovetta couldn't really mean that, could she?

"Aren't you even going to look?" Lovetta sounded taken aback. "I couldn't paint something half as lovely."

Penn looked to the mirror—perhaps the same mirror that Lovetta had thrown her fist through—and tried to focus on the rose, but it was no easy task. Not with her long, blonde waves spiralling haphazardly over her shoulders and her cheeks so rosy. Seeing herself so delicate, so feminine … It wasn't right. It wasn't *her*. Penn dropped her gaze and apologised to Lovetta.

"Don't you like it?" she asked.

Penn clasped her hands to hide her nerves, hoping she hadn't offended her. "The rose is beautiful."

"Then why do you look so miserable?" Lovetta asked, placing a finger beneath Penn's chin and raising it. She would do such things every now and then, as if Penn were a doll on her shelf. It never failed to make Penn's chest flutter.

"I don't think flowers suit me," Penn said, meeting Lovetta's gaze.

"And why is that?" Lovetta pressed, refusing to move her hand or drop her gaze.

"I don't know," Penn lied, looking back to the floor in shame. She wouldn't understand.

Lovetta made another clicking noise and stepped back. "Well, we ought to go down for supper." She sighed and walked to the door before turning back to Penn. "You don't have to wear the rose. You're beautiful without it."

Penn's entire body burned red, and her stomach might as well have fallen through the floor. Where on earth had that compliment come from? Penn swiftly followed Lovetta from the room, looking anywhere but at the woman before her.

Supper passed in an intoxicating haze of elation. No matter how many times she replayed Lovetta's words in her head, she couldn't believe she had truly heard them, and she could still feel Lovetta's finger on her chin.

Clare had to wave her hand in front of Penn's face to get her attention. "What is up with you tonight?"

"I have a headache," Penn lied, not knowing what else to say. Why was she so preoccupied with Lovetta, and was it normal? She didn't study Clare with the same intensity or second-guess the meaning of every word she said. She didn't play back their time together in her head, or flush at her touch. It couldn't be normal, surely!

Lovetta, who had chatted more animatedly to her sisters over supper than she had in weeks, said that she was too exhausted to stay up and read when they returned to her chambers.

"You don't have to stay in just because I am," Lovetta said as Penn unlaced the back of her gown. No matter how many times she had done it, undressing Lovetta still gave Penn a thrill.

"I'm happy to. Clare's busy tonight anyway," Penn said as she admired the curve of Lovetta's neck.

"Oh? What torture has Edony condemned her to this time?"

Penn laughed. "Nothing of the sort. They're drinking."

"What?" Lovetta exclaimed, looking cross. "Where was my invitation? Now I'll have to drink alone."

"You're not too tired, my lady?" Penn unhooked Lovetta's necklace and placed it on the dressing table to clean in the morning.

"To read, not to drink. Gods, I'm so sick of drinking alone."

Whether it was an invitation or not, Penn leapt at the opportunity. "Perhaps I could drink with you. If it pleases you, that is." It felt good to be bold.

"If it pleases me," Lovetta repeated, raising her eyebrows then murmuring, "If you knew what pleased me, you'd run for the hills." She cleared her throat then stood up. "Yes! Have a drink with me. It would please me immensely."

Quickly there Lovetta was, clad only in her underclothes, offering her a drink. Penn was ecstatic. Grinning, she took the small cup and raised it to her nose.

"What is this? It smells wonderful." Sweet and strong like a fruity perfume.

"Apricot liqueur. Taste it; it's to die for! Cost me a limb to get it off Edony."

"Then you shouldn't waste it on me!" Penn placed the cup on the low table by the hearth and sat on the rug. Lovetta joined her.

"It's not a waste, silly. I've had it for months and have been saving it to share with someone. Please accept it."

Penn hesitated, then took the cup from the table and tasted the liquid. "It's marvellous." Thick and warm, it enveloped her tongue like honey.

"It's from the market. A lovely little couple make all kinds. My favourite is the spiced apple."

"I'll have to keep my eye out for it," Penn said before taking another sip.

"They won't sell it to you." Lovetta laughed. "They won't even sell it to me. We're both too young."

"Perhaps they won't even know I was there," Penn said, raising a brow.

"You don't mean to *steal* a bottle, do you?" Lovetta said, eyes wide. "You wouldn't dare."

"No, I probably wouldn't," Penn admitted. She couldn't have Lovetta believing her a thief!

"What a shame," Lovetta said, then sipped from her own cup. "It would make for a brilliant story."

She *could* have Lovetta believing her a thief. Perhaps this was it, Penn's chance to truly impress her. She had swiped things from Theroulde's markets before without anyone noticing. Sure, it happened years ago, and it had never been much: a piece of fruit or some candy. But it had been easy.

"I don't have a cloak with deep enough pockets," Penn said, thinking up a plan.

Lovetta's eyes lit up like she had never seen before. "How deep must they be?"

"The size of a bottle. Or two," Penn said, and Lovetta's eyes went wider.

"And here I was thinking you a prim and proper southern lady, free from sin." Lovetta drank.

Penn laughed. "Me? You must be joking." She finished her cup and Lovetta reached for the bottle.

"I'm deadly serious. Oh, we should have had a drink sooner. If I had known..." Lovetta refilled Penn's cup, but not her own.

They both laughed, and it was a blissful thing. Was *this* what Lovetta had been waiting for all this time? Had Penn truly put her efforts in all the wrong places, steaming Lovetta's clothes to perfection when all she really wanted was a friend?

"Well, now you know. We're not all as we seem." Penn sipped. Gods, the drink was good.

Lovetta smiled warmly. "No, we are not. Goodness! What have you done to your finger?"

Penn looked down to find a smudge of blood on her cup. "Oh, don't worry yourself. I snagged it on a thorn when I was picking roses. I should have bandaged it." She searched her pocket for a handkerchief to no avail.

Lovetta rushed to the mantel and took one of her own, then returned to Penn's side. "You should have worn gloves." Gently, she wrapped the cloth around Penn's finger, then applied pressure.

"That's what Clare said." Penn sat still as a statue. Lovetta was so close that she could smell the sweetness of her breath.

Lovetta brushed her thumb ever so softly over Penn's hand. "Wear them next time. It would be a shame to mark such lovely skin."

Penn's breath hitched, and as she blushed, she noticed them. The faint raised lines upon Lovetta's knuckles, scars from months past.

"You flatter me," Penn said as she met Lovetta's eye. "Perhaps I could accompany you the next time Edony invites you for a drink. It could be fun, the four of us."

Lovetta drew back. "Of course. I imagine Clare would like that." Her smile had dropped, and Penn wondered if she had said the wrong thing.

"But this is fun, too. I'd like to do it again." She tied the handkerchief around her finger.

Lovetta's mouth twitched. "You aren't just saying that to spare my feelings, are you?"

"Of course not. I enjoy your company very much."

Lovetta quickly dropped her head, but Penn didn't miss the return of her smile. "I think I will go to bed now. Or else, I might..." she paused as if carefully considering her next words, then said, "Drink far too much and make a fool of myself. I'm quite good at that."

Penn finished her cup, savouring its strong flavour, then fetched mint water and cloth for their teeth. That night, she tossed and turned just as she had on her very first evening in Rocque. Over a month had passed, and Penn was still drawn to Lovetta in a way she didn't understand. Her dreams were funny, vivid things, full of drink and laughter, and then a scream and a shattering of glass. She woke with a start and got up to check the dressing table, but it was just as they had left it, and Lovetta slept soundly in her bed. There was still an hour or more until dawn. Penn walked toward Lovetta.

For a moment, she watched the rise and fall of Lovetta's chest and wondered what it would be like to touch her in the way she had been touched. To lift Lovetta's chin with her finger and place a rose behind her ear, or brush her thumb over her scarred knuckles, sitting close enough to feel the warmth of each other's breath. Since the evening they'd met, something deep inside Penn had been simmering. Now, standing above Lovetta, whose blankets and underclothes were in disarray, the thing began to boil.

* * *

The room was empty when Penn woke. It was well past dawn, a cool breeze accompanying the light that streamed through the window. Penn dressed in a panic, pulled up the bedcovers and moved as quickly as was ladylike to the dining hall. They would eat plainly, for the duke had donated a good deal of the food stores to struggling villagers, as he did every summer.

The hall was teeming with bodies, disguising Penn well as she shuffled onto a table a few seats down from Clare and Marion.

Beside her was a spindly young girl with short black hair called Tibby, who had recently become Dorett's maid. Across from her was Thamasin, Tibby's lookalike elder sister who had been Sarra's maid for years. Then there was Jinny, a scruffy brunette who worked in the gardens.

"Rough night?" Clare called across the sea of faces.

"Is it that noticeable?" Penn said, shovelling porridge into her mouth like the world depended on it.

Clare gave her a friendly smirk. "Your hair is kind of a mess."

Penn hadn't even thought about her hair. She had been too busy getting her shoes on the right feet. She ran her fingers through her waves in an attempt to smooth them out, but quickly gave up and returned to her meal. Penn barely had time to clear her plate before Lovetta rose from the dais and walked her way.

"Are you quite well this morning?" Lovetta asked, feeling Penn's forehead as if expecting a fever.

"Never better!" Penn buzzed at the warmth of Lovetta's fingers. "I overslept; that's all." Lovetta inhaled sharply, and Penn's stomach lurched, heavy with the porridge she had just devoured.

"It won't happen again, I swear." She bowed her head so low that her neck strained.

"Penn, look at me," Lovetta demanded, and Penn obeyed. "You're not in trouble. How you wake so damned early every day is beyond me. Oh, look at you! You've got moons beneath your eyes, and here I am about to force you onto a horse when you ought to be resting."

Penn immediately perked up. "Are we riding today?"

"Only if you promise not to fall asleep on Primula." They both laughed.

The two set off for the stables, a newfound giddiness in Penn's step. Primula had already been saddled, and she nuzzled Penn with a force that could only mean she was happy to see her. Lovetta mounted her mare as Penn looked around. "Where is everybody?"

"They won't be coming today," Lovetta said, stroking her blue roan's neck. She had named her Sapphire.

"Are you meeting with Lord Hazir on your own?" Penn whispered, her chest tightening in a very unpleasant way. Such a thing was not proper for a lady of Lovetta's standing, and the last thing she wanted was to watch the two huddled close and whispering, as if privy to something Penn was not. Feeling dejected, she mounted Primula and sat astride, lining up her mare just behind Lovetta's horse.

Lovetta laughed. "Oh no, nothing like that. I just feel like riding today. Come, ride beside me," she offered as they headed for the drawbridge. Honoured by the invitation, Penn urged Primula forward to trot alongside Lovetta. They rode the same path as they always did, with two of the duke's men quietly on their tail. Soon they came to a gallop, the speed whipping Penn's hair back and forth, in front of her eyes and occasionally, into her mouth.

Today felt different. Lovetta was riding for herself, no one else, and Penn would not sit quietly in the background, waiting to be forgotten. Something had changed between them, and it brought a wide, giddy grin to Penn's face. With the sun prickling her skin and the morning air crisp, Penn felt like a new woman.

They dismounted in the usual place and settled on the grass by the water's edge. The sky, though a vast and perfect blue, held a scattering of oddly shaped clouds that were reflected in the water. Penn stretched out her legs and looked across the lake where dense woodland bordered the banks.

"The Saraqs live over there," Lovetta said, watching Penn. She rolled onto her front and propped her chin up with her palm. "And the Dabneys and the Toustains. They all have Azorian blood, did you know that?"

Penn swatted at a fly and turned to Lovetta, who had not taken her eyes off her. "I didn't," she admitted.

Lovetta looked away and sighed. "It's important."

"May I ask why, my lady?" Penn asked with caution. Was this yet another thing she hadn't paid attention to during her lessons?

"They like to keep us together, so they can keep an eye on us, in case we suddenly decide one kingdom isn't enough and wage another war."

The tension between neighbouring Azor and Vastal was no secret. King Segarus Bondeville, Vastal's monarch, had spent decades preserving the fragile alliance between the kingdoms. Too much blood had been shed by his predecessors and both kingdoms decayed under the pressure of warfare. When the treaty was signed near twenty years ago, trade blossomed, and men could move between the lands without persecution, provided they had the right papers.

"Do you think Azor could?" Penn asked, watching Lovetta roll onto her back and face the cloud-streaked sky.

"They have twice as many soldiers as Vastal, and King Bahsayis is unpredictable. If you ask me, it's only a matter time." Lovetta exhaled dreamily and stretched her arms above her. The edge of her tunic rose past her hips, exposing her tight-clad thighs.

Gods, how bold she was! "How do you know all this?" Penn asked as she looked Lovetta up and down. Her body curved in all the right places, like an hourglass. She was perfect.

"Hazir," Lovetta said, closing her eyes.

Penn's stomach dropped. She didn't know why the idea of them being close should bother her, but it did.

"He was born in Azor, you know. Sahin and Zekeriya, too."

Though Penn wasn't surprised—the men had obvious accents—she was becoming more curious about the Bondeville's involvement with the Saraqs. "How long have you known the lords?" She settled onto her back beside Lovetta, separated by mere inches. "You all seem very close. Did they move here when they were young?"

"Well, no, not really. They've been here for six years, but we only started meeting with them about a year ago."

Penn wasn't sure whether this was a relief to her or not.

"Belsante and Zekeriya were the first to meet; we were all at court for the king's name day. It was a huge affair." Lovetta's eyes snapped open as she recounted the story. "You wouldn't know it now, but Bel took quite a liking to Zekeriya at first. They danced all night." She laughed. "It wasn't until we were just about to leave that Zekeriya introduced Edony and I to his cousins. Sahin and Edony got along straight away, but Edony was cautious. She saw him dance with at least four other girls that night, and, well, she's no stranger to jealousy."

From the stories Penn had heard from Clare, this came as no surprise. "And Lord Hazir?" she asked hesitantly.

"Hazir was so shy. He still is, but believe me, if you knew him then, you'd think he was a completely different person now." Lovetta made a high-pitched noise that could have been a giggle if Penn hadn't been determined to think otherwise. "I thought he didn't like me at first, but really he was just embarrassed. I think living with such an outgoing brother overshadowed him a bit. He always felt second best, and he had no confidence with women whatsoever." She laughed again.

Lovetta spoke of Hazir with such admiration; was there something romantic between them after all? "You know him quite well," Penn said, matter-of-factly.

"He's a good friend. He can be quite sweet when you get to know him. We read a lot of the same literature, and we both want to go back to Azor someday. Politically, we don't exactly see eye-to-eye, but I can understand why. He was raised in a very traditional household, and he grew up thinking it was normal to have slaves."

"He had *slaves?*" Penn was unable to disguise her revulsion.

"Oh, yes. His family in Azor still do," Lovetta said bluntly. "According to Hazir, they treat their slaves very well."

"But they're still his family's property." Penn couldn't believe that a man so close to Lovetta, whose own father had dismantled the slave trade in Vastal, could defend his family's actions.

"I know. I don't think it's right, either, but … some opinions can't be changed."

"Your father changed the opinions of an entire country." Surely Lovetta could change the opinion of one man! Or was she too clouded by infatuation to try? The thought only made Penn dislike the man even more.

"Anyway, enough about Hazir," Lovetta said, then yawned. "Did you know that the first time Zekeriya proposed to Bel, she almost said yes?"

Penn welcomed the change of conversation. "Really?" She couldn't hide her surprise. Zekeriya was the least talked about Saraq, and from what Clare had told her, he also had the least personality.

"It's true. On paper, they're a perfect match. He's handsome, a skilled swordsman, he comes from a well-regarded family, and most importantly, he's Azorian! Not that there's anything wrong with marrying into a Vastalian family," she added, then laughed. "If my mother hadn't, I wouldn't be here, would I?"

The mention of Lovetta's mother was a rare occurrence. In fact, the late duchess was scarcely mentioned by any of the daughters. All Penn knew about her was that she died on the birthing bed labouring a stillborn son, the only son she ever carried. It was a tragedy.

"I don't think Bel would marry a Vastalian, though. I don't think any of my siblings would."

"Why?" Though Penn had little interest in marrying any man, she couldn't understand why Vastalians were undesirable in Lovetta's eyes. Did she see Penn in the same light? The thought made Penn's heart squeeze.

"If we marry into Azorian families, we can go there whenever we want. And it's not that I don't love my father and my home, but Azor..." Lovetta sighed yearningly. "When my mother was still alive, we visited my grandparents and I fell in love. The country is so beautiful and rich with culture. If I'm stuck in Vastal for the rest of my life, I'll lose that part of me."

Penn turned to Lovetta and saw a great sadness in her eyes. She was beginning to understand her a little better. Without her mother, Lovetta's connection to Azor had faded, and she wanted to hold on to the little she had in any way she could. As a woman, her only way to do that was to marry the right person, someone who would travel with her as often as she liked, perhaps with a foot in both realms. Suddenly, Lovetta's whispers with Hazir made sense.

"It's not right that you have to worry about this," Penn said. "Nobody should have to worry about this. Azor is as much your home as Vastal." She felt a familiar flicker of fury. "If you were a man, you could do as you please without marrying anyone. Everything would be different."

"Yes." Lovetta exhaled and turned to meet Penn's gaze. "Everything certainly would be different." She smiled sadly. "Penn ... I want to apologise to you."

Penn became acutely aware of how close they were and shuffled back. "What could you possibly have to apologise for?"

"When you arrived, I wasn't as friendly towards you as I could have been. I didn't want a noble maid, and I made that clear to you. Too clear." She looked down. "I judged you before I got to know you. I thought you'd be just like Ariad." She gave a feeble laugh. "You must think me a monster. I don't mean to speak ill of the dead, truly, but she wasn't well suited to being a maid, and she seemed determined to make an enemy of me."

Penn sighed, feeling guilty. She had believed a life of service beneath her, just as Ariad had, until she met the lady she was to serve. "I don't blame you for thinking that, Lovetta."

"Ah!" Lovetta exclaimed, and Penn flinched. "You did it. You finally called me Lovetta!"

Penn blinked. She had called Lovetta by her name alone on the day they met, albeit uncomfortably. Had she truly not used it since? She smiled and hoped she didn't look as embarrassed as she felt. "I'm sorry it took me so long."

"Don't be. This is my apology, remember? I think if we had talked like this more often, I would have warmed to you sooner. Last night finally opened my eyes. You're not Ariad. You're nothing like Ariad."

"No, I'm not. I would never do what she did."

Lovetta paled as she sat up. "You do know about it, then. I wondered."

Gods, why did Penn always have to put her foot in her mouth? She pushed herself up with trembling hands. "I know there was a rumour and that it hurt you deeply. As for what Ariad said exactly—"

"It doesn't frighten you?" Lovetta interrupted, meeting Penn's eye.

She shook her head. "Of course not. Bullies will say any old thing to get a rise out of someone."

"But if the rumour turned out to be true?"

Penn laughed at Lovetta's joke. "I would oil myself up and ask if you preferred ginger or garlic."

Lovetta's eyes all but bulged from her head. "*What?*"

"It was a joke! I wouldn't really let you eat me. Who would light the fire?"

Lovetta exploded in a fit of laughter like nothing Penn had ever heard. "You can't be serious! You thought I ate people?"

"Only women. Gods, no! I didn't really think that. That was just the rumour."

Lovetta laughed so hard that she started to choke, and Penn belted her between the shoulders in a panic.

"I'm sorry!" she spluttered. "I'm okay, I'm okay." She spent a moment catching her breath. "Oh, bless you, Penn. Bless you."

Penn scratched her head. "I thought you knew of the rumour. That's why you didn't like Ariad."

"I knew of a rumour, but it certainly wasn't that one. Goodness, I think I pulled something in my stomach from all that laughing. Oh, I do wish we had talked like this sooner. To think you've been imagining me dining on noblewomen."

"Housemaids, actually. Noblewomen would be too conspicuous."

"You're right, they would. I'll keep that in mind if I ever have a craving for human flesh. It's a shame, though. You do look quite delicious."

Penn flinched. "You certainly know how to make someone nervous."

Lovetta smiled. "You have no reason to be nervous with me. I like you far too much to eat you."

Lovetta liked her. Those three small words hit Penn hard in the chest, filling her with joy. "Would you have eaten Ariad, then?"

"No, never. Far too stringy."

How crude it was for them to laugh as they did, and yet Penn didn't care. It was bliss. When she visited Clare in the hayloft that afternoon, she had a skip in her step.

# Six

When Duke Wymark returned from Tirel, he brought with him an invitation. The end of autumn was approaching, and Princess Roheisa had birthed her third child and first son. The princess was not as young as she used to be, and her hope for another child was thought to be lost. Naturally, there would be a celebration like no other to commemorate the occasion, and the Bondevilles were at the top of the guest list. According to Edony, so were the Saraqs. The event would take place in a fortnight, so they would leave in a little over a week.

In preparation for the trip, Penn spent a great deal of time on her needlework. Lovetta's new gown had arrived and looked dazzling, while Penn's was a little worse for wear. The hem had to be taken down an inch, and there was a small hole in the sleeve; sitting crumpled at the bottom of a trunk for two months hadn't helped matters. Clare would be spending her afternoons embroidering Edony's gown, who had insisted that the original number of roses was insufficient for such an occasion. Marion, who had previously spent several afternoons in the company of Penn, Clare, and their basket of thread, had stopped coming to the hayloft altogether.

"Have you noticed that Marion's been acting strange lately?" Penn asked as she unpicked the hem on her gown. It was a soft yellow with a high neckline and trumpet sleeves, tightening at the

waist and finishing in a sweeping skirt. To Penn's relief, it was free
from flowers, tulle, and anything that sparkled.

"I have noticed," Clare said, putting Edony's scarlet masterpiece
down. One of the ginger kittens, who had been chewing on a stray
piece of hay, suddenly pounced on Clare's shoe.

"The other day I said good morning and smiled at her, and she
looked away without a word. I'm sure she heard me. Do you know
if she's all right?"

"She's just annoyed with me," Clare said as she nudged the kitten
away from Edony's gown.

"Annoyed with you? Why would she be annoyed with you? You
two have been close ... forever!"

Clare kept her eyes on the floor and shuffled her feet. The tabby
pounced again. "Well, I don't want you to take this the wrong way,"
Clare made a point to avoid Penn's gaze, "but I think it's because
of you."

"Me? I've never been anything but kind to her!"

"I know, I know," Clare said reassuringly, nudging the kitten
away a second time. "I don't think it's your fault."

Penn, who was totally thrown by the news, dropped her sewing,
no longer able to concentrate on it. What could she possibly have
done to annoy Marion? Quiet, smiling Marion who always left the
largest drying cloth for Penn when they shared a bath. Why had
she stopped showing any interest in spending time with Penn and
Clare ... and the *kittens*?

"I don't understand," Penn said.

Clare looked uncomfortable. "I really don't think you've done
anything. I think she's upset because I'm spending so much time
with you, and it always used to be just the two of us."

Penn could hardly believe it. Marion was seventeen years old,
not a child. Could she really be jealous that Clare had made a new

friend? "That can't be it, surely? She's a grown woman. Us being friends doesn't take away from her friendship with you. I'd never even had a friend before you, and even I know that you can have more than one." The only reason Penn and Clare had spent so much time together when she first arrived was because Lovetta had shown no interest in Penn's company, which Marion was aware of. Now that Lovetta had warmed up to Penn, she wasn't taking up anywhere near as much of Clare's time as she had when she'd arrived.

"Grown women have feelings too." Clare picked up her needle to rethread it. The feisty tabby had taken to chasing its littermate's tail.

"But it doesn't make sense. If she thinks I'm ... I don't know, replacing her or something, why would she stay away?" Penn said, determined to prove Clare's theory wrong. "If she cares so much about being your friend, shouldn't she spend more time with you, not less?"

"We had a disagreement," Clare admitted, looking sheepish. "She wanted me to stay away from you, and I said no."

Penn balked. "Why on earth should you stay away from me? I don't bite." Penn started to laugh. "I don't have an *appetite for women*, as Ariad would say." Immediately, Clare flinched. "I'm sorry. I shouldn't have mentioned her."

"It's all right," Clare said. "I'll talk to her and set her straight, okay? Let's just forget about her for now."

They sewed in silence until the sun drifted closer to the horizon, and they returned to the castle earlier now that the days were growing shorter. When Penn's frustration had subsided, she made her way to Lovetta's chambers, but found them empty. She checked the library, sure she would find Lovetta there, but it too was empty. So, she scoured the dining hall, the bathhouse, the courtyards and the stables, all to no avail. After conceding that she would have no more luck on her own, she returned to the dining hall to seek help from her friends. But Clare did not look up to Penn with her usual smile that evening, and Penn wondered if she had already spoken to Marion, who sat right across from Clare, chatting to Tibby. Penn doubted she would have any luck with her. What if something had happened to Lovetta? She disappeared often, but Penn always found her. This time, not one person had seen her. It was like she had vanished from existence. There was no way Penn could eat while Lovetta was missing.

Penn left the dining hall and checked their chambers again just in case Lovetta had returned. They were still empty. Penn started to panic. She had to find Edony; if any of Lovetta's sisters had knowledge of her whereabouts, it would be her.

"Please tell me you know where Lovetta is," she said when she saw Edony in the corridor. "I can't find her anywhere."

Edony folded her arms and furrowed her brow, as if deep in thought. "I haven't seen her for a few hours. Was Saph in the stable?" she asked calmly.

Penn wracked her brain, trying to remember if she'd seen Lovetta's mare when she checked the stable earlier. "I..." she stuttered, feeling more nervous by the second, "I can't remember." Penn cursed herself for not checking.

Footsteps sounded from around the corner and Clare joined the two. "What's going on? You didn't eat." She sounded genuinely concerned. "Where's Lady Lovetta?"

"Excellent question," Edony said. "You checked the library, didn't you?"

"Yes, I've checked everywhere," Penn replied, trying to keep any irritation out of her voice. "Unless she's hiding in the bushes, she's not on castle grounds."

Clare and Edony looked at each other, as if they knew something that Penn didn't.

"You haven't checked everywhere," Edony said. "I think I know where she is. Come with me." Edony led them to the front courtyard, her steps fast and fists clenched. Unexpectedly, they veered to the left down the path that had lured Penn away from the castle when she'd arrived, despite it leading nowhere extraordinary. With little light, Penn took care not to slip on the moss. As they continued, she felt that same pull guiding her down the path. How were Edony and Clare so perfectly at ease? Did they not feel it too?

Just as the chill set in, Edony stopped in her tracks and turned to the shrubbery. She reached to the vines and swept them to the side, revealing a narrow arch in the thicket. How had she missed that? Edony walked through the opening with Clare on her tail, holding back the vines. Penn followed, feeling like a fool.

They entered a small clearing speckled with tiny flowers, and the force that urged Penn onward dissipated. In the centre, illuminated by moonlight, was a polished tombstone. Above the tombstone stood a human-sized statue of an angel, or a god, Penn couldn't be sure. Her stone arms were clasped tightly around a blanketed bundle held to her chest, and she gazed down at her baby. A bitter taste hit Penn's tongue. The grave belonged to Duchess Sefare Issa, Lovetta's mother, and the little brother whom she never had the chance to know. Was this where Clare meant to take her on her first day in Rocque?

Edony sighed. "I really thought she'd be here."

Penn approached the tombstone and touched the white roses laid out before it. They were fresh. "I think she was here. Is it the anniversary?"

Edony shook her head. "It was a few months back." Around the same time Lovetta had thrown her fist through a mirror?

"Then this could mean something!"

"We don't know who placed them, Penn," Clare reassured her.

"I do. I cut these just this morning. I left them on the dresser. I meant to refill the vase, but I was in a hurry. They were gone when I returned."

"Even so, it might not mean anything," Clare rationalised.

Edony stepped back through the archway. "No, Penn's right. It means something."

Penn pulled herself away from the sacred space, forcing the image of her own mother's face from her mind. This wasn't the time to grieve. All three hurried along the path toward the front of the castle.

"If Saph's not in the stables, we're going to find her," Edony declared, sounding truly worried for the first time since Penn had reported the disappearance. They hurried through the darkness to the stables, where, to their dismay, they found Lovetta's mare missing. Nobody made a sound as they hastily saddled their mounts and kicked them into a gallop, nearly flying through castle grounds. For the first time, the drawbridge was down. It was *never* down after dark. Worse still, Roderick and Sir Ulrich were nowhere to be seen. Panic set in. Were the men-at-arms with Lovetta, watching over her and keeping her safe, or were they disposed of early, and Lovetta snatched from the grounds in broad daylight? Was the missing mare a diversion, a strategy to disguise Lovetta's true whereabouts? No, Lovetta had gone willingly. Penn prayed the roses hadn't been her final goodbye.

Penn's fears only worsened when they reached the lake and found no sign of Lovetta. Edony surged forward, leading them further up the road than Penn had ever been. They rounded the great lake, hoof-falls softening as they pounded soils less travelled. Then, silhouetted in the distance, three willowy shapes emerged on the road, moving slowly toward the search party. Penn's heart faltered as the shapes became clearer. Three mounts carrying three riders, one tethered in the centre. It wasn't until they were mere feet apart that Penn could make out Lovetta's tear-streaked face beneath her cloak's hood. A relief like none other washed over Penn, and she swayed in her saddle.

"Thank the gods," Edony breathed.

Lovetta would not meet Penn's eye. Her hands clutched tightly to a roll of parchment and Saph's reigns. Penn fell back as Edony rounded on her sister, seething with fury.

"We were worried sick! You could have been killed! Do you have no regard for the people who care for you?" Edony said as they turned and headed back towards the castle.

"He said he was leaving for Azor," Lovetta croaked. "My only chance, gone!"

Hazir. Penn's heart sank.

"I had to find out if it was true, but his letter was so vague. What if I wrote back and he had already left?"

Edony was silent for a moment before responding. "I don't understand. I thought you didn't love him," she said, her previous rage subsiding.

"It's bigger than that!" Lovetta wailed.

Bigger than *love?* No, surely not. Lovetta had never pined over Hazir like Edony did for Sahin. She'd called him sweet and shy, a good friend! Had she secretly harboured affection for Hazir all this time?

Edony hushed her sister and tried to reason with her. "He wouldn't leave on a whim, Love, not without your answer."

At this, even Clare's head snapped to attention. Had Hazir *proposed* to Lovetta? Nausea danced like a thousand tiny worms in Penn's gut. Please let it be a lie.

Lovetta hiccupped and said, "How can you know that? I only have one shot. It wasn't worth the risk."

Penn could read between the lines. Hazir had proposed to Lovetta, undoubtedly enthralled by her, but marriage was a lifelong commitment, and Lovetta only had one chance to get it right. It was only natural that she couldn't decide right away. But she took too long, so Hazir left, believing her indecision a refusal. Maybe it was wrong, but Penn couldn't help but feel a little relieved that Hazir had gone home to his assemblage of slaves. As much as Lovetta was hurting, she deserved better. Thank the gods Penn knew nothing of love, or what it could do to a person.

When the castle came into view, the duke's men untethered Sapphire and watched until the women entered the stables. Lovetta was grey, saying nothing as she stumbled to her chambers. Penn followed her and silently untied her gown and let out her hair, pausing at the nape of Lovetta's neck to savour her scent. It was an intoxicating mix of lavender, sweat and coconut oil. How pleased she was that it was her hands on Lovetta and not Hazir's.

Penn guided her into bed. Lovetta rolled onto her side and stared out the window, her eyes emptied of all feeling. It wasn't until Penn had pulled back her own bedcovers that Lovetta whispered, "Stay with me."

Penn slipped into the empty space beside her. She would do anything to ease her pain.

\* \* \*

The days following Lovetta's disappearance were a blur. Lovetta had lost all vitality, dressing, eating and sleeping with barely a word in between, as if she had nothing else to give. A letter addressed to Hazir Saraq had left the castle the morning after the event, but no word had returned. They were drawing closer to their departure for Tirel, and an anxiety reverberated within the castle walls. Would Hazir's reply reach Lovetta before they left if he hadn't already?

Naturally, the duke was informed of Lovetta's adventure, so she had lost her independence. Penn was no longer permitted to leave her side, which meant no more visits to the hayloft, and no more lone baths for Lovetta. They established an unspoken agreement to keep their backs to each other, but it hadn't been quite that easy. Penn wanted to look at her, and she stole secret glances at her now and again, praying that Lovetta wouldn't notice. What was it about Lovetta that pulled Penn in? She had never looked at Clare or Marion's bodies with the same hunger. As the week drew on, she became bolder. She turned toward her more often and watched her for longer until, one day, she caught Lovetta doing the very same thing. They both flinched, looked away at once, and Penn burned all over.

Not every moment in Lovetta's company was quite so exciting. Penn discovered an entirely new world of boredom while accompanying Lovetta to her classes. She had two tutors, a matter-of-fact Azorian woman, who taught history and etiquette specific to Azorian culture, and a white-skinned woman who taught the Vastalian equivalents. Penn didn't mind the mornings with the Azorian tutor, but the afternoon tutor's rambling could put a bird to sleep mid-air. Penn and Lovetta visited Sefare's grave twice that week, and Penn thought of her own mother each time. The more she frequented the path, the less it seemed to call to her.

"I should have said this weeks ago, but I'm so sorry for your loss," Penn said as Lovetta placed fresh flowers by the tombstone.

"And I yours. Nobody should lose a parent so young," Lovetta said, then sighed. "It makes me wonder if there really are gods, and if my mother is watching over me as they supposedly do."

"I'd wager she can hardly take her eyes off you." Penn smiled, even though she didn't believe in life after death. She knew exactly where her mother was, her ashes piled into an urn in her father's study.

Lovetta shook her head, looking sheepish. "I need a drink. Fancy a trip to the market? Edony's still sour with me, so she won't give me a thing."

The duke had banned his daughters from riding following Lovetta's disappearance, so Edony had been furious to miss a meeting with Sahin.

Penn shrugged her shoulders. "That depends. Have you found me a coat with deep pockets?"

The marketplace buzzed with a chorus of squealing children and hollering merchants. Paths were clean and tree-lined, bustling with villagers from all walks of life. The wine peddler sat in the last row of stalls beside the artisan cheeses, talking up his sweet mead to a group of ladies not much older than Penn. It was hot under the coat, the stall in full afternoon sun, and Penn was already sweating. There weren't as many customers as Penn had hoped, so her timing would have to be precise. Thankfully, she had Lovetta to charm the peddler.

They approached the stall from opposite sides, Lovetta with a half-eaten caramel apple in hand and Penn a cob of corn. Blending in was key, and what better way than to do as locals did? Lovetta had called it a genius idea and made a fuss of buying Penn the freshest cob, which only made Penn more eager to succeed.

The merchant snapped to attention as Lovetta approached the stall. "A blessed day it is to be visited by a Bondeville," he said. Despite dressing plainly, the colour of Lovetta's skin declared her identity like a rooster announced dawn.

Penn wandered closer, studying the many bottles as she chewed on her corn. Another customer came forward, scanned the wares, then left with a loud sniff. Penn picked up a small, dimpled bottle and turned it over, then almost snorted at the price. A whole aur for such a tiny thing? Shaking her head, Penn set it down and moved on to the larger bottles with foreign names.

"Oh, how marvellous!" Lovetta said as she brushed a finger over a bottle. "The drawings on the labels—"

"All by hand and one of a kind, m'lady."

Penn scoured the shelf for the bottle she had seen in Lovetta's chambers.

"You must tell me the artist's name. I've been looking for a piece in just this style to sit above my bed."

There were a lot of bottles, and Penn could feel the sweat beading on her upper lip. Gods, why did the coat have to be so thick?

"You know, I've got his name somewhere. If it pleases you, I'll find it," the merchant said.

"That would be magnificent!" Lovetta exclaimed.

The merchant turned his back to the stall, and Lovetta shot Penn an urgent look. She moved faster.

"Blimey, it's here somewhere, I'm sure of it!" the merchant called as he rummaged under a shelf.

Grape wine, date wine, rum and something called honeyfizz ... there! She'd found it. The apricot liqueur Lovetta had shared with her, right beside a bottle of spiced apple liqueur: Lovetta's favourite. Frantically, Penn took the cob between her teeth and checked over her shoulder. When nobody was looking, she slipped a bottle into the coat's inner pocket with ease. Heart hammering, she looked back again. Oh, what a thrill! If only she could get that second bottle, Lovetta would be *so* impressed.

"Ah, here it is!" the merchant called.

With no time to lose, Penn stuffed a second bottle into her outside pocket.

The merchant straightened up and squinted at the card in his hands. "Lady Mary Rigelsford. A woman." He cocked a brow.

"You seem surprised," Lovetta said.

"Indeed I am. Never heard of a lady artist before. Bit funny, isn't it?" He handed over the card, then scratched his head.

"Well, I've never heard of your wines before, yet you say they're the best in the realm. Funny, isn't it?"

The sourness in Lovetta's tone didn't go unnoticed, and Penn's pulse quickened as she sidled over to the duke's men, who were deep in conversation with a woman offering samples of cheese.

The merchant coloured. "Perhaps m'lady is too young to know a fine wine when she sees one. I'm certain your sister can vouch for the quality."

"I meant no offense, sir." Lovetta laughed. "As you say, I'm too young to know much of anything about wine. Perhaps I'll give them a try when I come of age. Good day to you." Lovetta curtsied and turned her back to the baffled merchant, seeking out Penn with a look of frustration.

"Never heard of a lady artist," she scoffed, coming to Penn's side. They both walked along the row of vendors, breathing fast. The duke's men fell behind. "So? Did you get it?"

"Of course I did. Slow down!" Penn said as Lovetta overtook her. "Unless you want someone to think we're up to no good."

A firm hand grasped Penn's shoulder, and she spun around. Her stomach dropped. It was Osenna.

* * *

"Never in my time as housekeeper has a thief walked these halls," Osenna boomed. She had guided them straight to her sitting room, dismissing the duke's men and saying very little.

"Penn is no thief, Osenna. This is all a big misunderstanding," Lovetta said as she placed a hand on Penn's arm reassuringly.

"Respectfully, Your Grace, I think not. I saw her take that bottle with my own eyes, and no coin was exchanged. The evidence is before you now." Osenna indicated to the bottle on the table. "Perhaps your judgement is clouded by your affection for the maid."

"My affection?" Lovetta dropped her hand.

"Lady's maids are a conniving lot, always looking for a means to get ahead. They forget themselves." Osenna stared down Penn like she was a roach fit for squashing. She had never sweated so much in her life.

"You've got it all wrong, Osenna. It was I who asked Penn to take it! I'm the conniving one."

Osenna's eyes widened. "Your Grace! I don't believe it. She's put you up to this to save her reputation, hasn't she?"

"No, she would never! I'm telling the truth, Osenna. I asked Penn to steal a bottle for me while I distracted the man running the stall. I asked him about the artwork on the bottles—look—I have this card to prove it! I made him find the artist's name so that Penn could take it without being caught." Lovetta gave Osenna the card, a look of shame on her face.

Osenna's stare softened. "Oh, Your Grace. Why?"

"I wanted to drink. Needed to," Lovetta said, shrugging her shoulders and looking at the floor.

Osenna shook her head and sighed. "You are too young to be drowning your sorrows in drink."

"Sometimes it's all that helps," Lovetta said meekly, bringing a hand to her face.

"There's no need for tears, Your Grace. I won't be saying a thing to your father. I know how hard these last few months have been for you, but … I'm afraid I can't let you keep this. I've seen too many of our kind lose themselves at the end of a bottle."

Lovetta sniffed. "I understand."

Osenna turned on Penn. "As for *you*," she said with unrestrained loathing. "You are supposed to be her grace's guide. *You* are supposed to keep her safe. That means stopping her from making foolish decisions that could ruin her reputation. It would be wise for you to remember that."

Penn shook beneath her stare. "Yes, Mistress. It won't happen again."

"If it does, I'll make sure your family hears of it, and you'll have no reference from me. Do you understand?"

Penn nodded. "Yes, Mistress."

"Good. Now go make yourself useful and prepare her grace for the journey."

They left at once, taking the least public route to Lovetta's chambers through the servant's passageway.

"I am so sorry," Lovetta apologised as she pressed the door closed behind them.

Penn shrugged off the coat. "Don't be. What you said in there … it was my idea. You shouldn't have protected me."

"I encouraged you. You could have been sacked! And for what? Nothing, in the end."

"Oh?" Penn said, grasping at the contents of the coat's inner pocket. "Then what's this?"

Lovetta's jaw dropped. "You didn't!"

Penn laughed. "You fluttered your eyelashes for so long that I could have taken a dozen."

"You would have needed quite the coat," Lovetta said, then smiled wide. "Oh, Penn! This is brilliant. I could kiss you!"

"I can only imagine what Osenna would think of that," Penn said, her body buzzing with a thrill at Lovetta's words.

"Ignore her, she's all talk." Lovetta took two glasses from the mantel and popped open the bottle. "Gods, that smell is to die for." She filled the glasses and set them before the hearth.

"Clare's terrified of her. You don't think I should be? If she wrote to my father—"

"It wouldn't matter in the slightest. If someone truly came to take you away, they'd have to pry you from my cold, dead hands."

The buzzing, the warmth, the racing of her heart; it all intensified. Lovetta summoned Penn. "Come, drink with me. You've certainly earned it."

She joined her by the hearth gladly, and gods the drink was good! Sweet and buttery with notes of cinnamon and clove, it slid down Penn's throat with ease. They drank and laughed, and when they had drained the bottle of its last drops, they packed their trunks for their journey north.

A knock sounded from the doorway and Clare's head poked through. "Are your bags ready, m'lady?" Her gaze fluttered to Penn, and she offered her a heartfelt smile. It felt like they hadn't seen each other at all over the last week, and they were used to spending so much of their time together.

"By the dressing table," Lovetta murmured.

Clare fetched Lovetta's trunk and gown, then turned to Penn and hoisted her belongings under her other arm. Combined, the luggage was bigger than Clare.

"I'd help if I could," Penn said. Though she doubted Lovetta was in a fit enough state to run off to the Saraqs, Penn had promised the duke that she would stay by her side, and she certainly couldn't afford another visit to Osenna's sitting room.

"No bother," Clare said, struggling out the door. "I'll see you in the morning."

"Goodnight," Penn called out to her. When the door closed, she re-joined Lovetta by the hearth.

Lovetta sighed. "I'm sorry you have to spend so much time with me."

"There is nowhere else I'd rather be," Penn said truthfully.

The corners of Lovetta's mouth twitched. "You have to say that." She tucked a curl behind her ear.

Penn wrapped her arms around her knees. "I said it because I meant it, not because I had to. Just as I meant what I said the other night; I enjoy your company. Too much, sometimes." She wasn't entirely sure what she meant, but the words spilled out faster than she could think. "Anyway, I'd be a pretty lousy maid if I lied to your face." She smiled reassuringly.

Lovetta swayed in her seat. "Maybe it's not a maid I need."

Penn bit her cheeks to stop herself from grinning. "I can be more than a maid. I can be your friend." Saying it aloud felt good, childish, and wrong all at the same time. Lovetta, her friend, just as Clare was. Yet why did it feel so different?

She watched Lovetta fidget with her hair. "Just because I have a duty to serve you doesn't mean I can't be more." Lovetta's lip wobbled. "Oh, Lovetta. What troubles you? Please let me in. Is it Lord Hazir?"

"Ugh, don't call him *Lord*." Lovetta screwed up her nose. "No, it isn't him it's … just me." Her voice cracked. "I think I'm broken."

"That's absurd!" Penn stood and bravely took Lovetta's hands in her own. "Osenna was right. This year has not been kind to you. You deserve so much better than the cards you've been dealt."

They looked at each other for a moment, silent, Lovetta's hands hot in Penn's. It was strange. Penn spent much of her time close to Lovetta, unlacing her gowns and braiding her hair, and yet none of those moments felt as intimate as this.

Eventually, Lovetta dropped her gaze. "It's late. We'll be exhausted in the morning if we don't get to sleep."

Penn let go of Lovetta's hands, but her fingers still tingled as she pulled back Lovetta's bedcovers.

"Will you stay with me again tonight?" Lovetta asked, sitting serenely on the side of her four-poster bed. She had not asked this since the night she disappeared.

"Of course," Penn whispered. An intangible force led her to her bed space, undressed her, extinguished the candles, and tossed her into Lovetta's bed with limbs weak as a fawn. The pillow smelt of lavender, and it took some time before she was calm enough to consider sleep. Again, she wondered: What was it about Lovetta that inflamed Penn so? Why now, as she stared into the darkness, did she feel so compelled to stay awake and commit this moment between them to memory?

What had Lovetta done to her?

# Seven

Penn woke to the sound of the creaking door. She sat bolt upright, surprised by the sight of Clare in the doorway. Clare's face was devoid of colour, and she stuttered when she spoke. "You're late."

It took Penn a moment to realise that the room was brighter than it ought to be. She looked quickly to the orange glow at the window, and Clare was gone by the time she turned back. Lovetta stirred beside her and stretched her arms before climbing out of bed. They changed into travelling tunics and made for the stables with haste.

It was a cloudy morning, but the riding party was in high spirits, nonetheless. A well-oiled wooden carriage big enough to fit the entire Bondeville family and their maids sat by the drawbridge, tethered to half a dozen packhorses. Another dozen men-at-arms milled around on foot and horseback, heavily armoured and restless. Penn could see Roderick talking fast to Duke Wymark, gripping his helm tight over his protruding belly, his caterpillar eyebrow as animated as his talk. After spotting the latecomers, the duke gave Roderick a pat on the back and made his way toward them.

"Belsante and Edony will be on the road with me," he said. "You will not. You will watch over the others in the carriage, and I hope you will all be on your best behaviour." He glanced at the bulky vessel where Ysabell, Dorett and Sarra perched bleary-eyed, their maids huddled beside them. Penn wasn't looking forward to spending the next three days jammed between the maids. Tibby and Thamasin would talk them all into headaches, and Marion wasn't exactly her biggest fan. If only Clare and Jehane weren't riding with the duke.

The duke looked at Penn. "Lady Prestcote."

She bowed her head. "Yes, your Grace."

"I will be relying on your diligence while we are away." He gave Lovetta a disapproving look. "My daughter is stubborn and too smart for her own good. You would do well not to trust her. I do not expect you to be her shadow, but I pray that you will keep her safe."

Penn bowed her head again as he retreated.

"Stubborn, ha! Where does he think I get it from?" Lovetta teased.

The duke called an order, and his men were instantly in motion. Metallic clanking filled the air as they mounted their horses. Penn climbed into the carriage and, distracted by the commotion, tripped and landed on her hands and knees. Whirling around, she saw a glimpse of Marion's boot retracting from the threshold. Penn pulled herself up, grateful nobody else had seen her stumble. Marion avoided her eye as if completely oblivious, but Penn was sure she had done it on purpose. Letting it go, Penn helped Lovetta into the vestibule.

The carriage was far more extravagant than her father's had been. It was longer than it was wide, lined with tiny, curtained windows and plush seats adjoining the walls. Dividing the two columns of seats was a skinny table adorned with teacakes and tarts. A large bowl of ripe apricots, peaches and plums caught Penn's attention. They didn't grow in Theroulde, and by the time the merchants got their hands on them, they were too soft to eat. What a treat! Perhaps their confinement wouldn't be so bad, after all.

Penn squeezed her way through the carriage to join Lovetta, who was perched on a seat facing backwards. As soon as the travellers had piled in, a shout reverberated outside, and the horses kicked into motion. Quickly the vessel pulsed with chatter and the steady beat of hoofs hitting the earth. Lovetta reclined with her feet on the seat and looked wistfully out the window.

"You wish you were riding, don't you?" Penn asked.

Lovetta shrugged. "Not at this pace. I'd fall asleep on my horse. It's a shame you couldn't ride Primula, though. She would have liked a good run." Lovetta smiled. "At least we won't have saddle sores like the rest of them." She wiggled in her seat and flexed her ankles, while Penn sat still as a statue. "Oh, relax Penn! Osenna isn't here. Put your legs up, enjoy yourself. We'll be in here for a while."

Penn tentatively lifted her legs onto the seat, only to find that both her legs and Lovetta's legs could not fit without touching. She twitched with nervous energy, but if Lovetta had noticed the grazing of their calves, she didn't show it. Penn's skin prickled, but eventually, she relaxed into her seat.

The first couple of hours were long, the frivolous conversation between Tibby and Thamasin nearly lulling her to sleep. They stopped briefly to water the horses and relieve themselves, but they were quickly on the road again. Lovetta taught Penn an Azorian card game, but the rules were confusing, and Lovetta quickly grew tired of winning without a challenge. Once Lovetta had fallen asleep, Penn received a visit from Marion, who came with a strained smile and a large, ripe peach.

"You must be hungry after missing breakfast this morning. Clare told me you had a late night. Here." She passed over the piece of fruit. "They're delicious."

"Thank you," said Penn, surprised. Was that her way of apologising for the weeks passed? And if so, had Penn simply stumbled over her own feet earlier and wrongly cast Marion as a villain? Perhaps the drink still lingered in her blood and made her clumsy.

Marion returned to her seat, and Penn brought the offering to her lips, her mouth watering. She took a generous bite, and juice trickled down her chin as she savoured the taste. But something was off. It was too soft, too sour. Penn held the fruit into the light and nearly gagged. Beneath the skin, the peach was dark with rot. She spat the mouthful into her hand and cursed, then turned the fruit over in her hand. A tiny spot of mould was nestled in the furrow, fluffy and white. So much for Marion's apology!

Penn slid off the seat and marched over to a dustbin in the corner, looked directly at Marion, and threw the rotten peach out with a thump. Like before, Marion refused to meet her eye. If there weren't so many ears in the carriage, she would call her out then and there. Her appetite squandered, Penn retreated to her seat and seethed until her eyelids grew too heavy to keep open.

\* \* \*

A bump in the road woke Penn with a start. The carriage had come to a stop. Lovetta, who was wide awake and frowning, pulled back the curtain and peered out the tiny window. She sighed. "Just watering the horses."

They both looked across as the door clicked open. The light that filtered in was dim, and Penn wondered just how long she had been asleep. Needing desperately to stretch, they left the carriage. They had stopped on a well-worn road far from any villages, and a dark cloud blanketed the sky above them. The two navigated their way through the crowd in search of the remaining Bondevilles, each of the duke's men bowing as they passed.

"A storm is coming," the duke told his daughters as Clare handed out wrapped lunches. "We may be in for a rough night. Eat quickly. We need to be clear of the bridge before the worst of it."

Penn waited for Clare before opening her package of dried fruits and bread, her stomach a little queasy from the long ride. "I bet you're having a better time than I am," she said to Clare.

"I don't know about that," Clare grumbled, picking the seeds off her bread and eating them one by one.

"Why? Saddle sores already?" Penn teased, nudging Clare in the ribs.

"No, Penn. I suppose I'm just having a bad morning."

"You can talk to me about it," Penn offered, but Clare looked pointedly away. "Okay, if you don't want to talk about it, then listen. You wouldn't believe what happened this morning."

"I just might."

"No, really. It's been awful in there."

"Just *awful*, I'm sure," Clare said, her tone heavy with sarcasm. "A little awkward after last night, is it? Didn't it go according to plan?"

Penn swallowed her mouthful and frowned at Clare. "Didn't what go according to plan? Has Osenna said something?"

"Oh, you must think me so simple!" Clare jumped to her feet and walked off faster than Penn could scratch her head. She would talk to Clare that night and get to the bottom of her bewildering behaviour.

When the riding party was back in motion, Penn and Lovetta started on a round of chess. Much to Lovetta's surprise, Penn won consecutively, thanks to the many long, wintery nights in Castle Theroulde with her father.

Marion did not bother Penn again. Instead, she kept her eyes down, hunched over her embroidery for the rest of the afternoon. As the day drew on, the storm clouds began to thunder, though the first drops of rain did not hit them until they had reached the great Rocque Bridge. Penn craned her neck to get a good look at the famous structure through the window but could see little more than a few yards of stone through the fog. It was probably for the best. If Penn couldn't see the bridge, she couldn't see the bottomless lake beneath it either.

Night fell as they reached the end of the bridge, the rain now falling in sheets. Crown men-at-arms searched the party leisurely, soaking those on horseback to the bone. Thankfully, they arrived at their destination before the hail. The night would be spent at a small inn crammed with what seemed like every man from the village. Penn and Lovetta raced from the cosy carriage to the inn's door, squealing as water trickled down the napes of their necks. Edony glared, hair plastered to her head like a knight's helm.

The innkeeper was a robust, red-faced man with jittery hands. His bare head shone in the amber light of the inn as he welcomed the Bondevilles inside, a wide, giddy grin spread from cheek to cheek. The Bondevilles and their maids were taken up a creaking staircase and showed to their rooms. Shivering, Penn shrugged herself into a coat and lit the fire. The room was plain with a draft that made the flames dance. Cold and hungry, she followed Lovetta downstairs, where they were greeted by a deafening chorus of song. Something about a horseless knight in a storm; Penn didn't know it. Despite the weather, the cheer was infectious. Ruddy-faced villagers filled the long tables, downing flagons of ale and bellowing with laughter. The air hung with the smell of sweat, hay and roasted meats. Penn and Lovetta squeezed onto a bench across from Edony, Belsante and their maids, followed swiftly by the innkeeper carrying plates laden with baked potatoes, peas, chicken, several kinds of bread and an enormous boat of gravy; they would have to eat around the chicken.

Edony grabbed a discarded flagon of ale, only for it to be swiped from her eager hand by the innkeeper. "Commoner's drink, your Grace!" he shouted over the bedlam. "I'll bring you something more to your taste." Edony grinned wickedly as the innkeeper disappeared behind the bar, returning with a full tray of goblets. "Plum wine from Yasai. I've been saving it."

"You spoil us!" Edony said, exalted.

The innkeeper passed the pink liquid to each of the daughters and their maids with not a single drop spilled. "It's not every day we are blessed with royalty, your Grace. And something so fine would be wasted on this sort!" He grinned and waved in the direction of the villagers. Nobody laughed, and Lovetta cleared her throat. "Anyway," the innkeeper said, his expression suddenly nervous. "I dare not take up any more of your time. Drink up! There's plenty more where that came from." He sank into the crowd.

Belsante was the first to taste the brew, nodding appreciatively after a delicate sip. Edony dove in, quickly draining half of her goblet, followed by Lovetta whose swig rivalled a common man's. "I suppose it's okay, even if he was awful," she said with a sour look.

Penn laughed. "Awful? He gave us all wine!" She fixed her gaze on the goblet before her. It had a musky aroma that reminded her a little of Maud.

Lovetta snorted. "Yes, but he demeaned the rest of the room—his loyal, paying customers—while he did it."

"At ease, Love. Not everyone is a monster," Edony said, finishing her goblet and eyeing Lovetta's. "You know he was only trying to impress us."

"Belittling others doesn't impress me," Lovetta said, sliding her half empty goblet to Edony, who drank it rather than retaliate. Before trying the wine, Penn searched the hall for prying eyes. If Osenna got word of her drinking in public, she would be in strife.

"Oh, go on. None of her spies are here," Lovetta said, as if reading Penn's mind.

Penn swallowed hard. "She has *spies?*"

Lovetta laughed. "It was a joke. You're safe with me." Lovetta's hand took Penn's beneath the table, and Penn felt herself flush from her temple to her toes. She looked to Lovetta, who met her gaze and smiled sweetly, as if waiting for something.

"You're safe with me, too." It felt like Lovetta's hand had reached not to her own, but into Penn's chest and caressed her heart.

Lovetta scrunched up her nose like a mischievous child. "Then we can both make fools of ourselves. Come on, drink up!" When Lovetta's hand came away, Penn had to stop herself from reaching out and taking it back.

Penn turned her attention to the wine, and was glad her first sip was a cautious one. It was thick, sickly sweet and a little sour, like it had been bottled for a decade too long. No matter where it came from, the drink was no better than any old wine. She coughed involuntarily. "I think I prefer mead."

"I second that," Lovetta said wistfully. A few minutes later, two cups of mead materialised before them. At the end of the table, a young woman atop the lap of a drunkard nodded to Lovetta. She was exquisite, with skin like Lovetta's, curls piled high atop her head, and a little less clothing than the season called for. The man beneath her was nothing special, teeth rotten and hands grabbing at her hips greedily. Penn guessed that he had paid for her company. A shadow came over Lovetta's face as she acknowledged the woman, and Penn realised that she was blushing, a sight Penn had never seen. She liked it.

As the storm raged outside, they savoured their mead, ate and laughed merrily, save for Clare, who brooded between Edony and a woman with an ear-splitting cackle. It seemed that at every moment, Clare avoided Penn's eye. When the duke rose to retire to bed, they stashed their goblets under the table and tried not to sway as they climbed the stairs. Penn had been the victim of too much drink only a handful of times, but she had learnt quickly to recognise her limits. Lovetta, on the other hand, had trouble undressing herself. Giggling, she sat on the edge of the four-poster bed as Penn came to her rescue, pulling her gown over her head. Clad only in her underclothes, Lovetta turned to Penn and abruptly seized the sides of her face with her fingertips. "Penn! You're so much fun!" she cooed. "Oh, don't blush! There's no need to be shy with me." One of Lovetta's hands left her cheek and intertwined with Penn's hair, sparking a memory. Blurry and broken, it was of her smiling mother, her fingers moving through Penn's hair slowly. Penn had been mad at her and pulled away, and did the very same thing to Lovetta.

Lovetta seemed surprised, and she surveyed Penn with glazed eyes. "Why did you do that?"

"Do what?"

Lovetta touched the ends of her own hair instead. "Pull away when I came close."

"I didn't mean to. It's not you, it's my hair."

"Your hair?" Lovetta said with a doubtful expression. "Explain."

Penn sighed. "Having someone touch it—even just seeing it in a mirror—makes me think of my mother." Penn had never told anyone this before; how easily a little liquor loosened her tongue. "I've wanted it gone for years, but father never let me cut it. I don't blame him, really. I might have run off and pretended to be a boy. I'm joking! Well, I'm a little serious. Fancy that, life as a boy. All the opportunities I would have had!"

Lovetta tipped her head to the side and scrutinised Penn. "You'd make a very handsome boy."

Penn laughed. "That's a relief. I'd hate to look like my brothers."

Lovetta snorted. "They can't be that bad if they share your blood. Anyway, why not cut it? Your father can't stop you now, can he?"

"No, but it wouldn't be proper, would it? People might think I sold my hair for coin." Penn sighed, fingering the ends of her hair with contempt.

"Well, we're not a very proper family. I say if you want to cut it, you cut it. If anyone is offended by it, that's their problem." But where would Penn even find someone to cut her hair who wouldn't think her mad? "Oh, and you'd be the height of fashion in Azor. Edony says short hair is very popular with young women."

"Really?" Penn's knowledge of fashion was abysmal.

"Absolutely." Lovetta yawned and threw her arms above her head dramatically, then fell onto the bed. "It's wild how different Azor and Vastal are. Slavery is still legal in Azor, but women are treated better. Well, women who aren't slaves..." she trailed off, winding her fingers through the air in some kind of dance.

"In what ways are women treated better?"

"They can study and work, regardless of their family name. They can even own land. What can we do here but mind our manners and spit out babies?" She sat up and looked at Penn intensely.

"Nothing." Penn sat on the bed and crossed her arms. "We go from our father's property to our husband's property, and when they die, what do we get?"

"Pushed under another man to serve. It's wrong."

"It is!" Suddenly restless, Penn stood back up and paced by the hearth. "How is it fair for my brothers to inherit Theroulde, and I nothing?" She stumbled a little from the drink. "I'm older than Gillot, so I should be second in line, but because I'm a woman, I'm not even *in* the line. It makes me so angry. I wish I had been born a boy. I'd do anything—"

"No!" Lovetta cut her off. "How would that help? Men are the *problem.*"

Penn went quiet. She had said too much.

"Tell me. Do you truly want to become the very thing that limits us? Do you know what doing that would say to the world?"

"That I'm mad?"

"Maybe," admitted Lovetta. "But more importantly, it would say that you are ashamed of being a woman and that you agree that men are superior." How Lovetta had the mind to philosophise after the amount she had drunk, Penn didn't know. "Why perpetuate such nonsense when you can fight it instead? Then it isn't only you who benefits, we all do."

Penn laughed. "It's impossible, as wonderful as you make it sound." And at that, Lovetta dropped onto her back, her fire extinguished.

"All big things come from little ideas," Lovetta whispered, and Penn knew she had said the wrong thing.

Penn sighed. "Okay. How do we fight it?"

Lovetta sat up abruptly, charged with renewed energy. "That's the question, isn't it? Firstly, you do just as my father says. You stop believing that you'll never amount to anything, even if the world tells you so. It isn't easy, but it can be done. Look at Jehane. No one in their right mind would pick a fight with her. They'd call her a warrior in Azor."

Penn wracked her brains for the little she knew about the country. "Is it true that in Azor, women can take the throne?"

"Absolutely. Mention that to father, and he'll talk your ear off all night."

"He agrees with it?"

"Of course he does!" Lovetta laughed. "Duke Wymark Bondeville of Rocque, abolisher of slavery! Why do you think most of his workers are women? And commoners, at that!"

Penn shrugged. "I just thought he was kind, and perhaps didn't want any strapping lads around tempting his daughters into debauchery." The shortage of men in the Bondeville's service was obvious, and barely any of the women she had met in the castle had noble lineage. Lovetta had even made a point to detail the absurdity of hiring highborn maids, which Penn had thought a kind of prejudice.

"I hadn't considered that. A few years ago, there was a rumour in the village that he was a pervert. How absurd!"

Penn laughed. "I'm glad we've established that your father is neither a prude nor a pervert. So, he hires women over men to make a statement? And the common girls—"

"To give them a chance of a better life. His idea is to raise the status of women so that one day, we're equal to men in all ways, but it's not one of his more popular notions."

Penn was not surprised. "Neither was jailing slavers." The movement had been condemned by so many, and yet somehow, the duke had made it happen.

"All he had to do was plant the seed," Lovetta said.

Penn joined her on the bed, brain buzzing with all she had learnt. She repeated Lovetta's words. "All big things come from little ideas, indeed. So, how do we plant *our* seed?" she asked, mulling over the fantastic proposition.

Lovetta sat bolt upright, making the bed shake. "We cut your hair!"

"We *what?*"

"It isn't much, but it'll make a statement. That's a start, isn't it?" Lovetta said, pulling Penn upright.

As exciting as the thought was, Penn was doubtful. "Maybe we should keep thinking."

"Maybe." Lovetta sighed, deflated again.

Penn had scarcely seen Lovetta so passionate about anything. Maybe it was just the liquor talking, but her eyes blazed with a manic energy, and Penn was willing to do just about anything to keep her fire burning. "I suppose we could cut my hair anyway."

"Really?"

"Sure. Let's make a statement." Penn didn't believe for a second that it would make a difference in the grand scheme of things, but if it appeased Lovetta, then why not? Her father couldn't stop her, and Osenna couldn't sack her over something so trivial. "Where are we going to find scissors?"

"The innkeeper!" Lovetta shouted, stumbling to her feet and swaying.

Penn steadied her and brought her back down to the bed. "How about I go?" A disinhibited and scantily clad royal would not be the most inspiring sight for the common people.

"That's a good idea," Lovetta admitted, then closed her eyes. "I'll just rest for a while."

Penn left the room and made her way as quietly as she could down the creaky stairwell. The last thing she wanted was to run into the duke while she had drink on her breath. She found the innkeeper carrying a crate of liquor in the hall. He obliged her request with a quizzical look, and Penn tiptoed up the stairs with a small wooden box. Lovetta had already fallen into a light sleep but woke as the door clicked shut.

"Perfect!" she squealed, eyeing the rust-speckled silver. Penn was dragged over to the dressing table, her coat stripped off and her braid unfurled. Lovetta wet down the kinks, splashing water from the basin all over the table, then dragged a brush through her hair, apologising every time the bristles caught.

Penn considered herself in the mirror, bobbing her hair at different lengths with jittery fingers. She pointed to the base of her chin. "Cut it here."

Lovetta giggled. "Goodness, that is short! I like it." Penn gulped as Lovetta brought her hair behind her shoulders, then took the scissors from the box. "Close your eyes." She braced herself to make the first cut.

Snip.

"I did it!" Lovetta exclaimed, as if surprised by her own actions.

Snip, snip, snip. Penn covered her face with her hands until Lovetta finished, and it felt like hours until she heard the scissors return to their box.

"You can look now."

Penn lowered her hands and opened her eyes. Her jaw dropped. It was gone. The hair that she hid behind, red-faced and frustrated, was gone. Her eyes started to water.

"You hate it, don't you? Oh, what have I done!" Lovetta shrieked.

Penn turned her head from side to side, marvelling at Lovetta's creation. Blunt chin-length locks that tucked neatly behind her ears. No more waves, no more knots, and no more damned braids. The cut wasn't perfect, but Penn was ecstatic, nonetheless. "Thank you, Lovetta." She grinned, holding back tears. "I love it."

# Eight

It was no surprise that Lovetta had a splitting headache the next morning. Even Penn's breakfast remained untouched, and she welcomed the darkness of the carriage, but not the motion. The rain had not eased until the early hours of the morning, leaving the road slippery and squelching underfoot. Prying eyes followed Penn as she hurried to the carriage. Tibby was so impressed with her new look that she asked Lovetta to cut her hair too, but Thamasin quickly talked her out of it.

"Don't you want to get married?" Thamasin asked Penn in a tone of surprise.

Penn shrugged. "Not really."

"*See?*" Thamasin whispered to Tibby, as if Penn's fate had been sealed by her hairstyle alone.

"We all make mistakes," Marion said patronisingly.

"Speaking from experience, Marion?" Lovetta retorted, to which Marion looked down with cheeks bright as tomatoes. "Just ignore them, Penn." Lovetta placed her hand on Penn's shoulder.

Instantly, she was reassured. "I intend to. I like it, and I hear that short hair is the height of fashion in Azor."

Lovetta giggled, and they took their seats.

The second morning on the road was a quiet one, both women doing their best to sleep off their liquor. The party stopped for a long lunch at midday, and Penn sought out Clare, who seemed to be making a point of surrounding herself with as many people as possible. Unable to get Clare alone and tired of hearing 'oh, but you had such beautiful hair', Penn retreated to the carriage early.

Just before nightfall, they arrived at a town on the outskirts of Tirel and were greeted by a chorus of cheer. Townspeople lined the streets shouting blessings and prayers, honoured to receive the king's brother and his family in their humble town. Despite the welcome, it wasn't long before Penn missed the rickety, raucous inn from the night before. Their accommodation was much finer, but its luxuries came at a price. The duke and his family were seated on the dais for the evening meal, the maids and men-at-arms shuffled out of sight to dine. With Clare making every effort to avoid her, Penn had a quiet night. Afterwards, she was glad to find Lovetta in their shared chambers.

"I can't wait to be out of this place," Lovetta said, shaking her head. "We weren't permitted a moment of quiet all night, and the look of utter disgust on their faces when we didn't touch the duck! We might as well have been dancing naked on the tabletop."

Judging by the size of the crowd on the streets, Penn bet that every lord and lady within a day's ride had come to greet the duke and his daughters.

"I can't imagine anyone ever looking at you in disgust," Penn said instinctively.

Lovetta smiled sweetly. "I'll take that as a compliment."

Penn nervously changed the topic. "You'll never guess where I dined this evening. A barn. The innkeeper's wife insisted we make space for the good people who travelled far and wide to see a royal in the flesh," Penn said dryly.

"People seem to really struggle with the concept of abdication." Lovetta sighed. "I'm sorry. I should have said something."

"It's okay. It doesn't bother me that much," Penn lied. "I probably would have used the wrong fork and made someone faint."

"If they hadn't already fainted at the sight of your hair."

Penn reddened. "You said you liked it."

Lovetta laughed. "I do like it! Oh, you're so easy to tease. I like that, too."

Penn put her hand on her heart, feigning hurt. "Have mercy, m'lady! I'm but a simple country girl doing my best to please you."

Lovetta joined Penn in her theatrics. "Simple country girls mustn't forget their place," she said in an obnoxiously posh accent.

"How cruel you are! Do I truly deserve such treatment? To be fed on the floor of a barn, like an animal? I think not. I demand a seat at your table!"

"Oh, somebody fetch a healer! Something is terribly wrong with my maid! She has opinions of her own; I fear she may have gone mad." They both guffawed, and their theatrics came to an end.

"You too would go mad if you had to sleep on that." Penn pointed to a wooden pallet draped with a moth-eaten blanket. No mattress, no pillow. "Pigs sleep better."

Lovetta grimaced, then took a seat at the dressing table. "Do you honestly think I'd make you sleep on that? You'll fit just fine in my bed. In fact, so would the rest of my sisters and their maids. If I didn't adore keeping you all to myself, I'd invite them in to sleep over."

Penn blushed as she pulled the pins from Lovetta's hair. "If you did, there would be far too much tension in the room for anyone to sleep."

Lovetta reached out and took Penn's hand softly in hers. "Penn, what happened? You and Clare aren't speaking, and Marion was openly rude to you this morning, which isn't like her. Talk to me."

Penn allowed her hand to go limp in Lovetta's, her skin prickling as it always did when Lovetta touched her. "I don't know why Clare won't speak to me. Marion should be happy; she's been hostile for weeks now, all because Clare and I grew close. I think she feels like I've replaced her, but that isn't true. Clare only spends so much time with me because I'm a useless maid."

"Firstly, you're not useless, and you never have been. Secondly, I'm certain that Clare spends time with you because she enjoys your company, and Marion sees that."

"But Clare can have more than one friend. Marion's acting like a child."

"Penn, Marion is barely fifteen and she idolises Clare. It's only natural she's going to get jealous when somebody else comes into the mix. Have you spoken to her about this?" Lovetta let go of her hand and started unfurling her own braid.

"No," Penn admitted, helping Lovetta.

"Why not?"

"I don't know," said Penn, exasperated. "I've never had friends before. This is all very new to me."

"Well, if you want to be the bigger person, you need to be the one to reach out. Make her feel like she's important."

"You make it sound so easy. Do you have some kind of guide-book on friendship?"

Lovetta laughed. "No, but my family is the size of a small village, so I've had my fair share of disagreements. Mostly with Edony."

"But the two of you are so close," Penn said, helping Lovetta out of her clothes.

"Sometimes the closer you are, the more you bicker." Lovetta kicked the wooden pallet aside and climbed into the four-poster bed.

"Life was easier before I had friends," Penn said, climbing into the far side of the bed. The mattress was so plush it was like lounging on a cloud.

"But now that you know the feeling of their friendship, you'd be awfully lonely without them," Lovetta said through a yawn.

"Not if I still had you." Penn snuggled into the blankets, and Lovetta's hand found hers again. That was how they eventually fell asleep, laying on their backs with their fingers intertwined.

Lovetta refused to eat in the dining hall the next morning, walking straight to the carriage to share teacake and fruit with Penn instead. Despite her reluctance to try another peach, she couldn't say no when Lovetta held out her own for Penn to try. Without the sisters and their maids, breakfast in the wooden box was oddly intimate. Penn had rarely dined with Lovetta alone, so she was painfully aware of her etiquette. It was almost a relief when the others filed in, her chewing no longer so obnoxious.

On the road, Dorett and Sarra brimmed with excitement for the ball, showing off their gowns and accessories with pride. Tibby and Thamasin made a great deal of *oohs* and *ahhs*, while Ysabell and Marion remained buried in books and needlework. Penn practiced Lovetta's hair for the ball, and Lovetta fussed with her fingernails and a pot of red paint. Midday passed, and they did not stop for lunch, which Penn hoped meant they were nearing their destination. For an hour or so, Lovetta and Penn kept their eyes on the window, watching the horses pass sun-crisped fields and sleepy townships.

When the riders were stopped for another search, Penn knew they had arrived in Tirel. Through the window, a city stretched as far as her eye could see. Thick stone walls towered around a sea of thatched rooftops, and dirt roads teemed with bodies. Here, there was no grand welcome.

Tirel was unlike anywhere Penn had ever been but not in a desirable way. It was as if someone had painted a landscape in only greys, and the people did not care to be preserved one bit.

Where trees might have lined the streets, trash piled haphazardly. Smoke billowed from dilapidated rooftops, blanketing the city with an acrid stench. Barefoot, skinny-legged children chased chickens, and the few faces that looked to the carriage did so with contempt. These weren't the faces of people who drank to their good king's health, for they did not know such a king. Their king was the sort who built a wall to keep them out, who charged his people taxes to take up space, and who allowed them to live in squalor while he dined on pheasant and figs.

In Theroulde, the common folk lived off the land they worked. It was not their land, and every month they paid their taxes to Lord Prestcote, but their produce was their own. When summer came and the earth was too dry to farm, Duke Wymark sent cartons of produce. When the rains turned to flood, Penn's father gifted hay bales and absolved debts. It was clear there was no such kindness in Tirel. With homes built so close together, there was no spare land left to work. No citrus trees, no vines of green bean or paddocks for grazing. It was a sorry sight.

Once they passed the inner wall and entered castle grounds, tulips lined the cobblestones, and children wore tidy tunics. Here, people lived lavishly in cottages of timber. Women in garish frocks travelled in flocks, tittering as the duke walked forward on his steed. Lacquered doors creaked open, and shop bells chimed as maids, pages, butchers, and bakers looked out, keen to see the new arrivals with their own eyes.

A welcoming party met the Bondevilles at the front of the castle, a grand thing of buttery stone and trefoil archways two-men tall. Penn climbed out of the carriage stiff-legged, shivering in the shadow of the castle. They met the royal chamberlain, a svelte man near the duke's age with auburn curls and a manicured beard. He was nothing short of impressive in his high-necked tunic of black velvet, richly embossed in gold.

"Old friend!" the chamberlain called, embracing the duke. "It feels like only yesterday. Or was it? Any excuse for a party with this lot. Good thing you haven't got anything better to do."

"And he's at it already." The duke sighed in a friendly manner. "You know, Theo, I'd stop showing up if you'd stop inviting me. I age about ten years each time I cross that damned bridge."

The chamberlain guffawed and put a hand on the duke's back. "We'll set it on fire, then. After you've accepted my offer and relocated, of course."

The duke went rigid and whispered, "Later, Theo. Later." But Penn had heard it clear as day, which meant Lovetta had too.

"Apologies." The chamberlain cleared his throat. "I suppose you're tired from the journey, hmm? We've prepared the east wing for you," he continued as he showed the Bondevilles into the castle. The walls were lined with coppery damask, floors were waxed to perfection, and a grand toile hung in the foyer depicting woodlands drenched in wildlife. It was quite obnoxious after seeing the way the common folk lived.

"His Grace insists you meet him in the oratory before supper. A matter of great importance, I'm sure. Ten aur says he's praying for new dancing shoes."

"By the gods," the duke said with a look of open repulsion. "I shall go at once." He turned to his daughters and bid them farewell before setting off down a lamp-lit hallway.

The chamberlain cleared his throat again. "Well, then. If you all follow me, I think you will be very pleased with the changes we've made—oh, hello there!" He looked directly at Penn, examining her like a gem. "A new face, I see. And who might you be?"

"Lady Penn Prestcote of Theroulde, my new maid," Lovetta said.

"Prestcote, you say? Related to Lord Durant Prestcote, then?"

Did this man know her father?

"His daughter," Lovetta said, a little too bluntly.

His eyes widened. "An unbelievably small world this is! What a delight it is to meet you. Lord Theodore Carignan, royal chamberlain. An absolute pleasure." He took Penn's hand and kissed it lightly, and her neck grew hot with embarrassment.

"Lord Carignan." She curtsied after swiftly retracting her hand.

He laughed. "Please. Call me Theo."

"If you don't mind, we're rather tired," Lovetta interrupted.

His gaze lingered on Penn for a moment longer before he said, "Of course! My apologies, your Grace. This way."

As they walked along the elegant maze, Penn studied the chamberlain. Although he looked around her father's age, Durant had as little to do with the Crown as a lord could, and not once had she seen this man in Theroulde. Moreover, why did the chamberlain care to know her name? Surely, he didn't make a point to know *all* the staff in royal service.

Arriving in the east wing, Penn quickly forgot about the brief exchange. The east wing was exquisite. The sitting room held a dozen overstuffed armchairs upholstered in rich brocade and draped artfully with animal furs. The hearth—double the size of Lovetta's—was in the centre of the room, topped with a mantle of slick mahogany. Above sat a row of ornaments made from glass, and on either side, bookcases stretched from floor to ceiling. Once the chamberlain had taken his leave, Penn let her eyes feast on the finery.

Lovetta looked about. "It's a bit much, don't you think?"

Penn barely heard her. "I've never seen glass used this way," she said, surveying a carved swan on the mantle. "I can't even imagine how much it would cost." Her own father had gawked at the cost of outfitting Castle Theroulde with windowpanes, so they had gone without.

"My guess is enough to feed half the kingdom for a week."
Lovetta came closer, grasped the glass swan and scrutinised it.
The thought of putting her own clumsy hands anywhere near
the sculpture terrified Penn.

"I bet if I took this, no one would even notice."

"Why would you take it?" Penn whispered, hoping their trip to
the marketplace hadn't given Lovetta any wild ideas.

"Like I said, it's enough to feed half the kingdom." She put the
swan down just as a maid came into the wing. Penn stifled a laugh.
The woman wore a bright purple gown, too much rouge, and her
hair was piled high enough to hide a dagger beneath it. She spoke
with Belsante, then left to fetch refreshments.

"I'm so glad you don't make me dress like that," Penn said.

"I don't think I could look at you with a straight face if you did."

Penn snorted, then continued exploring the east wing. A dining
room adjoined the sitting area, and on the other side of the room,
a hallway that was lined with identical doorways, separated by delicate tapestries.

The maid returned in the company of two others dressed in the
same fashion, and the dining table was loaded with teas and petite
cakes. With the weight of the journey behind them, the Bondevilles
and their maids relaxed into their chairs and had their fill. Clare and
Marion, who had barely spoken to each other in weeks, were cosied
up, side-by-side. Although it was an unexpected sight, Penn was
glad. If Lovetta was right about Marion's jealousy, having smoothed
things over with Clare should put her at ease.

As the day drew on, Lovetta became agitated. Penn guessed she
was nervous about the following night's ball and whether she would
see Hazir. She had not spoken of the Saraqs for over a week, and
Penn hoped it would stay that way. She didn't know what it was
about him, but Hazir got under her skin in the strangest of ways,
and Penn prayed that Lovetta had moved on from whatever had

manifested between them. To Penn's disappointment, when they entered the dining hall, Lovetta's eyes darted all over the room, but Hazir was not there. Edony cursed at Sahin's absence, while Belsante didn't even mention Zekeriya.

The Bondeville daughters and their maids were seated at a long table already half-filled with new faces. The duke took his place on the dais a few seats down from an empty throne that belonged to King Segarus. "Father can't stand the spectacle of the procession," Lovetta had said to her earlier.

The sound of a trumpet reverberated around the dining hall, and the guests came to their feet. Penn craned her neck to see a band of purple-cloaked men and women enter the room, fronted by King Segarus himself, who looked much paler and leaner than Penn had expected. The fanfare ceased as the oldest Bondeville and the reigning monarch took his seat, followed by a trail of bejewelled brunettes. First came his son and heir to the throne, an unsmiling Prince Julien, then young Princess Anais, followed by a man just as tall and angular as the duke but with a salt-and-pepper beard: Prince Alistair, the king's first brother in the company of his wife, Lady Hermana. The last two to enter were the king's sister, Princess Roheisa, and her husband, Lord Wylam.

As the King gave his welcome, Penn couldn't help but stare.

"He doesn't look well, does he?" Edony whispered.

The king's face was gaunt, and he hunched over the table with a grimace. Even from a distance, Penn could see the shadows beneath his eyes.

"I wonder if that's what his meeting with father was about," Lovetta said.

"That, or we're all moving to Tirel," Edony whispered.

"Hard to say what's worse," Belsante chimed in.

Lovetta scoffed. "Father would never move here, not in a thousand years."

Penn scanned the faces before her. "I don't see the chamberlain," she said.

"Oh, don't call him that; his ego is big enough. He's probably off oiling his beard. I guarantee he'll be in the east wing later, chasing up my father for something."

The conversation was cut short by a mousey boy in purple carrying an armful of crockery. Without a sound, he made his way around the table serving the guests. Penn looked to the other tables and saw young, purple-clad boys at each one.

"The servers are all boys," she said out loud.

"Pages," answered Lovetta, sipping her drink. "It's part of their training."

Of course. Penn was so used to seeing Duke Wymark's household flooded with women that she had forgotten the typical way of things. She wondered how her younger brother, Gillot, had fared as a server when he was a page. While Florent was good-natured and well-mannered, Gillot had quite an ego. He would certainly think serving beneath him.

"You know they opened a school recently," Lovetta said, regaining Penn's attention. "For the common people, I mean. But they won't take girls."

"Why not?" Penn asked, making a start at her supper. Girls and boys from Theroulde were expected to take lessons from a governess, although never together. A boy's learning was a mystery to Penn.

Lovetta looked around and lowered her voice. "I'd say they want soldiers who can read, and they don't care where they come from. Girls, on the other hand..." She pulled a sour face. "If they're lucky, they might find work scrubbing floors. No noblewoman will take a common girl as a maid."

"They still deserve a chance," Penn whispered.

"I know, and father knows," Lovetta said.

After seeing the living conditions of the common people of Tirel, Penn was surprised the duke hadn't formed a personal army of peasant girls. She looked around the dining hall at the other guests, who were all draped in fine silks and adorned with heavy gemstones, then pushed back her plate. She felt sick. Smiling, Lovetta nudged her arm and pushed Penn's goblet closer. "Come on, Penn, have a drink. May as well make the most of it."

Once the Bondeville women returned to their chambers that evening, Penn and Lovetta tittered by the hearth in the east wing, tipsy on expensive wine. When the duke returned, he was in the company of Theo, just as Lovetta had predicted at supper.

"Lovetta, darling. Off to bed with you. It's late." He dismissed the two, and they left the common area before making fools of themselves. As soon as they shut themselves in their chambers, Lovetta dropped to the floor and put her ear to the crack beneath the door.

"What are you—"

"Shhh!" Lovetta hissed, pressing her ear closer to the gap. "Okay, it's clear. They're in the study." She had fire in her eyes when she stood. "Father has been acting strange for weeks, and I think it has to do with what Theo said to him as we arrived."

"The job offer?" Penn asked, recalling the short conversation outside the castle.

"Precisely!"

"Or it could be the king's health," Penn suggested. "He looks terrible."

"Either way, we need to find out what's going on, and the only way to do that is to eavesdrop. He'd never tell us if we ask."

Penn sighed. "This sounds exactly like the kind of thing your father and Osenna want me to stop you from doing."

"Honestly, Penn. If my father and Osenna told you to jump off the Rocque Bridge, would you?"

Penn pictured the lashing waves beneath the bridge and shuddered. "Of course not, but that's different. You heard Osenna—"

"Are you so worried about her withholding a reference? Have you another household in mind you'd like to serve?" Lovetta was frowning now.

"No! I'm not going anywhere, I just—"

"Well, that settles it. You're not going anywhere unless it's by my side. I'm going out there, and it would make me very happy if you joined me, but I won't force you."

Penn gave in. "Let's get it over with, then."

Lovetta smiled wickedly. "Brilliant! Whatever you do, keep quiet. If I take your hand and squeeze, get back to this room as quickly as possible."

"As you wish, Mistress," Penn joked, bowing her head low.

Lovetta giggled, then winked. "That's a title I could get behind. Are you ready?"

Penn nodded, warmth spreading within as she committed their exchange to her memory. Only then did she realise how much had changed over the past weeks. Penn had gone from being a servant, hoping to be noticed and desperate to impress, to a friend that Lovetta now included in her most dastardly of plans.

The thrill of adventure coursed in Penn's veins as Lovetta opened the door. They slipped into the hallway and tiptoed until they reached the only illuminated doorframe. Voices hummed inside.

Penn dropped to the floor and put her ear to the gap just as Lovetta had, and the conversation was quiet but clear.

"It's just a little convenient, don't you think?" came Theo's hushed voice.

"I don't disagree, but his own son? I have a hard time believing he would go to such measures."

"But you see it, don't you? The motive is there."

"Julien has no reason to think he won't take his father's place on the throne. We've all made sure of that, have we not?"

"If you're suggesting that my lips have somehow been loosened by the little prick, you seriously underestimate my interest in this cause."

"I'm not suggesting that at all, Theo. You have proven yourself to me more than once. But your concerns revolve around Julien having knowledge he couldn't possibly have. There are only five people who are aware of the plan, and I trust them all completely."

"I don't doubt your judgement, Wymark, but of this, I am certain. Somehow, he knows that someone is meddling with the line of succession, and he's not about to wait around for the throne to be snatched out from beneath him. Why else would he be in such a hurry to finish him off?"

"Segarus' health has never been spectacular. We all thought he would drink himself into an early grave. Why are you so determined to believe there isn't a natural cause to his deterioration?"

"Because I have spent an awful lot of time around the young prince, a damn sight more than you have, Wymark, and he is not the golden child his father makes him out to be. I've seen that boy do things that would turn even the strongest stomach. I do not trust him, and I do not want him alone with the king for even a moment. If that constitutes treason, then so be it."

The duke took a long, drawn-out breath, and silence fell. Penn and Lovetta glanced at each other. Lovetta looked as sobered by shock as Penn felt.

"What do you expect me to do with this information, Theo?"

"Move faster. I can't guarantee that I can keep the king alive for much longer. I've done everything in my power to find the source of his illness. It's not the food, the water, the wine. I won't stop looking, but I fear it may be too late, that we have already lost him."

"You're not doing a fantastic job of convincing me the cause isn't natural."

"I've found blood on his handkerchief three times this week. It's poison. I've seen this before. Soon his hair will be falling out, and he'll be bedbound. You must hurry."

"It cannot be rushed. If I move any faster, we risk being discovered, and if my case is not unassailable, we risk rejection. You know what that would mean for all of us."

"Five less heads at court is my best guess." Lovetta's hand flew to Penn's and grasped it. Penn flinched, ready to flee, but Lovetta held her hand firm to the floor.

"Precisely," the duke said. "Catastrophe. This is delicate work, my friend. You must try to keep Segarus alive until I'm finished. Under no circumstances can Julien succeed."

"On that we are in agreement. Gods, this would be so much simpler if you weren't so damned far away all the time."

"If, as you say, Julien does have suspicions, they will only increase if I leave Rocque. And you know what it would do to my daughters, my staff—"

"Half of them are old enough to be married with sons. There are plenty of eligible lords in Tirel, and if they don't want to marry, Princess Anais will gladly take on a few more ladies in waiting. Lady Ysabell has already been formally offered a position. Just say the word and I'll pull some strings."

"I won't play a part in orchestrating their futures. You know my promise to Sefare."

"There are ways to keep them safe, we've got—"

"No, Theo. If they know of the plan, they will want to be involved, and if they're kept in the dark, they will unknowingly endanger themselves. They are safest in Rocque."

"I know, I know. I just hoped that with the change of circumstances, you might be willing to reconsider."

"I'm sorry. If Ysabell chooses to stay I will support her decision, but I will not condemn the rest of my family to these walls. I don't want to hear of this again."

"I ... you won't, your Grace."

"You've just spent the last ten minutes professing my incompetence. Calling me 'your Grace' seems rather ill-fitting."

Theo guffawed, and the tension behind the door seemed to ease.

"Your Grace. Gods, I would have pitched myself off the highest tower if I'd been the firstborn son," said the duke.

"You keep telling yourself you're not a prince then." Theo chuckled. "Alistair was never this difficult."

"That's because Alistair has no personality. Rejecting that title was the smartest decision I ever made."

"*Oh, he's humble, debonair. A sharp mind, truly one of a kind,*" Theo began to sing.

"Not that song, please."

"*Honourable, warm and honey sweet, he cannot be beat.*"

"Theo! Save your dulcet tones for a good woman, won't you?" the duke pleaded. "What happened with whatshername, anyway? She was one of Roheisa's lot, wasn't she?"

Theo sighed. "I'm afraid my heartfelt gestures have proven insufficient yet again. I think she had a problem with the beard, and I'm sorry, but the beard comes first."

The duke groaned, and finally, Lovetta squeezed Penn's hand. The two crept back to Lovetta's room, where they could breathe freely again. Penn looked to Lovetta, who sat wordlessly on the edge of her four-poster bed. Her face had paled, and her eyes were wide.

"He's..." she began, looking up to Penn with confusion. "He's a traitor?"

Penn dropped to her knees and held Lovetta's trembling hands.

"My father is a traitor."

# Nine

The news of the duke's ambiguous plan stayed between Penn and Lovetta. "The more people who know, the more danger he's in," Lovetta had said the night before. "Until we know what he's planning, we must not tell a soul."

Penn had spent at least an hour trying to convince Lovetta that they couldn't be certain her father was a traitor. "He said himself that five people were in on his plan; King Segarus may have been one of them."

The next morning, Lovetta took every opportunity to steal Penn away to hypothesise on what her father was up to. They came up with several extravagant scenarios that seemed entirely possible until they remembered they were talking about Duke Wymark, Lovetta's adoring father: the man who had abolished slavery. Whatever he was up to *had* to be for the good of the realm. After all, he had called the young prince's succession a catastrophe. The pivotal question was this: who did the duke want on the throne instead?

Over breakfast, they were convinced it was Prince Alistair. The middle brother seemed the most logical person. He was next in line after Prince Julien, and he was known to be a sensible, no-nonsense kind of man. But this theory evaporated when Lovetta reminded Penn that her uncle had no children to succeed him, and he was far more interested in hunting boar than negotiating with emissaries.

Around midday, they considered the possibility of Duke Wymark seizing the throne for himself, but Lovetta couldn't keep a straight face as the words left her mouth. The idea was so uncharacteristic of the duke that it was laughable.

As they readied themselves for the ball, Lovetta concluded it had to be some distant cousin whose connection to the king was so obscure that Penn hadn't even heard his name. The man had three sons, and seven or so grandsons, but was arguably worse for the job than Prince Julien, not to mention bordering on senile. Weighing their options, Alistair still seemed the most likely candidate. They continued whispering fervently as they made their way to the festivities.

The ballroom was sleek, marble floored and lavishly decorated with cascading flowers of white and blue to announce the arrival of a son. A set of double doors sat open at the base of the ballroom, leading into the royal gardens that wound around several crowded pavilions. It was beautiful, but Penn couldn't help but feel out of place amongst the finery. She wore her newly-repaired yellow gown and her short-cropped hair loose, which drew more attention than she had anticipated. No one said anything though, not to her face, anyway.

"Unless he's found a way to bypass him and go straight to Malvern." Penn was only half-listening to Lovetta as they ventured through the garden. "It seems absurd, I know. But who else is there?"

"Hazir," Penn said, so stunned that she stopped dead in her tracks.

"Don't be ridiculous. Nobody with his bloodline could ever have a claim to the throne. The Azorian throne, maybe—"

"No, look!" Penn pointed to the centre of the pavilion where a cluster of giggling women surrounded three young, handsome, brown-skinned men.

"Hazir!" Lovetta exclaimed, wide-eyed. She looked at Penn with wild confusion. "I thought ... I ... he didn't leave?" she stammered, sounding utterly bewildered.

"Go on, then. Talk to him!" Penn said, nudging Lovetta toward the noisy group. Penn watched her go, something inside her twisting incongruently to her encouragement. She hated to admit it, but Hazir looked dazzling in wine red, his hair held back by a velvet cap studded with gold beads. Suddenly, Penn didn't feel like celebrating anymore, so she left the pavilion and walked through the winding gardens. The castle grounds looked magnificent, illuminated by the moon and multi-coloured lanterns. Positively romantic. Penn walked alongside the water until the sounds of the party faded, taking a seat on an empty bench half-hidden by a drooping willow. Light flickered and danced in the reflection of the water, and she pictured Lovetta and Hazir tucked into the darkness, locked in an embrace. Why did the idea of that hurt so much? Her eyes welled up, and one by one, tears trailed down her cheeks and dotted her gown.

"You had to wake up from the dream eventually."

Penn jumped as Clare materialised from the shadows.

"What dream?" Penn hastily wiped the tears from her cheeks.

Clare came closer. "The one where you and Lovetta rode off into the sunset on your well-mannered mares."

"I wish you would speak plainly."

"I saw Lord Hazir on the pavilion. I bet Lovetta's happy to see him."

"Of course she is," Penn said, tired of Clare's sour tone. "Why have you been avoiding me? I don't understand what I've done to upset you. And I see Marion's back in your good graces?"

"Don't pretend you don't know what the problem is. Just when you thought things with Lovetta were going according to plan,

Hazir shows up, and everything changes. Now she'll have to make a choice, and what chance does a maid have against a man like that?"

"What in the name of the gods are you talking about?" Penn was convinced Clare had lost her mind entirely. In what world did a lady have to choose between keeping her maid and marrying a noble lord? Even if Lovetta moved to Azor, Penn would follow her there. Penn would follow her anywhere.

"Don't play the fool. I saw you the other morning, curled up in bed together. You know, at first I thought I was making it all up when I suspected there was something between you, but Marion helped me see."

"Marion? *Marion* put you up to this? I'm not even surprised. She's been trying to push me away since we left Rocque."

Clare raised her eyebrows. "For good reason, it seems."

"Why, Clare? What have I done to upset you both so much?"

"You fell in love with Lovetta."

Penn's stomach lurched. "You're wrong. That's ... ridiculous. Impossible." She laughed. "Women don't fall in love with other women."

"I'm right. I can recognise an unrequited love when I see one." Clare's fingers tightened around her forearms. "I've experienced it myself."

"Have you now?" Penn suddenly very much wanted for this conversation to be over. "Who's the lucky man? The duke?" Clare had always looked at him with such affection. "Aim high, don't you? He's twice your age, you know."

"I don't love the duke," Clare said, her expression changing to one of frustration. "Gods, you couldn't be more wrong. I have watched you from the moment you arrived."

Penn stiffened, afraid of where this conversation might go.

"I have been here through it all, helping you, coaching you, consoling you. I welcomed you with open arms, but you never noticed me. Not in the way that I wanted you to. She has her hooks in you so deep."

"I'm not a fish."

"To her, you are. You're not her equal; you're her prey."

"Oh, please don't start on that ridiculous rumour—"

"Do you truly not see it? You idolise her; you pine after her. You even sleep next to her! Whenever you see her with Hazir you're miserable. It's not normal, Penn. Not for a lady's maid."

Penn couldn't speak. All she had wanted since she met Lovetta was to prove that she could be useful, and she had done that by becoming her friend. Penn had bent over backwards for Lovetta because she wanted to be a good maid, but it wasn't until she dropped her guard that Lovetta truly noticed her.

"She and I are friends. Maybe it isn't typical of a lady to befriend her maid, but I don't care. If I'm too abnormal for you—"

"That's not what I'm saying." Clare's voice softened. "Tell me this. Your friendship with Lovetta. Does it feel at all like ours does?"

"No, it doesn't," Penn said, struggling to meet Clare's eye. "But what you're suggesting..." Fear swirled in her stomach, and she couldn't find the words to defend herself.

"Is the truth, and it's okay! I don't think it's wrong like everyone else does. I just wish it hadn't been her. She's royalty, Penn. You don't have a chance. She'll play with you, she'll kiss you, but eventually, she'll grow tired of you. That's what they do to people like us. You should be with someone who understands you, like—"

"Stop it," Penn whispered. Clare's words were beginning to sting.

"You have no idea what you're talking about. What we are—"

"She's in love with Hazir. She's going to marry Hazir."

Penn squeezed her fists shut. "I said stop."

"She'll only hurt you. You'll never be her equal."

"*Stop it!*" Penn screamed, launching herself from the bench. "Don't act like you know anything about Lovetta and I! You've been ignoring me for days, and now you think you have the right to an opinion on what we are to each other? Lovetta has never treated me the way you are now. She's kind and warm and wonderful. If women could love other women in that way, then I would be proud to love her."

Clare looked away. "Marion was right."

"Then forget me and go back to Marion!" Tears of fury clouded her vision. Determined not to let Clare see her cry, she turned her back and walked away as fast as she could. It seemed Clare was no friend of hers.

As the path stretched and climbed, Penn's sobs found company. Hushed voices became steadily louder until Penn forced herself to stop. She knew those voices. Peering through the foliage, she saw Edony and Sahin standing feet apart, glaring at each other with contempt.

"If you aren't planning on proposing, then I'm done. I've wasted too much time on you already," Edony seethed. She didn't look hurt, she looked angry.

"How can you call it a waste? You break my heart, my darling," Sahin cooed.

"Ugh! What heart? The one you've divvied up between me and Corrin and Gerdy and ... whoever the hell that new one is!"

"They mean nothing to me, my sweetheart. I promise you're the only one for me." He sauntered forward and placed a hand on her cheek. "But marriage—"

"Let me guess. It just isn't for you? How nice it would be to have the luxury of choice. And how can I believe anything you say when you're full of empty promises?" She pushed his hand away. "I've given you a hundred chances, but you never change. I said if you lied to me again, it would be the end of us, and *I meant it*."

He laughed haughtily. "Edony, you're overreacting. Surely you don't mean to stop seeing me. You love me," he added, sounding nothing but obnoxious.

"You're right. I love tall boys with money and a good family name. But you know what else I love? My reputation, compassion, integrity and honesty. Traits that are unfathomable to you." She inhaled sharply. "Goodbye, Sahin." Edony turned away from the Saraq and let the air escape from her chest in a long, pained exhale. "From now on, my sisters will be riding without me." She left him alone in the garden, scratching the back of his head.

Only after she was out of earshot did he call into the wind, "Bitch."

Penn could hardly believe what she had just witnessed. She knew Sahin had been popular with many ladies, but she truly believed he was in love with Edony, something it seemed that Edony had foolishly believed, too. She fought the urge to chase after Edony and comfort her, knowing that she wasn't the kind to sulk on someone's shoulder, and Penn would likely have to explain her own puffy eyes. She let it be and retired to the Bondeville's chambers, comforted by the warmth of the hearth and the crackling flames, the only thing breaking the silence. Habitually, she wondered what Lovetta was doing, and her chest panged. Could she even look at her the same way after Clare's accusation, and why had her words hurt so damned much? They couldn't be true. Penn didn't even know how to love a man, let alone a woman. It just wasn't the way of things, and Penn couldn't afford to be any more abnormal than she already was.

A door clicked shut somewhere behind Penn. As far as she knew, the chambers were empty. The duke was at the ball, yet footsteps thudded in the hallway from the direction of his study. Her heartbeat quickened. Was somebody snooping around in the duke's possessions? No, of course not. It was only the chamberlain, Theo, looking as suave as ever.

"Lady Prestcote, was it?" he asked. His fingers jittered, and he smiled a little too broadly, like he was nervous.

"You can call me Penn."

He clasped his hands. "Lady Penn, then. I'm here dropping something off. Not one for merrymaking?"

Penn attempted to smile. "I have a headache," she lied, hoping the amber light masked the redness of her eyes. "Better to retire early and sleep it off than risk making it worse."

"Smart woman," Theo chimed. "You know, Duke Wymark is lucky to have you."

"Why do you say that?" It seemed an odd comment from someone she had only just met.

"Your father is a great man, and the apple rarely falls far from the tree. Not to mention how pleasing it must be to have such a pretty face bringing light into that castle."

"Sorry, but do you know my father?" Penn asked, a little uncomfortable with Theo's line of conversation.

"I do. We studied together, here in Tirel," he confirmed, running his spidery fingers through his well-oiled mane.

"At the university?" Her father didn't speak much about his time at university, and Penn never made a point to ask. Truthfully, she found philosophy a bore.

"Mmm, Duke Wymark too," Theo said, casually planting himself in the armchair across from her. "We were a force to be reckoned with."

"Is that where you all met?" she asked. Now she was interested.

"Not quite. Durant and Wymark were ordained in the same year, I believe. They spent some years on the road together doing the king's work, you know how it is. Then there was the accident." He paused, no doubt reminiscing about her father's leg. "And so, they decided to study the arts at the university, where I met them both." He smiled fondly. "I was much younger than they were, of course."

"So ... the three of you were good friends?" Penn remembered the day she met Duke Wymark and her distinctive feeling she recognised him. Had she been right all along?

"Three men of similar ambitions who spent a great deal of time together, so yes, I suppose we were." He shrugged.

"Similar ambitions?" Penn enquired, finding it hard to believe her sullen father had much in common with the duke or the chamberlain.

"Goodness, you are curious! Ambitions the same as many a good scholar." He chuckled. "The desire to change the world, ultimately. We certainly weren't alone in wanting that. There were five of us working together in the end."

Five. Had the duke not let slip the night before that five people were in on his plan? Penn's heart skipped a beat. Was *her father* involved in the duke's scheme? Surely not. He was about as passionate as a wet sock.

"Yes, I was very keen to learn from them all, especially your father. We called him the code master!"

Penn laughed. "He taught me a little about codes, too. When we were small, my brothers and I would write all kinds of silly messages to each other."

"How lovely," the chamberlain said. "He was certainly better at decoding things than he was at philosophy. I do believe Wymark was the only one of us who had a real love for it. Dreadful stuff, I'm telling you. But when that little Faintree girl came along, well, she gave him a run for his coin."

Penn wasn't sure she had heard him correctly. "Sorry, who?" He couldn't have said what she thought he had.

"Lady Betryse Faintree, bright girl around my age, I think. Although for the first few months, we all thought her name was Henry, and, well, that she was a boy." There was no mistaking her ears this time. "She was brilliant; everyone loved her. She went on to marry... oh, of course!"

"My father," Penn finished. Lady Betryse Faintree was her mother, but Penn had no idea that she went to university, let alone masqueraded as a boy to do so. Her ears burned with intrigue. "I can hardly believe it. I know almost nothing about her," she admitted.

"Oh. Well, grief takes us all in different ways. It must have been too painful to talk about. I'm sorry. She was your mother, so I shouldn't—"

Penn shrugged. "No, it's fine. I was so young when it happened. I wish I remembered more about her," she added, a little embarrassed.

"I see," he hummed. "Well, if you like, I could tell you about her. I knew her for quite a few years." He smiled.

"Could you?" A pang of homesickness hit her hard in the gut.

"Certainly. It's the least I can do for Durant. You're here for a few more days, are you not?"

"Well, yes, but can't you tell me tonight?"

"I'm afraid I'm needed back at the ball, Lady Penn. But I'm sure Wymark won't mind if I borrow you for an hour or so tomorrow." He winked. "Chaperoned, of course."

"Oh, that would be wonderful, but I don't want to be a bother. Are you sure?"

"Absolutely, it'll be a treat. Those days were some of the best of my life! Now, leave everything to me. I'll organise it all." He pulled himself out of the armchair and straightened his sleeves. "But for now, I must be off."

Penn stood up just as the door creaked open. Lovetta. A wave of heat washed over Penn. She had returned from the festivities far earlier than Penn expected her too, and Penn shamefully hoped it was because Hazir had rescinded his proposal.

"Theo?" Lovetta said, eyeing the two quizzically.

Penn had trouble meeting her eye, her conversation with Clare fresh in her mind.

"Father has been looking for you," Lovetta said.

"Then I'll find him at once." He walked to the door before turning back to Penn. "I'll fetch you tomorrow. Ten o'clock?" He smiled.

Penn gave the chamberlain an eager smile and thanked him. He disappeared behind the door looking chuffed. Penn turned to Lovetta, who looked at her with utter bewilderment.

"What was all that about?"

"You'll never believe this. He knows my parents, even my mother! He said he could tell me about her."

Lovetta started to smile. "That's wonderful."

"Theo says she studied at the university, Lovetta! Isn't that brilliant?"

"Goodness, really? How? Women can't—"

"She pretended to be a boy. Oh, I can't wait to hear more!" Her mother, a scholar. A *boy* scholar. The little she did remember was starting to make sense. Nights by the fire, her parents reading hefty volumes, discussing issues well beyond her understanding. The freedom she'd always been granted, and the wise words whispered in her ear as her mother parted her hair. Her mother, invaluable in their group of five, working to change the world. But something didn't add up. Her mother died eleven years ago when Prince Julien would have been a young child. Duke Wymark's plan couldn't possibly have been in place for that long. No, the number must be a coincidence. A little disappointed, Penn tailed Lovetta to their chambers and helped her pull the pins from her hair. "How was your night?" she asked hesitantly.

"Oh, not so bad. Bit of a disaster for the rest of them, though. Especially Edony."

"What happened?" Penn kept a straight face as she packed the pins away. For the first time, she paused before helping Lovetta undress. Her fingertips were hotter than ever, buzzing before even grazing Lovetta's skin. No, their friendship was nothing like the one she had with Clare. She was never alight with nervous energy in her presence. She never savoured the scent on the nape of Clare's neck, or let her hands rest a little too long on her shoulders. She didn't picture Clare as she went to bed at night, replaying every tiny moment of intimacy they had shared. Yet, Penn couldn't bring herself to believe Clare's words.

"Edony and Sahin had this huge row. I wasn't there, but apparently it was the worst they've ever had." She sighed. "Anyway, Edony ended it for good this time. At least I hope so."

"You didn't like Sahin, did you?" Penn finished unlacing Lovetta's gown and retreated with shaking hands.

Lovetta snorted. "He's certainly not to my taste." No, Lovetta preferred quiet, intellectual types, like Hazir. Clare's voice echoed in the back of her head, so Penn distracted herself with Lovetta's jewellery box, straightening her brooches and earrings.

"And there was drama with Ysabell," Lovetta added, flopping down on her bed. "Apparently she's not coming home, and she wasn't planning on telling anyone about it until the day we left."

"She accepted the princess's offer?" Penn said, surprised. Ysabell had made it seem like moving to Tirel was the last thing she wanted.

"I'm as stunned as you are. I can't believe she wasn't going to say anything. She's the least sisterly sister in the realm."

"If she didn't tell you, how did you find out?"

"Well, that's the third dilemma!" Lovetta said dramatically. Penn stopped fussing with Lovetta's things and sat on her own bed, a smaller and much less elegant version of Lovetta's, across the room in a corner. At least it wasn't a pallet. "I was walking through the gardens when I found Clare sitting by the water, bawling her eyes out."

Penn's stomach dropped. Had Clare told Lovetta about their fight?

"I asked her what was wrong, and she said she'd had an argument. That she had lost enough friends already, or something. It was kind of hard to hear her, you know, with all the crying. I tried to ask her what was going on, thinking that you might have approached her and had an argument, but then she said Marion was leaving."

A wave of relief rushed over Penn. She had mentioned Marion, not Penn. Then, she put two and two together. "Marion is Ysabell's maid."

"Exactly. She said she'd be staying with Ysabell. I was so shocked! I don't think she realised Ysabell hadn't told anyone. Poor thing cried even harder."

"I had no idea. Even with Ysabell staying, I thought Marion would come home."

"It seems they're all quite eager to have Ysabell. I suppose Marion was offered work so that Ysabell would be more comfortable staying."

"But why Ysabell? If they had asked Edony—"

"I know, she would have gone in a heartbeat. I've heard Princess Anais is a little ... a little behind. She has trouble with reading and the like, and she's rather impressionable. There have been rumours of wild parties her ladies have thrown at her expense. They don't sound like very kind people. I think they chose Ysabell because she's so different. She's well-read, responsible, and has a flawless reputation. She's the perfect influence. As much as I love Edony, I can't say the same for her. Why are you so far away?" Lovetta cocked her head in Penn's direction.

"Sorry," Penn said, walking over to join Lovetta on her bed. "It's been a strange night. I'm not feeling myself."

Lovetta sat upright. "Theo didn't do anything untoward, did he? I'll kill him myself if he did."

"Gods, no. But what you said before about Clare, that you thought I might have approached her. Well, I did. Marion wasn't the only reason she was upset."

"Oh. I suppose there's no sense in asking if it went well, then. I'm sorry. Do you want to talk about it?"

"I wish I could." Without Clare, Lovetta was Penn's only confidant. More than anything, she wanted to pry open her heart before her, spill out every word Clare said to her and laugh. But such simple joys felt out of reach now. What would Lovetta think of Clare's accusation? Would she keep her distance from Penn and shy away from her touch? It wasn't worth the risk. Things were just fine as they were. All she needed was to erase that evening from her memory, and they could go on as if nothing had happened.

"Do you need me to rough anyone up for you?"

Penn laughed. "No, but thank you for the offer."

Lovetta tucked Penn's hair behind her ear, and, this time, she didn't flinch. "You know, I'd do just about anything for you. If you change your mind, just say the word," Lovetta said sweetly.

Clare was right about one thing. They were so very far from normal.

"You are too good to me." Penn's body grew warmer by the moment, and the air seemed to escape the room. How she wanted to stay right there, to reach out and cup Lovetta's face in her hands and breathe in her precious scent. It was akin to hunger, but a kind that could never be satiated. It only grew stronger. Then, it came to her with a force that stole the breath from her lungs. The rumour.

*She has an appetite for women.*

In a moment, every tiny piece of Lovetta that she had shared with Penn fell into place, and as Clare's words knitted them neatly together, she finally felt at ease.

"Oh! I almost forgot to tell you of tonight's final scandal. Hazir is staying." Lovetta raised her eyebrows with a mischievous smile on her face.

How was it possible to be at peace in one instant and in the next in total turmoil?

"He plans to move back to Azor eventually, but not as soon as he hoped. His father wants to train him to be a healer," Lovetta said, winding her hair around a finger. "He's not terribly impressed by it, but he won't say no. I think it's fantastic!"

Penn knew she should be happy for Lovetta, but how could she be? Her entire world had turned upside down in one short evening. If Lovetta cared for women in the way that Ariad accused her of, why was she so glad to have Hazir stay?

"Are you ... going to marry him?" Penn stammered, the muscles in her heart knitting tighter than ever.

Lovetta's smile immediately evaporated and her body went rigid. "I wish people would stop asking me that. I don't have an answer. Not for him, not for Edony, not even for you. I'm sorry."

"Don't be." Penn's voice cracked. "It's nobody's business but your own." Penn slid off the bed.

"Penn, wait!" Lovetta caught her by the hand. "I didn't mean ... he could be my only chance to go back."

To return to Azor. Of course. Love wasn't even part of the equation.

*She called her a queer.*

Penn couldn't forget the revulsion in Jehane's eyes as the term came from her mouth. Was that what it meant to love a woman?

To be called awful names and to only ever be looked at sideways? That was no way to live.

"The only thing that matters to me is your happiness." Penn gently unlinked their hands and, feeling the threat of tears, turned away to compose herself. "Were you able to meet the little lord?" She needed a distraction.

"Oh, yes. He's a terrible conversationalist, though," Lovetta said with a smile that didn't quite meet her eyes. "You won't believe the name he's been given. Wystopher!"

Penn snorted. "That's atrocious." She walked over to her bed, yawning. "I need to get some sleep." She doused the candles and readied herself for bed.

As she climbed in, Lovetta spoke. "I'm really glad you'll be able to learn about your mother."

"So am I. But … it's odd thinking there's someone out there who knows my mother better than I did. Someone I'd never met, nor even heard of. I'm excited." It was the truth, even if she didn't feel it in that moment.

They said goodnight, and Penn welcomed the comfort of her down-filled pillow. In her mind, she recited a song her mother used to sing when she had trouble sleeping. It was the only way to keep Clare's words from toying with her, the words that made more sense each time she remembered them.

*You fell in love with Lovetta.*

Again, she recited the song. She needed to think of anything but those words because with them did not come the joy that true love promised, only pain.

Again, again, again.

# Ten

The sky was a perfectly undisturbed blue the following morning. After breakfast, they were to practice archery with the Saraqs and Princess Roheisa's daughters. Once they had eaten their fill, Penn and Lovetta returned to their chambers and changed into sensible tunics, then made their way to the field. They were quiet. Something fell between them now, like a shadow made tangible, and Penn was certain Lovetta felt it too.

Archery made for a good distraction. Penn had only used a longbow once before, and it had been strung so tight that she couldn't shoot a single arrow. Discouraged by her performance, she had never tried again. The Bondevilles, on the other hand, had practiced archery since they were very young. Competency in the skill was expected of Azorian noblewomen, with many Vastalians also partaking. With a sword, Penn could defend herself. With a bow, she'd probably kill herself.

The Saraqs sauntered onto the field accompanied by two young women in pristine gowns. Something like disappointment flickered on Sahin's face as his neck craned, likely in search of the absent Edony. It would take some time for her to face the philanderer again. Naturally, Clare had stayed with her lady, and Ysabell was so busy with her induction that she and Marion had not shown either.

Penn stood to the side as the newcomers greeted the Bondevilles. They were Princess Roheisa's daughters, Lady Beatris, who was tall, sleek, and articulate, and Lady Isadora, who was younger and fairer. They were all enthralled to see each other, and after a tumultuous hello, Hazir sidled over and extracted Lovetta from the crowd. So, Penn chose the company of Jehane over Tibby and Thamasin. They had always gotten along well.

"Always looks like he's plotting something, doesn't he?" Jehane murmured, tipping her head to Hazir who looked as serious as ever.

"He is. He's plotting to steal her away," Penn said, looking longingly at Lovetta.

The archers ambled about collecting longbows and quivers, and Zekeriya was the first to shoot. After one round, Sahin took over, but his aim was off, undoubtedly distracted. Penn stayed in Jehane's shadow and watched Lovetta and Hazir. They were having a heated conversation by the brambles; Lovetta's arms were crossed, and Hazir towered over her with a scowl.

*She's in love with Hazir. She's going to marry Hazir.*

The exchange was uncomfortable to watch. Penn couldn't bring herself to believe that Lovetta loved him. It hurt too much. If she married Hazir, it was for Azor. Nothing more.

Penn looked away and walked over to a bench in prime view of the archers. With any luck, her presence would go unnoticed, and she wouldn't have to let loose a single arrow in front of the well-rehearsed royals. Despite the gnawing discomfort that Lovetta and Hazir coupled together gave her, Penn found peace in the arrows soaring rhythmically through the air, like whistling birds.

Thus far, Jehane was the strongest archer of the group, followed closely by Zekeriya, Belsante and Beatris. Neither Tibby nor Thamasin had an aptitude for archery, and Sahin's brow remained furrowed, as if consumed by his thoughts. When Lovetta joined the archers with a vicious scowl on her face, she let loose three arrows that landed dead centre in each target, the sheer force of her final shot knocking the panel to the dirt. A great whoop came from her sisters at the same time as an outcry of frustration came from the others. Lovetta's party were in the lead, but Hazir had yet to shoot.

The young Azorian did not look in the mood for archery, and instead of heading for the collection of longbows and quivers, he took the empty seat beside Penn. They had never been so close to each other. The proper response would be to stand up and greet him with a curtsey, but Hazir didn't seem to notice she was even there. So, Penn gazed steadily ahead and watched proudly as Jehane and Lovetta took turns at the targets. The ruffling of Lovetta's tunic, and the rhythm of her hands on the bow, sent Penn into a trance. She could sit there all day, the sunshine relaxing her right to sleep.

"Beautiful morning, isn't it?"

Penn jumped. It was Theo, looking prim as ever in his usual black and gold. "I'm early, I know. Duke Wymark has generously granted you leave until noon. Shall we have a go of it?" He extended his arm. Penn took it cautiously and waved to Lovetta, who did not look impressed. They set off toward the castle, and Penn's excitement built with each step. Over a decade had passed since her mother's death. She had made peace with the fact that she would never know her like a daughter ought to, but that was all about to change.

Theo led Penn through the gardens at a leisurely pace, stopping here and there to show her exotic plants and extravagant marble statues. He talked and talked, and Penn nodded along politely, but truthfully, she didn't give a damn about where they grew the hibiscus in winter. She just wanted to hear about her mother. Although it was refreshing to be in the company of someone new, she found she grew bored of Theo rather quickly. She never grew bored of Lovetta. She liked all the Bondeville family, despite the drama that had ensued of late. For a moment, she wondered what it would be like to leave. To run home to Theroulde or to find someplace new. But even if she trained as a steward and travelled every realm, could she be truly happy knowing how it felt to be by Lovetta's side? Would she ever meet another that made her hunger in a way she never had before? Was this what it meant to be in love?

Theo stopped. They had arrived at a quaint but beautiful cottage. Yellow bell-shaped flowers were planted on either side of the arched doorway, and vines of ivy snaked around the circular structure like a scene from a fairy tale. Theo pushed the door open with a creak and ushered her inside, following closely behind. The bottom floor was cosy with a wide hearth and a row of stringed instruments, slick with oil. The most exquisite was a golden harp taller than Penn, glistening in the light of the fire.

Theo watched as Penn marvelled. "I'm quite the virtuoso, if I do say so myself. Perhaps I'll play you a tune some time. Would you like that?"

"That would be nice. I don't hear music very often in the Bondeville house." Penn had no intention of staying in Tirel long enough for Theo to follow through with his offer.

"Now that is a tragedy. If you lived here," Theo cleared his throat, "if you worked in the castle, you would be dancing every evening."

She widened her eyes in mock horror. "Oh, thank the gods I don't work in the castle. I'm a terrible dancer."

"So am I," Theo interjected.

Penn feigned a laugh before turning away.

There was a shuffling from above. The stairway to the upper landing curved along the stone wall, and light filtered down from a circular skylight imprinted with the image of stars. Descending the stairs was a woman much older than Theo, dressed in modest grey.

"This is Lady Penn Prestcote," Theo said, "and this is my housemaid, Ulga."

The housemaid curtsied to Penn with a toothy smile. "How lovely." She grinned, and Penn made her acquaintance.

Theo placed a hand on Penn's shoulder and gently steered her to the left. It was a little too familiar, but Penn dared not be rude. They entered a small courtyard filled with greenery and two caged birds in colours of the rainbow. Theo pointed to them. "Parrots. Lovebirds, actually. Beautiful, aren't they? Very rare."

Penn smiled to appease him. The birds may have been beautiful, but they didn't look happy.

"Make yourself comfortable," Theo said, pulling out a chair to a wiry table and offering it to Penn.

She sat and craned her neck for the housemaid. She couldn't have gone far; it wouldn't be proper to leave Penn alone with a man in his home.

The courtyard was darker than the front garden. Tall shrubs blocked out much of the morning sun and dampened the sound from the nearby streets. Cold seeped from the stone at her feet and made a home of her bones. She shivered as Theo took the opposite seat.

"Tea will be out shortly." He smiled. "Now, Lady Prestcote ... Penn ... I'm sure you have questions for me. It has been many years since I knew your mother, but I will do my best to help you. Every child ought to know their parents."

Penn clamped her hands together beneath the table. This was it. She finally had the chance to ask all the things she couldn't bring herself to ask her father. But where should she start? She thought back to her conversation with Theo the night before. "You said my mother went to the university as a boy. How did she do that? And why?" Penn could hardly believe that her mother had spent part of her life in disguise. Had her mother felt as she did? Trapped in a body that limited her choices and shaped the way people thought of her?

The housemaid reappeared and put down a tray laden with sliced fruit and two steaming teacups. Penn warmed her hands on the cup as Theo pondered her question.

"Well." He cleared his throat. "Betryse came from a family of boys, as you are no doubt aware. She had two brothers. If my memory serves me, one came to court to train in the arts of knighthood, and the other preferred the world of academia. His name was Henry, and he was ill for a very long time, sickly from birth with a strange illness. Nobody quite knew what it was. On his worst days, he could hardly walk. He was a year or two younger than Betryse, so she often took care of him. They were very close.

"Their father didn't think much of university, but he knew Henry couldn't manage much else, so he accepted that his son would never become a knight and paid a great sum to secure Henry a place in Tirel to study. But," Theo sighed, "when the time came, Henry was too frail to travel. He seemed to understand that he was dying and that the trip alone might kill him." Theo took a sip from his cup and looked away as he recounted the tale. "The only person who knew Henry had changed his mind about leaving was Betryse. He knew she wanted to go to university more than anything, so instead of telling his parents that he must stay, Henry switched places with his sister. Betryse loaded herself in the carriage before dawn, and Henry told their parents she was too angry at him for leaving to see him off. Henry said his goodbyes, climbed into the carriage, and a mile or so down the road, he slipped out the back unnoticed. What happened after that, I'm not entirely sure. But Henry made it home eventually, and I imagine their parents were furious." Theo chuckled.

"They couldn't leave to bring her back to the Orange Isles because there were no more horses—Henry's medicine and the sum paid to the university must have burdened them—so their only option was to wait until the riding party returned. By the time they did, Henry's health had declined markedly. They were too scared to leave him alone, so they did nothing."

"Just like that? They forgot all about bringing her home?" Her father would have clawed his way to Tirel on his hands and knees if it meant stopping Penn from doing something so reckless.

"I daresay Henry did everything he could to keep them from intervening."

"But it can't have been easy to pretend to be Henry. Surely somebody would have noticed that she wasn't a boy, I mean ... she would have, you know, *looked* like a girl," Penn said delicately, hoping that her point didn't need clarification.

"Ha! Well, she was barely fourteen at the time and had a thin frame. Not much to hide, really. The haircut and breeches were enough for a year or so, and when she..." he coughed and avoided Penn's eye, "when she became a woman, she found other means of disguising her femininity. I distinctly remember a lot of coats."

Penn sighed. "I just can't believe it." She envied her mother's brazen actions. Why hadn't she been more ambitious? Perhaps she could have found men's work if she had disguised herself and set off for someplace new. Was it too late? If Lovetta were to go with her, it would be like living a dream. Penn did her best to erase the image of taking off with Lovetta from her mind. After all, she was the king's niece, and Penn valued her life.

"So, you and the duke thought my mother was a boy when you met her. When did you discover that she wasn't Henry?"

"I was the first to find out about that minor misgiving. I'd like to say it was by accident, but I had noticed something odd about her. I never suspected *that*, but she was very secretive, very easily startled. I knew she was hiding something, and I confess that what I did was not honourable. It was a midsummer's morning when I saw her stash a letter inside her pillow. I thought it was odd, so when she took her leave, I reached in, retrieved it, and read it. I couldn't make sense of it. At first, I thought she had stolen it, but I kept reading and it all came together in the end. Henry had died, you see. Her father wanted her home for the funeral."

Theo looked at Penn searchingly, as if he were expecting the story to resurface some long-lost grief in Penn, but she had never known her uncle, so the news didn't make her feel anything other than hungry for more of the story.

"Anyway, she went home for the funeral, said it had been an uncle who died. I didn't confront her until she came back, but while she was gone, I told your father and Wymark because I trusted them. In hindsight, I shouldn't have done that. But at the time, well, I was young, and all kinds of things were going on in my head." He half-smiled.

"How did she react when she came back and found out you all knew her secret?" If Penn had been in her mother's position, she would have been mortified.

"She was scared. Thought we'd go blabbing to the world, and she'd be kicked out of the university in a heartbeat." He chuckled. "Drastically underestimated our friendship."

"So, you kept her secret?"

"Of course! We were all quite impressed with her. The audacity of it! And, as I said before, she had a real knack for philosophy. A brilliant mind through and through. We couldn't entertain the idea of continuing our studies without her, not for a moment. If it weren't for her, I'm certain we would all be very different people. Disengaged and ignorant of the many crimes of humanity. She birthed an idea that changed everything," he said, scratching his artfully-crafted beard.

"She did?" Without realising it, Penn had dug her fingernails so deep into the back of her hand that little white crescents painted her flesh.

"She did," Theo confirmed. "As you know, Duke Wymark has always held very ... unpopular views," he said, phrasing himself carefully. Penn knew exactly what he meant. "Betryse's experience was the first time we really saw it all in perspective. The complexity of human interaction and the roles that we play in this world. Wymark took it all very seriously. He now had a personal connection to the injustices of our way of life. Durant sympathised with her too, but I was so young. I'll admit it was all a little too complex for me. Things had always been the way they were, and for the most part, they still are."

Penn was starting to lose track of the conversation. "Do you mean slavery?" Duke Wymark's infamous cause was to abolish Vastal's ancient practice, and he had succeeded.

"No." Theo smiled. "That came after Betryse. Well after. What concerned Wymark first and foremost was *women*. The divide between the sexes. Where did it come from, and what purpose did it serve? Was it cohesive, or was it a hindrance to humankind's ability to move forward? He posed a great number of questions nobody could answer, or at least nobody at the university. Such discourse wasn't in their best interest; even I thought his ideas were far-fetched at the time. Despite knowing Betryse, I didn't truly see the problem. I didn't think the division *was* a problem. But eventually, I came to understand that the issue wasn't something I could overlook. I couldn't live with myself if I did. Since then, I've done what I can to support the duke and his cause."

Theo had woven a tapestry of information, and Penn had lost herself in it. Everything she knew about the duke made more and more sense. He hadn't simply decided he didn't like the way the world worked as Penn had assumed. Betryse's story had touched him so profoundly that he couldn't ignore the divide of the sexes any longer. That was why he treated his daughters so differently to other noble families and why he made a point to fill his house with working women, paying them reasonably and feeding them in the same hall as his own kin. The baths, the beds, the conversations. Every gesture he made, great or small, represented something much bigger: the need for change and his willingness to make it happen, despite the conflict it would knowingly evoke.

And her mother. Her mother had been his muse. Whether she had done so consciously or not was something Penn would likely never know, but she did know one thing for certain. She had inherited a great deal more from Betryse than her pink cheeks and fair hair. There was a reason Penn had always felt like she needed to do something bigger than herself. She remembered Lovetta's drunken speech from their first night on the road, and her fingernails dug deeper into her flesh. Lovetta said Penn had to give up on the idea of becoming a man and instead show the world she was worthwhile as a woman. She said that many things in Vastal weren't acceptable and that Azorians had a fairer view of women, that they were treated better.

Suddenly, something dawned on Penn that shook the chill from her bones. The conversation came back to her as clearly as if she were there, observing herself and Lovetta through an open window.

*Is it true that in Azor, women can take the throne?*

*Absolutely. Mention that to father, and he'll talk your ear off all night.*

Penn jumped to her feet, making Theo drop his teacup in surprise. It cracked down the middle, and its contents spilled all over the table and into his lap.

"I'm so sorry, Lord Carignan!"

"No matter, just Theo will do." He mopped the liquid up with a handkerchief. "Are you quite alight?"

"Yes! I've just remembered that I need to be somewhere. I'm so sorry, but I must go. I promised Lady Lovetta..."

Before he could respond, she took off through the cottage, out the front door, and into the maze of green. She ran in the direction of the castle, heart hammering, heels clacking and tunic ruffling in the wind. She found her way to the Bondeville's chambers without stopping for anything or anyone, despite the cramp in her side. By now, Lovetta ought to be back from archery practice and in her chambers. Indeed, she was. As soon as she reached Lovetta's doorway and saw her, all the words came to her at once.

"You were wrong. It's not your father, or Duke Alistair, or your great, great uncle or whatever!" she exclaimed, gasping for breath and clutching her side. Realising the door was wide open, she slammed it shut and continued panting. "It's Princess Roheisa! He's going to put Roheisa on the throne!"

# Eleven

Lovetta gasped. Evidently, she had not made the connection either.

"How didn't I think of that?" she exclaimed after removing her hands from her mouth. "It makes so much sense! Everything he stands for ... and she's the perfect leader."

Her reaction solidified Penn's suspicions, and for a glorious moment, she felt truly impressed with herself.

Lovetta smirked. "The prince would be furious."

"But she deserves it, doesn't she? She has a whole decade's advantage *and* an heir."

"Three potential heirs, actually. If she takes the throne, that means all her children could rule, in theory. They can't say no to Tris or Issy if their predecessor was also a woman. Oh, Penn. How am I supposed to keep this a secret?"

"You must. If the prince found out, who knows what could happen to her. You heard what Theo said to your father."

"Theo says a lot of things, and not all of them are true."

Penn hesitated, somewhat taken aback. Theo had just spent his morning regaling Penn with tales of her mother, and they *had* to be true. She needed them to be true.

Lovetta paced before the hearth and lowered her voice. "I think we need to do some of our own investigating."

"Gods, how would we even do that? We can't just drop in on the prince for tea."

Lovetta pondered, arms crossed and fingers drumming the flesh of her upper arms. "The prince has organised a meeting tonight. I heard Theo and father talking about it. I haven't a clue what it's about, but I'm quite certain that nobody is supposed to know about it. Or at least not father."

"That's promising, but we don't even know where it is. And how would we listen without being caught? This is the *prince* we're talking about. He'd have men standing guard, surely."

"We'll have to follow Theo," Lovetta said.

"But if your father isn't invited, surely Theo isn't either. Everyone in the castle seems to know they've been friends forever."

"Oh, I don't think Theo will be invited. He'll be up to the same thing as us."

"Spying, you mean?" Penn clarified. The grin on Lovetta's face was all the answer she needed.

"All we have to do is follow him and not get caught. It'll be easy enough. He'll be too preoccupied with his own intentions."

"That's sort of brilliant. Spying on the spy," Penn exclaimed. It was bold, and it already plagued Penn with guilt, but it made sense.

"Be quiet," Lovetta hissed, and Penn went beet red. "You're lucky we haven't left yet. If you blow our cover out there, we'll be skinned alive."

Penn swallowed hard. "You don't really think … if they found us, they wouldn't really hurt us, would they? We're only…" She wanted to say they were children, but this was no courtyard game, and they were both old enough to be held accountable for their actions. If they were caught invading the prince's privacy, there was no telling what might happen.

"If they did find us, we'd be painted as the prince's peeping fans, not threats," Lovetta said, sounding annoyed.

"Good point. So, we spy on the spy, avoid getting caught, and get to bed with all our limbs accounted for. A quiet night." They both laughed nervously. "When do we leave?"

"The meeting is at midnight when the streets are empty. I say we leave well beforehand. If we miss Theo, we don't have a chance of finding the meeting on our own."

Penn felt as giddy as a child playing a game of hide-and-seek. "Should we split up or stay together? One of us could watch his cottage, and the other could watch the castle."

"Gods, I hadn't considered that," admitted Lovetta. "I know where he works from, but I don't know where his cottage is."

Penn grinned. "I do. I was there today."

Finally, Penn had become useful, and not in an ordinary way. This wasn't like braiding Lovetta's hair or soaking a stain from her linens. This was bigger than anything she could have imagined, and it felt good.

Lovetta flinched. "You went to his cottage?" There was a tone of accusation in her voice.

"Yes, but we only talked about my mother. He collected me this morning, remember?"

"Oh, I remember," Lovetta grumbled. She clearly didn't like Theo.

"I'm happy to wait there. You can take the castle, since you know where he works."

"No." Lovetta shook her head. "I don't like it. We're safer together. We'll go to the cottage. It's more likely he'll leave from there, anyway."

Penn agreed and the two put their heads together to organise the finer details of their evening endeavour. An hour or so after supper, they clambered out of Lovetta's window and slipped into the gardens like shadows.

Penn led the way to Theo's cottage, keeping to the shrubs and poorly lit pathways. By the time they found the circular building, their evening gowns were laden with pulls and their shoes in need of retirement.

"There's light inside. He must be home," Lovetta whispered, crouching low behind a shrub so fragrant that Penn had to hold back a sneeze.

Penn joined Lovetta, crouching beside her. "It could be the housemaid."

"Oh, you've met his maid?" Penn was close enough to feel Lovetta's breath on her face. "It wasn't just the two of you?"

"Of course not. Did you think I'd knowingly sully my reputation by visiting a gentleman's house unchaperoned?" Did Lovetta really believe she'd do that?

"You know I don't think much of ladies who manage their maid's affairs," Lovetta said awkwardly.

Hearing herself referred to as a maid by Lovetta's own mouth was sobering, and it took Penn a moment to gather her words. "For what it's worth, he was perfectly honourable."

"I'm glad," Lovetta whispered. "His beard is ridiculous."

Penn muffled a snort. "Glad I'm not the only one who thinks so."

Eventually, when Penn's calves were well and truly aching, the cottage door swung open. Theo moved swiftly and silently through the garden, isolating himself to the shadows. Penn signalled for Lovetta to follow, and the two began slowly tracking him. Every now and then a cold-crisped leaf would snap beneath their feet, and he'd look over his shoulder, but Penn and Lovetta stayed well out of sight.

The further they walked, the deeper Theo sunk into the darkness and the swifter his steps became. All the while, Penn's pulse pounded in her ears and sweat slicked her palms. Eventually, Theo stopped somewhere along the western inner wall. A single thatched cottage sat on the far side of a deep sewer too wide to jump. Yards away, a narrow stone walkway, guarded by two men-at-arms, bridged the water.

Lovetta's expression was glum in the filtered light. "It's impossible."

"Then where is Theo? There must be a way across."

They slipped and squinted through the thickets until a flash of movement caught Penn's eye. "I see something." She nodded toward the sewer. A lone silhouette stood knee-deep in the water. It was Theo.

"How did he get there?" Lovetta whispered.

Penn studied their options. "Jumping would make too much noise, and the bridge is a death wish." Penn already knew the answer, but she didn't like it, and Lovetta would certainly hate it. Penn crept through the garden, her eyes scanning the ground beneath her feet.

"Where are you—"

"Found it." Penn beckoned Lovetta toward her. "He's entered from here. Look." She pointed to the ground, where a large metal disc engraved with a stag's head sat between rose bushes. "This is perfect."

"I hope you're joking. I'd rather die than wade through *that*."

Penn had to stop herself from laughing. "You're always talking about how you want to change the world, but you're scared of a sewer?"

"Yes, and rightfully so. They carry sickness of the most wretched kind, and that's exactly what you'll get if you go down there. I thought you of all people would understand."

Lovetta's words stung. She was referring to Penn's mother, who had died from the very same sickness that had killed the maid before her. "I'm sorry. Why don't you wait here and I go? If need be, I'll burn my clothes." Truthfully, she didn't want to do it either. Would anyone volunteer to wade through excrement?

"No, we're staying together," Lovetta said firmly. "And I'm going to be completely honest with you. I have no idea what I'm doing, and you seem to be a natural at this kind of thing. I need you."

Penn had never been needed by anyone before, and those words coming from Lovetta could have made her burst with happiness. So, she looked for another way. Scaling the wall would be an impossible feat in their evening attire, and there was every chance they could slip from a foothold. Neither had the upper body strength to monkey-climb underneath the bridge, and the sewer was out of the question. No matter which way she looked at it, the wall, looming eerily overhead, had to be the answer.

"Not the wall," Penn whispered, an involuntary smile stretching her face. "All we need is a tree." She looked up to the branches of a great oak. They stretched partway over the water, but not far enough to make a safe drop to the other side. "A bigger tree."

Lovetta recoiled. "I don't like where you're going with this."

"Honestly, where is your sense of adventure?" Penn said playfully. "This entire thing was your idea, so unless you have a better plan, follow me and keep quiet."

For a moment, neither said a word. Lovetta looked her up and down, and Penn took a step back and bit her tongue.

"Yes, Mistress," Lovetta said with humour in her eyes.

Penn could hardly breathe. "I shouldn't have said that."

"Don't apologise, I liked it. You should put me in my place more often."

Feeling hot from Lovetta's submission, Penn followed the curve of the sewer with a wobble in her step. She was far more to Lovetta than a maid.

It didn't take long to find it. A thick branch draped precariously over the muck, low enough to reach from the trunk, and just long enough to bridge the gap. With the men-at-arms and Theo out of sight, Penn put her hand on the great oak.

"Wait a moment." Lovetta held Penn back. She untied two long ribbons from her braid and gathered Penn's gown in her hands. "If you catch it on something, you might fall." She proceeded to secure the excess fabric behind Penn's back.

"Good idea," Penn said, enjoying the gentle tugging of Lovetta's hands. Was this how Lovetta felt when Penn fussed with her gowns of an evening?

Lovetta pulled tight. "You know what would have a been a better idea? Breeches."

Penn took the second ribbon and tied Lovetta's gown in the same fashion. "We're supposed to be inconspicuous. Also, I don't have any breeches."

They advanced on the tree. "As soon as we're home, I'm taking you to my tailor," Lovetta said.

"As much as I would enjoy that, I don't think Osenna would be impressed." Osenna might have turned a blind eye to Jehane, a fellow Azorian, but to Penn? Certainly not. She was already out of Osenna's good graces.

"Oh, how many times—"

"This isn't important right now. We need to get across the sewer." Penn cut Lovetta off and appraised the trunk. They would only have to climb a foot or so before they could scale the overhanging branch.

Lovetta took a step back. "You first," she said.

Having spent the latter half of her childhood in the company of trees, Penn didn't need any encouragement to climb the oak. She scaled the base of the trunk, swung herself onto the branch, and shuffled across with nimble hands. Lovetta, on the other hand, shook as she clambered across the branch. When Penn dropped to the ground on the other side of the bank, she had to coax Lovetta down and into her arms. A moment of bliss overcame Penn before she set Lovetta down. Had Lovetta felt it too?

Across at last, they tiptoed to the cottage and concealed themselves in the greenery beneath an amber-lit window. The voices inside were faint but easy enough to decipher. The two exchanged a triumphant glance. From what Penn could tell, there were at least three or four men inside. Most of their conversation was a bore. Trade deals, old slavers and a ring of thieves in the city. It wasn't until a fifth voice chimed in that their attention was caught. The voice was louder than the others with an edge of authority. Lovetta pointed to the window and mouthed 'that's the prince.'

"You'd be a fool to trust them," Prince Julien said. "Any of them. Sympathisers. If Wymark knew what was good for him, he'd take his lot back to where they belong. He must have been out of his mind to marry that woman. Her blood has no place in Vastal. Tainted, the lot of them."

Penn could hardly believe her ears. Had the prince actually just accused the Bondeville daughters of having tainted blood? If only she could cover Lovetta's ears.

"Couldn't have said it better myself, your Highness. A stain on our history if you ask me," added one of the unidentified voices.

"He'll answer for his crimes, I assure you. It won't be long now," the prince said.

"His crimes, your Highness?" came another voice that shook with age.

"The marriage! And those abominations he calls his children. Such things were crimes once; they will be made crimes again, as they should be." Silence fell in the cottage. "Weak, all of you," scoffed the prince. "No stomach for it, but it has to be done."

"Your Highness, I assure you that we are all in full support of your cause. Whatever you need can and will be arranged," the older voice trembled.

"Yes, whatever I need. Whatever I need," the prince reaffirmed, "or you will have no place in the new Vastal. None of you."

"We live to serve the Crown, your Highness. We will swear allegiance once more if it pleases you."

"That won't be necessary. I have no doubt you will continue to play your parts well. In fact, I wish to thank you. Your work so far has been ... formidable." The prince paused. "But there is still much to be done. Grimshaw's report confirms it. We need more recruits. Bahsayis still outnumbers us two to one."

"It is true, your Highness. However, our soldiers are expertly trained. Perhaps we could succeed with a smaller force."

"Perhaps is unacceptable! Bahsayis is notorious for his ability to command an army, and with his term ending, he'll be certain to put on a show. He will not hold back. We need *more*. Expand the schools, lower the age if you have to."

"But, your Highness, we have boys as young as ten fighting already. Lowering the age, well, they're just boys, your Highness."

"They'd as likely stab themselves as they would an opponent," another voice added.

"I don't care what you do, just get me more soldiers!" the prince shouted with such force that Penn quivered. She looked at Lovetta and saw a great sadness in her eyes. It was clear what the prince had planned was far more sinister than they had anticipated. Bile rose in the back of Penn's throat.

"We will not fail you, your Highness," submitted one the prince's minions.

"No, you will not. Now, what news is there of Yasai?"

"No news, your Highness. The emperor continues to evade us."

"Disappointing."

"We have some doubts about the agent in question, your Highness. If you could permit us to send another—"

"We cannot spare the men. If we have no news in a fortnight, any prior agreements with Emperor Umeji will be considered null and void."

The elder interrupted. "But, your Highness, without Bahsayis and without the trade, Vastal will suffer greatly. We need the emperor—"

"You think I cannot rule Vastal on my own?" spat the prince.

"It's not solely a matter of ruling, your Highness. The treasury will run dry, and our people will starve."

"I have no patience for old fallacies!" the prince shouted. A rustling from behind broke Penn's concentration, and before she could turn around, a hand clasped firmly over her mouth.

"Do not scream; you are safe," a voice whispered. Penn looked sideways to Lovetta with a hammering heart. A white, gangling hand held Lovetta too, and she could feel their captor's breath on the back of her neck. Penn looked closely at the fingers over Lovetta's mouth. She had seen them before. "I am going to let go, and you will make no sound. You will follow me in silence until I permit you to speak. Do you understand?" The two nodded in their captor's grip and one-by-one were released to breathe.

Relief washed over Penn as she turned and looked into Theo's eyes, but he was far from happy to see her. Saying nothing, he looked at the two with unbridled anger and led them away from the cottage. As they approached the water's edge, the prince's raised voice faded to nothing. Theo dropped soundlessly into a man-sized hole, then proceeded to wade knee-deep through the filthy water. Lovetta looked to Penn and shook her head violently. She took hold of the branch they had used to cross and clambered to the other side of the sewer, shaking all the while. Penn followed, and they met Theo at the other side. She opened her mouth.

Theo shook his head. "No. We're not safe." So, they traipsed through the gardens in silent shame until they reached his cottage.

Theo swung the door open and ushered the two inside, looking over his shoulder repeatedly before following them in. Only after the door was shut and locked did he breathe.

"What in the name of every god this side of the sea were you two *thinking?*" He towered over Penn and Lovetta with a snarl, completely unrecognisable. "Stupid and reckless—no regard for your own lives—total idiocy! Your father would be furious!"

"Please, Theo, don't tell father, he'll—"

"Send you to the convent? Perhaps that would be a wise decision, your Grace!"

"You can't mean that," Lovetta pleaded. Penn was lost for words.

"What were you even doing there? You followed me, didn't you? I knew I sensed something."

"We know about father's plan. We just wanted to help!"

"Help? You're barely eighteen, and you," he pointed to Penn, "are as reckless as your mother."

Penn couldn't help but smile.

Theo shook his head. "Oh, no, I'm not finished. She was reckless, but stupid? No, that's all you."

Penn's smile faded. She had just started to like Theo.

"Don't you dare speak to Penn that way!" Lovetta hissed.

Penn looked at her sympathetically. "It's fine."

"No, it isn't!" Lovetta rounded on Theo. "Penn was a genius tonight! If it wasn't for her, we probably would have been caught. I thought it was impossible to get across the sewer, but she ... she's brilliant. And the tree! I would have fallen without her help."

Penn loved hearing Lovetta's words, but she had a feeling that her argument would be her undoing.

"So, it was the maid who was responsible for all of this?" Theo exhaled.

"No, that's not ... what I meant was that she's the smart one. She kept us safe. Spying on the meeting was my idea."

"But you admit it was Penn who got you across the water?"

There was a brief pause. "No, I—"

"Yes, it was me. You don't have to lie for me, Lovetta."

"Good," Theo said. "Better a rogue maid than a rogue royal. Out of the love in my heart for your mother, I will implore the duke to be lenient with you, but, Lady Penn, what you've done is grounds for immediate dismissal."

"You can't be serious," Lovetta said, tears building in the corners of her eyes.

"She has grievously endangered your life, your Grace. No, you are not without blame, but your father need not know that this was your idea. The fact of the matter is that if it weren't for your maid, you would have turned around and taken yourself right back to your chambers."

"That's not true," Lovetta protested. "I'll tell father exactly what happened. He'll never believe you over his own daughter."

Penn was speechless, dreading the thought of facing the duke. It was her job to serve and protect Lovetta, not indulge or endanger her. Theo's fury was completely justified, as would be the duke's and Osenna's if she ever saw her again.

"I have known your father longer than you have been alive. I am his most trusted advisor, and I have never lied to him, not once. You, on the other hand, are a child who is meddling in affairs far beyond your comprehension. If you had been caught ... you have no idea what the prince is capable of!"

"But after tonight I do know what he's capable of. Waging war on my people, slaughtering *my* people. The prince called us abominations!" Lovetta shouted with fire.

"Mind your words, girl!"

"You dare call the king's niece *girl?*" Penn interjected in Lovetta's defence.

"Oh, I don't want to hear another word from you," he snapped. "I will hear no more from either of you. Whatever you heard you will forget. You will mention it to no one, not even each other. I will deliver you to your father tonight and tell him the truth of it. You will come *quietly*. If you do not, I will make it my personal interest to ensure you never have the pleasure of each other's company again."

Lovetta dissolved to tears, and Penn scrambled for a handkerchief, consoling her as best she could without a voice. Penn's heart broke. She would take any punishment if it meant she didn't have to see Lovetta cry ever again.

"Out," Theo demanded, holding the door open.

"I know what you're trying to do," Lovetta choked, fury in her eyes.

"You don't know anything," Theo hissed. "Now go."

When they reached the Bondeville's chambers, Duke Wymark was perched on an armchair by the fire, drumming his fingers on his knees. Belsante and Edony were talking at his side, and tension hung like a storm cloud overhead. As Lovetta crossed the threshold, the duke leapt from his chair and the tension dissolved. He held her forehead in his hands and planted a firm kiss. "Thank the gods! Your window was open. I was beginning to think the worst," he said, stroking the back of Lovetta's head.

"You almost had the worst," Theo said from behind them. "They were sneaking around in the dark. Followed me to the meeting we discussed earlier. The maid had her performing above water acrobats and nearly had her killed."

"That's a lie! I was never in any danger. Penn only did what I asked of her, and gods! I *climbed a tree.*"

Penn was touched that Lovetta cared enough to defend her, but truthfully, she didn't think she deserved it. Theo's version of events may have been exaggerated, but there was some truth to them. If Penn were a maid of any credit, she would have found a way to dissuade Lovetta from her plan.

"What is the meaning of this, Theo? You allowed them to follow you?" He sounded incredulous.

"I certainly did not. Your daughter seems to think she's good enough to spy for you, an idea put into her head by that reckless maid, no doubt!"

"You are such an ass," Lovetta seethed.

Penn became acutely aware of several open doorways in the hall. The rest of the Bondevilles and their maids had poked out their heads to see the commotion.

"Don't listen to him, father. Penn's the best maid I've ever had. She would never do anything to put me in danger. You can't punish her for following my command!"

Penn swallowed hard as she saw Clare staring straight at her, her eyes empty of all emotion.

"My darling, please keep your voice down," the duke said calmly. "What is important is that you're safe. Now, I must speak to Theo alone. You and I will speak in the morning. Get some sleep, the both of you."

"I'd have two men stationed outside their room if I were you," Theo said.

"I am not putting my children under guard, Theo. Give it a rest." He sighed. "Bed, now. All of you." He dismissed the two, and the many peeking eyes disappeared behind closed doors. They retreated to Lovetta's chambers, meek as mice. It was no easy task undressing Lovetta that night. She cried all the while, trembling and hiccupping her way to the bed.

"Everything is going to be fine. Your father dotes on you." She tucked a clump of tear-soaked hair behind Lovetta's ear.

"It's not me I'm worried about," she sobbed. "What if he takes you away?"

"No one is going to take me away from you, remember? They were your words," Penn reassured her. "Who would want me, anyway?" She laughed half-heartedly. A clumsy maid with no manners was a trophy to no one.

"Theo," she hiccupped.

"What? Why would Theo take me away?" Penn cringed. After their last hour, she couldn't think of anything worse.

"You heard him the other night. He's looking for a wife, and you're young, beautiful and unspoken for."

"That's ridiculous. He just informed the entire world how hopeless I am. And he was my mother's friend!" The idea was grotesque, but Penn couldn't help but smile. Lovetta had called her beautiful.

"Don't you see? That's how he plans on getting you. He knew you wouldn't say yes to a proposal, so he's discrediting you. He thinks father won't want a maid in his service with a poor reputation. Father will want to send you home, then Theo will feign chivalry and find you a position in the castle." Lovetta's breathing quickened. "Then he'll court you, and you'll marry him for lack of a better option. He's tried it before."

"Slow down." Penn put her hand atop Lovetta's to quell her shaking. As much as she didn't want to believe Lovetta, she remembered her conversation with Theo earlier and his talk of how different her world could be had she worked in the castle. Could Lovetta be right?

Lovetta looked up to Penn with swollen eyes and placed her other hand atop Penn's. "I don't want you to marry him."

"I don't want you to marry Hazir."

"What?" Lovetta said, sniffling.

"Nothing," Penn whispered. "You have nothing to worry about. Even if I have to work in the castle, I will never marry him. No matter how close he was to my mother or father. Even if tonight never happened and I still thought he was a decent person, I wouldn't. Marriage just isn't for me."

There was a moment of calm.

"Well, even so." Lovetta sniffled and tightened her grip on Penn's hand. "I don't want you to leave."

"I would never do it by choice. Not ever." There was a brilliant warmth in Lovetta's words, but fear niggled in Penn's gut. She would not be given the luxury of choice. She would be lucky to find work for a fishmonger without a good reference. But even if she did, could she ever be happy again? Nobody had made her feel as wanted as Lovetta did.

The longer they touched, the harder it became to move. It was as if their hands had been joined by needle and thread, their spirits by a force intangible. Eventually, as Lovetta's tears subsided, she let go. There was nothing that could be done. If the duke sent Penn away, she must grit her teeth, pack her things, and leave with her head held high, if only to spite Theo.

"Don't go," Lovetta whispered as Penn went to move away. "Sleep here with me tonight." Neither of them could make eye contact any longer. "It could be the last time."

Hit by a perplexing mix of dread and glee, Penn nodded. It made no sense at all to want to be so close to Lovetta, yet she did. Penn stripped down to her underclothes and climbed into Lovetta's bed. Inches apart, they faced each other without moving, without breathing, doing nothing but staring into each other's eyes, a most peculiar pastime for a lady and her maid.

"This is nice." Penn sighed. The warmth of Lovetta's bed swallowed her whole. Lovetta's gaze was water in a drought, urging her to do something, anything, to bring them closer together. Penn closed her eyes hoping to break the spell, but it didn't work. She could hear Lovetta's breath and she could smell her hair. Even without sight, her body pulsed with desire for Lovetta.

"You can't sleep yet," Lovetta whispered, stroking Penn's arm.

"I'm not sleeping." Penn swallowed, growing hotter by the second. "I'm restraining myself." Her heart pounded like a drum. Was this what it felt like to have an appetite for women? If it was, it couldn't possibly be wrong.

"What if I don't want you to?" Lovetta whispered. "Please open your eyes."

Penn obliged, the urge to pull Lovetta closer becoming unbearable. Lovetta had given her permission, and yet Penn laid frozen in her place. What was stopping her? It was Marion whispering in Clare's ear. It was Osenna standing over Penn in her sitting room, criticising lady's maids for forgetting themselves. It was Penn's father, who deserved a daughter who didn't raise eyebrows everywhere she went. Somehow, she knew that if she acted on her urge, she would be forever changed. Clare and Marion would gloat, Osenna would cast her out without a reference, and her father would never look her in the eye again. Shame would follow Penn everywhere she went.

She watched Lovetta. The rise and fall of her chest, the flick of her tongue as she wet her lips, and how the shadows danced and darkened the freckles on her collarbone; Penn had never noticed them before. Osenna was wrong. Penn could not forget herself before this woman. If anything, she was more aware of herself and her standing than ever, and it infuriated her.

"What are you thinking about?" Lovetta whispered. Her hand reached out and found Penn's.

"What I'm always thinking about," Penn said, tentatively lacing their fingers together. "You."

Saying it out loud soothed her, and she was reminded of something Lovetta said only days prior. Penn had to stop believing she would never amount to anything. Yes, she was a maid, but above that, she was a person. She was a sister, a daughter and a friend. The opinions of others should not define her, nor should her duties in the Bondeville castle. If she were to keep living her life in the hope of making her father proud, she would never find happiness.

Penn opened her mouth to speak but was swiftly silenced by Lovetta's lips. In a blink, the distance between the two dissolved, and Lovetta's body was upon her.

It was bliss. Heart hammering, finger numbing, lip quivering bliss. It was the confirmation Penn didn't know she needed, and it made sense of her entire world. Penn lost herself in Lovetta, drunk on her scent and the softness of her lips. No matter how hard she tried, she couldn't hold Lovetta close enough. Sunlight poured through her veins like something molten, and lightning sparked in every place Lovetta touched.

They lay intertwined for what felt like hours, and yet it was still not long enough. When they finally extracted themselves from each other, it was agony.

# Twelve

Penn woke early the next morning wrapped in Lovetta's arms. Orange light filtered through the window and settled on the bed, bathing Lovetta in the kind of glow reserved for gods. Penn wriggled out of Lovetta's grip, careful not to disturb her sleep. She dressed quickly and left the castle before the others woke, grateful to find the aviary empty of all but feathered friends.

From the prince's heinous conversation with his henchmen to Lovetta's reaction to the thought of Penn leaving, she didn't know what to make of the previous night. It all felt so surreal, as if the evening had occurred at double the speed. A completely new side of Theo had emerged, and it saddened her. Now she would learn no more of her mother through his memory. But what did Theo matter? What did any of it matter after her night with Lovetta? Just the thought of their kiss made Penn dizzy, and when she replayed it in her head, touched her lips and smelt the lavender on her hands, she could hardly breathe.

*She'll play with you, she'll kiss you, but eventually, she'll grow tired of you. That's what they do to people like us.*

Clare's words stung. Could the kiss have been a bizarre reaction to the stresses of the night and not a reflection of Lovetta's true feelings towards Penn? It was an awful thought, but it made sense. If Lovetta was a princess, Penn was a toad.

Despite Penn's worries, it was as if the sparrows sang only for her that morning. The sky was clear and blue, and the morning breeze held an early winter's chill. The birds flittered through the trees with flashes of blue and grey. They made her think of home. No, they made her think of Theroulde. Rocque was her home. She missed Theroulde's hilltop air, sunlight warmed cracked earth, and the sound of the stables in the early morning. But more than that, she missed Rocque's endless greenery, winding roads, and, most of all, Lovetta's chambers. The nights spent in each other's company by the fire, Penn polishing jewellery as Lovetta read sprawled out on the rug, both of them perfectly content without a care in the world.

Now that her future was uncertain, Penn knew exactly what she wanted. Although the prospect of becoming a lady's maid had once repulsed her, Lovetta had changed everything. They were not and never had been master and servant. They were friends, and after the night they had just shared, they were something far more special. Penn could conjure a thousand questions about the night, but none of them would matter. Whatever the night had meant to Lovetta, it meant worlds to Penn. It had peeled away her shell, made her vulnerable, and breathed new life into her. The feeling was terrifying, yet she welcomed it. She would welcome just about anything if it meant she could kiss Lovetta again.

In just a few days, the Bondevilles would begin their ride east, back to Duke Wymark's castle and the normalcy of their humdrum life. The image of herself by Tirel's inner gate waving a final good-bye to Lovetta was an unwelcome one, so Penn gave it no mind. The duke was known for his kindness for a reason. She couldn't believe he would truly send her away.

The chirping softened with the rising sun. Soon the duke would call for her and her punishment would be affirmed. Heart heavy, Penn came to her feet and made her way back to the Bondeville's chambers. To her delight, Lovetta was awake and sitting by the fire with Edony, talking softly over cups of tea, serene in sapphire silk. Penn flushed and stood in the doorway; her heels stuck to the parquetry until Lovetta looked her way.

Lovetta cleared her throat. "Penn, where have you been?" She gave nothing away, no hint of excitement, no shadow of remorse.

"I took a walk to the aviary," Penn said politely. "It's such a beautiful morning." She took a few steps in Lovetta's direction and hovered by an empty armchair, waiting for an invitation to sit. Lovetta nodded while Edony stared fiercely into the fire, saying nothing.

"I told her about last night," Lovetta whispered.

Penn flinched. Just how much of last night?

Lovetta's eyes widened as if she had read Penn's thoughts. "About the prince. Bel should know too, but not the others. They're too young. I don't want to frighten them."

Penn nodded stiffly. It was difficult to focus on Lovetta's words, on anything that came from those lips. Penn turned her attention to the red and blue blaze that flickered and licked its stone surrounds.

"Sorry you got caught," Edony mumbled. "It's my fault. When I saw the window open, I panicked."

"Forget about it." Lovetta shook her head. "I should be thanking you. If anything, you telling father that we were missing worked in our favour. He was just glad to see us alive."

Edony snorted. "You can thank me when he's had his say this morning."

They sat there in silence until the duke called their names from the hall. Then, sharing an uneasy glance, they made their way to his study, Edony remaining transfixed by the hearth.

"Come in, girls," he called. He was seated behind a desk as grandiose as its surrounds, all slick red wood and finely carved. He snapped a book shut with a puff of dust and crossed his arms. Penn and Lovetta loitered by the door, afraid of meeting his eye.

"Father, before you say anything, you need to understand that everything Theo said is a lie."

"Oh?" the duke said, sounding almost amused. "So, you didn't sneak out after dark and spy on a meeting that you ought not be privy to?"

"Okay, most of it was a lie," Lovetta said. "We did do that, but we were only following Theo. He wasn't meant to be there either."

"Theo was there on my orders. You had no place being there in any capacity. Either of you." He nodded to Penn, standing a foot behind Lovetta, her human shield.

"He'd been acting strangely," Lovetta said. "He'd invited Penn into his cottage unchaperoned just hours earlier. We only wanted to be certain he wasn't up to something unseemly."

Penn bit her lip and wished Lovetta had briefed her on their story beforehand.

"Admirable of you, but from what I hear, Lady Penn is more than capable of making decisions for herself. Skulking around in the night is hardly a way to protect her reputation." He scratched his head. "And above that, anything could have happened to you, and I would have been none the wiser."

"Places like this aren't safe for a lady of my colouring," Lovetta recited. "I know, father. After last night, I know more than I ever could have imagined. The prince called our blood tainted, and the way he talked of my mother—"

"Please, my darling. All I've ever wanted is to protect you from such vitriol. He is a disgrace to the Bondeville name." The duke softened his voice. "But that's not why I've asked you here."

"You're sending her away, aren't you?" Lovetta almost squeaked.

"Please let me finish. I'm concerned for you, Lovetta. Yet again, you have been reckless and senseless. When Lady Penn came to us, I hoped she would bring stability to your life as her father did to mine. That she could calm you and keep you from making such rash decisions. Yet, you seem as determined as ever to put yourself in harm's way. I'd send you to the convent at once if I wasn't certain they'd send you right back."

Penn had heard Lovetta threatened with the convent before. She was far more interested in what the duke had said of her father. He could calm the tide if he talked to it long enough. He'd calm it right to sleep. The duke, however, rarely gave his emotions reign. Perhaps he hadn't always been this way.

"I'm sorry for the way I acted and for bringing Penn into this," Lovetta conceded. "I just wanted to be useful for once, but I thought with my heart instead of my head. There is just so much injustice in our world, father! How can I stand idly by?"

The duke looked at her with admiration, and Penn had to hold back a laugh. How similar they were without knowing it.

"I'm truly grateful for everything you've afforded me, really, I am, but can I not help you rather than sit around twirling my hair? I'm certain that I was made for more than you think me capable of."

"My darling, darling girl. I'm sure you could command an army if I gave you the reigns, but that isn't the life we built for you."

"But you let mother help. She used to attend your meetings," Lovetta said.

"And it paid a great toll on her happiness. She did not want her children to know the things she knew, to feel how she felt. She wanted you to have a simple life full of love and laughter. Lovetta, you are too young to have such weight on your shoulders."

Lovetta opened her mouth as if to speak, then closed it again. She looked to the window, brow in a tight line. "She really wanted that for us?" she murmured. The duke nodded, and the last of Lovetta's fight left her. "I'll do better." There was a quiet catharsis for a moment, time enough to see the guilt on Lovetta's face manifest, and the duke to turn to Penn. She met his eye for the first time that morning.

"I'd like to speak with you privately, if you would be so kind," he said.

Penn was just beginning to think that the ordeal was over, her part in the scheme a blip on the duke's horizon. Relief would not come just yet. She nodded and stepped forward.

"Be kind, father. She's important to me." Lovetta excused herself from the room, glancing at Penn only briefly as if to wish her luck.

"Please, come closer. Take a seat." He waved her forward. Penn did so, wondering if she would ever sit in front of this man again.

"Contrary to what I've just told my daughter, when I agreed to take you on, I wasn't sure what, or who, I would be met with. Your parents were so very different." He spoke with a smile in his voice. "Your father said you were smart but stubborn. That you had your own ideas for your future, much like your mother, and that he hoped you did not bring me any trouble."

Of course he had said that. Penn picked at her fingernails in preparation for a scolding.

"Imagine my disappointment when you turn up, and not only are you an incredibly pleasant young woman, but Lovetta is enthralled by you. No drama, no trouble. Where's the excitement in that?" He chuckled, and Penn could finally breathe. "I don't blame you for last night. Lovetta has been struggling and acting out since her mother died. If anything, her behaviour has improved since you arrived. You may not feel like it today, but you've done well."

"It's kind of you to say so, your Grace." She felt the tension in her shoulders easing bit by bit.

The duke looked at her curiously, studying her. "But more importantly, are you happy?"

"Of course," she answered without a thought. "I like Rocque, and I like being Lady Lovetta's maid. At first, I thought I couldn't do it, but every day is a little easier than the one before. I don't want to leave."

The duke smiled paternally and crossed his arms. "I'm very glad to hear that. Your father would be proud."

"Do you think so? My needlework hasn't improved much."

"I don't think your father is overly concerned with your needlework. I think he would be glad to see you excel at something and find happiness in the small things. I also think..." he paused, studying her again, "that you and Lovetta have something in common, and that is why you shine in each other's company. It's also why your emotions may get the better of you, as Lovetta's do to her."

"I'm not sure I understand, your Grace."

"I believe, and forgive me for being so bold, that what unites the two of you is the loss of your mothers." Penn stiffened as his gaze intensified. "Yes, I see it. You lost your mother very young, and so did Lovetta. Robbed of the most complete and irrevocable love. Forgive me." He drew back. "I only mention this because I see it so clearly in my daughter. In all my daughters, to some degree, but particularly in Lovetta. She shared a connection with my wife that was very different to her sisters. I noticed it when Sefare was alive, but more so when she passed. The other girls, well, they miss their mother dearly, but not like Lovetta. Her grief was inconsolable. She withdrew for a very long time, struggled to engage with others, even Edony. I thought she might never be cheerful again. She threw herself into her classes and became a finer archer than Sefare ever was ... blistered fingers and shadows beneath her eyes. She barely slept. And other days, she couldn't leave her bed! Then she'd have these fanciful ideas and get herself into strife. It was exhausting for everyone. *Don't* tell her I told you this, please." As if her ear wasn't pressed to the door. "Anyhow, since you arrived, she has been happier. She still has her ups and downs, but not like before. Somehow, you've rekindled her fire, Lady Penn." He exhaled. "And that's precisely why I won't be sending you away."

Penn wanted to smile, but she couldn't. Not after all she had heard. "Thank you, your Grace."

"Cheer up. I won't be mentioning this to your father."

"What about Mistress Osenna?"

"Gods, no. That's one headache I could do without."

"You are too kind, your Grace," Penn said, her gratitude toward the duke catching in her throat.

He waved. "Nonsense, I simply detest gossip. You know, I owe your father a lot, Lady Penn. That's why I agreed to take you in when he wrote to me."

Penn's breath hitched. That wasn't right. It was her father who had granted the duke a favour, wasn't it?

"Nothing against you personally, of course. But as you must know by now, I try to bring in girls whose futures are a little more ambiguous. Girls who aren't looked after quite so thoroughly."

"You took me in because my father asked you to?"

The duke nodded. "As simple as that. I would do anything for Durant, and I daresay I would have regretted turning you down." He smiled, blissfully unaware he had just unravelled her father's lie.

The duke never wrote to her father seeking aid; her father wrote to him in a plea to rid himself of a troublesome daughter. Penn's fingernails dug deep into her palms. She barely heard the duke dismiss her or ask for Lovetta to return. Had she curtsied or just walked out? All she knew was that she needed to leave the castle as quickly as she could because if she didn't, she would scream until her throat burned.

Breaking into a run, she made for the wall. If she ran fast enough, she couldn't feel the tears. She whipped through the garden maze and narrow streets until the inner gate came into sight. Everything stung, but she welcomed it. Anything was better than the feeling that her father didn't want her anymore. She couldn't breathe.

On the other side of the wall, two guards manned the exit that would take her to the outer circle of Tirel. The castle and all its grandeur made her sick. Penn stopped at the gate and watched the desperation of the townspeople who begged for food, silver, medicine or mercy. The guards retaliated by grunting, spitting, and kicking back those who came too close. They weren't even decent enough to feign compassion.

"Let me out," Penn demanded.

"Y'dun wanna come out 'ere, missy. Trust me," said a dopey guard as he shoved a woman and her baby back into the crowd. He had a round middle, red hair and a snout-like nose that ought to be accompanied by a curly tail.

"It's not your place to tell me what I do or don't want. Let me out," she said fiercely.

"Easy," slugged the second guard, a tall, thin and pockmarked man. "There's nothing for a lass like you out there. Go on home now, or you might snag your dress."

Dopey laughed. "Yeah. Poplolly like you won' last long out 'ere with this scum."

Penn walked forward and put her face close to the redhead's. He smelled of sweat and old cheese. "The only scum I see here is you. Let me out, or Duke Wymark Bondeville will hear of this."

"Duke Wymark Bondeville!" he exclaimed. "I'm real scared now, missy!"

They guffawed, and for a moment, the taller of the two loosened his grip on the hilt of his sword. Without thinking, Penn shot her arm through the bars and seized the weapon, pulling it through the gate with ease.

"Oi!" he shouted. "That's mine! She swiped me cutter!" He flailed around, and the crowd of peasants quietened. "Give that back!"

"I'll give it back if you let me out *and* give me your word that you'll start taking their pleas seriously," she demanded. Holding a real sword was exhilarating, even if it she had no intention of fighting with it. Did Florent and Gillot feel this powerful? She swivelled the hilt in her grip, testing its weight and balance. It was heavier than a sparring sword and cool to the touch.

"Crikey, imagine wanting out of the castle that bad! Yeah, all right," he conceded, sounding bemused.

"All right what?" Penn teased. She was enjoying her moment of power.

"All right, I give you my word I'll listen to the rats!" Penn smiled. "You lot, stay back while we open up, or you'll regret it!" he bellowed.

They fell back, and the gate swung open just enough for Penn to pass through. When she was safely on the other side, she held the sword out in front of her. The guard swiped at the hilt, but Penn was quick. Instead of handing it over, she flung the sword into the bushes and dived into the crowd. A roar sounded from behind her as she ran.

"It's worth at least ten aur! Sell it and divide the coin!" she shouted to the cheering crowd. When she was out of sight, she looked back and laughed. A few townspeople were scattered in the bushes, one holding up the blade triumphantly. The rest had swamped the guards. Dopey cowered on the ground, and the other clung to the gate for protection. Penn laughed until her sides ached.

# Thirteen

In a mingled state of self-satisfaction and distress, Penn dawdled along the streets. She took in everything from the scantily-thatched rooftops to the pungent odour of human waste. It was obvious that folk from the inner circle of Tirel did not frequent the outskirts because heads turned in Penn's direction on every corner, so she trudged on with her head down and her senses alert.

The Tirel marketplace was quite unlike that of Rocque and Theroulde. Her past home's stalls had been small, but the merchants were charismatic and the produce always fresh. Rocque's markets were the biggest Penn had ever seen, full of fun and fuss and freedom. The torn walls and broken-wheeled carts that stood before Penn now were no happy sight—except to the rats, of which there were too many to count.

Faces behind stalls looked out without life, many of the merchants too old, too tired or too hopeless to promote their wares. The people were so thin that knees and elbows protruded through clothes, frail enough to snap at the lightest touch. Some had swollen bellies, but Penn knew it was because they were so ill. She had seen starved bodies before, but not in numbers like this. It appeared that merchants had long given up on business from highborns and their servants. Penn fingered the coin purse she kept tucked into her gown and looked the marketplace over. She wasn't in need of anything, but it felt wrong to have silver stashed away when there were others who needed it to survive.

Nestled between a cart of spices and a cloth merchant, a wrinkled woman sat hunched over a mouldy table. She smelled stale, and her hair was so sparse that she looked bald from a distance. Penn walked closer and saw that her eyes were tainted by a grey cloud. Sitting centred atop her brow in black ink was the mark of blindness: an eye with no pupil. Penn approached the table, wondering what kind of wares the woman sold. Before she could ask, the woman moved.

"What have you come for?" she rasped. The table was full of odd trinkets.

"To look, ma'am," Penn answered, evaluating the worth of the old woman's goods. She noticed something familiar amongst the junk, something that was likely worth more than the entire market-place combined. "This is from the castle," Penn murmured, carefully picking up the glass swan that Lovetta had held only days earlier.

"Do you call me a thief?" the old woman said with a tone of incredulity.

"No, ma'am." She placed the swan back down. She had a good idea of how the ornament had made its way from the Bondeville's chambers to the dingy stall. "But it's very valuable," she continued in a whisper. "You shouldn't leave it on the table like that. Someone might steal it."

"I appreciate your concern, girl, but I haven't been stolen from in thirty-five years." Penn wondered how that could be possible. "Just because I'm old and blind doesn't make me weak."

Penn flushed. "I meant no offence." She looked over the other trinkets. A row down from the glass swan sat a silver brooch in the shape of a fox. It was tarnished in places but otherwise in good condition. Penn reached out to pick it up, but as her fingers grazed the silver, a voice squeaked from behind her, and she flinched.

"You can't have that one. It's mine!"

She turned and saw a scrawny girl no older than seven or eight. She had dirty blonde curls like Maybelle and an open cut on her right cheek. "I'm sorry, I didn't know this one had been sold." She smiled and moved her hand away from the brooch.

"It hasn't," the old woman said dryly.

The girl was feisty. "Toldya to put it aside, three-eye!" she yelled, stamping her bare feet. "I said I'd getcha the money, and I will."

"You haven't a shred of silver to your name, girl. And I don't take kindly to customers who resort to name-calling." The woman crossed her arms.

"Either way, I don't need the brooch. I was just looking," Penn reassured her.

On hearing Penn speak, the little girl's demeanour changed dramatically. "You're from the castle, aren't you?" she asked, wide-eyed.

"Not quite. I'm visiting the castle. I'm from a long way away."

"How long a way away?" she inquired, and Penn laughed.

"Well, I was born in Theroulde, but now I live in Rocque." The girl looked at her blankly. "A three-day ride," she simplified.

"Wow!" shrieked the girl. "Is it fancy? Are you rich? Are you a *princess?*"

Penn laughed again. "I'm just a maid. But my father is a lord, which makes me a lady." The girl's jaw dropped. "He isn't really rich, but he has a lot of land. He sent me to a fancy castle to become a maid, and the family I work for is very rich."

"Wow!" the girl said a second time. "Name's Heather. I live over there." She grinned, shook Penn's hand, and pointed to a collection of large rocks that were piled haphazardly on top of each other, creating a tiny cave. The sight of it made Penn's heart ache. "Made it myself. Ma reckoned I coulda' been a builder if I was a boy." She puffed out her chest with pride.

"And where is your ma?" asked Penn.

"She's long gone," Heather said in a very detached manner. "Don't look all sad about it. She's better off up there," she added, pointing to the sky. "She was real sick."

"I'm sorry to hear that." Penn wondered if anyone had a living mother anymore. "Do you have anyone else?"

"Whatcha mean?"

"To look after you. Or are you alone?"

Heather shrugged. "S'been just me for a while now."

The idea of this tiny girl on the streets in such a harsh terrain was absurd. What was she eating? How did she stay warm in winter? What would happen if *she* fell ill?

"Well, we need to clean that cut," Penn said. "If it gets infected, you'll be in a lot of trouble."

"It's nothin'. I've had worse." Heather crossed her arms.

Penn turned to the old woman. "Where can I find spirits and clean cloth?"

Before the woman could answer, Heather bounced beside her. "I know the way!" Tugging on Penn's sleeve, she led her to a cart manned by a couple too young for the grey streaks in their hair.

"That's a nasty cut you got there, mischief," the woman said with a sad smile. Her male counterpart took no notice of his company; he was thoroughly cleaning a stained vial with an old rag. No matter how hard he rubbed, the stain did not budge. Still, he persevered.

"Wasn't my fault this time." Heather shuffled closer to the merchant woman and looked up at her with doe eyes. Maybelle's eyes.

"Enough of that now, enough of that. I can't keep patching you up for free, mischief. I've got taxes to pay."

"That won't be necessary. I'm happy to pay," Penn interjected. She took notice of Penn for the first time, looking her up and down twice over.

She shrugged as she eyed Heather's cut. "Suit yourself. Won't need a stitch, just a good clean."

Penn extracted the coins from her purse and placed three silvers in the woman's pale hands. She looked pleasantly surprised by the amount.

"Come 'ere, mischief," the woman beckoned, pulling the stopper from a small glass bottle and soaking a clean wad of cotton in its contents.

"It'll sting," Penn warned Heather.

"S'all right." Heather shrugged, standing perfectly still as the merchant worked.

"There," the woman said, rubbing the area dry with a clean piece of cotton. Penn nodded at her appreciatively.

"Don't you go getting her hopes up," she said just loud enough for Penn to hear.

"Sorry?" Penn leaned in, but the merchant had already turned away. How bizarre.

"Thanks, Marge!" Heather called. "And thanks, lady!" She smiled at Penn.

"You don't have to call me lady. My name is Penn." She guided the girl away from the marketplace and toward the pile of rubble that Heather had called home. Heather dragged two wooden crates from her collection of rubbish and set them on the side of the street. She sat down, her legs barely long enough the skim the ground, and beckoned for Penn to sit with her.

"It must get cold in there in winter," Penn said, taking a seat.

"Dunno, wasn't here last winter. Ma was still alive. We lived in a three-wall 'round the corner."

"A three-wall?" Penn enquired, having not heard the term before.

"Like a house with four walls, but with one less. But we did have a roof!" Heather said proudly, as if that were an exceptional feat.

Perhaps it was for a girl who now lived on the streets. Truthfully, Penn was surprised that Heather could even count.

"What happened to your three-wall?"

Heather sighed. "Got kicked out. Tough crowd around these parts. What's your house like?" she asked, changing the subject and swinging her legs as though eager for the answer. The wave of guilt that rolled over Penn could have knocked her over. "Ma used to tell me all kindsa stories 'bout ladies like you. They were my favourite. But I never thought I'd see a lady in real life. Maybe the gods have been listenin' after all."

"You believe in the gods?" Penn smiled. Heather was sweet but naïve. What god would allow little girls to roam the streets and starve?

"'Course I do! Don't you?" Heather's brows came together in surprise.

"No," Penn admitted. "My father once told me not to believe in anything you can't see with your own eyes."

Heather giggled. "That's silly. You can't see love, but I know Ma loved me."

Penn was shocked by Heather's wisdom. "I think you can see love," Penn said. Her chest fluttered as Lovetta's face came to mind. "It's in the things people do. Like hugging, kissing ... and generosity," she said, the glass swan poking at her consciousness.

Heather shrugged. "I guess. But the gods do exist; I'm sure of it."

"Maybe they do," Penn said simply. There was no proof either way, and if faith had kept Heather going thus far, it might be more powerful than Penn thought.

Heather's legs bounced up and down again. "I still wanna know about your house. Pretty please?"

"All right." Penn sighed theatrically. If it made her happy, it was worth Penn's guilt. "The castle is *so* big. Not as big as where the king lives, though, but I like it better. The gardens are long and winding and so beautiful. We mostly grow roses. I like the white ones the best. They grow near the stables, so I always visit Primula while I'm there. She's my horse." Heather's face lit up. "Have you seen a horse up close before?" Heather shook her head violently. "Well, they're bigger than you think."

"You ride her every day?" Heather squeaked.

"No, but often. Lady Lovetta loves riding, and because I'm her maid, I accompany her wherever she goes."

"Even when she poops?"

Penn laughed. "Okay, not everywhere. She's permitted some privacy."

"What kindsa places do you go?"

"The markets, the lake, the orchard. Sometimes we go with her sisters and their maids, too, but I like it best when we go just the two of us. She's brilliant. We have a lot of fun together." Penn warmed at the thought of their early morning talks in the long grass. Lovetta had taught her so much about the world, about friendship, even about herself.

"What kinda fun?" Heather pressed.

Penn couldn't breathe back the redness in her cheeks now. "You know, talking. Finding shapes in the clouds … that kind of thing," she stammered. At that moment, Penn realised that Heather had asked her about her home, and yet, she was talking about Lovetta. Was she her home now?

The unlikely friends talked for a while longer, Penn learning much about the girl's daily life and Heather making constant expressions of awe at Penn's stories. When the sun moved high up in the sky, Penn knew she ought to find a way back into the castle. Her stomach was beginning to rumble, and Lovetta would likely be looking for her. But Penn felt awful for leaving Heather, despite only having known her for a couple of hours. *Don't go getting her hopes up*, the merchant had warned her. But a little more time couldn't hurt, surely.

"Heather, do you know where I can buy breeches?" Penn asked.

"You mean them things boys wear on their legs?"

"Precisely. I would like to buy a pair."

Heather's eyes widened. "You got a fella *too?*"

"Goodness, no. I would like a pair for myself."

Heather looked intrigued. "Ma never told me ladies wore 'em too. I know just the place!"

Penn was swept further into the marketplace, Heather's small hand clinging to hers like her life depended on it. Penn was fuelled by her anger at her father and her exasperation with this awful city and everything it stood for. She would no longer force herself to be something she wasn't, and no one could stop her. The duke wouldn't send her away over an unconventional change of dress, her own father had already cast her out, and if Osenna refused her a reference, she'd get one from Lovetta herself. Penn did not need to assuage anybody.

Finally, they came to a three-wall with a thatched roof, manned by a boy who couldn't be older than Penn was. He looked at her with a coy smile.

"An honour to make your acquaintance, m'lady." He knelt and kissed Penn's hand.

"And yours ... sir," Penn said, feeling awkward until he released her hand.

"What can I do you for?"

"Breeches," Penn blurted. "For me. Have you any that might fit?"

He raised his eyebrows. "I've got everything you need, m'lady. Come inside."

Half an hour later, Penn emerged with two new pairs of boots, one for herself and one for Heather, half a dozen pairs of socks, a blouse in the same blue as her maid's uniform, and a pair of walnut breeches. She would not return to Rocque in a tunic and hose. Her mother had given them up, so why couldn't she?

"I'm not sure I can find my way back to the castle from here. Could you take me to where we met?" Penn asked Heather, who delighted at the chance to continue playing host. When they returned to the centre of the hustle and bustle, Penn fixed her eyes on the old woman's stall, full of glittering trinkets.

"Tell you what, mischief. I bet that brooch would suit you better than all the other girls in town." It wasn't much, but it was something.

"Y'reckon?" Heather squeaked, a smile pulling at the corners of her mouth.

Penn nodded and approached the stall, seizing the silver brooch from the table without hesitation.

"Back again?" the old woman asked.

"How much for the fox?" Penn asked, withdrawing her coin purse.

"Twenty silvers," she answered stoically.

That was a *lot* for a tarnished bit of jewellery! Still, the woman needed the silver more than Penn did, so she withdrew the coins from her purse without question and placed them in the woman's outstretched hand.

"Bless you." She almost smiled. Penn turned to Heather, then remembered the glass swan. "Please, ma'am, the swan. Sell it to a glassmaker or keep it hidden. If the guards were to see—"

"There hasn't been a guard in these parts for years, sweet child. Go on home now."

Penn hesitated, then turned away from the stall to a bouncing Heather. She crouched down and showed her the brooch. "I want you to look after this," she whispered.

"I will!" Heather exclaimed. "Foxes are my *favourite*. Canya put it on for me?"

Penn fastened the brooch to her tattered tunic. It looked handsome as it glinted in the sunlight, even if it was worn in spots. Heather squealed and jumped on the spot, completely enthralled by the gift.

"I have to go now," Penn said, and Heather's joy immediately vanished.

"Wish I could go with you."

"If I could take you with me, I would." She placed a hand on Heather's bony shoulder. Heather looked at the ground in disappointment. "If you need silver, you can have mine."

"That's nice, but no thanks, lady." Heather frowned. She was Maybelle again.

"All right then. Stay out of trouble, now," Penn croaked, ruffling Heather's hair.

Heather gave her a weak smile. "Seeya, then."

"Seeya." Penn turned away from her with a heavy heart.

The outskirts of Tirel were busier now that the early hours had passed, and it quickly became a challenge for Penn to retrace her steps. After walking the same street for the third or fourth time, Penn looked around for something even remotely familiar but didn't find much. What she did find, however, made her smile. A dirty blonde-haired girl peering out from the side of a shack, watching Penn intensely.

"I can see you," she called. Heather jumped at least a foot into the air. "What are you doing out here?" she asked as Heather skipped over to her. "You're a long way from home."

Heather shuffled her feet. "Forgot to say thank you."

"You're very welcome," Penn said with a smile. Heather didn't budge, so Penn improvised. "Can you help me with one more thing?"

"Sure!" Heather squeaked, her enthusiasm returning.

"I really need to get back to the castle, but I'm hopeless with directions." Penn looked up and down the street for the umpteenth time. "Can you show me the way?"

"Oh, I know the way! Easy. Follow me!"

She bounded down the lane, and Penn followed her through a labyrinth of broken homes, continuously reminded of the poor conditions Tirel's people were forced to live in. Her father wouldn't stand for it in Theroulde, and neither would Duke Wymark in Rocque. They would starve themselves before letting their people do the same.

The conversation she'd had with the duke earlier that morning squeezed at her heart. She couldn't think about her father right now.

They continued through the squalor until, eventually, the castle came into view. The townspeople had done a thorough job of terrorising the guards; one had scampered up a tree, and the other was nowhere to be seen. Penn approached the trunk and looked up at the dopey-eyed guard. He shook violently in the branches.

"Drop the key, or I'll send them back to finish the job," Penn called. The guard didn't think twice about Penn's threat and sent a heavy brass ring clattering to the ground. Smiling sweetly, Penn turned the brass in the keyhole and swung the gate open with a creak, then locked it behind her. She slipped through the opening and turned to Heather to say goodbye for a second time, but Heather wasn't there. Penn snapped her head back and forth until she found her bobbing around in the castle gardens. How had she snuck through the gate without Penn noticing?

She looked at Penn with big, wide eyes. "I just wanna see the castle up close once in my life, lady."

Penn sighed. "I can't stop you, but if the guards catch you, there's nothing I can do," she said as she dropped the key onto the dirt.

Heather grinned. "Betcha they won't even see me!"

Penn succumbed and took a quiet route through the gardens. Heather's jaw dropped at every turn, her eyes feasting on a world that, without Penn, she might never have seen. Every few blocks, they would pass a lady or a squire, and Heather would stop to stare. As they approached the castle, a small crowd gathered by the stairs came into view. Just as Penn was about to tell Heather to turn back, Lovetta emerged from the circle and called out her name with a distraught tone.

"Where have you been?" she shouted, hands firm on her hips. Penn ran forward, hoping that Heather had fallen back into the bushes. "You can't just run off like that!" Lovetta exclaimed, drawing the attention of the rest of the Bondeville daughters and their maids, Clare and Marion included.

"I'm sorry. I went beyond the wall."

Lovetta eyed the bag slung over Penn's forearm. "And went shopping? Gods, I thought something awful happened to you. And you're filthy!"

Penn couldn't count the number of times she had wandered off in Rocque, and not once had Lovetta so much as questioned it. Why was she so upset now? What had happened to the infinite freedom Lovetta had always afforded her? Speechless, Penn came closer still, and Lovetta's expression softened. "If you're uncomfortable around me now, I'll fix it. Whatever it takes, I'll make it better. But you can't just leave me like that," she whispered. "I didn't know what to think."

The gradual warming Penn had felt the night before returned. If they hadn't an audience, she could reach out and touch Lovetta's cheek and ease her fears. She could hold her and tell her that nothing in the world felt as good as being by her side. For now, with Clare and Marion's eyes burning into her like the fire of a thousand suns, Penn had to settle for something less intimate. "I have no reason to want to leave you." Briefly, she squeezed Lovetta's hand, then let go. "I don't know why I went out there. I just needed to think. I needed to get away from all of this for a while."

Lovetta crossed her arms and looked away. "So, it is my fault."

"No, Lovetta. It's everything else. You're what brought me back," she said, praying their onlookers couldn't hear. Lovetta didn't uncross her arms. "Something the duke said about my father upset me. It's silly of me to care so much."

The tension left Lovetta. "Caring is never silly. What did he say?"

The sting hit Penn hard again. "All this time, I thought your father invited me to Rocque, but that's not true. My father wanted me gone. He asked the duke to take me away."

"That's awful," Lovetta said, glancing sideways. "Let's go inside. We don't have to talk about it here." She smiled faintly, reaching out and taking hold of Penn's forearm. There was some comfort in Lovetta's words, but Penn couldn't leave with Heather still on castle grounds. If she was caught, she would be arrested for trespassing. As Lovetta walked forward, Penn resisted.

"I think I dropped something in the gardens. Can you give me a moment?" The onlookers had lost interest in their conversation, but Lovetta looked taken aback. "Wait here," she said before hurrying to the last place she'd seen Heather.

"Heather!" she hissed, crouching down in the greenery. "Where are you?"

"Here, lady!" her small friend whispered, poking her head out from a thorny shrub.

"You need to head back now, okay? There's a big group of people outside the castle, and if they see you, there might be trouble. Do you understand?"

Heather nodded, but her eyes betrayed her. She didn't want to go back to the marketplace, and Penn couldn't blame her.

"I wish I could stay here."

Penn raised Heather's chin. "I wish that for you too, but..." If only this were Rocque, and it were the duke Penn had to plead Heather's case to. Theo was her best point of contact in Tirel, and she had no chance of swaying him after their last exchange. "Are you so sure this is what you want? To live within these walls? The realm is so much bigger than Tirel. You could go anywhere."

"Like the place you live? Could I go there?" Heather said with a hopeful expression.

"In theory, yes, but..."

"But what?" Heather pressed.

Penn made her decision. She would plead Heather's case to the duke. "I'm going to try to help you. I need to leave to talk to someone, but until I come back, you can't be seen. Can you do that?"

Heather nodded enthusiastically. "Yes, lady!"

"Keep your voice down." She bent down and kissed Heather on the head as if she were Maybelle. "I can't promise anything, but I will try. You absolutely can't be seen, got it?"

Heather stiffened, and her eyes went wide. "I think it's too late, lady," she whispered, and Penn spun around.

"A child?" Lovetta said. "You dropped a *child* in the garden?"

Penn breathed a sigh of relief. Lovetta would understand.

"She wanted to see the castle," Penn explained. "Her name is Heather. She has no family, no silver, and she lives in a pile of rocks."

Heather scowled. "They're good rocks, lady." She turned to Lovetta and studied her. "Why are you so dark?" she squeaked.

Penn gasped. "Heather! Don't be rude."

"I'm not being rude. She's different. *Why?*"

Lovetta raised her eyebrows. "Because my mother came from a much nicer place than here," she said tartly. "A place where little girls are polite, and *your* skin is what's different."

Heather didn't spend long in contemplation, replying with a single 'wow'. The tension lifted.

Lovetta touched Heather's forehead. "What happened to your face?"

"Who are you, lady?" Heather asked with a mischievous smile.

"She's Lady Lovetta Bondeville, daughter of Duke Wymark, the king's brother," Penn explained, watching Heather's eyes bulge.

"Does that mean you're a *princess?*"

Lovetta groaned, brought her hands to her face, and mumbled something incoherent.

"It sure does," Penn said, revelling in Lovetta's embarrassment.

Heather bounded up and down so violently that Penn felt dizzy. "A princess! I met a real princess!" she squealed. Eventually she stopped and attempted to curtsey but tripped over her feet instead.

"All right, that's enough. You're supposed to be keeping quiet, remember?" Penn laughed and helped Heather up.

"And absolutely don't be seen until you come back," Heather said seriously.

Lovetta shifted beside Penn. "What's going on?"

"I'm going to talk to your father and see if he'll give her work in the castle," Penn said.

Lovetta smiled and moved closer to Penn. "That's bold."

Penn shrugged. "I'm trying something new." Heather was on her toes against a tree, straining to reach a butterfly. "Do you think it's a bad idea?"

Lovetta's eyes lit up with a plan. "No, I think it's marvellous. Heather, when was the last time you had a good meal?"

Heather came bouncing back, then shrugged. "Depends what you call good."

Penn and Lovetta shared a knowing glance.

"All right, you're coming with us," Lovetta said, taking Heather by the hand.

"Really? Right now?"

"Princess' orders," Penn said.

The look of awe on Heather's face was priceless. Penn took Heather's other hand and they walked from the gardens as a single unit. The Bondeville clan had dispersed, and the guards hadn't the right to question Duke Wymark's daughter. Without conflict, the trio made for the servant's quarters, where Heather could eat and bathe out of sight of the other royals. A reluctant maid fetched her a clean tunic.

Lovetta fingered the brooch on Heather's rags admirably. "This is lovely." She ran a polishing rag over the blackened spots. Penn smiled with a mouthful of cheese and bread.

While Heather bathed, they were alone in the quarters. Penn's awkwardness from the morning had not completely subsided, so their conversation was clunky at best. Nevertheless, she was glad to be beside Lovetta once more.

"I saw something interesting out there in the market," Penn said as she brushed her crumbs into a pile. "A glass swan for sale. I could be wrong, but it looked an awful lot like the one from the east wing."

"How unusual," Lovetta murmured. She moved the brooch from Heather's old clothes to her new ones. "Perhaps there was a thief in the night."

"Or," Penn began with a cocked brow, "perhaps I'm not the only one sneaking out."

Lovetta looked at Penn with a smile in her eyes. "That would be rather out of character of me." They both laughed.

# Fourteen

Lovetta spent a good deal of the afternoon in Duke Wymark's study convincing her father to take on a new maid. She wouldn't allow Penn to put herself in the line of fire and insisted that she could easily win over her father. When Lovetta emerged tear-free and composed, Penn knew she had succeeded.

"We decided she might be better suited to tending the gardens," Lovetta relayed when Heather was out of earshot. "Considering her aptitude for building and resourcefulness ... and because she didn't take kindly to the proposition of regular bathing."

"I'm sure Mabs and Jinny could use the help," Penn said. Mabs was the Bondeville's head gardener, and young Jinny was her only assistant. Between the two, they kept the Bondeville's land in pristine condition, but the work was never ending.

That night, a maid set up a bed for Heather in Lovetta and Penn's chambers. After the intimacy of the night before, Penn didn't know how to feel about Heather's presence. She was an intruder, but also a necessary distraction to the many images assaulting Penn's mind. Of Lovetta's legs wrapped around her waist, their underclothes in disarray, Penn's shaking hands and the growing heat between her thighs. If it weren't for Heather, Penn might have marched over to Lovetta and stripped her bare, right then and there. Gods, had Clare been right all along? Had *Marion*? No, Penn didn't know anything for certain. Kissing Lovetta had been the most brilliant thing she had ever experienced, but until Penn understood exactly what it meant, she ought to keep her hands to herself. She would not be a plaything, not even for Lovetta.

As she laid in bed, a cacophony of thoughts kept her from sleeping. She pictured Hazir and wondered what he would think if he knew about the night they had shared. Would he consider Lovetta impure because of it? Perhaps he wouldn't think anything of it at all. To him, Penn was just a maid, not an equal. Now that the Saraq was staying in Vastal, Penn assumed that he and Lovetta would carry on as they had before. Penn would endure endless hours of hushed voices and nervous laughter, all the while hoping that Lovetta would decide she couldn't possibly marry him, or any other man.

It was jealousy. That was the reason Penn had begrudged Hazir for so long. She had been jealous of the man from day one, but only now could she acknowledge it. She wanted those close, quiet moments with Lovetta by the lake. She wanted Lovetta to laugh at her jokes, to grow shy at her touch. Was it possible for Lovetta to feel the same way about Penn? To have kissed her because she desired nothing more than her skin on Penn's? And did Penn liking it make her a queer, as Ariad had called Lovetta?

When Penn closed her eyes, she felt the pressure of Lovetta's lips against hers. Warmth prickled in her fingers and toes, coursing through her body and lighting a fire in her core. That night, Penn lived blissfully in the memory of Lovetta's touch. She created a chasm in her mind of Lovetta—only Lovetta—and she would visit it every night, even if their skin never brushed again. She prayed there were more of such memories to come.

It was early the next morning when Penn woke from a sleep coloured by dreams of Lovetta's body before her. The sun had yet to rise, but only she and Lovetta remained in the bedchamber. Heather was gone, and they were due to leave Tirel at first light, so she dressed quietly in her new clothes. The breeches were snug across her hips, but the blouse fell just long enough to hide her behind if she stood up straight. The outfit revealed more of her body than she had ever shown to the world beyond Theroulde's courtyards and the Bondeville's bathhouse, yet she wasn't uncomfortable. Men dressed like this every day, and nobody gawked at them, so why should she be any different? Feeling confident, Penn left the room in search of the Bondeville's new gardener. Heather was by the fire in the common area, entranced by the flames. Even as Penn sat across from her, she couldn't look away.

"Always thought fire was a bad thing," Heather whispered. "But it can be beautiful too. Might never have known." The hint of a smile played on her lips, and Penn knew that she and Lovetta had done the right thing. Penn could have cried. Was this feeling why the duke made it his mission to help girls like Heather?

"Do you think you'll miss it here?" Penn asked. The town may have been unsightly, but it was all Heather knew. Every memory of her mother would feature a dingy, grey backdrop and the stench of sickness, smoke and human waste.

Heather broke away from the fire and looked at Penn. "Dunno, never gone anywhere else," she said logically. They were quiet for a moment, and Heather frowned.

"Your ma would want you to be safe," Penn reassured her. "She would want a nice long life for you."

"But what if she comes back and I'm not here?" Heather said morosely. "I know she's dead. I saw it and everythin', but sometimes I think ... I wonder if maybe she'll come back somehow."

Penn stood and moved closer. She placed her hands on Heather's shoulders and pulled her into a tight embrace. "She can't come back. Moving on is hard, but you need to put yourself and your future first. It would make her happy to know you're warm and fed come winter."

Heather returned the embrace and sniffed. "I'll be fine, lady." She smiled and hopped off the chair.

Penn smiled too. "I know you will be. You're strong. Now, go and wake Lady Lovetta. We'll be leaving soon."

Heather shot down the hall, energised by her mission.

Before long, the family was assembled outside of the castle kissing Ysabell goodbye and giving Marion their regards. Penn wished Ysabell luck, though the young Bondeville wasn't one for sentiment. When she approached Marion, she didn't know what to say. They stood stiff and silent until Marion said, "The hair wasn't enough of a statement?" She eyed Penn's new clothes.

Penn took a deep breath. "I'd like to part ways on a good note."

"Can you promise not to hurt Clare again?" Marion said.

"I never meant to hurt her at all," Penn defended herself. "I still don't really know—"

"She *loves* you, you blind fool." Penn flinched. "And she knows you don't feel the same way. She knows you want her," Marion said, tipping her head in Lovetta's direction.

Penn lost her words entirely. Marion had confirmed Penn's suspicions from the night of the ball, the real reason Clare had been so upset. Penn had fallen in love with the wrong woman.

Penn cleared her throat, avoiding Marion's eye. "Good luck in the castle. Watch out for Theo. I hear he has a thing for young maids."

"Thanks, but I can look after myself just fine," Marion said with an air of arrogance.

Penn said goodbye and turned away faster than she could take a breath. There was no saving their friendship, but there was still a chance of salvaging what was left of Penn and Clare's.

When they climbed into the carriage and set off, Heather took Ysabell and Marion's place, entertained by Tibby and Thamasin's gossip. Penn relaxed at the front of the carriage with Lovetta, sitting in silence for longer than was comfortable. Why was everything such a mess? If she were a man, she wouldn't get caught up in such ridiculous squabbles. She'd be too busy drinking with her companions, singing songs at the fireside and comparing the size of their swords. If she fell in love with Lovetta, no one would question it. Her life would be simple. She wondered if her mother's life had been easier when she attended the university disguised as a man.

Lovetta broke the silence. "I'm so glad we're going home."

"It doesn't seem right to be leaving when so much is going on though," Penn whispered.

Lovetta sighed. "It's not like we would be of any use in Tirel anyway. You heard father." She crossed her arms.

"Hey," Penn said, reaching out a fraction but stopping herself before making contact. She saw Lovetta pretend not to notice. "Remember when you said we have to stop believing we'll never amount to anything? Well, you're not off to a very good start."

"I told you it was hard," she reminded Penn. "But maybe this just isn't a war we can fight."

"Or we haven't found our way to fight it. Wars aren't all blades and savagery." Lovetta nodded. "I had a lot of fun spying on the prince, you know." She chuckled. "Well, before we got caught."

"You were pretty good at it," Lovetta admitted. "Maybe one day you'll be a spymaster."

Penn grinned. "That'd be a dream. I wonder how Theo does it all. Look after the king, organise balls, investigate the prince and take care of the castle. How chaotic. But it sounds kind of fun, doesn't it?"

"Gods, maybe you should have stayed with Theo."

Penn gagged theatrically, and Lovetta laughed.

The two succumbed to another bout of silence that lingered for most of the day. When night fell, they stopped at a village a little further along than they had anticipated. The innkeeper was hospitable, and the rooms warm, but they couldn't get away with sipping mead under the duke's watchful eye. Again, Heather shared their room. The whole party woke the next morning well-rested and eager to be on their way. That day, Lovetta grew restless in the carriage. Penn wished there was something she could do for her, but they were trapped in the wooden box. Even Heather's company was beginning to suffocate the small space. Perhaps they all missed the feeling of moving air.

Their second night on the road was spent at the same inn they had visited at the beginning of their westward journey. The inn-keeper was overjoyed to see the party return, though Edony ensured that he did not waste any more of his fine wine on their immature tongues. With Heather tucked under Tibby and Thamasin's wings, Penn and Lovetta were free to drink their weight in mead with the others. Unsurprisingly, the group had a roaring time. Even Clare relaxed into her seat. Penn tried her best to strike up conversation with her old friend, but she could hardly hear her from across the table. What was she to say, anyway? That she thought Clare mad until she and Lovetta kissed? That perhaps Clare had been right all along?

*Oh, the kiss.* Penn loved thinking about it. The more they drank, the more Penn forgot about the awkwardness induced by her night with Lovetta. They talked as freely as they had before and brushed shoulders without pulling away. Each time they caught each other's eye, they shared a long, heated look. Finally, they retired to bed with red cheeks, heavy eyelids and Heather in tow.

\* \* \*

The final morning on the road had an air of relaxation to it that the previous days had not. When Heather was out of earshot, Penn and Lovetta tried hopelessly to give themselves a role in solving the duke's problem. They could not fathom how he was going to put Princess Roheisa on the throne or whether he'd be able to do it before King Segarus passed; he already looked so frail. Now there was no opportunity to spy on the royals themselves, Lovetta was convinced that they would have to spy on the duke instead.

"It's the only way," she justified. "He won't tell us anything, no matter how hard we try."

"But what if he finds out? You're already banned from riding. Maybe he really *will* send you to the convent," Penn fretted as Lovetta sat and continued to scheme beside her.

She laughed. "Oh, you heard him. They would only send me back. And my ban ends the second we get home. If he catches us, he'll only ban me again. I'll survive," she said bluntly. "Besides, I don't need to ride. I have you to entertain me now."

Penn shifted in her seat and tucked her hair behind her ears, feeling hot. She had to stop reading into Lovetta's jokes so much. "Do you think we'll even gain anything from spying? We're on the same side."

"Look, I don't love the idea of it either, but if there is anything we can do to help father, we must. He won't trust us until he sees us as capable."

"I suppose."

"And don't forget that you're rather good at spying. I doubt we'll get caught," Lovetta said to Penn's delight. "But when we get home, we should do as much riding as possible. Just in case." She grinned.

"The Saraqs will be sick of us," Penn said.

Lovetta frowned. "Oh, not to see them. After what happened between Edony and Sahin, I can't imagine we'll be visiting them for a while. We'll ride just the two of us."

Penn smiled. "I'd like that."

Though Penn was grateful they had a plan, she was nervous about spying on the duke, and of what might happen the next time she was alone with Lovetta. But that was a problem for when they got home. For now, Penn could simply throw her head back and close her eyes.

The carriage pulled into the castle well before dusk, and the party was welcomed by a tumultuous greeting. Sarra and Dorett climbed out of the carriage first, immediately flopping down on the grass and moaning with relief. Heather was more reluctant to leave her newly familiar confines, and Penn and Lovetta had to coax her out. She had been so eager to see the royal castle. What was holding her back now?

"Come," Penn whispered. "Let me show you something." She led Heather to the place she had visited during her first weeks in Rocque when she too needed comfort. The hayloft had not changed since the Bondevilles had left for Tirel, but it was noticeably emptier. The kittens had grown over the few months Penn had known them, and only two were present, a dark tabby and a ginger.

"They yours?" Heather asked as she approached the sleeping ginger.

"They don't belong to anyone, so we all take turns looking after them. You can visit them whenever you like." Heather bent down to pet the ginger kitten and giggled as it curled into a tighter ball, its face hidden in the coil of its tail.

"Me and Ma used to have a cat that visited us," Heather said. "I liked it. But it was old and real skinny. One day it just stopped comin'." There was a moment of silence, and Penn wondered whether bringing Heather to the hayloft had been a good idea.

Unexpectedly, Heather smiled. "I wanna be their friend." She tickled the pink pad on the ginger's back foot, and they both laughed as it twitched.

"I bet they want to be your friend too," Penn said, beginning her descent of the short ladder. They made their way up to the castle, Heather silent and wide-eyed as she took in its grandeur. She was going to be just fine.

That evening, Heather's absence left a quiet void in Lovetta's chambers. As a gardener, she would sleep with Jinny and Mabs in the dorm by the stables. She would like it there. Penn worried that without Heather's presence, she and Lovetta would be forced to acknowledge their heated night together, so Penn delayed to save her nerves. Instead, she sought out Clare after supper but could not find her. By the time she returned to their chambers, Lovetta was snoring softly with a flask by her pillow. Penn took herself to her own bed. Had it always been so cold?

After daybreak, Penn rose to an empty room. Lovetta had been summoned to the duke's study and didn't return until after breakfast.

"Remember how I said father would lift my riding ban when we returned?" Lovetta looked dismal.

"Oh, no," Penn said as she approached the hearth. "He went back on his word?"

"No." Lovetta flopped onto her just-made bed. "I can ride, but he's given me another punishment for sneaking out with you."

"What is it?" Penn asked, rising to stoke the fire.

"I have to teach archery." Lovetta groaned, glaring at the ceiling.

"Archery?" Even though Lovetta was a brilliant archer, the punishment was unusual.

"Sarra and Dorett are kind of useless," Lovetta explained.

Penn was quietly mortified. When the Bondevilles had practiced in Tirel, Sarra and Dorett had hit the target with every shot. If that was what Lovetta considered useless, what would she think of Penn's ability?

"You know," Penn retorted. "In some circles, Sarra and Dorett would be considered rather advanced."

"Well, I don't think those circles exist in Azor." Lovetta propped herself up on her elbows. "It's not their fault, though. We haven't had a tutor since our mother died."

Penn abandoned the hearth and moved to sit on the edge of Lovetta's bed. "Who taught you before?"

"She did," Lovetta said without emotion.

"Gods, I wish my mother had taught me something. Like how to dress like a man."

Lovetta looked Penn up and down. "You seem to be doing just fine without her. I like it, by the way. The new look. I meant to say it sooner."

"Thank you," Penn said. Jehane and Tibby had praised the change, but Thamasin was less impressed. Clare continued to evade her, and shockingly, Edony made a point to tell her that she had fabulous legs.

Penn shuffled closer to Lovetta, acutely aware that they were alone, and the door was closed. "To have taught you all you know, your mother must have been quite the archer."

"She was magnificent," Lovetta said with the ghost of a smile. "But I suppose all Azorian noblewomen are."

Penn recalled her favourite story as a child. It was about an Azorian peasant girl who dreamed of joining an expert group of archers who consisted entirely of highborn women. They fought alongside men and were heavily respected. Penn had idolised her, even if the girl wasn't real.

"When you were young, did you ever hear the story of Arjani?" Penn asked Lovetta. "She entered an archery competition disguised as a foreign noble's daughter and won."

"That's right," Lovetta murmured. "And they invited her to join the Kalasanti."

"And then she revealed herself," continued Penn, "but they let her stay because she was the best archer in all of Azor. She changed everything."

Lovetta nodded and sat up. "She did. She was the first peasant to ever join the Kalasanti, and now she's famous."

"Wait. Do you mean to say that the story is true? That Arjani was a real person?"

"I think so. Almost all Azorian folktales are true."

Penn laughed. "You can't be serious. Most of the stories I heard when I was young *were* Azorian folktales. Are you saying that dragons and firebirds and Shakalha are real?"

"Well, I don't know about the dragons and firebirds, but Shakalha certainly are," Lovetta said.

Penn could hardly believe her ears. "You're joking. People who can turn into animals? That's ridiculous!"

Lovetta's smile vanished. "There's a little more to it than that. Shakalha are gods. Gods aren't defined by the same rules that humans are."

Penn cocked her head. "You believe in the gods?" The only time Lovetta had mentioned the gods was when she cursed them.

"Why are you fightin'?" came a third voice from the doorway. Heather had snuck in during their disagreement.

"Heather, you shouldn't enter a lady's room without knocking," Lovetta said, instantly composed.

"I did knock, but you were too busy fightin'," Heather retorted. "Probably didn' hear me." She walked forward and her eyes lit up as she took in Lovetta's room for the first time.

"What are you doing up here?" Penn asked, a little grateful for the intrusion. Lovetta didn't back down easily from a challenge.

"A man on a horse came. He wanted to give you this." Heather held up a roll of yellowed parchment and handed it to Penn.

"For me?" She looked the parchment over, touching the wax seal. It was her father's mark. She stiffened, unsure of whether she wanted to open it or not. Her father had asked the duke to take her away. She held the parchment in her hand until her sentimental side prevailed, and when she unfurled the parchment, she found three separate letters. The first was written in her father's academic scrawl, the second in Maybelle's scribble, and the third...

"Florent!" she exclaimed, gripping the third piece of parchment hungrily. "I can't believe it! That means—he must be—may I be excused?" Penn pleaded, desperate for the long-awaited news from her brother.

"Suit yourself," Lovetta huffed.

Penn rushed from the room with parchment in hand. Perhaps when she got back, Lovetta would have forgotten all about their exchange. Penn took the servant's labyrinth to the back courtyard and cursed the castle for its unnecessary size. Florent had been away from Theroulde for years. The last time they had seen each other, he had been a gangly boy no taller than Penn. Now he would be a man, respected for his training in the arts of knighthood and making history with every passing day. Naturally, Penn had to read his letter first. She plonked herself onto a bench and uncoiled the parchment carefully, savouring her brother's handwriting.

*Dearest Penn Penn,*

*I am so sorry to have missed you. Father informed me that you are serving in Duke Wymark Bondeville's household now. You can imagine my surprise. Thankfully, my work in Port Sollers is over, and I am being repositioned closer to the capital. There is a new training regime in Tirel that they need instructors for. They seem to think I have what it takes for the job, and I am certainly grateful for the opportunity. As soon as I found out, I was out of Port Sollers before you could say poppycock.*

*We sailed to Port Greslet a few weeks ago, and it was an unmitigated disaster. You know how I feel about boats. Needless to say, I am quite certain I will be called a green knight until my dying day. As I had some time before reporting, I stopped in Theroulde for a few days. I am there now. I will be passing Rocque on my way to the capital, though I imagine that you will be in transit, so I will not be stopping. The news of Princess Roheisa's son is wonderful. I hope you have the chance to meet him.*

*It is strange being home without you, but I am glad that you have started to take your future seriously. The change will be good for you. I think the change will be good for me, too. Port Sollers was a difficult place to work in so many ways (slavers are an awful lot). Anyway, I am not sure when this letter will reach you. The weather has been treacherous here. The gods know the land needs it.*

*Now that I will have a base, you should write to me. Just address it to the Training Academy. Be cautious with your words, though. Anything that goes beyond the bridge is checked vigorously. If I have news from Gillot, I will let you know. Keep warm this winter, Penn Penn. I hope to hear from you soon.*

*JMPWFZPV, your brother Florent*

The letter left Penn with a familial warmth and a grin. They hadn't written coded messages to each other since they were small, but Penn remembered the one Florent used. It meant 'I love you'. Penn wiped a tear from her cheek and cleared her throat. There was a lot in Florent's letter to digest. Firstly, was it normal for men to be promoted so early in their knighthood? And what was this new training regime? Could the academy have anything to do with new soldiers the prince was after? If so, that meant Florent would be playing a part in the prince's despicable plan without even knowing it. Oh, she hoped she was wrong.

On top of Penn's many questions, how could she have come so close to seeing her older brother but missed out by just a few days? If it hadn't been for Princess Roheisa and her son, Florent would have stopped to see her. She cursed the princess then felt awful for it. If only she could have held the baby in just a little longer! Penn picked up Maybelle's letter next and flattened it out to read. It was much shorter than Florent's, and the handwriting was a challenge to decipher.

*Penny Penn Penn Penn,*

*You should write more. Daddy and I miss you. I think Maud does too because she talks to me a lot more. Not seeing you makes me sad so Mama had a new dress made for me. It's pink and has big long sleeves. I like it. I'll wear it for you when you come to visit. Can you come soon? It's raining really bad right now. Daddy says the land needs it. I hope it's sunny and nice in Rocque. I drew a picture of us but it got wet. I'm sorry. Please write back soon.*

*From Maybelle*

Penn was touched by Maybelle's words. The thought of visiting Theroulde entertained her for a while, but her opportunities to return home as a maid were scarce. Perhaps the Bondevilles would grant her leave over midwinter, but would her anger towards her father have subsided by then? Penn flicked to the final letter and read, frowning before she even began.

*Dearest Penn,*

*I imagine that you are angry with me. I have no doubt that by now, you have discovered the truth about your place with the Bondevilles. If you haven't, it's time you were made aware. That I received word from Rocque requesting your service was dishonest. It was I who wrote to Duke Wymark seeking a place for you in his household, and I beg your for-giveness for misleading you. I hope you will respect that my decision was not made lightly. Since the day you were born, everything I have done for you has been to ensure your safety. It is imperative you understand that this has not changed.*

*I regret that we will not be able to see you this midwinter. We will be visiting Olivia's parents in Port Greslet. She misses her father dearly. In other news, the rains have come at last. The farmers are thanking the gods—the land needs it. Until I see you next, behave yourself. Listen closely to Duke Wymark and stay by your lady's side. Make me proud, Penn.*

*From your loving father*

For a long time, Penn sat and stared at the sheet of parchment. One thing was for certain: Penn would not be visiting her family over midwinter. But something about her father's words didn't sit well with her, and she couldn't put her finger on why. Firstly, Durant was about as emotionally available as a teaspoon. He was quiet, a man of few words, and to ask her to make him proud? It wasn't like him. Had he *really* written this? Determined not to forgive her father so easily, Penn crumpled up the third sheet of parchment and returned to Lovetta's chambers.

The room was empty when Penn arrived. Lovetta had returned to unescorted tutoring sessions, and Heather would have resumed her work in the gardens. The fire burned low, so Penn added a log to the ashes and sat by the hearth with the poker. As she prodded the crackling mess, her father's words stayed with her. Unable to take her mind off the letter, Penn withdrew the crumpled ball of parchment and straightened it out the best she could. She had to read it one more time.

# Fifteen

Lovetta did not seem interested in talking to Penn that evening, or the morning that followed. The letter Penn had almost tossed into the fire now lay flat under her pillow, secure and at arm's reach. The more Penn had scrutinised the parchment, the more she had discovered hidden in her father's words.

At first, she had thought the bizarre softness was an attempt to sugar coat the part Durant had played in manipulating Penn's future, but the more Penn thought about it, the more she was convinced that the letter was, in fact, a warning. When Lovetta returned from her classes that afternoon, Penn showed her the letter.

"It looks like a perfectly normal letter to me," Lovetta said frankly after scanning the parchment.

"You didn't even read it." Penn pushed it closer to Lovetta. "This is important. *Really* important."

Lovetta sighed, took the parchment in her hands, and read it again. "This part is a little strange." She pointed to the middle of the letter. "It sounds kind of forced, the 'imperative that you under-stand' bit."

"That's what I thought. None of it sounds too abnormal, but there are little bits that just don't sound right. See here?" Penn put her finger on the crinkled letter. "It says that my stepmother misses her father dearly, but that's impossible. He used to beat her and his wife senseless."

"So why would she want to go back?" Lovetta said as she leant closer to Penn. Her mood always eased when a problem needed solving.

"She wouldn't. Not even for her mother."

"So, why go?" Lovetta asked again.

"I don't think they are going. They're going somewhere, but it isn't Port Greslet."

"Interesting," Lovetta hummed. "Do you think he said they were going there to throw off anyone who intercepted the letter?"

"Yes. And he wrote that she missed her father because I'd know it was a lie. I bet father was hoping I'd decode this. I think that's what he meant by making him proud." As her tongue unravelled each suspicion, her blood pumped a little faster. Lovetta was taking her seriously, and there weren't many feelings better than that.

"Maybe," Lovetta said with a shrug. "I don't know. You could just be overthinking it all."

Penn stiffened. Perhaps she had worked herself up at the sight of her brother's code, and Lovetta was merely humouring her. "I don't think so. He sent me here for my safety because he's in some kind of trouble. They all are. That's why they're leaving. He wants me to stay by your side, which I think means I'm not meant to stray far from the castle."

"Or that I'm in danger too," Lovetta suggested.

"I hadn't thought of that. But that would make sense, after all the awful things the prince said about your family."

"Yes," Lovetta mumbled. "Something I would rather not be reminded of."

"Sorry," Penn said, grateful she hadn't been more explicit. "Anyway, he's probably behind this." Penn shook her father's letter in the air.

"But what motive does the prince have to go after *your* father?" Lovetta asked. "Our fathers don't have much to do with each other anymore, do they?"

Part of her conversation with Theo came back to her. "There's something I didn't tell you," Penn admitted. "When Theo spoke to me on the night of the ball, he said something that got me thinking." She cleared her throat. "They all went to university together, right? Well, Theo said they were a group of five." Lovetta responded with nothing but a vacant look. "Don't you remember when we listened outside your father's study?"

"Sure, but ... oh! He said there were five people who knew of his plan, didn't he?"

"And he trusted them all completely. Sounds an awful lot like an old group of friends with the same values, doesn't it?"

"But who were the other two? I'm guessing Theo told you since you're so close now," Lovetta teased, and Penn began to doubt herself once more.

"He told me about one of them, but it was my mother." Penn sighed. "That's why I never told you. I figured it had to be a coincidence because my mother has been gone for years. The plan can't possibly have been in place for that long."

"No," Lovetta agreed, scratching her head, "but that doesn't mean you're wrong."

"It doesn't?"

"Just because one of the original five is gone doesn't mean the rest of them aren't involved. Father could have had another friend who took your mother's place."

The sentence hurt. How could anyone take her mother's place?

"I suppose that would explain father's involvement," Penn admitted. "I guess Theo was right."

"About what?" Lovetta asked.

"The prince knowing. I don't know how, but he must know of your father's plan. That's why everyone else is in danger. But then why would my father send me here? If this place ... if the duke's plan is the root of the problem, then aren't I in more danger here than I would have been in Theroulde?" A perturbed silence drifted between the two. In that moment, their entire theory came undone at the seams.

Lovetta was the one to break the silence. "Maybe there's more to the story. Everything you've said so far has made sense. What do we do now?"

"Well, this last part here," she pointed to the letter, "says to listen *closely* to Duke Wymark. It's an odd way of saying be on your best behaviour, don't you think?"

Lovetta looked at the parchment curiously. "It's almost like he's telling us to spy on him." She unfolded her arms. "Why would your father want you to spy on mine? Why not just talk to him directly? They're on the same side."

"I don't know," Penn admitted. "But can you think of any other reason he might say that?"

Lovetta shook her head. "No. I guess, well, it won't do any harm, will it?"

The realisation of what Lovetta was suggesting did not excite Penn like her scheming usually would. It didn't feel right to sneak around *this* castle, not when the duke had been nothing but kind to her.

Was this how a real spy felt when they received an assignment? Or did they feel as Penn had on the night they'd followed Theo to the prince's meeting? Nothing had seemed too frightening or uncouth, and even though they were caught, Penn had enjoyed herself. That night she had felt truly useful. It was so intoxicating that she was desperate to have that feeling back. But the duke wasn't like the prince. He was no villain.

"I don't think I can do it."

"What are you talking about? You were awfully good at it before," Lovetta reminded her.

"Actually, I got us caught. But that's not it, that's not why. It just feels wrong. Sneaking into his study, reading his mail."

"Oh, that's a brilliant idea! Why didn't I think of that?" Lovetta beamed, compounding Penn's guilt.

"Are you sure you want to do this?" she asked her pleadingly. "This is your father."

"We have to," Lovetta said matter-of-factly. "It's the only way to put this puzzle together. We deserve to know. We're being proactive. We're preparing ourselves." She smiled, making Penn feel marginally better.

"I guess," she replied. "I wanted to show you the letter last night, actually. When I read it, I just knew something wasn't right, and the only person I wanted to talk to about it was you."

Lovetta shifted her weight on the bed. "I was upset last night," she admitted. "You know I'm better off alone when I'm like that."

"But why were you upset? Was it something I said?"

They had both been bitter after their disagreement, but Lovetta rarely stayed bothered for long. Lovetta nodded.

"I'm sorry, I was rude. It's okay to have different opinions. I just don't believe in those stories."

Lovetta tensed at her words. "You don't understand," she said tersely. "Shakalha aren't just a story in Azor. They're the foundation of our religion. Our *gods*. To say that they don't exist or that the idea of them is ridiculous is more than rude. It's offensive, Penn." Lovetta looked her dead in the eye, as if challenging her.

"I didn't know they were real for you ... I mean, that they were real. I'm sorry." Getting the right words out was harder than she thought. "It's just difficult for me to understand because I've never believed in the gods, not one of them. But I don't think you're wrong for believing in them. I was just surprised. My father told me the gods didn't exist, so I believed him. I assumed you thought the same."

"It's okay; you didn't know. I shouldn't blame you for that. I think you should read this, though." She got up from the bed and collected a book from her bedside table. "I couldn't sleep last night, so I stayed up and marked some pages for you." She handed the hefty black volume to Penn, who flipped open the cover with curiosity. "I want you to learn about them. I want you to understand, even if you don't believe."

Penn thanked Lovetta and smiled as she studied the pages. It was somewhere between a recount of ancient history and a religious text, tightly scribed with at least a thousand pages. Penn opened to the section Lovetta had marked and looked at the heading. It was written in a language Penn didn't recognise. Beneath the complex characters sat a smaller heading that she could read. It said 'DIVINE CREATORS'.

"You don't have to read it now," Lovetta said as she lit the candle on her bedside table. The light in the room was dimming as the sun sank and supper approached. Penn closed the book and carried it to her corner, tucking it safely beside her pillow.

"I'll read it tonight, I promise. I want to understand." If the Azorian gods were a part of Lovetta's life, Penn needed them to be a part of her life, too. She would try to believe.

When the candles were lit, Penn and Lovetta readied themselves for supper. The hall was as elegant as usual with the Bondeville's table set for seven, despite Ysabell's absence. Clare, who would usually be beside Marion, sat instead with Jinny, who was across from Heather. The young gardeners had matching smudges of dirt on their noses. When Heather spotted her sidling along the table, Penn had little choice but to take the empty seat across from Clare. Perhaps they could finally talk.

"You're late!" Heather squeaked with a look of accusation. "I don't think you're a very good maid."

Penn laughed at the harsh truth. Even Clare cracked a smile. "Would it not be rude to leave my lady before she's ready?" Penn tested her.

Heather mulled this over with a thoughtful expression. "Sometimes I think everythin' is rude," she decided with a shrug.

Penn chuckled. "Be thankful you work in the gardens." She eyed the spiced pumpkin on Heather's plate. It was the last piece. "Are you going to eat that?"

Heather shook her head. "I don't think so. It tastes funny."

"Thanks." Penn scooped the leftovers onto her plate, then began filling it with the remnants of the other dishes. "You'll get used to the food. You'll even come to like it." Penn winked.

Heather looked doubtful but nodded, nonetheless. Penn began eating and tried to make conversation between bites. "What did you do today?" she asked Heather.

"I helped fix the moat!" Heather exclaimed, her face lighting up.

"Oh," said Penn, feigning a look of concern. "And what was wrong with the moat?"

"There was a leak. It was turnin' the ground all mushy. We had to fill it with stones. Nothin' I haven't done before," she added, her chest puffed out.

Penn fought the urge to laugh but was distracted by a glint of light. Fastened at the top of Heather's tunic was the brooch Penn had given her. She hadn't seen her without it since that day in the marketplace. Even though the trip to Tirel had been dismal, some good had come out of it. She had met Heather. Another memory of something that had happened in Tirel pulled at the corners of her mind, but Penn immediately pushed it away. If she thought of Lovetta's lips now, her face would show it.

"Clearly we picked the right person for the job," Penn said. Heather's laugh fully regained her attention. Clare and Jinny were talking amongst themselves now. "Do you like it here?"

"A whole lot! It's real big, though." She giggled. "I keep gettin' lost."

"That's all right; I still get lost sometimes." Penn realised she didn't have any plum with her rice, and it always tasted better with plum. She leant forward and surveyed the table, but the dishes were all but empty. Just as she gave up her search, Clare lifted her plate and pushed it in Penn's direction. Atop the crockery was an untouched plum halve, surrounded by its own juices. Clare said nothing, and her eyes were glued to the table, but the offer was there.

"Thanks," Penn said in surprise, scraping the fruit onto her rice. Clare returned her plate to the table, recommencing her conversation with Jinny just as Penn turned back to Heather.

The two chatted about the castle and its many nooks and shortcuts for at least half an hour, and when Penn finally looked up from the table, she found that the hall had nearly emptied. Lovetta and the duke were the last two left on the dais, talking softly over grape juice. By the look on Lovetta's face, the conversation wasn't going in the direction she hoped for. Across from Penn, Clare was still seated, picking the grains out of a dense roll. When Heather and Jinny took their leave, Penn made to follow, but stopped.

"Why didn't you eat the plum? You love plum," she said to Clare.

"It was the last piece. We don't have it often, and you love it even more than I do."

"Oh. That was really kind of you," Penn looked down. Why was she suddenly so nervous?

"Well, I've been a bit of an ass." Penn couldn't disagree with that. "I never told you I like your hair."

Penn laughed. "Thanks. What about the rest?" She put her hands on her hips and widened her stance, bold as a man.

"The clothes suit you. You look happy."

Penn smiled. "I am. Today I wear breeches, tomorrow I conquer the realm."

Clare laughed, a sound Penn had almost forgotten. "Penn, I want to apologise. What I said in Tirel, well, I shouldn't have." Penn sat back down. "There was just so much happening in my head. The things that I said to you ... I'd been wanting to say them for so long, but not in the way that I did."

"It's okay," Penn said, struggling to find words of comfort.

"It's just that I've been around women, *only* women, for so long now, and sometimes I think I see things that aren't really there. You know, between other women. I think they're like me," Clare whispered. "That they love women too."

An intense heat washed over Penn, and she prayed that Clare would stop talking immediately.

Clare cleared her throat. "When I said all those things, I was trying to tell you something, but you weren't hearing me."

"I heard you," Penn said, looking pointedly at the table. She remembered the fight so vividly; she was outraged, determined not to believe anything that came out of Clare's mouth. Incidentally, that included Clare's own confession.

"Oh," Clare said. "Well, it doesn't matter anyway. I was wrong," she added, half-smiling. "I might have been that way in the past, but not now. Not with you."

Penn was both surprised and relieved by Clare's words. Clare was Penn's first friend in Rocque, and she had always enjoyed spending time with her. She didn't want anything to change between them.

"And if I was wrong about me, I was probably wrong about you, too," Clare added. She looked as if a weight had been lifted from her shoulders. "It was silly. I don't know what came over me, thinking that you loved Lovetta."

"I do," Penn said matter-of-factly. "You were right." Finally, she could look Clare in the eyes. "I love her, and I hope she loves me too." Saying it out loud was cathartic. It was like something had unlatched itself from her chest, and the air that she breathed was crisper than before.

"Wait, what?" Clare stuttered, her face turning white. "But ... what about Hazir?"

"I can't speak for her feelings toward Hazir," Penn admitted. "But she kissed me. *She* kissed *me*," she repeated, letting her own words sink in.

Clare's face contorted in shock, and it took her a moment to grasp for a reply. "I can't believe it," she whispered, turning to the Bondeville's table and looking at Lovetta. As she did, Lovetta and the duke pushed out their seats and began their descent from the dais.

"I need to go," Penn said as she came to her feet. "I'm sorry for not believing you. I should be thanking you, really. I might never have realised I loved her without you." Penn smiled, then fell in line behind Lovetta as she exited the dining hall, leaving Clare to digest her revelation alone.

When they returned to her chambers, Lovetta grumbled about her conversation with the duke. "I tried so hard to get father to open up to me, but every time I asked him something he didn't want to answer, he just pretended he didn't hear me and turned away. He wants me to focus on my education and draw up a schedule for archery practice," she finished with obvious distaste.

"You know, that's not a bad idea. Personally, I'd rather my lessons were private. My abhorrent lack of skill might offend the others," Penn joked.

"Ha ha," Lovetta said sarcastically. "Do you really want to learn? You don't have to."

Penn began to unlace the back of Lovetta's gown. Her fingers fumbled more than usual, but she took her time. "I don't know," she mused. "Maybe I could be the next Arjani." Penn smiled. Any time alone with Lovetta was a blessing, and learning a new skill couldn't do her any harm, even if she did make a fool of herself in the process.

Lovetta laughed as she stepped out of her gown. "That's very ambitious."

Something about Penn's conversation with Clare had left her feeling bolder than usual, and she spoke without thinking. "How do you feel about Hazir?" she blurted. She had wanted to ask the question for some time, but not quite so directly. Penn looked at Lovetta's back, and although it was covered by her underclothes, the thought of her bare skin ignited a heat in her body. She wanted to see it again. Standing before the dressing table, Penn had a clear view of Lovetta's face in the reflection. She was frowning.

"Hazir?" Lovetta repeated, her arms folding in front of her. "He's okay, as far as men go."

Penn reached out and unfurled Lovetta's braid. She knew Lovetta was capable of doing it herself, but she wanted to touch her. "It's just..." Penn slowly ran her fingers through Lovetta's hair, separating each curl, "everyone seems to think there's something between you two. That you care for each other." She heard the nerves in her own voice. Was this line of questioning wise? If Lovetta truly did care for the Saraq, Penn would prefer that Lovetta said nothing at all. She watched Lovetta's face in the mirror as her fingers intertwined with her hair. Lovetta's mouth was a hard line and her brow creased with displeasure.

"They're wrong," Lovetta whispered. "We're only friends."

"He wants to marry you," Penn said, dropping her hands. "And when he left, you ran after him."

"I don't want to talk about this," Lovetta said. She walked toward her bed, then turned to Penn.

"I do," Penn said fiercely. "I need to know if you love him."

"*Love him?* Of course I don't *love* him. I've never felt that way about any man. You of all people should know that." She looked away. The grip on Penn's heart loosened. She didn't love him.

"Does he know that?" Penn pressed. Lovetta nodded and sat on the end of her bed. "And he still wants you to marry him?" she asked sceptically. "Why?"

"Marriage is more of a business proposal to Hazir than it is a celebration of love." Lovetta frowned. "And although I do see the benefits of such an arrangement, there would be certain expectations of me as a wife." She dropped her gaze. The image of Hazir's hands unlacing Lovetta's gown came to mind, and Penn flinched.

"You're still considering marrying him, aren't you?" Penn said, feeling hurt. "I don't understand. Even if you don't love him, you seem to admire him an awful lot. Why? His family have *slaves.* He doesn't care about the same things that you do. How could a marriage possibly work?"

"He thinks the way he does because he was raised to," Lovetta said in an exasperated tone. "It's not like he just decided he was going to have these opinions. They're ingrained. They're ingrained in most old Azorian households. You wouldn't understand."

"But he knows his beliefs hurt people. You said yourself that you tried to sway his position on slavery, but he wouldn't even hear your opinion."

"That doesn't make him an inherently bad person. He grew up with people who thought a man's worth was equal to his swordplay. Do you think Vastalian men are any different? They're not, Penn. You and I were both lucky enough to grow up with scholars for fathers, and you know how much criticism they've both received for holding the opinions they do. Where do you think that criticism comes from? It's not from Azor." She took a sharp breath. "Hazir doesn't call Vastalian blood *tainted.*"

Penn wanted to rebut Lovetta, but she couldn't. Her points may have been valid, but Penn's opinion on the Saraq couldn't be shifted. She could not sympathise with someone who owned slaves, but it seemed Lovetta couldn't find fault in the man. There was silence as Lovetta climbed into bed and extinguished her candles.

"I'm sorry for bringing it up," Penn said softly as she put out the fire.

"I'm sorry for getting mad all the time," Lovetta whispered.

Penn undressed, climbed into bed and eventually whispered back, "I just don't want you two running off into the sunset together." Penn thought she heard Lovetta laugh, but it could have been the wind.

With wide eyes and a brain too busy for sleep, Penn picked up the book Lovetta had given her and flipped to the dog-eared page that marked the chapter on 'DIVINE CREATORS'. Beneath the title was an illustration sketched roughly in black ink. It was a figure with many limbs, heads and tails. The torso looked human, but each projection represented an animal of some kind. Altogether, the creature looked hideous, like a demon from a nightmare, deformed and terrifying. She tore herself away from the picture and began to read the first paragraph.

*In the beginning it was the Shakalha, otherwise known as the shifting gods, who birthed the forms that became ani and anak. First came ani, crafted from the pelt and bone of Shakalha Hiji, built to carry the gift of life. Second came anak, crafted from the blood and talon of Shakalha Hiji, built to deliver the seed of creation. The forms were mortal and unshifting, capable of autonomous thought and action. The Shakalha were so impressed with ani and anak that they gifted their creations with food, water and lands to flourish, and in time ani and anak became many. However, ani and anak did not possess the supreme qualities that the Shakalha were bound to, thus the mortal lands suffered greatly. It is said that Shakalha Hiji came down from the god's land to intervene on many occasions, gifting the spirit of the gods to chosen ani and anak. The chosen could hone the Shakalha spirit and shift forms at will, bringing justice and prosperity to those they surrounded themselves with before succumbing to their mortality. The chosen were named for their creators and supreme leaders: Shakalha, messengers of the gods.*

Penn lowered the book. The stories of Shakalha she had heard as a child were very different to how Azorian history described the gods. Penn had never heard of ani or anak, only that there were people who could turn into animals. Wolves, foxes, rabbits, dogs, usually for some self-serving purpose, the story climaxing with a moral that few children took seriously. The stories never spoke of the divinity of the gods themselves, or why they sent messengers to the mortal lands.

That night, Penn's dreams were haunted by many-faced gods, snarls, whimpers and screams intertwined with Lovetta's lips.

# Sixteen

That week there was no meeting with the Saraqs. Three days after Penn and Lovetta began to spy on the duke, they woke to the sound of rain pelting the stone walls outside, and the chill of a cold, dark room blanketed in cloud. Penn lit the hearth, which was soon roaring with life, and lit some candles, and both women bundled themselves in woollen garments to keep their shivers at bay.

Since they had begun to spy on the duke, they had observed very little of interest. At first, Lovetta was enthusiastic, but she soon grew bored with their lack of results. Thankfully, Penn didn't mind doing the mundane things, like regularly checking the visitor diary. With Penn's access to the servant's passageways, she had it easy. Unlike Lovetta, her whereabouts rarely had to be accounted for. She could snoop around during Lovetta's lessons, and no one would bat an eyelid, save for perhaps Osenna. The visitor's diary was in the housekeeper's private sitting room, so she always took note of Osenna's comings and goings before entering.

The duke's study, however, had proven difficult to infiltrate. If it was unoccupied, it was locked, and Penn hadn't picked many locks in her time. On several occasions, she forfeited her attempts and returned to Lovetta empty-handed. The feeling of uselessness only drove her to work harder, and eventually, she could pick the lock in seconds.

To their dismay, the duke's mail was a bore and revealed nothing of Tirel's current affairs. With the capital's careful monitoring of imports and exports, Penn and Lovetta had doubts the duke could receive word from his associates at all. It wasn't until the discovery of two letters written in a foreign language that Penn knew they were on to something. No, not a foreign language. A code. The messages were short and completely indecipherable, and Penn had no idea how to approach the jumbled mess. She flipped, rotated, mirrored and skipped symbols, but nothing worked.

One morning as breakfast was due to commence, Penn decided she needed to change her approach. She left the hall early and went to the duke's study, insisting to Clare that she had eaten too much the night prior. Once inside, instead of trying to crack the codes, she laboriously copied the complex characters onto the back of her father's letter and took it to Lovetta's chambers. But even with the additional time, she was at a standstill. When Lovetta returned with a tray of food in her hands, Penn hadn't made any progress at all.

"Is everything all right? You didn't eat."

The look of concern on Lovetta's face warmed Penn. She explained her absence and showed her copied note to Lovetta. "It's so frustrating. I just don't get it! I've never seen anything like this."

The code was made up of symbols, not letters or numbers, or even a combination of both, which was rather common.

Lovetta shrugged. "I'd be a little worried if father was receiving coded letters that could be cracked by a seventeen-year-old girl in a couple of days."

Penn frowned. "It sounds silly, but most codes are quite easy to crack. A lot of people assume they're complicated, so when they see a code, they think 'oh, it's too hard' and don't try." But this code *was* too hard.

"How do you know so much about codes anyway?" Lovetta set Penn's breakfast up by the hearth, a role reversal that almost made Penn laugh. Three months ago, she never would have imagined herself sprawled on the ground, waving her feet in the air and cursing in her lady's company. "Penn?" Lovetta said, regaining her attention.

"My father. Theo called him a code master, believe it or not."

Lovetta raised a brow. "And yet you doubted your father's involvement."

"He's just so different now. He stopped including me in things like this when he remarried, even though I enjoyed it. Was it because I'm a girl? Surely not! He met the love of his life while she was disguised as a man." Penn laughed dryly. "Why was it okay for her to push boundaries, but it wasn't okay for me to?"

"Perhaps your mother is the reason. You must remind him of her, and he just wants to keep you safe."

Penn sighed. "Maybe ... anyway, the most interesting things I learned came from the books in my father's study. The ones not even Florent was supposed to look at. And before you say anything, I checked your father's study for a book on code-breaking, and no, he doesn't have one."

Lovetta narrowed her eyes. "But you haven't checked the library, have you? There could be something in there that might help us."

"*Of course* I haven't checked the library," Penn scoffed. "There are thousands of books in there. I wouldn't even know where to start."

Lovetta's smile twisted into something wicked. "I do."

So, the two made for the library, the crinkled letter folded in Penn's pocket. The stone-walled emporium smelt strongly of parchment and mildew, each aisle bursting with loosely bound books, topics ranging from foreign fables to the humble family history. As Lovetta searched, Penn wandered about the aisles. She had only been in the library on a handful of occasions, and they weren't for leisure. It was beautiful but intimidating. Penn wasn't used to having so much choice. Books were expensive, so her father's library had been modest, its primary contents of a scientific or philosophical nature. The duke's collection, however, had no bounds.

"You won't find much down there," Lovetta called from the second landing. "It's mostly almanacs. Not this year's though. That's in father's study."

Penn giggled. The duke didn't seem the auspicious type. Then again, he did believe in Shakalha. Penn took the stairs in twos to find Lovetta perched precariously on the back of an armchair, rummaging through the contents of the highest shelf. Penn winced. "There's a perfectly good ladder over there." She ought to steady Lovetta's hips with her hands, but just the thought of it got her all flustered.

"I'll only be a moment," Lovetta said, wiping the dust from a battered volume. "Found it!" She slid a hefty blue book from the shelf. "I knew I'd seen something about codes before." She tucked the volume under her arm and twisted her feet on the wingback. Just as Penn feared, the chair couldn't take the shift of Lovetta's weight, and it began to tip. Penn frantically grabbed at the air as Lovetta lost her footing, squeaked and tumbled into her. They both landed in a heap with Lovetta's face cushioned by Penn's chest. Penn groaned, lifting her head from the stone to find Lovetta straddling her. With the hint of a smile on her face, she climbed off as Penn's face burned scarlet.

"Are you all right?" Lovetta asked, retrieving the fallen book then holding out her hand.

"I can't complain." As she was pulled up, Penn's left leg buckled, and she gasped. "Actually, yes I can." Her knee had landed on an odd angle, and something wasn't quite right. She extended her leg to test her weight on it, and a sharp pain shot from her ankle to her thigh. "Ah. That's not meant to happen."

"I'll help you." Lovetta wrapped her arm around Penn's back. They hobbled down the stairs and out of the library with great difficulty, but Penn didn't mind. She was eager to decode the message, and with Lovetta pressed up against her, the pain was bearable. Still, it was a relief when Lovetta finally set Penn on her bed to rest.

"This is a bit of a problem, isn't it?" Penn shifted her leg onto a pillow. "How am I meant to sneak about like this?"

"Spying on my father is the least of your concerns right now," Lovetta said, gently palpating Penn's knee and ankle. "Well, I don't think anything is broken."

"How do you know?" Penn asked, chewing on her lip to distract from the pain.

Lovetta shrugged. "You would probably be screaming."

Penn mumbled her thanks and cursed herself, then let her head fall back on Lovetta's pillow. "Don't blame yourself. I fell on you," Lovetta said, collecting a pastry from the tray she brought earlier. "You should eat something, or you'll take longer to heal."

Penn took a bite from the fruit-filled tart as Lovetta poured her a flagon of grape juice. "Thank you." She swallowed, put the tart in her lap, and reached for the book they had found in the library. "Do you mind passing me some parchment?" Penn asked absent-mindedly, touching the smooth cover.

"Penn, you're hurt. You don't have to try and decode those messages now."

"I don't think I'll be washing the linens, and you've got classes. I may as well make myself useful."

Lovetta sighed, picked up the parchment, ink and quill and gave them to Penn. "Suit yourself," she mused. "You'd better have eaten the rest of that by the time I get back." She glared at the tart in Penn's lap.

"Yes, mother dearest," she joked, and Lovetta bopped her head with a cushion. "You make a good maid, you know. Have you ever considered a life of service?" Lovetta made an obscene hand gesture and left the room. Laughing, Penn retrieved her breakfast with one hand and fingered the book's cover with her other hand.

The lettering was embossed in gold and written in a language Penn didn't know. Somehow, it seemed familiar. It was just like the strange symbols in the book on Shakalha. Penn flipped open the cover, and at the sight of the first page, she groaned. Not a single symbol was decipherable. As she chewed on her tart, Penn flicked through the book page by page, hoping to find something recognisable, but it was no use. The entire book was written in the foreign language. How did Lovetta expect Penn to decipher a code with a book she couldn't understand? And how had Lovetta known it was the right book in the first place?

Penn picked up her sheet of parchment and looked over the two codes. The symbols were similar in style to those in the book, but without a translation chart, she wouldn't have a chance at deciphering the messages. But Penn was determined to make sense of the letters; she couldn't just throw the book down and give up. It was only a code. *All* codes could be broken, and she had the tool to do it in her hands. She just had to figure out how to use it.

The next two hours were spent scouring the volume and flipping from chapter to chapter in the hope of finding a single symbol that matched up with one on her parchment. Penn was still buried in the text when Lovetta returned with lunch, which she ate at record speed. It wasn't until Lovetta was halfway through her afternoon class that Penn found something useful.

"I know you!" she shouted at the book, pointing to a symbol in her own tongue. Penn turned the page over to find a lengthy chart, no different from the several she had already encountered, except that this one made sense. On the left-hand side of the page sat a column of foreign symbols: the language of the code, and on the right, columns of simpler characters: the translations, written in Vast. Penn traced her finger along the page, matching the symbols from the letters to those on the chart and scribing the translations on her parchment. Her heart raced. Lovetta would be so proud of her.

Her eyes darted from the book to the parchment over and over until the message was complete, and when Penn looked it over, she recoiled. The unintelligible scrawl had come together to read something sinister.

*I HAVE FAILED. SNAKE COMING. DO NOT LOOK FOR ME. L.*

Penn's mind swam with possibilities. Who was L, and what had they been trying to accomplish? Did 'snake' mean the prince? If so, where was he going? Determined to understand the meaning of the message, Penn decoded the second message with haste. It was shorter than the first, but when Penn read it, it was no less harrowing.

*WILL STRIKE BEFORE MIDWINTER. RUN. L.*

She read it four or five times, and each time her stomach churned. When Lovetta opened the door an hour later, Penn could barely bring herself to speak. There was lump in her throat the size of a peach.

"I think you should see this," she croaked, her mouth dry as a bone.

Lovetta hurried over and snatched up the parchment. "You did it," Lovetta whispered, then her expression hardened. "No. It can't be." She shook her head. "Father would have said something. He would have moved us," she reasoned. "Look, it doesn't say the strike is here. It could be anywhere. And it could be about anyone." She laughed, but there was no humour in her eyes.

"It says 'run', Lovetta. Your father wouldn't have these if they weren't meant for him."

Lovetta dropped to the side of the bed and shook her head. "Why?" she whispered.

"I don't know." Penn leant forward and put her hand on Lovetta's shoulder. "But midwinter is only a month away. If whatever is meant to happen *does* happen, that means we only have a few weeks."

"At the most," Lovetta said, coming to terms with the new information. "What do we do?" She looked at Penn with desperation.

There was nothing Penn could say that would make Lovetta's fear disintegrate, but she had to at least try. "Come here." She patted the unoccupied side of the bed. Lovetta climbed over her cautiously but, despite her efforts, nudged Penn's injured leg with her knee. Penn's hands instinctively flew to her leg and she yelped.

Lovetta froze. "I'm sorry!"

"It's fine," Penn said, breathing through the pain. She shuffled down the bed and laid her head on the pillow as Lovetta did the same. They looked to the ceiling, and neither of them moved for a while. Penn wanted to comfort Lovetta, but their bodies were so close. If she turned to look at her, she would see the same tear-stained cheeks that had glittered in the low light of their chambers in the east wing. She would see the same lips inching closer, as warm and inviting as they were forbidden. Penn felt a hot trickle from her neck to her toes, and she turned to see Lovetta staring back at her, the sad desperation in her eyes no different from her memories. It would be so easy to kiss her, and gods, did she want to.

Lovetta's hand was limp in the space between them, and Penn didn't have to think for her body to respond. Her fingertips ignited as they laced around Lovetta's, the corners of Lovetta's mouth curling as their bodies moved closer. Penn knew what was going to happen, but this time, she didn't wait for Lovetta to bridge the distance. Instead, Penn leaned in, pressed her lips to Lovetta's, and kissed her softly. If the pain in her leg returned, she didn't notice.

Penn closed her eyes and her hands searched for Lovetta's hips, no matter how flustered they might make her. Cold fingertips found her face, drawing her closer. The kiss deepened. With a great effort, Penn slid her injured leg over Lovetta and rolled her onto her back, straddling her just as Lovetta had in the library. She paused to gaze into Lovetta's eyes, and they both smiled. Penn kissed her fiercely and ran her hands along the curves of her waist. Lovetta pulled her closer, and Penn felt a surge of power. Why on earth hadn't she done this sooner?

"Your leg healed awfully fast," Lovetta said as they parted for a moment.

Penn laughed before silencing Lovetta with her lips. This wasn't anything like the last time. Then, every touch had been cautious, and they had looked at each other as if it were for the very last time. Now, touching Lovetta was like seeing sunlight after a night spent in the dark. The world around Penn muted, and the fears she harboured only moments before turned to dust.

Lovetta found the small of Penn's back and pulled herself upright, their legs and Lovetta's skirt a tangled mess between them. As they pressed together, Penn committed every touch, every movement to her memory, her mind filling until she knew nothing but Lovetta. It was blissful and dangerous, and everything she had been waiting for.

Desperate to be closer, Penn moved her hand to Lovetta's thigh, and no sooner than she had, the creak of a door jolted it away. They broke apart with violence, Penn's heart hammering as she heard a squeal, a slam and the pitter patter of footsteps echoing in the hall.

"Heather," Lovetta panted, her eyes wide with fear.

"*Heather!*" Penn screamed, disentangling their limbs. She jumped off the bed, buckled under her own weight, and crashed to the floor for the second time that day. "*What have we told you about knocking?*" Penn bellowed as she gripped her throbbing knee. The pain was intense, but the fear of what Heather's discovery might mean kept her present.

"I'll handle this," Lovetta said, her voice trembling. She bounded off the bed and out of the door. After a series of clatters, bangs and shushes, Lovetta returned with the struggling child in her arms.

"Geroff! Lemme go!" Heather thrashed.

"I'll only let you go if you promise not to run off," Lovetta said, dodging the girl's flying limbs.

"Okay, okay!" Heather shouted, her violence ceasing the moment she was set down.

Penn dragged herself over to Lovetta's armchair and hoisted herself up to standing, hoping that Lovetta knew what she was doing. Penn certainly didn't.

"Tell me what you saw," Lovetta said in her most maternal voice as she guided Heather toward the hearth.

"I dunno," she replied, avoiding both of their faces. "You was doin' the married people thing, I think," Heather mumbled, scratching her nose.

"That is not what we were doing!" Lovetta said shrilly.

"Looked like it," Heather said.

Lovetta started playing with the ends of her hair, a nervous habit she reserved for the most stressful of events. "Okay." She exhaled. "You see, Heather, well, what we were doing—"

"Was practice," Penn interrupted. Lovetta looked horrified.

Heather scrunched up her face. "Practice for what?"

"For when Lady Lovetta gets married, of course! She has to be able to please her husband, and how else is she supposed to learn?" The words left a sour taste in her mouth, but they were the best she had.

Though Heather was young, she was a pint more mature than most her age. "You're gettin' married?" Her eyes widened.

"Of course," Lovetta mumbled after a threatening look at Penn.

"Who ya marryin'?"

"Hazir Saraq," Lovetta improvised. Penn's eye twitched. She wished she had used some other name. *Any* other name. "He's from Azor, where my mother was from. His family live across the lake," Lovetta said, relaxing into her story.

Heather grinned. "Is he as rich as you?"

Lovetta laughed. "Almost. In Azor, his mansion is one of the biggest."

"Sounds fancy," Heather said. "But I didn't know you was allowed to practice for gettin' married."

Penn cleared her throat. Lovetta had done enough talking. "Some people think it's not very ladylike, so it would be best if you didn't mention it to anyone. They might question her intentions."

"And don't mention Hazir, either. I haven't formally accepted his proposal yet," Lovetta added.

Heather's eyes narrowed and she nodded slowly. "All right, lady."

Penn and Lovetta looked at each other with relief.

"Well, that's settled then. You can run along now," dismissed Lovetta, and Heather dashed for the door.

Lovetta moved closer to Penn and put a hand on her waist. "Do you question my intentions?" she whispered, suppressing a grin. A frantic banging came from the door, and the two snapped apart again. Lovetta groaned. "Come in."

Heather reappeared in the doorframe. "I almost forgot. I came to tell ya somethin'! A man is here. He came on a horse and asked for the duke. I remember him from Tirel, but I think somethin' might be wrong."

"What does he look like?" Penn asked. Was it 'L', or another of the duke's secret comrades?

"He's got red hair and a funny beard," Heather recalled.

"Theo," Penn and Lovetta said in unison. "Okay, Heather, you can go," Lovetta dismissed again.

"Yes, lady!" The door closed, and they listened for the fading sound of stamping feet.

"What would Theo be doing here?" Penn asked, massaging a particularly tender spot below her knee.

"It must be serious," Lovetta murmured. "The last time he was here was when my mother died," she confirmed. "It could be about the prince."

"Maybe he's on his way. This is *bad*," Penn said.

Lovetta shrugged and gave her a tempting smile. "Bad news is still bad news in an hour." Her hand returned to Penn's waist and slipped under the hem of her blouse.

"Gods, I don't want you to stop, but..."

Lovetta pulled away, then sighed. "I know. We need to hear what he has to say."

"Later?" Penn suggested, then briefly pressed her lips to Lovetta's neck.

Lovetta's breath hitched. "Definitely."

Penn giggled, then looked to her leg. "I don't know how well I'll walk."

"So *now* your leg is a problem."

Penn blushed. "I'm serious!"

"You should stay here," Lovetta said. "I don't want to be responsible for any more injuries today."

"You're not going without me. You're an awful spy, and you know it. They'll hear you coming from a mile away." Lovetta crossed her arms and offered Penn a sour look. "I'll just have to manage," Penn said.

"All right," Lovetta gave in. "But take care."

"I will," Penn reassured her, and the two began their laborious venture to the duke's study. Lovetta kept hold of Penn's arm, her touch a constant reminder of the heated moment they had just shared. Penn refused to put the images out of her mind as she had after their evening in Tirel. She was more than a plaything.

When the two emerged from the hallway, two men-at-arms were stationed outside the duke's study, which was a rare sight. The men turned to the girls with a metallic clink, but before they could speak, Lovetta steered Penn into the next room. It was a small sitting area with an unlit hearth and a scattering of unusual artefacts. Penn hobbled to a dust-coated armchair and wondered how she had never entered the room before.

"That was quick thinking," Penn whispered. "But we won't be able to hear anything from in here."

"We might," Lovetta said, putting her ear against the adjoining stone wall. She frowned. "Flipping frogspawn, I can't hear a thing."

Penn looked around the room for anything that might help, but all she found was a pile of tarnished junk. "What is all of this stuff?"

"Who knows." Lovetta sighed. "Stuff just gets thrown in here. Father hates this room."

"Why?" Penn took a miscellaneous sphere from the table and turned it over in her hands. The spot where it sat was several shades darker without the accumulation of dust.

"It's the room my mother died in," Lovetta said, her mind elsewhere as she weighed up their options.

"I'm sorry," Penn said.

"Never mind about that, focus. You're the expert here. What do we do?"

Expert was a stretch. Penn scanned the room again, grateful she hadn't upset Lovetta. Her eyes fell upon the window, its curtains shifting limply in the breeze, and she had a thought.

"If you put your head out the window, can you hear anything?" She knew there was a window behind the duke's desk. If Lovetta leaned out far enough, they should have no problem overhearing the conversation.

Lovetta rushed to the windowsill and poked her head into the wind. After a moment, she withdrew back into the room with a shake of her head. "Barely," she murmured. "I think they're talking quietly."

Penn pondered until another solution came to her. "Is there a ledge beneath the window?" she asked, remembering the architecture of her home in Theroulde.

"I think so, but there's no way I'm standing on it, if that's what you're suggesting."

Penn rolled her eyes. "I meant me, obviously. Can you check?"

Lovetta stuck her head back out the window. "There is, but it's narrow. There's no way you can do it." Lovetta waved at Penn's dud leg.

"Well, someone has to," she pointed out.

A moment of quiet passed, and again, Lovetta's fingers intertwined with the ends of her hair. "Okay, I'll do it," she succumbed. "But I'm not going far. Just a few feet."

Penn watched as the colour slowly drained from Lovetta's face in anticipation. "Are you sure?" Penn was undoubtedly the better climber of the two.

Lovetta gulped. "Yes. But you need to hold my hand. If I slip, you need to stop me from falling. It's a long way, and I'm not ready to die. I'm still a virgin."

"You're not going to die." Penn's cheeks burned as she hobbled over to the windowsill with Lovetta. She looked down to Lovetta's feet and had a moment of panic. "Take your shoes off, or you *will* slip."

Lovetta nodded. "Right." She slid off her skinny heeled boots and climbed onto the windowsill, pausing as she straddled the stone. Gently, she lowered herself down to the ledge, which wasn't *that* narrow, then grabbed Penn with a shaking hand. "This was a terrible idea," she whispered, looking down at the four-storey drop.

# Seventeen

"Lovetta, look at me," Penn whispered, grasping Lovetta's clammy hand as if both of their lives depended on it. Maybe they did.

Lovetta shook against the wind. "I forgot to mention I don't like heights."

The pit of anxiety in Penn's stomach deepened, and she regretted not hauling herself out the window. "I need you to look up and face me, okay?" Penn quietly cooed, squeezing her hand as tight as she could. If Lovetta slipped, Penn would either save her or tumble to the ground by her side, and a four-storey drop was bound to hurt.

"Mm." Lovetta trembled, withdrawing her gaze from the sea of green below. "Talk me through this, would you?" She met Penn's eye.

"Okay. I'm going to stay right here and keep hold of you," Penn explained. "And you're going to move across the ledge very slowly. Keep your other hand on the wall as you go, and when you want to come back in, you need to squeeze my hand as tight as you can." She looked at her own hand, which was blue-tinged and rapidly losing feeling. "You might have to ... to just loosen your grip a *little* before squeezing. Can you do that?"

Lovetta gave a stiff nod and took a deep breath. Slowly but surely, she shuffled her feet until she was so far along that Penn's torso hung out the window with her.

From her position, Penn could only make out snippets of the duke's conversation with Theo. They never mentioned the prince by name, but the conversation didn't sound like a friendly one. Words like 'traitor' and 'abomination' were loud, flippant and frequent, and at least fifteen minutes passed before Lovetta signalled to come back inside. By the time she edged her way back to the windowsill and into the room, her face was almost as white as Penn's.

"Thank the gods," Lovetta inhaled, legs shaking. "We need to get back to my room. Right now."

"What is it?"

Lovetta shook her head. "Not here."

"Lovetta, every second counts. Just—"

"Not in *this room*." Lovetta's expression was pleading. "Too many terrible things have happened here already."

"Right. I'm sorry," Penn said, then took Lovetta's hand. "Let's go." They hobbled back to their chambers as quickly as they could manage, ignoring the men-at-arms and their curious glances. The second the door closed behind them, Lovetta exploded with everything she had heard.

"He *is* sending us away!" she shrieked. "I don't know where, but Theo was saying that the papers were all in order, and that we'd need to travel in small groups. That's why he's here." She paced the room as Penn dropped into the armchair. "He's got it all with him. Father said we had to go by different names."

"This is unbelievable. The prince really *is* going to attack Rocque." Her tongue went slack. If Lovetta was to leave Rocque, what did that mean for Penn? Where would she go? Her father was leaving Theroulde, perhaps he had already. She would be alone. "This can't be happening."

"It is," Lovetta said solemnly. "He'll sack the castle and everyone in it."

Fury boiled under Penn's skin. Through the abolition of slavery, Duke Wymark had saved thousands of lives, and this was how the Crown chose to repay him? "Sick, vile, hollow-headed cock of a warthog," Penn fumed, putting her head in her hands. She was powerless, and it infuriated her.

"Penn!" Lovetta exclaimed.

"Sorry."

"Oh, don't apologise. That was quite creative. Anyway, the person who sent those codes, I think I know who it is."

Penn dropped her hands. "Who?"

"Loxias Marisco. I heard his name several times." Lovetta sat on the side of her bed and looked out of the window. Night was falling. "And I just have a feeling—"

"Do you know him?" Penn asked, having not heard the name before.

She sighed. "No, and my father hasn't ever mentioned him. I think he has something to do with Ysabell. There's a plan to get her out of Tirel, too."

Penn stretched her leg out before her and tested her weight. "He could be one of the five, couldn't he? It makes sense." Her leg had neither improved nor worsened. "He knew the duke well enough to send him codes that only he could decipher. I doubt there are too many people in Vastal who can do that. What language were they written in anyway?"

"Old Azorii." Lovetta's voice cracked, her attention lost in the purple sky. "Nobody uses it anymore. Barely anyone can read it. I only know a few symbols."

"Are you okay?" Penn asked, wishing she could bridge the distance between them without limping. Lovetta laughed dryly. "Silly question, I suppose."

"Well, my family is about to be split up and sent off to somewhere only the gods know. Would you be okay after finding that out?"

"My family are on the run," Penn reminded her. "And I don't know where to, or why. Florent will be in the capital, right in the middle of the danger, and Gillot … gods. I haven't heard from Gillot in a year. More. For all I know his body is floating in the Black Sea." The image of her younger brother stiff and cold brought a sour taste to her mouth. He was no diamond, but he was family.

"We've certainly done something to anger the gods," Lovetta said, unfixing her gaze and coming to her feet. She circled the room, lighting the candles one by one.

Penn pulled herself up and added wood to the hearth. "Did your father…" she paused, poking the ashes. "Did he say when you're leaving?" Her words were barely audible over the crackling of the flames. Tightness gripped her throat as Lovetta walked toward her and touched her cheek.

"I'm not going anywhere if it means leaving you," Lovetta said. Penn looked into the fire and let the heat prickle her cheeks. She must look desperate as a child. "And no, I don't know when. But Theo said everything was in place, so it must be soon." She took a step back from Penn and crossed her arms. "We should go down for supper. Do you think you can walk on your own?"

"I'll be fine," Penn said. Her knee was the least of her concerns.

The two left Lovetta's room and made their descent of the marble stairs. "Will you tell Belsante and Edony?" Penn asked as they walked.

"I have to. Father won't say anything until the final hour, and that could be weeks away. It's not fair on them, and I can't keep a secret for that long. If I were them, I would want to know sooner rather than later. I'd want to prepare myself."

"And the others?" They turned into the main hall.

"I don't know," Lovetta whispered. "If Ysabell were here, she might be able to handle it, but Dorett and Sarra … they're so young.

They'll just lose sleep. Oh, maybe this is all a terrible idea. I don't know what I'm doing. I should just talk to father—"

"Lovetta, calm down," Penn hissed as they approached the dining hall. They were starting to draw attention. "We'll figure it out. I'll see you after supper." She tried to smile, then dropped into her usual bench. It was a surreal feeling, sitting beside her friends, all blissfully unaware of what would soon befall the castle. Would the duke give them all fair warning or only his daughters? It wasn't right for the castle to wake in the middle of the night to whinnying horses and war cries, but to warn them early might create panic.

Penn could barely remember serving her food. Even though Heather sat beside her, she felt so far away. It was otherworldly. Her movements were not her own, and there was a fog before her that dampened all sound. So, she breathed and looked at Lovetta. The duke had yet to come to the dining hall, and Lovetta's face was huddled close to her elder sisters. Sarra and Dorett were in a conversation of their own, smiling as innocently as young Heather. When the hall began to empty, Penn knew that the duke was not coming. She looked down at her plate, which was empty. Did she eat? She must have. Someone was saying her name, but the sound was distant, somewhere far away.

"Penn?" said the voice a little louder. "Penn!" A shout this time. It was Clare, sitting across the table, looking at her as if she had two heads. "Are you all right?"

The fog started to recede.

"Yes," Penn said, knowing her face said otherwise. She looked down the table, hoping nobody was in earshot. "There's something I should tell you." They waited for the last of their friends to retire for the evening, then Penn explained everything to Clare, from the very first conversation she had overheard in Tirel to the danger they were all in at that very moment. Clare's face cycled through a range of emotions before she made a peep.

"I can't believe it." She was clearly in shock. "I knew the duke was up to something during all those trips to Tirel, but..." She massaged her temple. "I never thought it would be something like this."

"You know, I was expecting this new life to be such a bore, but I ended up really liking it here. I like it more than Theroulde, but for all I know, the castle will be in tatters in a week. Ironic, isn't it?"

Clare looked even more shocked. "Gods, I hope you're wrong. The girls don't even know where they're going. What if they don't see each other again? Why hasn't the duke warned them? It's horrific."

"I suspect he'll have to after tonight," Penn said as she rubbed her forearms. The hall was so much colder once all the bodies dispersed. "I think Lovetta's already told Belsante and Edony, and I doubt Edony will keep quiet about it."

"That's true," Clare said. "She's probably in his study now, waving a flaming torch at his collection of Yasan poetry. I'm surprised we can't hear her shrieking from here." The two laughed half-heartedly but quickly fell into a hopeless silence. The candles were burning out one by one, and Penn wanted to get back to Lovetta. She pulled herself up from the bench and wobbled on her feet.

"What's wrong with your leg? I saw you limp on the way in."

"I had a tumble in the library." She shrugged. "I'm sure I'll be fine tomorrow."

"I wouldn't mind a tumble in the library," Clare joked, and Penn had to bite her tongue. If only she knew.

As they reached the top of the stairs, muffled voices disturbed the usual quiet. Lovetta was in her chambers, sitting by the hearth and looking grim. With her were Belsante and Edony, perched on the side of the bed. Seeing Edony, Clare followed Penn inside.

"Does she know?" Edony asked Penn with an almost hostile look. Penn nodded and closed the door.

"We went to father's study," Lovetta said lazily. "He said ... some things." A goblet was on the table. Lovetta had been drinking. Edony had her own goblet lying empty in her lap.

"What did he say?" Penn asked Belsante, the token sober sister.

"We leave in three days. That includes yourself and Clare," she explained, putting down the parchment.

Relief washed over Penn like the first rainfall of summer. She wasn't leaving Lovetta.

"We go to the Saraq's. Lord Carignan has been in contact with Lord Master Yusufhan and some rather questionable types who have kindly provided us with the provisions we'll need to get away."

"Get away to where?" Penn asked.

Belsante continued as if she hadn't heard her. "Once we've arrived, we'll be given our papers and will familiarise ourselves with our new names. Our stories. That is where we'll say goodbye to each other, setting off in groups of three or four to avoid suspicion."

"But *where* are we setting off too?" Penn asked again.

Lovetta snatched her goblet from the table and raised it to the ceiling. "To *Azor!*" she shouted, taking a great gulp and dropping the brass to the ground.

*Azor?* She thought they might relocate a few villages south or try their luck north of the Vastal Headlands. Azor was half a world away!

"I can't go to Azor," Clare said just loud enough for Penn to hear.

"But my family ... and it'll take weeks!" Penn fumbled for words.

"Longer," Edony drawled. "Can't sail around Tirel because it's not safe." She yawned. "We have to ride to Mirs, sail from there to Port Sollers, then ride from Orlebar through Raynor and hope to pass the wall without too much of a fuss."

Penn was speechless. The journey could take months.

"And then we have to get to the capital, Zutar." Edony hiccupped. "That's where we'll need our papers. They don't like foreigners in the city."

"Can't we just ... hide out in the Orange Isles or something?" Clare asked, her tone about as confident as a mouse. All three Bondevilles shook their heads.

"I second that. My mother was from the Orange Isles. I hear it's quite nice," Penn stammered. "Excellent citrus."

"Anywhere the Vastalian Crown touches won't be safe," Belsante said.

"Why?" Clare battled. "Surely the prince won't really come after us."

"You're right; he won't come after *you*," Lovetta said with a cruel look. "Not with that lovely white skin of yours."

Edony and Belsante turned to Lovetta as if to say something, but Clare beat them to it. "What does that have to do with anything?"

"This war isn't about catching Vastalians; it's about catching people like us," Lovetta said.

Clare crossed her arms defensively. "You honestly think this is going to come to war?"

"Is it really worth the chance?" Lovetta rebutted.

"If the king dies before our father changes the line of succession, every Azorian man, woman and child will be slaughtered on sight," Edony contributed. "Prince Julien hates our family not only because we have Azorian blood, but because our father knows more about him and his dirty deeds than he'd like. The prince is looking for an excuse to go to war with Azor. I don't know why. Maybe he skipped his history lessons as a child. But he'll do anything to keep our blood out of his precious country."

"Well, if it's only you who are in danger, why are *we* coming with you?" Clare tipped her head towards Penn.

Penn exhaled. "The prince will think we know their where-abouts. He might torture us for information or use us as hostages. He knows how kind-hearted Duke Wymark is." She hadn't given the possibility much thought until then. "We'd become bait."

"Right," Clare squeaked. "But there are so many in the castle. How can we all flee unnoticed?"

"You won't all be," Belsante said impatiently. "Only our maids and the few Azorians. Nobody knows the names of the others in the castle."

Penn stiffened. "What about Heather and Jinny? They're *children*. Where will they go?" She looked to Lovetta for backup, needing her to be as outraged as she was, but her head had fallen on an unusual angle. The wine had put her to sleep.

"Jinny's from Urry," Clare said. "There's no sense in her riding across the country when her old home is only a few days south. She's resourceful. She'll find work."

"And Heather? Should we send her back to the capital, back to her pile of rubble right in the middle of winter?"

"I don't know about Heather," Belsante admitted, getting up from the bed. "I'm sure she'll be okay on her own. She was before she met us."

Penn raised her voice. "*Okay* isn't good enough. She has nothing and no one! We can't just abandon her—"

"Okay, okay!" Belsante said as she approached the door. "I'll talk to father and see what we can do."

Penn's panic lessened, but her heart still beat strong in her chest. "Thank you," she croaked.

"It's fine," Belsante said. "We should all get to bed. Sleep off some of this stress … and wine," she added, glaring at the semi-conscious Lovetta before taking her leave. Edony followed with Clare in tow, leaving Penn to rouse Lovetta and ready her for bed. She prodded her awake and helped her undress, setting her on her bed in her underclothes. It wasn't the first time she had dealt with the aftermath of her drunkenness, and it likely wouldn't be the last. With Lovetta in a deep sleep, Penn limped around the room to tidy up.

When the goblets were wiped clean and the candles extinguished, Penn sat on the end of her bed and looked at her trunk. She was going to spend the next few months on horseback, so she would need to pack light. That should be easy; she already wore the same thing every day, save for the days her clothes needed a wash. Her mind too frenzied to sleep, Penn rummaged through her trunk and packed her few essential and sentimental possessions into a bag she could tie to her back. When her head finally hit the pillow, a crackling sound jostled her. It was her letters from Maybelle, Florent, and her father. Without hesitating, Penn rolled them tight and stashed them safely in her bag. She would not lose them.

Sleep evaded her for an hour or so, coaxing her to pick up the book on Shakalha and read pages at random. She inhaled the words, but nothing seemed to stick. Soon the very last light by her bed burnt out, and she was forced to close her eyes. For a while she tossed and turned, too anxious about the days ahead to settle. Eventually, she decided that her pursuit of sleep was pointless, and she got up. She walked aimlessly through the castle, shivers rippling her flesh as she squinted through the darkness and her knee protested.

Whether Penn had meant to or not, she ended up in the bathhouse. It was completely empty, the water as black as the night sky and billowing steam. The smell of lavender drew her in, and she spent a long time soaking in the scented pool, thawing out her limbs and letting the air sear her nostrils. Her line of thought flung from one thing to another, lingering on Lovetta each time she appeared in her mind's eye. Only days ago, she had pushed thoughts of Lovetta away, but thoughts of her, of them, now begged for Penn's attention. Alone here in the pool, there was so much to think about as she drifted in the hot water, recalling the long day as if it had all been a strange dream.

Penn closed her eyes and replayed that evening's kiss with Lovetta, imagining what might have happened if Heather hadn't interrupted. Lovetta had pulled herself closer, and Penn's hand had brushed her thigh. What would she have done? What would Lovetta have done? What *did* women do to please each other? There were so many possibilities to imagine, and Penn was soon drunk on a wine of her own making. She had wanted Lovetta's hand on her waist so badly, the memory of it sliding underneath the hem of her blouse making her twitch in pleasure.

The heat of the water combined with Penn's racing pulse urged her to the surface sooner than she would have liked. After pulling herself from the pool, her leg felt a little better, but she only wanted Lovetta even more. She dried off and dressed quickly, the cool air in the changing bay tickling her skin. Lovetta was still asleep when Penn returned to their chambers, and a thought occurred to her. For a moment, she stood in silence, caught halfway between Lovetta and her own empty bed. She hesitated and then chose Lovetta.

# Eighteen

Early the following morning, Penn woke with her fingers laced through Lovetta's. She remembered waking in the middle of the night from a frightful dream, but she couldn't picture what it was. Something with scraping, grinding, and the colour red. All she knew was that Lovetta had soothed her, and her sleep had been peaceful since.

With sleep-crusted eyes, Penn rolled out of the four-poster. The air was bitter, and the stone cold on her feet. Archery practice was due to start at first light, but Lovetta did not look as if she intended to wake.

Penn dressed, tucked her hair behind her ears, and approached her sleeping companion. "You should probably get up," she whispered, stroking Lovetta's cheek with her finger.

A groan escaped Lovetta's mouth, and she rolled over, a moment later sitting bolt upright. "What's happening?" she asked, rubbing her eyes vigorously. "Is he here? Is it time?"

"No. It's dawn, and you're supposed to be teaching. Archery practice starts today, remember?"

Lovetta grumbled again and dropped back to her pillow. "It's too early, Penn. Come back to bed and hold me," she whined.

"I'd love to, but I don't fancy being walked in on again, which *will* happen if you stand up your sisters." When Lovetta didn't respond, she took her by the shoulders and shook. "Get *up!*"

"Okay, okay!" she whimpered, shaking Penn off. "Gods, my life is awful."

"Yes," Penn said sarcastically as she walked toward the door, her leg sturdier than the day before. "Absolutely horrific. Can't imagine anything worse. Now get dressed. I'm going to the armoury."

"You're not going to wait for me?" Lovetta pouted, finally pulling herself out of bed.

"We're already late, and you're capable of dressing yourself." Penn limped out of the room. When she closed the door behind her, she smiled. The previous day had made her bold. She knew Lovetta wanted her around for her company, not her service. She had found her equal, even if the world didn't see them in the same light as she did. When Penn walked through the castle, she felt lighter than air.

The armoury was beneath the ground floor, not far from the bathhouse. Penn had only been inside the alcove twice before, once to feast her eyes on the duke's iron goods (which to her dismay had been locked out of sight), and once to collect an extra quiver of arrows for Jehane, the second greatest archer of the house.

The room was an eternal winter and smelt faintly of rust, little light filtering through the gaps at the head of the walls. The Bondeville's longbows were wrapped in cloth, hanging on the wall in a line. Penn took them down and fetched a mangy-looking practice bow for herself. It was much smaller and, by the look of it, hadn't been used in years. Before leaving, she tossed four quivers over her shoulder and snatched a handful of strings. Dorett and Sarra were making their way across the clearing when Penn emerged brandishing their equipment.

"Lovetta's running a little late," she said, handing the girls their belongings.

Sarra, the youngest of the Bondeville siblings, was barely taller than her bow. "If Lovetta's not here, can we go? It's cold, and I don't even like archery."

Dorett didn't look overly impressed at being up at dawn either. Penn wondered who exactly the duke was trying to punish when he'd suggested the activity.

"Look," Penn said, pointing across the clearing at a familiar silhouette. "There she is. Now you *have* to stay," she teased.

Dorett and Sarra groaned.

"Why do you two look so miserable?" Lovetta asked as she caught up to the group, her scarlet tunic a sight for sore eyes. She was breathtaking in bold colours.

"It's freezing!" Dorett exclaimed, rubbing her forearms. "Why do I have to be here? My archery is fine!"

Lovetta collected her bow from Penn and strung it tight. "According to father, you both need to work on your technique. You might not like it now, but I'm sure you'll thank him when you're older."

"Fat chance," Sarra snorted as she shivered.

"Oh, cheer up," Lovetta said. "You're young, and you don't have any real problems. Not yet anyway."

Penn smiled grimly as she strung her bow, envying Sarra and Dorett's ignorance.

"You know my knees get bad in the cold," Dorett said.

"If you want to warm up, run three laps of the field," Lovetta suggested.

"Run?" Dorett said incredulously. "That's not fair!"

"Neither is father forcing me to teach you a skill you don't care about." Lovetta poked her tongue out at her younger sisters. "Now, enough nonsense. Get in position," she demanded, evidently eager to be done with the session.

Penn took her bow and quiver and stood in line with the younger Bondevilles. There were no obnoxious targets nestled in the tree line at the end of the clearing, which meant Penn's failures would be less obvious. The two Bondevilles took suave stances and Penn tried to emulate them.

As Lovetta inspected the line, she frowned at Penn. "What are you doing with your elbow?" she asked, her eyes narrow.

Penn looked at her bow arm. "I don't know. What *am* I doing with my elbow?"

"I'm not really sure, but it's wrong," Lovetta said, moving closer. Penn was frustrated already. "Oh, you've rotated it the wrong way," Lovetta confirmed as she placed her hands on Penn's arm. "You need to hold it like this." She shifted the position of Penn's forearm an inch.

"Right," said Penn. "Got it."

"Now, your feet. Move your left leg back a bit." Penn dragged her injured leg back two inches with a grunt and Lovetta sighed. "You really shouldn't be on it if it's still sore."

"It's not sore," Penn lied. "Is this position better?"

Lovetta stood back and scrutinised her. "Your hips aren't quite right," she said as she walked in front of Penn. "Bring them closer to me." She jolted them forward. "Too far."

Penn was about to throw down her bow and leave. Surely a shift in positioning couldn't make that much of a difference.

Lovetta moved close behind her and put her hands on Penn's hips, pulling them gently towards her. Her backside hit Lovetta's pelvis, and she lost the grip on her bow. It thumped to the ground. Penn coughed, retrieved her bow and straightened up.

"You were saying?" She hoped her face wasn't as red as it felt.

Lovetta repositioned her hips, then stood back. "Much better. Now get ready to draw," Lovetta said with a smile that rivalled Penn's own.

Penn nocked the arrow as best she knew how and began to pull the string back. The tension was excruciating.

"Not yet!" called Lovetta. "Unless you want your arm to fall off. Wait for my command."

Penn softened her arm with relief. Even her beginner's bow was weighted too heavily for her. She looked at skinny Dorett and Sarra who was just a child. Their bows were hulking, malevolent looking things that gleamed in the light. How could they have enough strength to draw, but Penn, a grown woman, couldn't?

Lovetta talked her through the drawing process as the younger Bondevilles yawned and fidgeted. Her inexperience was shameful, and she felt guilty that the others had to tolerate her presence. Without her, the practice would be over in a heartbeat. Eventually, Penn loosed her first arrow. It shot a few yards ahead and thudded weakly to the ground. Lovetta's shot hit a trunk at the edge of the clearing, and she instructed her sisters to aim for a foot below it.

Dorett came close to the mark, but Sarra's arrow missed the trunk by a hair's length, soaring silently though the tree line. Over the hour, the sisters improved their accuracy, and Penn gained slightly more control over the bow. It was clear that Dorett and Sarra were already decent archers, but Penn, however, was useless. By the end of the session, the grass was studded with her failing arrows, and her fingers were red and raw from handling the string.

"I'm impressed," Lovetta panted, having returned from the tree line with arrows in hand. Dorett and Sarra had escaped the moment practice came to an end.

Penn rolled her eyes. "Don't lie. I'm terrible at it." She unwound the string from her bow and coiled it around her hand.

"You can't expect to be wonderful on your first try," Lovetta said, noticing Penn's blisters. "That looks nasty. I should have warned you."

"Your hands are fine," Penn noted glumly. "And I bet *you* were wonderful on your first try."

"Don't be ridiculous. The only reason I'm as good as I am is because I've practically been doing this since I could walk. And look." She held out her hand. Between two fingers, a slight swelling had appeared. "I should have worn my glove. Any longer and my fingers would be as bad as yours."

Again, Penn noticed the faint scarring on the hand that had flown through Lovetta's mirror and remembered the duke's words in Tirel. Penn wasn't the only one who had grown through their friendship. Somehow, she had changed Lovetta.

"I've never told you about those, have I?" Lovetta said softly.

"No, you haven't. You don't have to, either." Penn took Lovetta's hand and kissed her scars lightly.

Lovetta laced her fingers with Penn's. "It's okay. After Hazir proposed, I hurt myself."

"Why?" Penn whispered.

"I don't know. Everything was wrong, or that's how it felt, at least. I knew he would ask me, and I needed him to, but I didn't really want it. I didn't want him. I felt awful, and I didn't know what to do. I was so alone. I wanted an escape."

Penn looked into Lovetta's eyes, and they were filled with sadness. "Do you still feel like that?"

Lovetta nodded slowly. "Sometimes, but not like I did then. It scares me to think about it, but then I was so ready. I could have escaped in my own way. Now, the thought terrifies me. *Death* terrifies me. I think it's because I'm not alone anymore."

Penn smiled with tears in her eyes. "You'll never be alone again." She leaned in and kissed her, twining her fingers through Lovetta's hair and breathing in her scent. The heat returned, and Lovetta's fingers found the skin beneath her blouse. Penn gasped at her touch, then pulled her closer.

Lovetta broke the kiss. "Maybe we should—"

"No, I don't want to stop," Penn groaned.

Lovetta giggled. "I was going to say that maybe we should move over there." She tipped her head to the tree line.

"That's a magnificent idea," whispered Penn. Abandoning their weapons and the open field, the two ran hand in hand into the woods.

Lovetta pushed Penn against the trunk of a tree. "This will do nicely."

Penn pulled Lovetta's hips into hers. "How long do you think we have?"

"Oh, I'm in no rush. No one will find us here."

"We might get arrows in our backs," Penn said.

"They'll be worth it." Lovetta pulled up the hem of Penn's blouse and trailed her fingers up her spine. The goosebumps were instantaneous.

"How do you do that?" Penn cooed.

Lovetta smiled wickedly. "Do what?"

"Light my body on fire every time you touch me." Penn fumbled with Lovetta's tunic, reaching for the hem.

Lovetta whispered close to Penn's ear. "Imagine what it was like for me, all those times you slowly unlaced my gowns and ran your fingers through my hair. It's only fair that I get a turn." Lovetta found the ties beneath Penn's bosom and took them in her teeth, then pulled. Her blouse loosened, and Penn's legs wobbled.

Lovetta abruptly straightened up. "Is your knee okay?"

"My knee? Oh, I forgot about that."

"How convenient," Lovetta said with a cocked brow. "In that case..." Lovetta pulled off Penn's blouse and fumbled for the button on Penn's breeches.

A bolt of anxiety hit Penn, and she stilled Lovetta's hand. "I'm a virgin too."

"I assumed." Lovetta shrugged, then put her lips to Penn's neck.

Penn started to laugh. "I don't know what I'm doing."

"Neither do I," Lovetta said against her neck, then pulled away. "I can stop."

"That's completely unnecessary," Penn said as she hiked Lovetta's tunic up over her bosom.

"You sure do want your marriage to work, don't you, lady?" came a voice that tore Penn and Lovetta apart. "Ma always said practice makes perfect, I 'spose."

Heather stood before them with a frog in her hands, and the look that Lovetta cast her had enough power to kill a man. Penn simply stood there, topless and mortified, while Lovetta pulled down her tunic.

"*What* are you doing out here?" Lovetta said through her teeth.

"Gardenin'. That's my job," Heather said, looking Penn up and down. "Whaddya call this?" She held out the slimy creature for them to see, and Lovetta stepped behind Penn.

"That's a frog, Heather. Put it back where you found it," Penn said as she shrugged back into her blouse.

Heather sighed. "You're no fun." She didn't move.

"Now, Heather," Lovetta ordered.

"Yes, lady," Heather said, and she bounced away, frog in hand. Penn relaxed, then looked at Lovetta with a half-smile.

"Don't look at me like that. You brought her here, remember?" Lovetta said, crossing her arms.

Penn laughed. "She's harmless." She slid her hands around Lovetta's waist and pulled her in.

"No, Penn! Now all I can think about is frogs. They're disgusting," she groaned.

"All right, let's head back," Penn said, a little disappointed. "Unless you want to shoot another round?"

"Not until you're properly geared up," Lovetta said. They set off to collect their bows and quivers.

"There's no point. I'll probably break my arm the next time we practice."

"Gods, Penn. I didn't think you were one to give up so easily." Lovetta laughed. "You'll never accomplish anything if you don't put some hard work in."

"No amount of hard work will get me anywhere near your level. Damnit, why are you so good at everything?"

"I'm not. You see what you want to see. Everyone has faults." Lovetta stopped and lifted Penn's chin. "But if you really want to stop, that's okay. It means less work for me." She smiled. "Besides, we have more important things to worry about. We're leaving in two days. Trying to learn anything while you're stressed is impossible."

Penn looked at her raw hand, then closed her fist over her wounds. "Maybe. But I don't want to stop. I'm just being a sook," she admitted.

Lovetta shrugged. "I know."

"Then why did you ask?"

"I wanted to hear you admit it." Lovetta grinned. "Get yourself a glove and an armguard from the marketplace, and we'll practice again tomorrow."

That afternoon, Penn set out with her coin purse to do just that. Despite her poor performance, Lovetta's words had motivated her. She had spent her whole life telling herself she couldn't do things

262 | S. R. HOYER

because she was a woman when, in reality, the only difference between her and her brothers was that they could practice free from
judgement. If her father had never remarried, and if her mother
was still alive, perhaps she would already know how to wield a bow.
If she worked hard at archery, she could be good, too. Besides, the
kingdoms could be at war in a few weeks. It was only sensible to
find another way of defending herself if the worst were to happen.

The marketplace in Rocque was a happy place. It was so easy to
peruse the lines of stalls sampling goods and making small talk, and
she wished Lovetta had joined her. The smell of sun-ripened fruit
lingered in the air, making Penn's stomach rumble and drawing her
toward the fruit merchant. A half-filled crate of peaches sat on the
table, fruit flies buzzing overhead.

"How much?" she asked a white-bearded man with a cowbell
in hand.

"Two a coin, Miss!" he bellowed, ringing the bell with vigour.

"But I only want one." A villager nudged her in the back. The
crowd was suffocating.

"Sorry, Miss, twos and fives only," he hollered over the ruckus.
"Gotta clear the crate before nightfall, and that sun is starting to
set." In disappointment, Penn tucked her coin purse back into her
pocket and a second nudge jolted her forward.

"Watch it!" she shouted as she spun around. But the person
before her was no villager; it was Osenna, and Penn's body instantly
tensed.

The thickset Azorian raised an eyebrow. "A servant has no use
for a sharp tongue."

"Forgive me, Mistress Osenna." Penn bowed her head.

Osenna's nostrils flared. "I hope you're not off castle grounds to
make trouble. *Again.*"

"Absolutely not. I've come on Lady Lovetta's orders." Penn smiled nervously. "Her perfectly honourable orders," she clarified.

"Of course," Osenna said as she scrutinised Penn. "Those breeches..." Penn prepared herself for a scolding, "look like they were made in a barn, and the fit is all wrong. Does the good duke not pay enough for you to visit a tailor?"

The tension in Penn's body eased. "You're right, the duke is a very generous man. I will do just that. Thank you, Mistress Osenna."

"Gunther keeps fabric aside in the house colours, and his workmanship is far superior to Opal and Rose. Don't waste your coin there."

"Thank you, Mistress Osenna," Penn repeated, a little shocked by Osenna's hospitality. "I'll be going now."

"What about your peaches? I'll have one."

"Sorry?"

Osenna's nostrils whistled. "Mathematics, child. Peaches are two a coin, and you now have two people who want one. Your problem is solved." She smiled mockingly. "You can show your thanks by paying."

"Oh," Penn said, feeling hot. "Of course. Excuse me!" She shouted to the merchant. "I'll take two!"

"Wise choice," he said as he put down the cowbell. Penn retrieved her purse and extracted a single silver, handing it to the merchant's assistant as he wiped the peaches clean.

"Fresh as from the tree." He flashed half a mouth of rotting teeth. Penn thanked him and handed Osenna the larger of the fruits.

For the first time in history, Osenna smiled at her. "You're all right."

Not in Penn's wildest dreams had she ever expected praise from the stern housekeeper. They backed out of the crowd, and Penn bowed her head, still in shock. "If you'll excuse me, Mistress Osenna."

Penn sidled into the crowd on the opposite side of the path and headed for the tanner, peach in hand. She looked it over carefully, sceptical after Marion's prank, then took a small bite. It was as ripe and delicious as it ought to be. With a satisfied smile, Penn chewed and wandered until the flesh was gone, and the tanner was in sight.

"Lady of her Grace!" came a powerful voice as she entered the shop. The bald and burly merchant known as Jon emerged from behind the counter, a pot of oil in hand. "What can I do for you, sweetness?" He towered overhead with a beam. He was a kind man.

Penn smiled at him. "I've decided to take up archery, and I've been instructed to purchase an armguard."

The tanner looked at her with excitement. "Certainly, my lady!" He moved closer and withdrew his hand from the pocket of his apron. "If I may?" Penn held out her arm and let the tanner inspect it. He moved his fingertips along her forearm, evaluating its size and shape, turning her wrist this way and that. "Small," he commented. "But I think I have just the thing." He winked.

He disappeared behind the dusty countertop and rummaged through his goods with several clanks and bangs. A moment later, he reappeared with a piece of black leather and handed it to Penn to feel. The underside was soft on her skin.

"It'll wick away sweat and water, and it's reinforced. Makes a good light armour, actually, not that you'll be doing much fighting around these parts." He chuckled.

"You never know," Penn mused. "I wouldn't mind a bit of protection. Just in case." She looked over the guard admirably. The hand piece was patterned with tiny silver studs in the shape of a bounding rabbit. "Sir!" she exclaimed. "It's my house crest! How did you know?"

"Your brother, actually. He passed through not long ago on his way to Tirel. I made them for him, but they were just shy of a good fit."

"I can't believe it. Wait." She paused. "You said *them*. What else did you make him?"

"Oh, there are two." He moved to the counter, withdrew a second armguard, and handed it to Penn.

"Brilliant," she said, feeling the strong exterior.

"Give them a try, then!"

Penn held her forearms out, and one by one, the tanner turned over the undersides of her arms and slid the sheets of leather beneath them. They laced together with black cord through metal rings, sitting snug just where they ought to.

Penn waved her arms before her to get a good feel. The guards followed the curve of her forearms perfectly, moving with her joints without chafing or sliding. She surveyed the silver rabbit design with pride. The only things women carried brandishing crests were brooches and hairpins. This was *so* much better.

"I love them, Jon. They're perfect." Her cheeks ached from smiling.

"Ingrid will set you up with a nice pair of gloves to match, if you like." He wrapped her purchase in cloth, and she thanked him more times than she could count, tipping him five silvers before leaving the shop.

"Lady Prestcote!" he called after her. "I almost forgot. Would you kindly tell Miss Jehane that her boots will be ready tomorrow morning?"

"Certainly, Jon!" Penn waved from the path then tucked her purchase under her arm and set off to see Ingrid, the village glover. She was an enigmatic woman who wore far too many jewels and looked surprised no matter what the situation.

Penn pushed through the door to a metallic dinging and breathed in the heady aroma. The store was full of dangling, delicate ornaments and accessories, gloves occupying only a third of the room.

Penn browsed the wares as Ingrid flitted about the back room, humming to herself. Specialty gloves sat on a counter at the back, propped up by wooden wedges and separated by price markers.

One pair of gloves stood out above all others. They were black, three-fingered, and wrapped around the wrist with a thick strap, fastened by two silver buckles. They were simple but matched the armguards perfectly. The price marker read one gold aur, which was *a lot*, but with her wage, she could afford it.

Penn tried the pair on and, when she was satisfied with the fit, took them to the counter. Something silver caught her eye as she rang the bell. Nestled on the counter in a pile was a glistening locket. Just like the brooch Penn had bought Heather, it was tarnished and engraved with the shape of a fox.

"How much for this?" she asked, picking up the locket inquisitively. Heather's life was about to be upturned again; a treat would do her good.

"That old thing?" Ingrid murmured whimsically as she wrapped Penn's gloves. "You can have it for ten silvers. It's real; I promise you that."

"I'll take it," Penn said as she tossed the locket into the glover's hands. Her day was becoming an expensive one; the tailor would have to wait.

Penn left the marketplace to a backdrop of setting sun, her spirits high. The days ahead would be challenging, but she would have Lovetta by her side and Heather under her wing. They would hide out for a few months, and when the threat of war dissolved, they would come home to a perfectly undisturbed castle. Perhaps they could do some sightseeing while they were away.

By the time Penn reached the castle, the sky was dark and the air still. It was quieter than usual. Penn walked up to the gate to find it closed, guarded by four heavily armoured men who she recognised, but didn't know by name.

"State your business," one man grumbled through an iron helm.

Penn hesitated. The men-at-arms never wore helms on castle grounds.

"She's one of the maids, Kalum. Let her in." The men clanked about and opened the gate. "Quickly, my lady," said another, ushering her inside and resealing the gate.

Penn narrowed her eyes and advanced on the castle. The duke had tightened their security rather soon.

Neighs and nickering broke the silence as Penn approached the stables. Who would be saddling up so late? It wasn't safe to ride at night at the best of times. Changing her course, Penn ambled into the barn. A troop of stable hands were talking as they saddled several horses, Primula included.

"What are you doing?" she said as she caressed the side of Primula's face.

One of the stable hands snapped her head around with a frightful look. "You best get inside, my lady. It's not safe out. I'll have her ready for you."

At that, Penn knew something was wrong. She hurried to the castle as quickly as her leg permitted. It was beginning to throb, but the pain was bearable. Barging through the castle doors, she found an empty foyer and her stomach dropped. The candles had been doused, and an unnatural silence hung in the halls. Where was everyone?

"Lovetta?" she called to no response. "Anyone? Hello?" But only her voice bounced back. Penn's throat tightened, and her body tensed. It was suppertime—everyone should be downstairs. She rushed through the ground floor of the castle in search of another soul, *any* other soul, but found no one. Her trip to the marketplace had only taken an hour or so. What had happened in her absence?

Lovetta's chambers were empty, and as she checked the rest of the bedrooms, she started to panic. They were gone. They were all gone. As a last resort, she climbed to the fourth floor, her leg protesting at each step.

"Duke Wymark?" she called, panting as she hobbled to his study. "Duke Wymark!" she called again. "Where is everyone?"

A familiar figure appeared in the doorway, and Penn breathed a sigh of relief. "Theo! What's going on?"

His face was paler than usual, and his hands trembled. When he spoke, his voice shook. "You should be underground with the others."

"Why?" she demanded. "Is he here? Is the prince coming?" she stammered, following Theo back down the stairs. There were three possible reasons the others could be underground, and Penn doubted they were all having a bath or a drink in the cellar, which meant they were in the armoury—the safest part of the castle.

"The plan has changed," Theo said as he clattered down the stairs. The prince's forces are on their way. I saw them when I left this afternoon and came back to warn Wymark."

"We're leaving now? Tonight?" she asked, her breath ragged and leg throbbing as she tried to keep up with him.

"Yes, if it isn't too late already!" His voice was booming in the deadened castle. "He's accusing Wymark of treason, and he has no sympathy for little girls, so you best hurry!"

Penn paused on the stairs, her knee buckling. Her bag was in Lovetta's room, and she couldn't leave without it. "I need to get my things." She made for the third-floor landing and raced to Lovetta's chambers, Theo calling after her. She ran through the pain, and when she got to the room, she had never been more grateful for her pre-planning. Her readied bag sat open by her bedside. She stuffed her purchases in and cinched the fox locket around her neck.

As she threw on her travelling cloak, Penn surveyed the room. Was there anything else she might need? She was bound to have forgotten something, but there was no time. Her foot tapped instinctively. *Yes*, there was something else. Penn ran back to her bed and withdrew the two books from beside her pillow. The codes she cracked might not be her last, and the history book might come in handy. If only they weren't so damned heavy.

Penn darted from the room and leapt down the stairs, terrified she might have kept the riding party waiting. Theo had sped ahead, and when Penn reached the underground, she found Lovetta's sisters in the armoury, hoods up and longbows in hand. Lovetta wasn't with them.

"Where is she?" Penn panicked as she found Clare. "Where is she?" she repeated, her eyes wild.

"Looking for you," Clare said calmly.

Heather broke through the crowd and clung on to Penn's thigh. They both wore heavy cloaks like Penn and were unarmed. "Where did you go?" Heather demanded. "We were worried!"

"I was just at the market, but I ... I didn't see her. Why isn't she back? Something could have happened to her ... and Osenna. She was at the market too!" Penn felt suddenly hot.

Edony spotted her in the doorway and strode forward. "Oh, good. She found you. Now we can—"

"No, she didn't," Penn interrupted. "I never saw Lovetta. We have to find her and Osenna!"

"I'm touched," Osenna broke through the bodies and tipped her head in Penn's direction.

"Thank the gods," Penn said. "But Lovetta's still out there. We have to go!" She panted as she bolted from the cellar. Clare, Heather,

Edony and Belsante chased after her, and despite the pain, Penn moved faster than she ever had in her life.

The search party raced from the underground through the servant's passageway and up to the ground floor—the fastest way out of the castle. As they moved, Penn's mind tortured her. Every possibility of Lovetta's whereabouts that came to mind terrified her, and she blamed herself for putting her in a precarious position. Why did she have to go to the marketplace that afternoon? Why didn't she predict that something like this might happen?

With every leap, she cursed herself. The group raced up the hall to their own chorus of foot-clattering and gasps, desperate to reach Lovetta before the prince's forces arrived. As the foyer came into sight, the front doors swung open. Nobody slowed as a silhouette emerged from the darkness and clambered into the castle. Penn kept running, vowing only to stop when she found Lovetta.

"Penn!" the new arrival called. There was no mistaking that voice. Penn slowed, her lungs burning from exertion, as the figure came into focus. Lovetta stood before her, flushed and panting with her longbow in hand and a quiver across her shoulder. The bow clattered to the floor and the two embraced, Penn silent as she found the nook of Lovetta's neck.

"You're okay," they exhaled at the same time.

Lovetta took Penn's face in her hands and brushed her forehead with her lips. "We need to go now," she said firmly, looking over Penn's shoulder at her sisters. "They're here."

# Nineteen

"They're here now?" echoed Edony, wiping the sweat from her forehead. Nobody questioned the embrace after Lovetta's harrowing news.

"We should be long gone," Belsante said. "Get to the stables. I'll fetch the others," she ordered, sprinting back down the hallway.

"Heather, you should go with her," Edony said, patting her on the shoulder affectionately.

Penn's insides twisted, and she pulled the wide-eyed girl out of Edony's reach. She wasn't ready to say goodbye.

"Father will keep her safe; you don't have to worry," Lovetta cooed.

A tear escaped the corner of Penn's eye and trickled down her cheek. *No.* This wasn't how it was supposed to be. If they only had a few more days, Belsante and the duke could have found a way to include Heather in their plan. They could have forged more papers or found some other way to sneak her into Zutar. The duke's goodwill wasn't enough. Penn had to protect Heather herself. She was her responsibility.

Edony took Heather's hand and tried to pry it from Penn's blouse but failed.

"No, I won't stay!" Heather squealed, pressing closer to Penn. More tears fell from Penn's cheeks.

"Edony," Penn croaked, "please." She looked at the Bondeville in-charge pleadingly. There had to be a way to make this work.

"We don't have time for this!" Edony said with a look of distress. She put her hands to her face and fell silent for a moment, shaking her head as she thought. "Fine. Bring her. We can't stop you."

There was no time to rejoice. Penn took Heather by the hand and the group surged forward, a current of clanging and war cries assaulting their ears as they crossed the threshold. Penn couldn't see anything from within the inner walls, but she pictured the duke's men-at-arms stationed outside the gate in a long line around the perimeter, furious and waiting for the command to strike. She prayed they were all as loyal to the duke as Roderick and Sir Ulrich.

For a second, Penn's naivety got the best of her. She slowed, preparing to stop and fight, but her gut warned her against it. Bravery was useless without skill, and no matter how many years she had pelted makeshift swords against trunks, she could not fight. If she dared try, she would likely be slaughtered in a heartbeat. Instead, she sprinted to the stables with the others, refusing to let go of the girl at her side. Heather needed her more than the duke's men.

The horses were ready and waiting when they arrived. Penn took a swig from her flask as Clare disappeared into the hayloft. When she returned, she was wide-eyed and empty-handed.

"They're not here."

"Who isn't?" Penn asked, hoisting Heather into Primula's saddle.

"The kittens!" she shrieked. "What if something happens to them? If the castle is sacked, they could be killed!"

The kittens had been the last thing on Penn's mind. Clare had cared for them since they were born, and she hated to be apart from them for long.

Myrtle, a stable hand, squeezed through the line of horses. "They're fine, Clare. They're in the village," she said with a comforting hand over Clare's.

Clare sighed with relief. "I thank the gods for you every day."

Penn slipped into the saddle behind Heather, surprised by the display of affection.

"Try not to pull out her hair, okay? She won't like it," Penn instructed Heather, who looked up at her with fearful eyes. "Don't worry. I'll hold on to you really tight. You're going to be just fine."

Heather nodded, and Lovetta walked her mare forward and settled beside Primula. Her hand disappeared beneath the hem of her gown and withdrew a cloth-wrapped dagger, which she handed to Penn. "Just in case," she whispered as Penn's fingers laced around the hilt and unfurled the cloth.

Penn looked at the weapon hungrily. The blade was double-edged and in pristine condition. Though the hilt looked old with tarnished filigree, it had probably never been used. "Where were you keeping this?" Penn asked, looking at Lovetta's form-fitting tunic.

"Close." Lovetta winked. "Do you know how to use it?"

"Of course I know how to use it. Stab blindly and pray you don't hit a friend. I just hope I don't have to." She wrapped the dagger, tucked it into her pocket and felt a little more confident about the journey ahead.

"You shouldn't have to," Lovetta said. "I can loose eleven arrows a minute with this." She indicated to her bow. "You'll be safe with me."

Penn looked away, ashamed. "I'm supposed to be protecting you."

"You should know by now that I don't need protecting. She, on the other hand, does." Lovetta nodded to Heather, and Penn tightened her grip around her.

Primula walked forward as the remainder of the Bondevilles made their way into the stable, nervous and panting. Jehane looked deadly in chainmail with a bow in one hand and a sword sheathed at her side. Penn's eyes bulged with envy. A real sword. A *woman* with a real sword.

"Where are Tibby and Thamasin?" Clare asked as her horse grunted and whinnied. No amount of riding had strengthened their bond.

"I couldn't find Tibby," Belsante breathed, throwing herself atop her enormous stallion. "Thamasin wouldn't leave without her, so they're both staying. It can't be helped." She sighed. A moment of silence passed between the women before they left the stables. The sister maids were so close to Dorett and Sarra that their absence would be sorely missed. Penn prayed the duke could keep them hidden, because of all the maids in the Bondeville house, they liked to talk the most.

Belsante led the troupe around the back of the castle to a covert entrance hidden in the overgrowth. It was so densely covered that Penn doubted it had ever been used. With her blade, Jehane sliced at the vines, freeing the gate and ushering the riders into the outer rim of the castle. The space between the inner and outer walls was negligible, and the shouts from outside amplified. They walked ahead, and as they did, a horn sounded from beyond the wall. A cold shiver ran down Penn's spine as a great cheer erupted, signalling the commencement of battle. She looked to Lovetta as the shouting and scraping came together to form one blood-curdling symphony. Her eyes were as wide as Penn's.

Duke Wymark would be out on the battlefield, putting his life on the line for his family and a cause few believed in. His force was not large, but Penn had to put her faith in his men. Even a mediocre knight was worth at least ten good soldiers.

The outer wall of the castle didn't have a back gate as the inner wall did. Instead, it had a weak spot. A white boulder marked the place where stones were packed loosely, disguising a hole big enough for a mount. Penn flung herself from Primula and helped Jehane pull the stones free, replacing them once the group rode through. Beyond the wall was a narrow bank of land, separated from their destination by a dense body of water. Penn had almost forgotten about the moat. How were they supposed to cross when the bridge was at the head of castle, swarming with soldiers? Belsante dismounted and crouched low at the water's edge.

"What are you doing?" Clare whispered.

"There's a marker, like the boulder," Edony explained, craning her neck to check for eavesdroppers. It was so dark they couldn't be sure what lurked beyond the waterline.

"A marker for what?" Clare whispered back, squinting through the shadows.

"There's a shallow strip of the moat," Edony whispered. "The land beneath the water was built up so that we could wade through if we ever needed to escape. Bel's looking for a white rock like the one inside. It should be right here."

The design was clever, but Penn was far from enthusiastic. She did *not* like deep water. Belsante signalled to the group to move forward and mounted her stallion once more. She had found the marker a few yards over, barely visible in the dark.

"I'll go first," Jehane insisted, bringing her mount to the water's edge. "And pray that the land hasn't gone soft."

Penn closed her eyes as Jehane and her horse plunged into the moat with a slight splash. A sigh of relief reverberated through the group, and Penn opened her eyes. The water was level with the horse's hock. Jehane led her mount in a straight line and reached the other side with ease.

One by one, the others followed. When it came to Penn, her hands were clammy on the reigns, and Heather shook in the saddle. It wasn't the shallow strip that made Penn nervous, it was the rest of the moat. One step too far either side meant they were both going under, a thought that chilled Penn to the bone. When Primula dropped onto the strip, Penn held her breath. The others had crossed safely. If she handled the reigns right, everything would be fine. As they crossed, she held the air in her chest, letting go only when Primula's hooves touched dry land. Penn's entire body felt weak.

Clare was the last to cross, and Penn bit her lip and hoped that her mount cooperated. After some coaxing from the others, Clare took the plunge and began her wade. The terror on her face was clear from the waterline, and when she made it across, Penn gripped her shoulder.

"You did it," she whispered, grinning wide. They both did it. Noticeably too shaken to reply, Clare simply nodded.

Quietly, the riders sunk through the tree line and into the woods. It wouldn't be safe to come to a gallop until they were clear of the castle. Penn walked Primula forward, hearing only the intake of Heather's breath, the distant cries of battle, and hooves in the underbrush. Eventually, the land began to slope downward, and their guard steadily dropped as distance wedged between the riders and the castle walls.

The foliage became denser the further they rode. With her head ducked low and her eyes focused on the mounts before her, Penn let the filtering moonlight guide her. She had never been so deep into the woods and didn't much care to revisit them. Every shadow haunted; every noise was a potential danger. Heather shivered beneath her grip, but despite the early winter's air, Penn wasn't cold. Her nerves were ablaze with fear, and she thanked the gods when a thick beam of light broke through the trees in the distance. They were nearing the edge of the woods.

"Ouch!" Clare hissed with a rustle and a snap.

Penn turned to her at once. "Are you okay?" she whispered, coming up beside Clare's mount.

"Just got hit by something. Right in the face."

Penn returned her focus to the underbrush, her senses prickling. She had that feeling, like when something was too close to her nose but not quite touching. Something in the air had changed, and she wasn't the only one to notice it. Was this how her brothers felt when they were on the road? Constantly on edge, flinching at every hoot and crackle?

Belsante signalled for the group to stop, her eyes scanning the shadows. The calls of the wildlife had vanished, and heavy footfalls stole their attention. All at once, a band of soldiers emerged from the trees, whistling and whooping at their discovery. There were half a dozen or more of them loitering in the shadows, swords glinting at their sides. Immediately, the Bondeville's formation tightened and arrows nocked, ready to draw at Belsante's command. Penn pulled Heather close with one hand and withdrew the dagger with the other. Her earlier desire to stay and fight felt more foolish by the second.

"Would ya look at what we got 'ere!" jeered a long-faced man, half-obscured by the shadows. "What's a prim an' proper lot like you doin' out these parts?"

Penn's fingers clamped tighter around the hilt of the dagger, blood rushing in her ears.

Belsante cleared her throat. "There's nothing quite like an evening ride in the forest. The waning moon has a certain magic to it. From your presence, I imagine you think quite the same."

The soldiers skulked in the shadows, evenly distributing themselves around the group. If the exchange managed to end without bloodshed, Penn would dedicate the rest of her life to serving the gods.

"It's a nice story, innit? Moonlit ride for the ladies?" said the frontmost soldier as he advanced on Belsante. Without hesitation, every arrow was drawn and aimed squarely at his chest. "Now, now. No need to be like that, misses! Me an' my men just wanna be friends," he said as his hand flexed toward the hilt of his blade.

Belsante snorted. "What kind of friends?" Her arm was starting to shake from the weight of her drawn bow.

"The kind that don' point arrows at each other," he said threateningly. "So why don' you put that thing down, eh? Because if you don', well ... I can't promise that the rest of me men wanna be 'just friends'. See, they're from a little place off the coast of Mirs. Maybe you've 'eard of it?"

Penn stiffened. There was only one place off the coast of Mirs, and it was a prison reserved for the foulest of mankind. The men before them were not soldiers at all; they were criminals, and they were proud of it.

"I'm thinkin' they might 'ave different intentions, so you'd best be puttin' that down."

"You leave me no choice." Belsante sighed as she lowered her bow.

Penn's jaw dropped. What was she doing?

The leader of the gang kept his hand on his blade and smiled. But nobody else had lowered their weapons.

"You lot 'eard her. Put down your toys!" he snarled.

"Forgive me," Belsante began, "but you never asked my friends to put down their weapons. Only me."

"I'll make myself clearer, then. *Put down your toys!*"

Nobody but Belsante stirred. "See, I don't think that's going to happen." She smiled. "I might be willing to negotiate with you, but they, see, they might have different intentions."

Penn's eyes widened at Belsante's fearlessness. Was she *trying* to get them all killed? The criminals started to jeer, and their leader spat at the feet of Belsante's mount.

She frowned, sniffed, then smiled. "Loose," she commanded, and every woman with a bow sent an arrow sailing in a different direction. There was a great clamour and clattering as the men advanced and the horses panicked. The leader fell dead with an arrow in his throat. Some of the women had dismounted and were fighting the men face to face, but Penn was frozen. As she scanned the crowd for Lovetta, Heather slipped from her grip and out of sight with a squeal. Penn's body went cold.

Heather was gone.

She threw herself from Primula and held her dagger close as she clambered away from the onslaught. The others were locked in a battle of shadows, grunting and parrying as the criminals attacked. Was Heather in the brawl with the others? Penn panicked as she watched Jehane block a blow aimed for Belsante's stallion with a mighty clang. The weapons had collided just inches from Lovetta's hanging leg as she sat astride her horse, loosing arrows at an incredible speed.

Penn's heart urged her to join the fight, but her head told her she needed to find Heather. She looked around wildly, trusting that the Bondevilles could defend themselves. Edony had a dagger to a man's throat with Sarra and Clare mounted between her and Jehane. Dorett took her boot from the stirrup and aimed a kick at another's face, while Belsante loosed arrows from the ground.

Everyone was there except for Heather, her squeals indecipherable from the whinnying horses. Where was she? Why did it have to be so dark? Limbs were flying and heads were bobbing, but there were no bouncing blonde ringlets. If she wasn't in the fray, where had she gone?

Penn started to round the group, keeping low by the underbrush. Her ears pricked at the sound of a scream, and a glisten of silver caught her eye. There Heather was, thrashing in the tree line. The moonlight on her brooch had revealed her. Penn ran toward her as she was dragged into the shrubs, Heather's raw scream piercing the air.

Gripping her dagger with her teeth, Penn dived into the undergrowth, landing on her protesting knee as her fingers flexed around Heather's vanishing ankle. But instead of heaving the child out of the shrubbery, Penn was pulled along with her. She rolled into a clearing and lost her grip on the girl, her side colliding with something solid.

"She's mine!" snarled a helmeted criminal, aiming a foot at Penn's sprawled out body. She rolled too late, and his boot rammed into her ribcage. A *crunch* sent Penn roaring in pain, and the dagger dropped from her mouth. Clutching her side with one hand, she fumbled to find the hilt. Heather whimpered as Penn pulled herself to her feet, staggering from the pain. The two were only yards away, and the man stood over Heather with his back to Penn. She limped over as he held the terrified and wet-faced Heather down, humming a verse in an attempt to subdue her.

"Don't cry, sweetheart. I'll take real good care of you."

Penn stood behind him and watched, bile climbing up her throat as he stroked Heather's cheek. He would not have her. Hatred smouldered within Penn, and devoid of any other option, she ripped the man's head back and dragged the dagger in a deep line beneath his jaw. There was a sickening gurgling as blood spilled from the cut in his neck, and he fell on top of Heather, saturating her in sticky, scarlet ooze.

It took a moment before Penn could comprehend what she had done. Her body swayed. She heard her name being called in the distance. Her mouth was too dry to respond, and she had the overwhelming urge to vomit.

"Over here!" Heather squealed, bringing Penn back to her senses. She surged forward and pulled Heather out from under the seeping body, her fingers numb. Heather locked her arms around Penn's neck, and Penn carried her out of the shrubbery. Lovetta was at the tree line looking at her with horror. They were both drenched in blood, and there was no way to tell whose it was.

"She's fine," Penn panted. "Take her, please," she groaned.

Lovetta detached the shaking child from Penn's side and held her close. The pain in Penn's side was awful, but the fight was over, and that was all that mattered. Looking at the bloody, fallen criminals, she wondered just how many arrows had been Lovetta's.

"What happened to you?" Lovetta fretted.

Penn slumped to the ground, her hands clutching her side protectively. "Kick to the chest." She grimaced. "I think he broke a rib."

Clare rushed over and put her hands on her, inspecting her body for any more injuries. "It's not her blood," she said in relief. "But she's probably right about the rib."

Penn laid back on the dirt and closed her eyes. Just a moment of rest wouldn't hurt.

"Pull up her blouse," Lovetta ordered. "You need to strap her. We have nearly an hour's ride ahead of us, and she's going to be in a lot of pain if we don't."

Hands fumbled with her blouse and tickled her skin.

"She's going to be in a lot of pain even if we do," Clare said as she felt Penn's ribs. "It's bruising already. Penn, you're going to need to sit up. I can't wrap you if you're all slumped over."

"Okay," Penn croaked, pushing herself up with agony. The faces of the others blurred and swayed, and she felt her bustier rip open.

Heather dropped down from Lovetta's arms and knelt at Penn's side, blood clotting in her hair. "You saved me, lady," she squeaked.

Clare started wrapping her chest tight, and she flinched.

"No," Penn grunted with closed eyes. "Your fox saved you. I wouldn't have seen you without it." She felt two small hands grasp her wrist in gratitude. "Is anyone else injured?" Penn asked, her awareness coming back to her.

"Cuts and bruises, mostly," Lovetta said. Penn opened her eyes to see her standing close. "Edony and I took down a few, and Bel shot another right through the eye."

"And the others?" Penn grimaced.

"Jehane got her sword wet," Lovetta said with a straight face.

In that moment, it was hard to believe Penn had ever wished to wield a sword of her own. There was no glory in taking a life.

"Does the last one ... does he need finishing off?" Lovetta pressed, her eyes darting to the clearing.

"No," Penn said, her mouth dry. "No, I cut his throat." Sickness brewed in her stomach and tears began to fall as she thought about what she had done. She had snuffed out his life like he was nothing more than an insect, and it had been easy. "I never even saw his face."

Clare, who had just finished bandaging Penn's chest, caressed her cheek. "It's better that way."

# Twenty

Free of the woods and the threat of capture, the riders were clear to move hard and fast into the night. From the road they saw the castle, but the sea of man and steed was barely visible in the dark. Battle sounds faded as they rode on, rounding the village and passing the great lake. Penn had never travelled further than the lake, the water like a bed of jewels in the moonlight.

Months ago, she might have thought the journey ahead a grand adventure: the stuff of children's stories and tavern songs. Was this what she had wished for all those years in Theroulde, mimicking her father's lunges and parrying with her brothers? Penn had never thought herself so juvenile. With Heather's limbs wrapped around her torso and her face nestled in Penn's chest, Primula powered through the shadows. Penn's splintered ribcage ached under Heather's weight, but she could not deny the girl that small comfort.

It took almost an hour of hard riding before Belsante's stallion came to a trot, signalling for the remainder of the party to slow down. With the lake out of sight and the trees thinning, small villages dotted the horizon. They followed the road through the sleeping settlements until they reached a hilltop manor, guarded by a dozen or so Azorians.

As Belsante approached the gate, she lowered her hood. The men did not stop her; instead, they bowed low to the ground with their right arms extended and their palms facing up as if beckoning for Belsante to come forward. It was a gesture Penn had never seen.

"He's expecting us," Belsante said, showing the men-at-arms something Penn couldn't see.

"You are most welcome here, your Grace," one the guards said. Cleared to enter, the gate opened, and the riding party climbed the hill to the entrance. Penn dismounted with Heather in her arms and tried to set her down, but the girl would not relinquish her hold.

"Will you come to me?" Lovetta asked, touching Heather's face. She nodded, and Lovetta lifted her from Penn's throbbing side.

"Thank you," she whispered, limping forward.

From the outside, the manor looked much like those of the families Penn had lived near as a child. It was made from bricks of light stone and had two floors with pointed rooftops, free of the turrets and towers that had adorned her own homes. The walls were interrupted by arched windows paned with glass, the hallmark of a wealthy family. Vines snaked across the exterior of the manor and crept underneath the front archway, leading the group to a set of doors with a brass knocker that Belsante hastily rapped.

A moment later, the doors opened to reveal a young Vastalian woman dressed in a peculiar fashion. Her tunic was knee-length and bejewelled, patterned in pink and gold. Underneath, she wore breeches just as a bright and shoes too soft to be worn outdoors. A long sash draped over her shoulder elegantly, tasselled at the ends. Her hair was piled high, and her eyes lined with kohl. The stain on her lips was a deep pink, too deep for her light skin, and her finger-nails were coloured red. She bowed low to Belsante and her sisters, just as the men-at-arms had. "Lord Master Yusufhan welcomes you," she said with a stooped head.

"We haven't met," Belsante said with a rare smile. "What is your name?"

"Lianthi, your Grace. I am new to the Lord Master's house." She kept her eyes down. "Please, follow me."

Penn stayed at Lovetta's side as they were led through a warm and musky hallway. The walls were decorated with portraits of Azorian women in varying states of dress, the paintwork glittering in the candlelight. They were provocative but beautiful. Curtains just as colourful as Lianthi's clothes hung over doorframes, and a subtle smoke hovered overhead. At the end of the hallway stood a sitting room, seeping with warm, hazy air. The woody aroma mingled with something more potent that tickled Penn's nostrils. As she stepped inside, her eyes began to sting.

"Oh my," Clare said, a hair's length from her ear. The room was blanketed by a rainbow, and it was magnificent. Candles bundled in bright glass cylinders projected their colours on every surface, flames feeding the warmth of the room. Penn blinked away the stinging in her eyes, hungry to see more. In the centre of the room sat a low table surrounded by cushions, and lounging on one with a smoking pipe was a man a decade or so older than her father. The Azorian's once-black hair sat atop his head in a knot, and his outfit was just as bright as his servant's but of blues and greens. His angular jaw, thick brows and curved nose gave him away as a Saraq. The man was Lord Master Yusufhan Saraq, father of Hazir and Sahin and uncle to Zekeriya. Seeing the new arrivals, Yusufhan dropped his pipe and came to his bare feet. He bowed low to the women, and they bowed back. Penn's attempt was a crippled, clumsy thing.

"Dearest Khojani, you've come at last!" Yusufhan said with a paternal smile. *Khojani.* She'd ask Lovetta what it meant later. The man crossed the room and took each of the Bondeville's faces in his hands, kissing their cheeks softly. To the others, he made a hand gesture which could have been a blessing or a curse, then looked twice at the blood-soaked Heather.

"You have had trouble on the road, I see. Have you any injured?"

"Only one needing treatment," Belsante said. She summoned Penn, who came forward limping.

"Closer, nhijani," Yusufhan said.

Another term she didn't know. Penn took another step forward, wishing she knew just a little Azorii.

"That's better." He smiled. "Now, don't be afraid." The Saraq put his right hand over his left and placed his palm on Penn's forehead, closed his eyes, and hummed for a time. When he stood back, he had a thoughtful look. "You have a cracked rib and a tear in your knee," he murmured.

Penn couldn't hide her astonished expression. How could he have known that from simply placing his hands on her? Was he touched by the gods like the Shakalha supposedly were? Her history book had mentioned many healing gods, but this man couldn't possibly be borrowing their power. The idea was absurd! No, this man was just perceptive. He saw her limp and clutch her side, and he made a lucky guess. That had to be it.

"Lianthi will take care of you," he said.

"Sorry?" Penn said as the servant woman walked toward her.

"You are in pain. You cannot travel this way." Yusufhan touched her face. If any other strange man had done the same, Penn might have slapped him. But Yusufhan looked at her as a father would. He may have been different, but he did not strike her as a threat.

Lianthi led Penn back through the hall and into a room very different from the first. A bed was laid out on the floor, and the air was cleaner. The shelves were packed full of herbs, poultices, cotton, thread and sharp implements that Penn preferred not to think about. It was without doubt a healer's room. "Please take off your top clothes and lay down," Lianthi said as she pulled the curtain.

Penn took off her coat and shoes, hesitated, then removed her blouse and breeches. She settled herself on the bed in only her undershorts, her chest naked if not for Heather's locket and Clare's makeshift bandages. At least the room was warm.

After rummaging through the shelves, Lianthi came to her knees before Penn. Her hands touched her chest, then tore away the bandages in one swift movement. Penn felt vulnerable as Lianthi ran her fingers over her chest, feeling for abnormalities and inspecting her bruises. She took a jar of dark green poultice from the shelf and began to spread it over Penn's bruises with a spatula. It was cool and soothing on her skin, but she couldn't help but wince.

"It will ease the pain. Not completely, but some. I'm not *that* kind of healer," Lianthi said with a smile. What kind of healer did she mean? "You need to be gentle with yourself while your body mends."

Penn nodded, then laid her head flat as Lianthi worked. The thickness of the air could almost send her to sleep. What she would give to lay down for an entire day, dreaming of innocent things and forgetting all about the scraping, shouting, and spilling of blood.

Lianthi used a concoction that smelt of honey on Penn's knee. The sticky substance prickled and warmed her skin like chilli did to the tongue. It was a strange sensation, but she liked it. Once her joint was coated, Penn sat up to be wrapped. Lianthi bandaged her much tighter than Clare, so tight she could barely move. Wherever she was headed next, the ride would not be pleasant.

With a clean tunic and breeches, Penn left the room feeling drunk. The poultices had masked the worst of her pain, but her limp had only worsened, thanks to the bandages. She found the Bondevilles in Yusufhan's sitting room, crowded around a table laden with food. There was no sound, save for the rustle of parchment.

Clare handed Penn a scroll as she lowered herself to the floor. It was slim and neatly scribed with the Crown seal. She unfurled the parchment and started to read, but the document wasn't making sense. It was a letter from the capital about a girl called Adelisa Janyn. She was to attend a school called Mayalri under the guidance of someone called Seyari Tukkai. Penn frowned at the document, then turned to Clare. "What is this?"

"It's your new name. It'll help you get into the city," Clare explained.

Oh. She had to become this woman to enter Zutar.

"Who did you get?" Clare enquired, and Penn showed her papers. "That's the archery school! It's famous. Seyari Tukkai. I guess that's Lovetta. You're going together."

"We're going to archery school?" Penn asked with a hint of excitement. Perhaps becoming somebody else wasn't such a terrible thing. Maybe she really would become the next Arjani.

"Well, no. The duke wants us to hide. These are just formalities. We can't stay in the city if we don't have a legitimate reason for travel."

"But, if we have the papers, what difference does it really make?" Penn asked.

Clare shrugged. "If you'd asked me yesterday, I would have said this whole thing is terribly over the top, but after tonight, well, I don't really know what to think."

Penn surveyed the room. The others were talking amongst themselves now, comparing their papers with snickers or scowls. "What does yours say?" Penn asked as she leant over Clare's letter.

Clare lifted it and read the contents aloud. "Milisent Royce, accompanying Chintya Vanniyan—that's Edony—in proposition of marriage. Boring." She feigned a yawn.

"In proposition of marriage?" Penn asked, taking Clare's paper and rereading it.

"To find a husband," Clare simplified.

"I know what it means, but is it allowed? I thought you had to be married, or at least betrothed." Penn handed back the paper.

"You do unless you have a full-blooded Azorian to give you away," Clare said as she glanced across the room at Edony, who was chewing on a roll with little interest. "That's why Zekeriya is coming with us. He's posing as Edony's cousin, returning home to present her at court and find her a suitable husband. I think it was meant to be Sahin, but he backed out, thank the gods. I don't think I could handle travelling with *that*."

"Do you think he backed out because of her?" She took a pastry from the table and bit into it. She wasn't hungry, but she ought to be.

Clare turned back to Penn. "According to Lord Master Yusufhan, he's staying to fight if need be. But I'm sure Edony had something to do with it."

"Wouldn't it be safer if all of the Saraqs left with us? The prince will be after them, too."

"Lord Master Yusufhan refuses to leave. He sent half of his men to help the duke, and a whole lot of them are Azorian, some of them villagers, too. Besides, he's the village healer. He can't leave his post when he has so many to protect. Belsante was begging him to change his mind earlier, but he wouldn't budge." Clare sighed. "It's awful. He knows that if the castle falls, he's next."

Penn finished her pastry feeling glum. The rest of the Bondevilles were huddled in conversation, Heather still attached to Lovetta's side. Her tunic had been changed and the blood wiped from her cheek; she looked like a little girl again. Penn pulled herself up, crossed the room, and sat on the floor beside the two. Lovetta was in a daze, and Heather's face was nestled into her tunic.

"What's the plan?" she whispered, stroking the back of Heather's head.

Lovetta jolted and straightened herself up. "We're waiting for the Saraqs," she croaked sleepily. "Gods, I wish they would hurry up. I don't want to pass out on my horse."

"Where are they?" Penn asked, rubbing her own eyes for good measure.

"With one of the villagers helping secure their home."

"Who knows how long they'll be. Let's just go."

Lovetta shuffled beside her. "We can't. We need Hazir."

"What do you mean?" Nobody had mentioned anything about the youngest Saraq when discussing their travel plans, and if Sahin was staying, wouldn't his brother do the same?

"He's my doting husband," Lovetta said nonchalantly. Penn froze. "Only on paper, of course. Didn't Clare tell you?"

"That you're playing husband and wife?" Penn recoiled. "No, she didn't."

Lovetta paid no mind to Penn's reaction. "It's all part of the plan. See, we're Lord and Lady Tukkai, and you're our maid. You and I are going to study at Mayalri, the archery school in—"

"*That* part I'm more than okay with. It's the *married to Hazir* part that I'm going to have trouble getting my head around."

Lovetta sighed as Yusufhan's voice boomed through the room.

"Khojanak!" he called with outstretched arms, his eyes on the archway. Zekeriya and Hazir had arrived at the worst time imaginable. "We have waited long. It is time," Ysufhan said, coming to his feet with a groan. The Bondevilles roused themselves and stood, and Heather detached herself from Lovetta. Hazir smiled in their direction, and Penn turned away. His affection was not meant for her.

The young Saraq sauntered over and put his head close to Lovetta's while the others formed their groups. The sight of him so sleek in his blue and silver tunic only made Penn angry. She surged out of the room and into the hallway, too frustrated to make polite conversation. Why did it have to be *him?* Of all people, she could have tolerated Zekeriya, even Sahin, but not Hazir. He was too close to Lovetta. He had already proposed to her, and she still hadn't refused him. What if this make-believe marriage and all of its benefits were all Hazir needed to finally win Lovetta over?

Suffocating in the smoky hall, Penn led Heather outside. She breathed the crisp air slow and deep. It felt so much colder without the battle-warmed blood pounding in her veins. Heather looked up at her with Maybelle's eyes.

"Don't cry, lady," she whispered.

Penn hadn't even felt the tears fall. She crouched down and squeezed Heather tight, focusing on her breath until the others filtered out onto the grass.

"We're taking the road along East Bay," Hazir dictated. He walked so close to Lovetta that their arms brushed, and Penn's anger reignited. He didn't deserve to touch her. He didn't know her like she did. With a heavy heart, Penn walked toward the pair.

"It's the longest route of the three, but it's the safest," he continued. "If you ask me, I think we ought to swap with Belsante's group. They're taking Nariha's Pass, and that's much more dangerous. Without a man, they ought to have the easy road."

Penn narrowed her eyes.

"Belsante is a strong fighter, and Jehane can keep the others safe," Lovetta reassured him.

"She's an archer, not a fighter. They're different."

Penn cracked her knuckles.

"I'm an archer," Lovetta said tersely. "The best archer this side of Tirel. My arrows have taken lives. Am I not a fighter?"

"You're different," Hazir reasoned. "You're not like the others."

"Are you so sure about that?" she challenged.

"Of course. You have your priorities in order. Bel and Edony spend too much time on their hair." He smiled. "If you want to be taken seriously, you have to make sacrifices. You understand that."

Hazir had made one ignorant remark too many. Penn came forward into the light and glared at him poisonously. "Say that again after fighting Bel or Edony one on one, *if* you're still alive afterwards," she snarled.

Lovetta gave her a warning glare, but Hazir only laughed. "I always said your father wasn't selective enough with his servants. Why did you bring one that talks back?"

Penn's entire body tensed. She wasn't going to wait for Lovetta to defend her. "Because I have certain qualities that Lovetta quite enjoys," she snapped, helping Heather onto the back of Primula. Every other conversation had fallen quiet.

"You're a maid," Hazir laughed. "Your personality is irrelevant."

"*You* are irrelevant!" Penn spat.

"Enough!" Lovetta shouted. "Both of you." She turned on Hazir first. "Don't you ever speak to her that way again! She is *not* a member of your house, and if that's the way you speak to your servants, you should be ashamed of yourself. And you." She turned on Penn, eyes full of disappointment. "I need a word with you in private." Lovetta took Penn by the arm and pulled her down the hill.

"You don't have to drag me; I'll come without question. All you have to do is order me to, and I will, your Grace," she said scathingly.

"What is the matter with you?" Lovetta hissed, grabbing Penn by the shoulders.

"You really need to ask? Remember when your father banned the word servant? Do you remember why? It's because it means we are *less than*." She knocked Lovetta's hands away.

"You know I don't think of you as a servant or a maid. I don't even think of you as a friend. You know you're more than that."

"Do I? To be honest, most of the time, I have no idea what you think." She threw her hands in the air. "Understanding you is a nightmare, Lovetta. You like it when I sleep in your bed, you like it when we kiss, but now you're standing beside your fake husband saying nothing while he compares me to an object!"

"I did say something."

"A little late," Penn scoffed. "And you don't seem bothered by the thought of playing his blushing bride at all. How did you think that would make me feel?"

"I didn't choose this, Penn. I didn't make the plan."

"But you probably would have!" Penn started to shake. "In fact, why pretend to marry him? Why not just do it? It's been months, and you still haven't said no."

"I haven't said yes, either. Why don't you notice that?" Lovetta rebutted, taking Penn by the shoulders again. "I only see him as a friend. I've told you this before. Why would I string him along for so long if I did want to marry him?"

"Don't act like you never considered it. The first time we went riding alone, you couldn't stop yourself from talking about how sweet he was, and you said if you were going to marry someone, it'd be an Azorian. Forgive me if I find it hard to believe you when you say he's just a friend."

"Of course I considered it!" Lovetta squeezed Penn's shoulders. "But it wasn't because I loved him. Do you remember why I said I'd marry an Azorian? It was so I could go home. That's all that mattered to me then. *I do not love him,* but gods, I wish I did. It would make my life so much easier, but my life wasn't meant to be easy. If you want me to choose between the two of you, I'll choose you, Penn. Please, hear me."

"You ... you chased after him in the middle of the night and then cried for days," Penn stammered, her hands in her hair. "Why were you so distraught when he ... wait, what did you say?"

"I'll choose you." Lovetta looked away. "I don't want to be his wife, on fake papers or not. I don't want to hide how I truly feel, but I'm scared." She started to cry, and Penn cupped her face. "I'm scared of what people will think. What *he* will think. And I ... I don't want to break his heart."

"Lovetta." Penn caressed the tears from Lovetta's cheeks, trying not to smile. "I'm not sure that he has a heart."

"You're cruel." Lovetta laughed, setting herself down on the grass. "I can't believe I once thought you fancied him."

Penn almost choked. "You've got to be joking." She dropped to the ground beside Lovetta.

"It sounds ridiculous when I say it out loud, but when you first arrived, I was a little paranoid, thanks to Ariad. You asked about him, and the way you used to watch us when we went riding, I thought it was because of him."

"I was looking at you," Penn whispered, warmth returning to her limbs. "It was always you."

Lovetta's mouth twitched, and her eyes darted to Penn, then back to the ground. "In Tirel when I kissed you ... I thought you didn't like it, so I decided not to do anything like that again. You could just continue being my maid and everything would be fine."

The tension in Penn's shoulders softened. "It was hard to let go, but I tried." She looked away from Penn. "But you made it so damned hard, and then you kissed me, and everything came flooding back. I was confused all over again. I still am," she admitted, her voice wobbling.

"What are you confused about?" Penn asked softly, her gut fluttering madly. Lovetta couldn't hold her gaze for more than a moment.

"How you feel about me," she mumbled, her hands fidgeting in her lap. "If it's real, or if it's just a game to you." Penn laughed. "I thought you knew. Everyone else seems to." Without hesitation, she took Lovetta's face in her hands and forced her to meet her eye. "Lovetta." She smiled, tracing her cheekbones with her thumbs.

"Yes?" Lovetta whispered, putting her palms atop Penn's.

"How I feel about you ... how I've felt for the longest time," she grinned, her entire body tingling. Lovetta looked at her pleadingly, and it was complete and utter bliss. "I—"

"So sorry to interrupt," Edony called from the incline. Penn and Lovetta jerked apart and turned around, Penn's heart hammering like a hailstorm in the quiet. "Honestly, I am *so* sorry, like the sorriest I have ever been about anything, but there's only a few hours until dawn, and we need to get out of here before Hazir sets both of your horses on fire."

Penn grasped Lovetta's hand and squeezed, hoping that her unspoken words had been heard. They shared one last longing look before climbing up the hill behind Edony and joining the others to say their goodbyes. Edony locked eyes with Penn and mouthed 'sorry' for the umpteenth time. Clare hugged Penn tight, and they promised they would see each other again soon. It had been hard enough not talking to Clare for a few days, let alone weeks, or even months. With tears in her eyes, Penn returned to Lovetta's side.

"Are you absolutely certain he has to come?" she whispered, eyeing Hazir as he loitered by his horse. "We've never needed a man to protect us before."

Lovetta laughed as she put her foot in the stirrup and hoisted herself on top of her mare. "By the time we're in Azor, you two will be the best of friends," she teased.

Penn made a gagging motion and slid into her saddle behind Heather, who immediately clung on to her. She had a surge of gratitude for the pain-relieving poultice Lianthi had applied.

"Who is this?" Hazir asked as he walked his horse toward Penn and Heather.

"Her name is Heather," Penn said in the mildest tone she could muster.

"What is she doing here?" he demanded, and Heather clung tighter. "She's not coming. She's not part of the plan."

"If you even think about touching her, I will hurt you." Penn smiled sweetly, affirming her grip on the girl.

"We have no papers for her!" Hazir exclaimed. "This could ruin everything. You will leave her here."

"We can't leave her here!" Lovetta said at Penn's defence. "She's our responsibility, Hazir. We have to keep her safe."

Yusufhan walked forward with his servant Lianthi. "If you would permit it, we could find work for her here," the older Saraq offered. "My son is right. You will not get her into the city without a letter from the capital."

Heather looked up at Penn with pleading eyes. "Don't make me stay, lady," she whispered.

Penn looked from Hazir to Yusufhan desperately but did not relinquish her hold on Heather. "Her home is with us." Penn shook her head. "With all due respect, Lord Master, I cannot leave her with you."

Hazir walked his mount closer and looked at Penn with an intense dislike. "I will not permit you to bring this child along and put us all at risk," he growled.

Penn's anger was reigniting with force, and Heather was starting to shake. "You *do not* command me, you heartless son of a—"

"I'll take her," interrupted Belsante, walking forward. "I have a letter for a maid that didn't make it out of the castle. If she comes with us, she can use it."

"Fine," Hazir barked, backing away from the two. "As long as she's not my problem."

Penn looked at the girl before her affectionately, her hands trembling on Heather's waist. She didn't want to hand her over to anyone. It didn't matter that it was Belsante, or that Jehane could kill a man with her eyes closed. Heather had put her trust in *her*, nobody else. As Belsante approached and opened her arms, Penn cried.

"Let go of Penn, little one. I'll keep you safe," she cooed.

Heather hesitated and looked at Penn, her eyes wet, seeking permission. Penn squeezed her tight, and she sobbed into Heather's hair. The faintest hint of lavender clung to her locks.

"I'll see you again, okay?" Penn croaked, wiping away the sadness that stained Heather's cheeks. She kissed her forehead and handed her over to Belsante, her tears turning to ugly gasps.

"Promise me!" Heather squealed as Belsante wrapped her arms around her.

"I promise I'll see you again." Penn smiled. "Promise me you won't get yourself into any mischief." She tried to laugh.

"I promise," Heather said with a forced smile.

Belsante said goodbye, then led her stallion away.

"Let's go. We're well behind schedule," Hazir said with an air of frustration.

Feeling empty, Penn couldn't take her eyes away from the spot where Heather had just been.

"Give her a moment," Lovetta said, putting a hand on Penn's thigh.

"No," Penn said, shaking the grief from her body. She walked Primula forward with a sniff. "Let's just go."

Yusufhan called goodbye as the groups dispersed, their mounts kicking into a trot. They rode lightly through the sleeping village and branched onto three separate roads. As they separated from the others, Penn looked steadily ahead. Without Heather, the space before her was bare, the saddle cold. She missed the hands that clutched her tunic and the eyes that were so like her sister's.

They rode east for hours before Penn noticed the hard, rhythmic bouncing against her chest. She had completely forgotten about Heather's locket, and now she was gone.

# Afterword

Just do it. No, not a Nike billboard, these were the wise words of a woman I once knew who self-published her debut novel at nineteen. Stop doubting your writing and just do it. *Write. The. Damn. Book.* So, I did. Mid-university degree and probably a little buzzed from anti-anxiety meds, *Her Grace* came to life in a few short months. Okay, that was the first draft and a good five years before I started typing this afterword. But the point is, I stopped overthinking it and just did it. Instead of writing about things I thought would get published (and getting bored after fifty-odd pages), I started writing about things I cared about: womanhood, sexuality, identity politics, covert heroism. I wrote until I built a world I couldn't let go of. I let my values and my identity be my lens, and I persevered. I used a dozen cherished books to inspire me in some small way. Young adult fantasy and science fiction were always my favourite genres, although my heart has a special place for historical fiction (especially Japanese). I've spent many months in Japan, filling my mind with future stories, and have used much of the country's imagery in the sequel to *Her Grace*. (Stay tuned!)

There isn't a lot I don't enjoy writing, but what I'm particularly fond of is young of heart, whimsical, and occasionally angst full. I love characters who stray from heteronormativity, challenge authority, and, of course, a strong female lead. I enjoy writing love in all its forms: platonic, romantic, sexual, invisible, and most of all, forbidden. I write the stories I craved as a young teen, the stories that were nowhere to be found in a conservative Catholic high school library. I write with the hope that in ten years' time, my book will be one of many titles in an aisle bursting with medieval lesbian prose.

If any part of my journey resonates with you, take a deep breath and just do it. Write. Make art. Play music. Whatever your thing is —do it. Even if it's one sentence a day, it's progress and it's valid. *Perfectionism feeds anxiety.* The only way I could move forward with my writing was to dramatically limit my editing. Each time I sat down to write, I allowed myself to read through and tweak the previous paragraph, and no more. Otherwise, I could sit there for hours and rewrite the same paragraph fifty times and never be truly happy. That's perfectionism. I only needed to have a little faith in myself, like my high school English teachers did. (I had gold stars coming out the wazoo.) I remember using the phrase 'acrid stench' in a creative writing task in year nine and seeing four red ticks screaming beside it with approval. It was one of the most exciting moments of my teenage life, and that's how I knew I was meant to write.

# Credits

So many people have helped me on my journey to publishing this book. To my very first audience: Alycia, Chrystal, Tom, Stephanie, Amber and Ammar; I thank you from the bottom of my heart. You are all golden. To my family, thank you for encouraging me to pursue my dreams and for always showing enthusiasm in my work, no matter how very different it might be from what you're used to reading.

To Lachlan, my sweet husband, thank you for making a conscious effort not only to support me in every endeavour, but for your open mind. I've never felt as secure in myself as I do when I'm by your side. You acknowledge and respect my bisexuality in a way that no other partner has been able to, and for that, I'm truly grateful. I love you to the moon and back.

Finally, to my editor, Kathryn Moore. There isn't a day that goes by that I don't feel utterly blessed to be your client and friend. I can't thank you enough for all that you've done, Kat. My manuscript is living its best life thanks to your belief in it, and in me.

# GRACE, FIRE & REIGN

*more to come*

❤ ❤ ❤ ❤ ❤